Rise Of The Walker King

Walking Between Worlds
- Book II -

Rise Of The Walker King

Walking Between Worlds
- Book II -

J.K. Norry

Rise of the Walker King
Walking Between Worlds Book II

www.SuddenInsightPublishing.com
Indie publishing for the Indie Author

Acknowledgements

Publishing the first book in this trilogy did not just set the tone for publishing the two to follow; it also set the stage for all the books to come. In the spirit of the series, and a truly well-rounded acknowledgements page, I would like to start with the demons and devils that helped us choose the path we did...

Thank you to all the publishing companies out there who have done such a fantastic job rejecting or exploiting so many talented artists. If not for all the authors' notes about the way you treat the talent and the reputation you have earned, the world would not have changed and our little publishing company might not be possible.

The angels that have acted to create this new world are true guardians of literature, and sincere thanks go out to every bright soul that toils behind the scenes to fill it with hope and possibility for today and tomorrow's writer.

Many thanks to everyone reading my books. It has been a special delight to hear your feedback, and to know that I am not the only one excited to see this through.

Thanks to my mom, Leslie, for being so supportive and excited about both the behind-the-scenes story and the published one.

Thanks to my dad, Larry, for getting so lost in the first book that you forgot who wrote it as you read...

Most of all, thanks to my "Awesome Girl", Dawn. The only person who can say she has worked as hard as me to make my writing a success and my books a reality is her. The doors she has opened to me enable me to see further ahead than ever before, and my thanks to her are many.

Special thanks to Quebon of Zorbon, The Great Bright Light...God, if you will...

And final special thanks to The One Who Shall Not Be Named...

Oh, wait...I named you, didn't I?

For my mom, Leslie...

CHAPTER 1

Kris approached the doorway, hesitating before walking through it. Waking up was not what it used to be, and he hadn't grown accustomed to the new way just yet.

Girding himself against the confusing wash of colors and sound, he closed his eyes as he stepped through. Some of the Guides said it was like being born; Kris didn't remember being born, and he suspected the Guides didn't either. It was darkness and it was light and it was neither and it was both. It somehow swirled through him till he felt he had forgotten himself, or the Universe had. Then it was a kaleidoscope of colors and a rushing river of sound, even when he woke to a dark and quiet room.

The feeling was even more explosive and sudden than before, as his consciousness permeated his dead body. Every cell of his ghostly form crackled with sensation, with aliveness.

He was through the doorway.

Kris felt the weight of Jessica's head on his chest as she slept. Flowers and strawberries filled his nose pleasantly, tied together in a sweet sultry sulfur scent. Tangling his fingers in her honeyed blonde hair, the Guide smiled softly.

Since he had died, everything had just gotten better for him.

He'd never felt so alive as he did in death.

Now he just needed to get used to sleeping, and waking up.

He could feel her hand moving before he realized her breathing had shifted. It drifted from where it lay on his chest slowly down his torso. Light and aimless, her touch delighted his tickled abdomen like her scent delighted his nose, like her closeness delighted his heart. As her hand found what he had hoped she was reaching for, she opened her eyes and turned her head slightly to look up at him.

Her eyes were big and round and blue and beautiful, and Kris let his heart sing the only song it knew as he lost himself in them.

Jessica's hand moved with curious certainty under the sheets, and her bright blue eyes began to swirl seductively with deep crimson smokiness as she watched him.

"I have never felt so satisfied and so full of desire all at the same time," the Guide murmured, not breaking the sacred eye contact. "I've wanted you so much for so long, I thought it would be impossible for you to live up to my hopeful imaginings about you."

He paused as she kneaded him gently beneath the covers in a particularly pleasurable way. A low moan escaped his dead lips.

Then her hand was still, her eyes expectant.

"And now…?" she prompted.

Smiling at her with all the love that burst in brilliant colors in his heart like an eternal fireworks finale, Kris replied, "Now I realize you are so much more incredible than I ever imagined, or ever could have hoped or dreamed."

Sighing softly, Jessica closed her eyes and kneaded his flesh again, smiling as he moaned.

"There's something you said to me," she spoke softly into his chest, her eyes still closed. "It was not the night I finally told you, you know, that I could see you and hear you."

"That was last night, Jess," he reminded her, his words more moan than words.

She giggled, and Kris closed his eyes to listen to one of his favorite sounds in the world since he had first heard it.

"It's been a long night, lover," she responded, her touch changing as she felt his body move, and his voice moaned and sighed. It was a long sweet moment before he could link enough thoughts to form a coherent sentence. He was happy, though, and she was the reason why. He thought she should know that.

"Last night was the most incredible night of my life," Kris said honestly. "I feel like I have lived my whole life in black and white, my soul longing for color."

When he opened his eyes she was looking at him earnestly, her eyes sky blue and human and vulnerable and brimming with tears.

Gazing at her, smiling softly, Kris whispered, "Last night you brought color to my life, to my heart and my mind, to my body and my soul. You woke my slumbering heart from a long dull nightmare to a love like I never imagined."

He watched her as closely as she did him, and when her eyes went wide he remembered why they had gone from touching to talking. Smoothing her hair lovingly, Kris felt his soft smile turn to a look of seriousness. He narrowed his eyes as they held her gaze.

"The other night I told you something, not knowing you could hear it," he murmured. "I said that I may sound a fool for what I am about to say, but if you can't hear me it doesn't matter and if you can I need to say it."

Her body relaxed against him, her hand kneading him gently and her eyes so open and vulnerable it might well have been her speaking.

Struggling mentally to keep his train of thought from derailing at her loving touch, Kris went on. "From the moment I first saw you I thought you were the most beautiful thing I had ever seen. I told Paul when we were leaving that I was no longer agnostic, because I had just seen an angel."

Jessica giggled. "I'm not an angel, silly," she whispered, like it was a secret. "I'm your horny little devil. Sorry to disappoint."

Her hand held hard evidence that the Guide was far from disappointed, and he laughed.

"What did Paul say?" she asked him.

"He said, 'You mean the blonde? Sorry, buddy, I didn't notice.'" Kris laughed quietly again. "Paul never liked blonde girls, and he had just gotten with Brenna anyway. Since they met she may as well be the only girl in the world, as far as Paul is concerned."

He shrugged awkwardly, lying there with his arm under her and his hand tangled in her honeyed tresses.

Her pretty unlined forehead crinkled in a pretty little frown. "The way you feel about me?"

"Precisely," he responded, smiling.

"Awww…" Jessica brightened. "You're so sweet."

Kris nodded, then let his fingers run gently through her hair along her skull. Closing his fist around a handful of her thick soft mane, he pulled back her hair until he saw her eyes widen and flash with fire. One night had been enough to learn much of what she wanted from her lover, and he was happy to be playful and serious and dedicated and occasionally a little obsessed and forceful.

Her playful hand got serious again in response, and he had to fight the urge to let his eyes roll back into his head as all linear thought exploded from his mind.

"Since that day," he went on, narrowing his eyes again with a sober look that held hers, "I have woke every morning thinking of you. Each night as I drifted off to sleep I would wonder if you were awake, what you were doing. I would promise myself that I was going to ask you out the next day, and that was the only way I could get to sleep. Even when I was sleeping with another girl I would promise myself that I would ask you out the next day, and break it off with her if you said yes."

She made a moue, an adorably furious and vulnerable swirl of red and blue in her eyes.

"Next time you tell this story you can leave out the other girls." Her hand did not squeeze him hard enough to hurt him, just hard enough to let him know that she could if she wanted to.

Letting go his firm grasp, he petted her hair soothingly.

"As you wish," he smiled. "I watched you, I thought of you, I suffered merciless teasing from Matt, and over time I realized I was not going to stop feeling this way."

He let his hand drift from her hair to alight on her cheek as tears welled in his eyes.

"It may sound silly, I barely know you despite all the time I've spent stalking you. But I love you, Jessica. I love the way you smile and the way you laugh. I love how every time you move it is with a sweet grace that delights my eyes to watch. I love your body, so sexy and perfect and always modestly but attractively dressed. I love how you frown just a little tiny bit when you say 'good morning' to someone and they don't respond. I love how sometimes your eyes are dark blue pools of stormy sea and how other times they are beautiful chips of ice, light blue sky stretching vast into eternity. I love you, Jessica. I love everything about you. Everything I learn about you makes me love you more, and I would give anything to have the chance to make you the happiest and most loved girl in the world." He stroked her cheek as he spoke, brushing away half of her happy tears while the rest puddled on his chest.

Her eyes were huge and blue and luminous with tears.

"Would you say it again?" Her voice was thick with emotion.

Letting his hand fall gently to her jaw, he tilted her chin slightly to make his serious words more serious.

"I love you, Jessica." Kris held her gaze as he uttered the words.

She blinked through the tears that still fell.

"I love you too, Kris," she whispered. Then her eyes swirled red and black and blue as she climbed on top of him, a grin on her tear-stained face. They sighed together a moment later, and her sigh carried the sweet words to his ears again. "I love you."

When the cell phone started buzzing and playing Katy Perry's 'E.T.', there was only a moment's hesitation before Kris felt her grind against him again in sweet desperation.

The song played on, the rise and fall of her hips keeping time with the music.

CHAPTER 2

Roche hung up the phone without leaving a message. Much as he wanted to get the machine moving, he'd rather the cogs and sprockets be happy and late than on time and miserable.

He tried Paul again, hanging up at the beginning of his long but pleasant message prompt. "Hi, this is Paul. Sorry I can't—"

Slipping his phone in the pocket of his dark slacks, the devil turned to Matt with a frown.

"This place needs to be ready in thirty-six hours," he growled darkly.

Matt let his gaze wander a slow circle around the room. All the furniture had been cleared to one side and stacked, save one table in the center of the floor flanked by two simple straight-backed chairs. Wood of all lengths and sizes were stacked in random haphazard piles, filling the space with the fresh scent of cut lumber. Table saw and a nail gun were cast with a crew of circular saws and belt sanders and hammers to make the production seem possible. The boxes of unopened nails and complete lack of sawdust told the truth of the matter, however, as did the papered unchanged windows and stark bare walls. The place was a shambles, gutted but for the coffee bar and the disarray of tables and chairs.

Matt gave a low whistle and grinned, unconcerned.

"Yeah, that's not going to happen," he mused.

"It is, though," the devil insisted. "I just need a good cup of coffee and a little help."

Spreading his hands, Matt arched an eyebrow at Roche. "Are you kidding? It's not humanly possible."

His clouded countenance cleared, and the devil grinned.

"Good thing I'm not human," he said through pointed canines. "And neither is my help." Digging his phone impatiently from his pocket, he frowned as his beefy fingers punched buttons.

"You still have the Walker's key?" Roche snapped.

Matt's eyes narrowed as he remembered, narrowing further as he dug in his pockets with a frantic lack of success. The devil held up his free hand between them, his meaty thumb and forefinger pinching a thin platinum chain dangling a glinting platinum key.

"You should keep better track of that," Roche reprimanded Matt as his hand curled about the key. He hung up again without leaving a message.

He sighed. The devil needed a cup of coffee.

Opening his mouth to speak, Matt closed it again as Roche barked at him angrily.

"Take it!" the devil shouted. "Get Paul! Hurry! Why are you still here?"

Matt examined the object for another moment.

"That's not my key," he protested. "It's gold, not silver."

"Paul got an upgrade," Roche growled through clenched teeth. "It's platinum."

"Cool." Matt palmed the key and headed for the front door, moving with casual slowness.

"Don't walk, jackass!" the devil took up shouting again. "Use the key! Close your eyes and think of the Walker! Engage your imagination! It's all you've got!"

Roche shouted until he was yelling at an empty room, then quieted and crossed his arms across his broad chest in satisfaction. Eyeing the coffee bar warily as he approached it, he slipped through the swinging door and stood before the great holy machines of mystery that turned bean to brew. Just as he was considering crushing a handful of beans in his beefy paw and heating a pot of water with a small fireball, the door that had been frustratingly closed all morning opened.

Jessica stepped into the cafe, disheveled blonde hair over penguin pajamas over penguin slippers. She was adorably cute and beautiful all at the same time, wearing a happy soft smile that reminded the devil why life is worth loving. Kris came in behind her, looking happy and a little sheepish as his robed frame floated soundlessly into view. At the sight of the pair the devil felt anger and frustration and impatience drain out of him, and he grinned broadly at them.

"There's the happy couple!" The devil was happy to hear happiness in his own voice.

They both flushed, and Kris stepped forward to put his arm around her shoulders and pull her close.

Roche nodded his satisfaction. "Good morning, you two. Jessica, would you be a dear and make a pot of coffee?"

She kissed the Guide's cheek and stepped away, leaving Kris to accept the devil's happy nod of approval.

"I sent Matt after Paul," Roche said. "Would you find out what's taking them so long?"

CHAPTER 3

Kris appeared in the familiar living room, a silly, sleepy, satisfied smile still tugging at the corners of his mouth. As the scene coalesced into his reality, his eyes grew round and his lips tightened to the thin line of a fierce frown.

"Paul!" he cried. "Paul, what are you doing?"

The Walker had Matt pinned to the wall with his forearm at his throat. He was naked, every muscle in his body taut with fury as Matt's feet kicked helplessly at the wall inches from the carpeted floor. A spray of dried purple blood was splashed across his darkened visage. Ignoring the Guide, Paul glared at Matt as he struggled for breath.

"What are you?" Paul demanded, his short sword appearing suddenly in his free hand.

His eyes bugging out of his head, Matt gasped wordlessly and spread his hands.

"Paul. Paul!" The Guide finally got the Walker to turn his head. "You're killing him. Let him go!"

Kris felt a chill as he looked into Paul's eyes, cold and full of rage. Then he blinked and stepped toward Kris, letting his short sword go back to wherever it came from as Matt crumpled to the floor. The Guide took an instinctive step back, but Paul just turned and collapsed to the couch. His bloodied face watched his gasping friend warily as he absently tossed the throw from the back of the sofa over his lap, somewhat covering his nakedness.

"Brenna." Paul's voice was suddenly loud, angry again. "Brenna is a devil. You're her brother." He looked past Kris to peg Matt with his furious gaze.

"What are you?" Paul demanded again.

Kris had to turn to see Matt's reaction, and was surprised that he was squirming uncomfortably under the Walker's accusing stare.

He turned again to Paul.

"What happened?" Kris asked.

"She came at me," Paul responded, his voice flat and toneless. "She came at me and I killed her."

It was Matt the Guide ended up restraining, standing to catch him as he launched himself unthinking at the Walker. Whatever Matt was, he wasn't any stronger or faster than the Guide, and Kris was learning to think success into his movements.

Holding him, his mouth right next to the Guide's ear as Matt shouted, "You killed my sister? You killed my sister!" Kris tossed him back into the chair he had sprung from. It rocked back precariously, and then fell forward to land with a loud thump.

Kris moved before the chair, blocking him from standing. He could hear Paul's low chuckle behind him as the Walker sat fearless, not even bothering to manifest a weapon.

His back to the Walker's dark laughter, Kris watched the man before him deflate from rage to bewilderment. Matt looked helplessly up at the Guide, whose gray eyes went from demanding peace to demanding answers.

"What are you?" he echoed the Walker's question.

Matt stirred uncomfortably in the chair, opening his mouth to speak only to shut it again. Finally his handsome mien relaxed, he sunk deep into the cushioned chair, and he shrugged.

"I don't know," he said simply.

"What do you mean, you don't know?" Paul was standing suddenly beside him, glowering down at Matt. He clutched the blanket over his bare belly, so it covered him to the floor.

The Guide nudged his naked shoulder.

"Put something on, would you?" he asked. "And maybe clean up the, uh…" Kris circled a finger round his face, not wanting to point out the blood to either of them.

Turning his head slowly to land his dark gaze on Kris, the Walker's face was suddenly clean over the collar of his leather duster.

They both turned their attention back to Matt.

"I don't know," he said again, squirming uncomfortable under their combined curiosity.

"Let's find out," the Walker snarled.

There was a glint of steel and a blur of leather, all too fast for the Guide to see.

He did see the light gash that appeared suddenly on Matt's naked forearm, welling red blood before he realized he'd been cut.

"Hey!" Matt jerked his arm away far too late, succeeding only in getting a few droplets of blood on his shirt.

"You cut me!" He covered the cut with his hand, glaring up at Paul.

"He's human," the Walker said to Kris, ignoring him. "Or at least his blood looks human."

Holding Paul's gaze long enough to let him know he did not approve of his methods, the Guide knelt beside Matt.

"Are you okay?" he asked.

"He'll be fine," Paul said dismissively. "It's just a scratch. There might be some bandages in the bathroom. I don't need them anymore."

Matt shook his head.

"It's okay," he said, though he still clutched his arm. "Would you guys please sit down? I don't know much, but I'll tell you what I do know."

The supernatural duo exchanged a glance and a shrug then sat again. Matt ran his fingers through his dark hair and sighed.

"You guys remember the accident?" he asked.

They both nodded.

"Well, up until then I thought I was living a pretty normal life." Matt grinned, forgetting himself. "Charmed, but normal."

"And since the accident?" Kris prompted.

"During the accident," Matt clarified. "Something happened, I don't know what. Brenna and I were…I guess, transported. To another place. Another world, really. I don't know."

"I remember that!" Paul snapped his fingers, and Matt started at the Walker's sudden movement. "There was, like, a wave of energy that swept over everybody. It was strange. It was like you and Brenna disappeared for a second. Then you were back. Then…"

Paul frowned, remembering.

"No," Matt shook his head. "It wasn't for a second. It was like an hour."

The Guide turned to Paul. "It sounds like they went above."

"No." The Walker spoke firmly. "Brenna is a devil. They went below."

Matt nodded agreement. "Yeah, someone asked what she was doing below. Some weird dude in a monster costume."

He frowned. "A devil. I'm so stupid."

"What happened?" Paul pressed him.

"Brenna said she needed to see someone, some lady's name."

"Was it Lilia?" The Walker asked.

Kris turned to look at him curiously.

"Yeah. Yeah it was. Lilia." Matt's response transformed his curious look into a questioning scowl, but the Guide turned back as he went on. "We went down this long hallway, and Brenna told me to wait outside. She went into a room and came out a long time later. Then we were back."

"That's it?" the Walker frowned. "That's all that happened?"

Matt shifted uncomfortably in his chair.

"Well, no." He glanced between them, looking for sympathetic eyes, settled on the Guide. "I kind of made a deal. The guy…the devil that met us said he could help me, that all I had to do was one little thing."

They both spoke at once.

"Help you with what?" Kris asked.

"What one little thing?" the Walker demanded.

"He said he could help with, you know, money. Success. He said he could turn my bad luck around," Matt shrugged. "It's what I've always wanted, to show Brenna and everyone that I can do it."

Paul snorted derisively. "By making a deal with a devil? You're a cliché, jackass."

"What did you have to do?" Kris asked calmly, trying to ignore the Walker.

"Nothing," Matt shrugged. "I mean, hardly anything. I just had to give her something and say that it was from me. It was just a pair of earrings, and they were pretty. I didn't see the harm in it."

Paul shook his head slowly, recalling his final seconds as a human being. "You didn't look real peaceful when you came back."

"No, no I wasn't," Matt agreed. "I remembered something, I remembered everything, and I was shocked stupid by the possibility of unintended consequences."

Kris and Paul exchanged a bemused look. It was not like their friend to consider unintended consequences at all, much less be emotionally distraught by them.

"What did you remember?" Kris asked.

"I don't remember," Matt replied. "The feeling passed and when I found the earrings in my pocket later at the hospital I gave them to Brenna."

"And then your luck changed," Paul said.

Matt nodded.

"Yeah," he said. "Yeah, it did. I told you guys about that stock, but that wasn't all. I can't buy a lottery ticket without winning something. A few hundred here, a few thousand there, I can't miss."

"So Roche hitched his wagon to your rising star," Paul mused. He arched an eyebrow at Kris. "Do you think he knew?"

CHAPTER 4

"Look at you, such a sweet pretty human." Her voice was beautiful and mocking, cruel and flinted. She stood with her hands on her hips, the curves of her full breasts and thin waist and rounded hips accentuated by her stance and the scant scrap of material barely covering it all. Flaming red hair and swirling eyes of orange and crimson and black animated the cold smooth breathtaking countenance of scarlet skin.

Looking down, hate burning in her heart and in her eyes, she glared at the head of dark silky hair hanging over the woman's face. Slender, delicate hands hung limp above her head on either side, a sturdy wooden stock closed around her slim and graceful neck and wrists. The thick grained frame and base of the simple restraining device blocked the view of the rest of her body, and for her lack of responsiveness she might have been a disembodied head and hands.

"Ximena!" the devil hissed.

Still the hands hung limp, the long dark hair unmoving. Lilia crossed her arms across her abdomen, squeezing her ample breasts together in a deep valley of cleavage. She sighed and smiled.

"Brenna," she said quietly.

The girl looked up, big dark eyes under a slight vertical line creasing the smooth pale skin of her forehead. She met the devil's eyes, unflinching and unfamiliar. Drawn and tired, her face was all the more beautiful for the dark circles under her eyes and the dark hollows under her high cheekbones. Her thick, full lips were parched and chapped, and she moistened them so they gleamed full and red before she spoke.

"I don't know where I am," she said calmly. "I don't know who you are. I don't know why you're doing this to me. I don't know how many times I have to repeat myself for you to hear me."

Brenna held the devil's eyes the whole time she spoke. After, she let her gaze wander the small stuffy room that seemed carved from reddish-brown rock. Awful things hung on the walls, sharp daggers and wrought iron pokers filed to a dull point. There were clamps and manacles and vices of all sizes. A long handled single-head battle axe that looked clean and sharp glinted in the guttering light of the torches that punctuated the walls regularly and spewed out black smoke interminably. There was no door, only rock walls and ceiling and floor discolored by the gathering smoke. Her round dark eyes watched the devil take the axe down and heft the weight of it as she turned.

"Please don't." They were two simple words, formed carefully by her thick glistening lips. The words held no fear, no anxiety, and no tone of supplication. She may well have been answering someone asking if she'd like them to add pickles to her sandwich.

The devil scowled, the sharp striking features of her face twisted but no less beautiful. "Tell me who I am. Tell me who you are. Tell me why you are here."

She shook her head as much as the thick wooden crosspiece would allow, long thick silky waves of inky black hair swaying lightly back and forth. "I told you. I don't know who you are. My name is Brenna Blanco. I don't know why I am here. I don't even know where I am. Please let me go."

Raising the glinting curved blade, the devil's eyes held hers. Her pupils were slits, and the slits widened as the arc reached its zenith.

"Tell me who you are," she hissed.

"My name is Brenna Bl—"

The blade swung, a spray of red blood splashed the devil's dainty scarlet feet, and the pretty little human head struck the floor and rolled. Big dark eyes stared lifeless up at the devil, a strand of hair across Brenna's face as a bloody puddle formed under her lifeless visage.

CHAPTER 5

"What do you think, Roche?" The Walker had taken the time to shower and dress, but his hand still went to his unshaved face, as if to wipe something away. The devil had heard the whole story.

"I think we need to get this place ready for tomorrow night," he growled, looking around the open empty unfinished room.

Paul folded his arms across his chest. "Kris has never been a real hands-on kind of guy," he said flatly. "He's sharp as a tack, very perceptive, and the most morally upright person I know, but he's no woodworker."

He glanced sidelong at the Guide. "No offense."

Kris shrugged. It was true. "None taken."

The Walker jerked his thumb at Matt. "And this one is useless in any real-life scenario that requires any level of any kind of skill."

Matt scowled. "None taken."

"So," Paul crossed his arms again, resolutely, "if you're not up for talking I'll leave you to your work and find my answers elsewhere. If you would like my skilled and speedy hands, however, you'll have to tell me what you know. Or what you think. Or what you think you know."

Roche sighed. "Jessica, would you get me another cup of coffee? And something to put in it?"

Paul gave the girl a weak smile. "Your white mocha making machine isn't ready to go by any chance, is it?"

She smiled prettily. "Coming right up." Squeezing his hand, she looked up to Kris. "Do you want anything?" He gave her a confused look and shook his head. "Matt?'

"Yeah, Jess," he replied. "Coffee. Thanks."

Kris watched her walk away, more entranced than ever as his imaginings were taken to a new level.

"You want something in your coffee, Walker?" Roche asked. "Sounds like it's been quite a morning."

Paul frowned, running his hand over his stubbled jaw. "Isn't it a little early?"

The devil shrugged. "Haven't you noticed? When's the last time you were drunk? Good and blasted?"

"It's been awhile."

"When's the last time you caught a decent buzz?" Roche pressed him.

He shook his head. "I don't know."

"I hate to be the one to break it to you, but immortality ain't all it's cracked up to be." The devil put his hands on his hips. "Poison won't kill you, but booze won't get you drunk either. You could shoot heroin all day and have nothing but a series of very brief highs and no needle marks."

"Have you?" Matt asked, curious.

"We've got some Bailey's back there," the devil suggested to Paul, ignoring him.

The Walker nodded. "Okay, Bailey's and coffee then. Heavy on the Bailey's." He considered for a moment. "Hey Roche, can I bum a smoke?"

"Take it outside, please," Jessica called to them. She arrived shortly bearing four cups of steaming brew with practiced ease. Devil and Walker took theirs with thanks and headed for the front door. Matt took one look at Kris and Jessica coming up close to each other. Their eyes were locked, Kris arching an eyebrow suggestively while she bit her lip in a demure provocation.

Matt turned and followed the sodden immortals outside.

When the door closed behind them, Jessica set her coffee on the lone table and put her arms around his waist. "You know, sweetie," she said, pressing against him. "You don't have to be like other Guides unless you want to."

He ran his hands through her honeyed hair. "What do you mean?"

Raising herself up on her toes, she kissed him. "You can drink coffee. Or beer, or whatever you like. You don't have to wear a Guide's robe." She kissed him again.

"Why doesn't anybody like my robe?" Kris frowned playfully. "I love it. It's timeless, it's easy to put on, it breathes. I can hide my hands while I twiddle my thumbs so I look wise instead of bored. What's not to like?"

Raising her hands to tousle his hair, she kissed him again. "Robes are for fat old men. You have a sexy body under there. I like the way you used to dress." Her mouth pressed against his again, her tongue flicking over his lips.

Kris cupped her face tenderly, kissing her deeply, tasting her sweetness. When he pulled away, her eyes were swirling blue and red and her breaths were coming fast.

"Let's go back to the apartment, you can see my room and I can change my clothes," he suggested.

When she bit her lower lip, the Guide's heart fluttered. Sometimes she did it to draw him in, seductively; other times she would stop in the middle of a sentence and bite her lip for a moment, searching for words; this time she looked nervous.

"That's so adorable," he murmured.

She cocked her head to the side, prettily. "What?"

"When you bite your lip like that." He bent to kiss the lip she had been biting.

"Oh, don't tell me that," she giggled. "I'll start to do it all the time."

He smiled. "You already do. That's how I know it's so adorable."

"What if I do it on purpose?" She bit her lip, blinking rapidly like a cartoon character in love.

"Then it's even more adorable." Kris nuzzled her thick soft mane, murmuring softly in her ear. "It's one thing to watch you from afar, falling in love with the way you move and the way you talk and your little mannerisms as they occur naturally. It's another thing entirely to tell you I adore something about you and have you do it deliberately for me. That means you not only listen to me and hear me, you also make an effort to do the things I tell you I like. That makes an adorable mannerism even more adorable, because now my love for you is a part of it. Every time you do it, you're both seeking my appreciation and sending me your love, especially if you do it deliberately. The simple act of biting your lip becomes a way of asking me to take a moment to adore you while showing me that you want to please me by doing the things I enjoy."

Pressing her hips forward into him, she leaned back in his embrace to look in his eyes and flatten her palms against his chest. Her eyes were a light luminous blue, holding his. "You've really thought about this, haven't you?"

He nodded. "Sorry."

A pretty frown darkened her features, storm clouds in the clear blue skies. "Sorry? For what?"

"I've been told that I analyze love to death," he muttered darkly. "I don't want to make you feel scrutinized, I want you to feel loved and appreciated."

She giggled, her hands still over his heart while his arms encircled her slim waist.

"Sounds like a stupid girl, or a deceptive one." She smiled as he raised his eyebrows in pleasant surprise. "I invite you to constantly analyze our love, to deliberately scrutinize my behavior. I have the opportunity to love an amazing human being with the heart of an angel. I know you want to be my perfect love; but to be that, you have to realize that I want to be your perfect love, too. If something I say or something I do seems less than loving, don't leave it alone. Talk to me about it, so I can stop doing it or you can understand why I do it and not be bothered by it. By the same token, when I do something that makes you feel loved or appreciated, let me know. Chances are that's why I did it, and knowing it made an impression will make me do it more."

His heart tingled under her hands as she spoke to him, and his eyes filled with happy tears. Others could be grateful for life; the Guide was grateful for death.

"I love you, Jessica," he said softly. "I want to say that everything you do makes me fall more in love with you, but it somehow doesn't sound right."

Pressed against him, she could feel his physical reaction to her loving words.

"We're not falling in love," she murmured, gazing into his eyes as hers swirled crimson and black with devilish desire. "We're rising in love with each other. We're not going to fall into a normal comfortable routine; we're going to rise to the happy challenge of loving each other more every day. Our love is important to me, and I'm going to tell you so and I'm going to show you. Everything you say and everything you do makes me rise more and more in love with you."

Jessica smiled and bit her lip. "How's that?"

The little brass bell jangled then, and the trio entered talking loudly. Jessica turned, staying in front of Kris so his excitement didn't show.

Maybe pants are a good idea, he thought.

"Awww," Matt called out, grinning. "Look at the lovebirds cooing softly to each other."

"Actually," Jessica threw a quick smile over her shoulder at Kris, "we were just analyzing our love to life."

Matt's face clouded in confusion.

"Uncle Roche?" Jessica spoke again, tentative. The Guide laid his hand light on her shoulder. "Could I go with Kris to his apartment?"

The devil's face twisted into a fierce frown.

"Shit, I'm sorry, girl." Roche glanced at the others. "We need a minute."

"It's okay," she said, in a sea of confused faces. "You can do it here."

Surprised, his eyes grew wide and he spread his beefy paws. "What do you want?"

She spun slowly in place and looked up at Kris, a shy smile on her lips. "Do you want me? Do you want all of me?"

All of their eyes were on him, he could feel them. Only hers mattered, though, and he smiled. "I want all of you, always."

Her soft smile became a little girl's delighted grin, and she rose to kiss him lightly before she turned again to Roche.

"That's what I want," she said, resolute and happy.

The devil stepped toward him, and Kris tried to match his look of seriousness despite having no idea what was going on. Standing before them as she moved to the Guide's side and clasped his hand, Roche reached out to take their free hands in his meaty paws. He bowed his head, and when he looked up again his eyes swirled with scarlet fire.

"I release you, Jessica," he intoned gravely. "I hereby transfer ownership and guardianship of you to the Guide Kris, severing all involuntary ties between you and I."

Kris felt a tingling in his hands, a current of energy passing into him from both devils. He kept his head bowed, solemn. When Roche released his hand it was burning, and the Guide held it before him for inspection. There was a symbol seared into the flesh of his palm in flaming orange and red. As he watched, it faded and his palm looked and felt whole again.

"Severing all involuntary ties?" he heard the hurt in Jessica's voice. "Does that mean you don't want me here anymore?"

The devil waved his hands.

"No, no," he shook his head. "It means you are free to do whatever you want."

Still holding the Guide's hand, she clenched it tightly. "What if I want to keep my job and my apartments? What if I want Kris to be here with me, and that's what he wants too?"

Kris squeezed her hand in reassuring response. It was one of the many things they had talked about and agreed on immediately.

Roche broke out in a broad grin and stepped forward to put a hand on each of their shoulders. "That would make me very happy."

The Walker cleared his throat loudly.

"This is all very sweet," Paul said flatly. "But I just killed my girlfriend, and I sure would like to know why." He rubbed his jaw absently while he looked from Guide to devil to Matt.

"It sounds like she was possessed," Roche offered with a shrug of his beefy shoulders.

Kris shook his head. "Then why did the body disappear? Lots of bodies disappear when you, uh, behead them: demons, devils, dragons, Guides, angels. But not possessed humans. They revert back to human form in death."

"Always?" Roche asked reproachfully.

The Guide shrugged, remembering his most important learnings.

"There's no such thing as always," he admitted. "Anything is possible in this world of imagination."

"My imagination didn't kill Brenna," Paul snapped. "My sword did. What did I kill? Where did she go?"

Roche was sipping his medicated coffee busily.

The Guide smiled, wondering if the devil was being evasive or chasing a high.

"What happens when a devil possesses a human?" Kris asked Roche pointedly.

Still sipping, the devil harrumphed. "It doesn't happen very often. It only takes one possession to realize that being human isn't half as fun as being a devil, and word spreads fast."

"But what happens?" Kris pressed.

"The possession is seldom a complete one." Roche made a show of draining his coffee and casting about for his bottle.

"What happens if the possession is complete, dammit?" Paul cut in, his patience clearly worn thin.

The devil sighed. "Well, then the body would probably disappear. The soul would be lost, and the human body would go to Hell."

"It sounds like she was a devil," Kris ventured. "In that case, she disappeared because she went back to Hell. If she was human and the possession was complete, maybe her soul was driven out by the demon or devil before you killed it. Were any of her demons growing dangerously large?"

Paul shook his head. "Brenna didn't have any demons."

Jessica and Roche both laughed, then broke off when they saw that the Walker was not amused.

"Everybody has demons," Jessica said gently. She put her hand on Roche's shoulder. "Even God."

"You don't," the Walker retorted. "Roche doesn't. Kris doesn't. Brenna didn't."

"Do I?" Matt asked.

Paul ignored him.

"You can only see the demons of humans," Kris explained, watching Roche staying awfully busy filling his cup and foregoing the coffee. "You can't see the demons of angels or devils or Guides or Watchers. They're not yours to deal with, the supernatural have their own ways of dealing with their demons and angels."

Paul sipped his own coffee mixture, thoughtful. Suddenly it smelled and looked so good to the Guide; he hadn't had a cup of coffee in days. Licking his lips, he turned to find Jessica watching him and giggling quietly.

"Cream and sugar?" she whispered, still giggling.

Kris nodded and squeezed her hand gratefully. As her fingers left his, he arched an eyebrow at Paul. "So? Does that help? Either she was a devil and she attacked you and you sent her back to Hell; or her soul was driven out by a devil or demon that used her body to attack you."

"Then what would happen to her soul?" Matt asked, alarmed.

Kris shrugged. "It could be lost. It could be in Heaven. It could be in Hell."

"I think it's lost," the Walker nodded grimly. "Every time I try to see her, I see nothing. I go nowhere. I can usually go to someone just by thinking of them, in Heaven or Hell or on Earth. But she's gone."

"If she was a devil, it was the best disguise I ever saw," Roche added. "I never thought Brenna was anything but human, and as far as I know I've never been fooled." He paused a moment, looked at Jessica.

Her honeyed hair swayed with the slight shake of her head. "She seemed completely human to me," she agreed. "Although she was just a little too perfect. Maybe she was an angel. Maybe she's in Heaven."

The Walker grimaced.

"So," he said flatly, "to sum up: Brenna could have been pretty much anything, and her soul could be pretty much anywhere. As far as you all know. Am I missing anything? Is there anything anyone knows about Brenna that they're not sharing?"

They exchanged glances, but no one said a word.

Kris shrugged. "Sorry, buddy."

Paul's eyes hardened.

"Let's get to work, then," he said abruptly. "What's the plan, devil?"

"A stage over there," Roche pointed. "Another bar over there. The coffee bar won't have taps, but it will have booze and bottles. All the liquor is in the back. If we need more, or anything else, someone needs to go get it."

"Roche." Paul stopped the devil. "Details. Priorities. Dimensions."

The devil grinned. "That's your job. You're the manager. Manage."

"Matt." He stood to attention as the Walker acknowledged him. "Go inventory the booze and then take the list to a couple bars where you know people and ask how it works and if we have what we need. If we don't, buy more booze and bring it back here."

"How do I buy the booze?" Matt asked.

"Buy a lottery ticket," Paul waved his hand dismissively. "Hurry. There's lots to do."

He was already turning back to Roche. "Those look like twelve foot boards. We'll make the stage twelve by twelve and three feet high. Start cutting three foot lengths with the table saw while I mark the plywood."

CHAPTER 6

Mason woke and stretched lazily. He smelled bacon and toast. Smiling, he propped his pillow against the headboard and sat up straight, soft sheets still covering his naked lower half. There was an ashtray on the nightstand, shiny and blue and clean. There were three joints in it, at three different stages of burnt. Leaning over, he grabbed the dish and set it on his lap. Next he retrieved the pack of cigarettes that waited by the ashtray, and then he was having smoky breakfast in bed.

"Smells good," he called out, exhaling a plume of white smoke that hung as a cloud before dissipating.

"It sure does." Sarah came into the room wearing only his tee shirt, a Metallica concert print. When she walked and sat on the mattress next to him, he could see her naked hips and ass under the swaying material. She leaned over and took the joint from his lips and kissed him, took one hit and then another. Holding it in, she smiled as her pretty pale face reddened slightly under her dark straight bangs.

"Hungry?" she asked, putting the joint back between his lips.

He nodded.

"Good." She stood up and walked back to the kitchen, exhaling a cloud of smoke as he watched her walk away. Her slender legs met in a tantalizing shifting shadow that made him wish he bought smaller shirts.

When she returned with two plates laden with hashed browns and eggs and bacon and toast, Mason took them both so she could slide in under the covers beside him.

"I like the sheets," he said, handing her a plate and taking a fork and napkin from her. "You were right, I admit it. Thread count matters." The fork dove indiscriminately into his food, mashing eggs and meat and browns into a small mountain of whitish goo streaked in yellow and flecked with brown. He balanced a mound of the goo on his fork to his mouth, and then followed with a bite of toast.

"Mmm!" he said, chewing.

Sarah smiled.

"I love feeding you," she said. "You seem to appreciate it so much."

Mason nodded his agreement, shoveling another mound in his maw.

"I'm excited about tonight." She picked up a piece of bacon and took a tiny bite.

He swallowed. "It's a new club, isn't it? Don't get up."

She turned to look a question at him, then her eyes blinked and went round. "I forgot the coffee!"

Mason leaned over and kissed her. "I got it."

CHAPTER 7

Pacing in front of the limp hands and dark hair hanging to cover the pretty face, Lilia stared at the red blood stain on the floor.

"Look at me," she snapped, her voice beautiful and musical and cruel.

Brenna lifted her head, met the devil's eyes.

"Why are you still here?" she demanded.

The girl's smooth brow crinkled in consternation. "You have me locked up. Please let me go."

"I cut off your head. Now you're fine. Explain that to me." The devil stopped pacing, brought her face a breath from Brenna's. "Who are you?"

She blinked, and her face cleared. "I am Brenna Blanco. Please let me go."

Lilia's eyes swam with fire, and she slapped the girl stingingly across the cheek. Two fine lines of red blood stood out on her pale skin where long fingernails had slashed. Brenna's face turned sideways from the blow, a spray of hair across it. She let her head fall forward again, her dark mane cascading to obscure her features.

"It won't be so easy this time," the devil said coldly, turning to make a selection from the wall of cruelty. "Tell me who I am. Tell me who you are. Tell me why you are here."

She selected a small sharp dagger and turned to her captive.

Brenna raised her head as best she could, warily tracking the devil's approach.

CHAPTER 8

The stage was completed and the bar was well under way by the time Kris and Jessica returned from the apartment. Kris watched Walker and devil blurring back and forth with amazing speed, opting for hand tools more often than not. Roche was driving nails with a single swing, one after another like a machine, when he missed and struck his thumb.

"Dammit!" The hammer flew to bounce harmlessly off the side of the sturdy stage.

"Are you okay?" Kris asked, concerned.

The devil gave him a wry smile. "Yeah, I'm okay. Thanks."

Paul halted his flurried activities.

"Did you dent another hammer?" he snapped.

Roche shrugged and looked away, sulking. "Maybe."

"It looks great in here, you guys." Kris surveyed the room while Jessica went to make more coffee.

"The Walker knows how to build," Roche nodded, obviously impressed. "We'll be done by two, three o'clock. Nice duds for a Guide."

Kris felt relaxed in his jeans and polo, loafers instead of sandals. When his girl brought him a fresh cup of sweetened coffee, he thought again that it was good to be dead. He couldn't imagine a better life for himself.

"You guys need any help?" Jessica asked.

Paul nodded. "If you can help Matt with booze and attend bartending school by tomorrow night, that would be great."

Roche exchanged a smile with Jessica.

"Don't be silly, Walker," Roche chided him. "We're devils. We're booze scientists. You got your bartenders right here. Kris and Matt can cover the door. You just manage."

"I won't be here," Paul shook his head. "I'm busy all night tomorrow."

"What?!" the devil roared. "You have to be here, Walker. It's opening night."

He frowned and stroked his shadowed jaw, considering. "All right. I need to leave now then."

Paul raised his voice slightly, cutting off further protestation. "Andre."

The Watcher coalesced into view, his spectacled round face appearing over his plain brown robe. Book and quill were tucked under one armpit. He looked disapproving at the Guide, dressed like a human being and sipping coffee.

He lowered his head. "Walker King."

Kris felt Jessica shudder beside him.

"Please don't call him that," she muttered darkly.

All eyes turned to her but Paul's, who seemed not to have heard. He stepped forward and let his hand fall on the Watcher's shoulder.

"I'll be back," he said.

Then they disappeared.

CHAPTER 9

Andre looked around, uneasy. The landscape was truly unappealing in every way, at least to him. Perhaps Tim Burton or Dr. Seuss' dark side could revel in the twisted dark rock that described every feature in fissured floor and jutting formations. Thick acrid smoke filled the air and his lungs, and the Watcher was glad he didn't need to breathe.

"Where are we?" he whispered.

Paul shushed him, staring intently into the shadows.

"You're in Hell, Watcher." A voice came behind them, and Andre turned. She was beautiful, short and lean. The taut muscles of her legs and arms stood out in defined lines as she held a spear threatening between them. Long dark silky hair and a few scraps of well-placed leather made her more feminine than frightening, although Andre still took a step back.

"Take me to Lilia," Paul demanded, stepping forward as the Watcher stepped back.

"Oh?" She looked at the Walker's plain human garb, jeans and pocket tee stained and torn by the morning's rapid construction. "And who are you, to be on a first name basis with the Queen of Hell?"

His eyes wide, Andre turned to Paul. "The Queen of Hell?"

"Relax," Paul frowned, bunching his shoulders and clenching his jaw visibly. "It's going to be fine."

He nodded at the devil. "I'm Walker Paul, King of the Walkers."

The pretty devil clenched her spear more firmly, rocking back as if to strike. Andre watched her taut muscles ripple under smooth crimson skin while orange flame lighted her slitted eyes.

"You want me to take the Walker King to the Dragon Queen?" she hissed, incredulous. She nodded, her pretty eyes narrowing. "Very well. One piece at a time."

Her spear thrust forward suddenly, and Andre could see that the end was not just pointed but beveled to a wooden blade. It would have neatly penetrated the Walker's throat if he had still been there, but instead two blades flashed. Paul stood next to her as her body crumpled to a lifeless heap at his feet, her pretty head and severed spear falling beside her with a thump and a clatter.

Paul sighed as Andre watched purple blood pump from her neck to puddle near the hem of his robe. He stepped back and looked up, and beheld the Walker King. Paul's armor had appeared, and he still held his swords crossed before him. The short blade was streaked with a wet purple smear.

"Sorry," he frowned under the wide leather brim. "I wasn't expecting that."

Shadows took shape around them then, and a dozen devils menaced the duo. Ten male and two female, they all sported curved swords or daggers and chain mail over their leather outfits. They looked mean and angry, and Andre knew they could take out a human army in an hour. He was surprised to see Paul's weapons disappear at the sight of them.

"Please," the Walker growled, his tone hardly supplicatory. "Take me to the Dragon Queen."

One devil was approaching from behind while another stepped toward Paul to keep his eyes forward. The Watcher saw, and opened his mouth to warn Paul; but both bodies dropped headless to the ground before he could speak. In a flash, the Walker stood in the same spot with two gleaming blades stained purple.

"I can do this all day," the Walker snapped. "I'm not here to kill devils; I'm here to talk to the queen. Attacking me is suicide. Please don't—" One of the females rushed forward, six feet of crimson and steel blur. A moment later Paul stood over her severed head, shaking his head while blood spattered his boot.

"I'm telling you," he insisted, kicking the head away. "I'm not here to pick a fight."

Another figure emerged from the shadows, a shining silver suit of armor with a curved sword sheathed at its waist and a long crimson forked tail jutting from the buttocks.

"Walker King," a muffled voice intoned from behind the slitted visor. "The Dragon Queen will see you now."

Andre sighed with relief and followed devil and Walker, skirting his way around puddles of blood and headless bodies and disembodied heads.

Paul fell into step beside him. "How much time do we have?"

The Watcher shook his head. "I haven't figured out the exchange rate yet. It seems to shift constantly. The higher you go or the lower you go, the longer the relative minute. Your key should tell you."

Platinum key suddenly in his upraised palm before him, Paul clicked the watch face open with the press of a button.

"See the dark brown hand? The middle one?"

Paul nodded. "It looks black."

"All the time trackers do, until you focus in on one. Then they appear dark red or brown or blue. The middle one is a twenty-four hour single hand indicator of Earth time. See the watch numbers?" He asked.

Paul nodded again.

"Not even noon. It's barely moving," The Walker noted, satisfied. "Looks like there's a demon on the menu tonight."

They followed the eerily quiet suit of armor around a smoking chasm and into a cave. Soon the rock walls became hallways, and soon the hallways led to a door.

The animated plate mail pushed the door open wordlessly.

Andre slowed as he entered the hall, turning in place to take in the colors and textures of the alien room.

The Walker brushed by him and approached the throne.

"Where is she?" Paul demanded, his broad armored back blocking the Watcher's view of whomever he was addressing. He looked instead at the dragon heads meeting above the throne in exquisitely crafted detail.

"I told you that you would come back to me."

To say the voice was beautiful was to say the ocean was wet. Her tones were flinted music, every word a song to win a dozen hearts. Andre took two quick steps to see if she was as impossibly beautiful as her voice. And she was, her hair flaming red and her body a compelling collection of curves that challenged a scant wave of black silk to cover it all. Her eyes swirled crimson and orange and black, with the slitted iris everyone seemed to be thinking more and more sexy.

Maybe it was just him.

Thick full lips smiled alluring at the Walker.

"Still no manners, even as a king," she laughed. Her laugh was a song Andre would play over and over in his mind, he knew it the moment he heard it. Rich and mocking and playful, he sighed as it died away. "Where is who, Walker?"

"Brenna." Andre couldn't see Paul's face, but he was sure it was twisted with rage the same as his voice. He took a step closer, and the swirling beauty of her eyes shifted to him.

"Your Watcher looks as confused as I am." It was hard for him to focus on her words as his heart listened to the flinted song of her voice, and for a moment Andre didn't realize she had given him a cursory acknowledgment.

The Watcher shuffled his sandaled feet nervously under his robe.

"Where's Brenna?" Paul demanded.

Her eyes narrowed attractively. "Who the Hell is Brenna?"

"Matt said they came to see you." His voice was still accusing, but there was an undertone of uncertainty in the Walker's statement.

She spread her hands and glanced again at the Watcher. "And who the Hell is Matt?"

Andre opened his mouth, compelled to do anything that might keep her attention on him. "Matt is—"

Paul gave him a sharp look sure to silence him unless the Walker addressed him.

"You didn't meet with him," Paul turned his stern gaze back to the scarlet lady. "You met with Brenna."

"Says who?" She arched pretty eyebrows over the flames of her eyes.

"Matt." His voice was flat, uncertain.

When she smiled, Andre saw sharp long canines that were as sexy as they were deadly. "Someone who didn't meet with me claims I met with someone I've never heard of, is that right? Did he say 'Brenna met with Lilia', or 'Brenna went to have a drink with the Queen of Hell last Thursday'? Did he know my name?"

"No," Paul admitted. "But he recognized it when I said it. He described the hallways."

Her laugh was purely mocking then, still beautiful in its way but ugly in its scorn. Andre promptly forgot the sound of it. "Nine worlds, each infinite compared to yours, with endless leagues of tunnels and hallways and half a hundred lesser queens and you bring this to me? How in Hell did you become a king, Walker?"

Andre didn't realize he was smiling until her beautiful scornful song pointed it out.

"Even your Watcher thinks you a fool," she laughed.

His face was stone as the Walker turned.

Paul's bunched shoulders relaxed in a sigh, but he worked the muscles of his jaw so fervently Andre thought he could hear teeth grinding.

"When I heard you were asking for me, I hoped you were looking to climb the royal ladder. Walker King marries the Queen of Hell, worth thinking about for both of us." She looked Paul up and down shamelessly. "You even started growing your beard and your hair for me." Andre felt a little awkward being in the room.

Paul shook his head, although the Watcher noticed he seemed to be considering a thought he found less than disgusting. Even Andre's mind went a little too far along the path of living in Hell. Devil girls were just plain sexy.

The Walker removed his hat. "I'm sorry, Lilia. You're right, I am acting a fool, and it is for love. But it is not for my love for you."

Paul let the words stand between them for a moment, giving her time to read between the lines. "I am in love with a human who was possessed by a demon or a devil." He lowered his head.

The swirling in her eyes stopped for a moment, and a slow sly smile spread across her full painted lips. It faded before Paul raised his head again, and she met his sad blue eyes with a look of genuine concern.

"I killed her," Paul muttered. "And now I can't find her soul."

"And you think she came to Hell and met with a devil? Based on the sketchy account of this Matt fellow?" Her scornful song's sharp notes bounced harmlessly off the Walker's duster. "How reliable is he?"

For a moment, Andre thought Paul was actually going to smile. He frowned and rubbed his rough jaw instead.

"I apologize again," the Walker said. "You are absolutely right. I was rude to you, and I am sorry. You have never done anything but help me; I should be thanking you and not accusing you. I owe you, Lilia, at least the benefit of the doubt."

"You owe me more than that." The devil was pressed against Paul in a heartbeat, and Andre was beginning to feel uncomfortable again. "Make it up to me, Walker King. Make me Queen of the Walkers. Or just be the king of my bed for the night," she breathed.

Trying to watch and look away all at the same time, Andre was glad when the Walker disengaged from the devil gently.

"Lilia," the Walker's voice was low and thick as he stepped back, "You are amazingly, achingly beautiful, and...and so much more."

Paul glanced at Andre and cleared his throat. "I am in love with someone else, however. I couldn't...I can't...I'm not here for that." He looked as though he regretted saying it, even as he said it.

"Well," she crossed her arms under her voluptuous breasts, and the silk slid tantalizingly both up and down her generous scarlet curves, "if your demon-possessed human girlfriend doesn't turn up, maybe you should consider it. You know what they say: 'If you've never had a devil, you've never really had it.'"

"Had what?" Andre asked, forgetting himself.

The long moment they both looked at him was his coldest memory of Hell.

"She might be a devil," Paul turned to the queen again. "Brenna. She bled purple and disappeared when I…when she died."

Lilia shrugged, her breasts bouncing over her folded forearms. "I don't know any devils named Brenna. I'll keep my eye out if you'd like, though."

Paul nodded his thanks. "What if she is lost?" He looked up at her, his blue eyes clouded with concern. "Do you know how to find a lost soul?"

The devil smiled sadly at him. "No one knows how to find a lost soul, that's why they call them lost." Her words could have been sarcastic, but her tone was flinted kindness. "I am sorry, Walker. I don't know what to tell you."

"Thank you, Lilia," he nodded sadly and planted his hat on his head again. "I apologize again for my behavior and my intrusion."

The devil waved her long slender fingers dismissively. "Water under the bridge, darling. Stop by anytime. I'll put the word out so you might pass …unmolested."

She smiled a shameless seductive sharp-toothed smile.

"By anyone but me," she added.

Paul shrugged. "It was nice to blow off a little steam. Thanks again, Lil." His hand fell on Andre's shoulder, and suddenly they were in the living room of Paul's apartment.

"Damn," the Walker swore, his armor gone. "That was my only lead."

The Watcher looked around the normal room, still reeling from the experience.

"Paul," he said. "Can I ask you something?"

Rubbing his jaw, Paul nodded for him to ask.

"Why did you take me to Hell with you?"

"Two reasons," Paul answered. "First, to keep me from…being tempted."

Andre nodded, smiling his understanding. "I thought so. But why me? Why not Kris?"

"The second reason," the Walker replied. "You were raised Catholic, right?"

Andre must have mentioned it, but he was surprised that Paul remembered if he had.

"Yeah, strict hardcore Catholic," he agreed.

"I wanted to show you it was real."

Andre nodded, happy. "Thank you, Paul."

CHAPTER 10

It was a completely different space. Kris looked around, allowing himself to be amazed anew at the transformation. There was no coffee shop here, no oversized space starving for customers. Every square foot was utilized in a balanced array of stage, dance floor, tables and bars.

Paul had returned with renewed energy and imagination, although Kris felt more than once that the Walker's constant fluid motion was more welcome distraction than joyful creation. The only times he stopped moving, it was either to sip at the drinks Jessica kept making him, or to talk about what needed to be done with whoever he thought needed to be doing it.

The drinks became more Bailey's than coffee as the day wore on, and the Walker's sips became gulps. No matter how much he drank, Kris never once saw Paul either waver or smile. Gathering them all together, he had pointed out how high the ceilings were. Then his hand was a blur, holding a fat marker over a flattened cardboard box. The drawing was a little confusing to the others, but Paul spoke with such excitement they all agreed it was a great idea.

Leaving Paul alone with Roche and the project, Jessica had helped Kris make a few trips back and forth to grab some things from the apartment. They had ended up in bed on the last trip, making love and falling asleep in each other's arms. While the Guide adjusted to his new touch and his new love and walking through that strange doorway once again, Paul had worked tirelessly through the night to turn coffee shop to nightclub.

Looking at it now, the Guide realized it really was a great idea. Twin staircases climbed from two opposite walls furthest from the entrance and flanked the stage. Twenty-three enclosed steps brought the climber to a wide balcony, wide enough for a table of four to sit undisturbed against the low wall while the climber passed. Half a dozen such tables and chairs were spaced in mirrored regularity along both walls. Above the entrance, the balcony widened to become a second floor. Another bar had gone up directly above the clanking brass bell Roche refused to take down, and they had sent Matt out again for more booze to stock the added service station.

Climbing the stairs, watching Jessica's slim shapely flexing buttocks as she ascended before him, Kris called down to Paul and Roche. "This is incredible, you guys. Everyone I know seems to be revealing fascinating facets of themselves that I can only be impressed by."

Jessica turned to smile sexy promises at him over her shoulder, then they both thought of Brenna at the same time. Kris felt himself flush.

"Where did you learn to build like this, Paul?" He asked loudly before the Walker could similarly relate the comment. When he looked down, Paul was frowning and staring into his tall coffee cup. It looked like it was pretty much just liquor from here. As he watched, the Walker tipped the cup and gulped twice, draining it. He licked his lips distastefully and glanced up at Kris cresting the steps.

"What do you think I've been doing the past five years?" Paul asked the Guide.

Kris shrugged. "What, you mean telecom installation? I thought you said it was mostly running cables and cutting connectors. You never mentioned woodwork."

"You're right," Paul admitted. "Most of what I built was metal fastened to existing concrete floors and ceilings. This whole structure is concrete, floors, ceilings and walls. Everything we built is wood around steel framing and supports attached to eight inch thick concrete with anchors as fat as your thumb. My lack of woodworking background came in handy here; the place just got hugely overbuilt to compensate. Long after this building has fallen down, the framing we built today will hold its shape." It was the longest bit of talking he had heard from his friend in a while. The Guide was pleasantly surprised when he continued.

"There's a countdown going on, buddy. For tonight. Afterwards I want to show you something. Any way I can have you for an hour or two about nine tonight?" Paul set his empty cup on the bar and looked up at him.

"Hang on," Roche roared. "It's opening night. I need you both here from eight until close. I need everybody here, especially the damned general manager. Not tonight, Walker."

"That's just it, though," Paul spoke calmly to the enraged devil. "I am a Walker. I am the Walker King. I have one job that I must do when duty calls, or another soul could be lost. Kris is my Guide." The Walker glanced up at him, and he couldn't help but stand a little straighter. "His job is as important as mine, and I need him now more than ever."

Roche was drinking directly from the bottle. Knowing him, it was a scotch that cost more than the plain outfit he wore and would be gone within the hour. Looking down on them, Kris thought how much they looked like drunken louts one bad decision away from homelessness. They both wore jeans and tee shirts and work boots, and the clothes that had looked fairly new yesterday morning now resembled the tattered rags worn by survivors of a shipwreck or hurricane. Cut and torn and even bloodied in places, their flurried activities had taken their toll on their threadbare ensembles. One of Paul's boots was open where sole met leather, and the white sock beneath was brown and frayed.

"You can handle one little demon by yourself, Walker King," the devil scoffed. "In a half hour."

The Walker frowned. "Fine. I'll do it alone. In however long it takes."

Paul eyed the devil's bottle. "What are you drinking, Roche?" Without waiting for an answer, he held out the cup he had emptied and the devil filled it with the syrupy brown liquid.

Jessica came to stand beside Kris and watch them drink. "Why don't you two get together after we close tonight?" She put her arm around his waist and pulled him closer.

"That's a great idea," Kris nodded. "What do you think, Paul?"

The Walker sniffed at the scotch, sipped at it cautiously.

"Sounds good," he muttered, not looking up. He tilted the cup and drained it, and when he set it down his features relaxed with a contented sigh.

"First you two need to get cleaned up," Jessica called to the ragged duo. They looked themselves over and laughed.

"And shave," she added, as an afterthought.

"Yeah, Paul, when was the last time you shaved?" Kris laughed. "My funeral? Since when can you grow a beard in two days? Is that a Walker power?"

The Walker stroked his whiskers thoughtfully. "Who says it's only been two days?"

Roche nodded, filling Paul's cup again. "I like it, Walker. A beard fit for a king. Hear, hear." He lifted the cup and they drank, Roche draining the bottle as Paul emptied the cup.

Jessica took Kris' hand and led him to the bar for a lesson. Since they had added the second tier, they were going to need another bartender.

CHAPTER 11

Sarah edged her little blue Accord against the curb a few paces behind the van. She set the parking brake and curbed the wheels, then turned with a smile.

"I'm excited," she gushed.

"Me too." Mason nodded coolly.

"Do you want to go check it out?" Sarah asked.

"Oh." Mason let his face fall in mock disappointment. "You mean the club. I thought you were talking about us."

She leaned over to kiss him, his lips, his nose, his cheeks and chin. He chuckled happily as her soft lips pressed against him again and again.

"Us is why I'm excited about everything," she murmured, her lips finding his again. "The club, the band, my life. Me is us now, baby. And I am very excited about us."

He kissed her back, cupping her head with his hand to pull her in close. "Let's go see."

Tyler and Jason waited for them on the sidewalk, looking up at the sign.

"Devil's Brew," Tyler said, bobbing his head in excited approval. "I guess they make their own beer."

Jason continued looking at the sign, his thumbs tattooing a beat only he could hear on his stomach.

"And coffee," Sarah added as they came together. "The owner is a cool old guy. He mixes the coffee blends, his manager brews the beer. Good coffee, too. I didn't try the beer."

"Well, it better be good or I'm not playing," Tyler squeaked, then elbowed Mason playfully. "Just kidding."

Mason looked up and down the street, quiet in the early evening hour. "Where's Mikie?" he asked Sarah. "And Robert?" A black Acura rounded the corner as he spoke, engine revving as it pointed their way.

He watched her dark hair brush her slender shoulders as she shook her head. "I don't know, sweetie. Want me to call them?"

"Nah." He took her hand and squeezed. "Let's go see if they're ready for us." Turning, he arced an eyebrow at Tyler. "Looks like your brother turned up. Can you guys start unloading? I'll be back to help in a few, after we go talk to them."

"We'll be back to help," Sarah added, clasping his hand and leading him to the door, glass set in steel. Mason reached the handle before her, opening the door and holding it for her from the sidewalk. A bell jangled loudly over his head when the steel swung inward, and Mason felt a sudden stab of pain, like a spike being driven into his skull. He winced, and Sarah noticed.

"Are you alright?" she asked, her pretty face clouded with concern.

Mason nodded. It had passed. "Come on."

Looking up at him doubtfully, Sarah stepped past him and Mason followed for two strides before the door hit the bell again as it swung closed behind them. The clang drilled a searing hole through his brain, and it was all he could do not to cry out. Sarah turned to see him scrunching his face against the pain, and she rushed to put her hands on his cheeks. Her cool palms were ice on fire, and he sighed at the contact.

"Everything okay?" A loud gruff voice called out from across the open room. They turned together to see the two men sitting at the bar. One was an older guy, stout and round and dressed neatly in shades of dark blue, suit and tie and jacket between black fedora and black patent leather shoes. The other wore black shoes and slacks and suit jacket, the only color in his outfit a dark purple shirt buttoned to leave the collar and one fastening undone. A small triangle of black showed that he had a tee shirt on under the buttoned purple shirt. His hair was a little shaggy, not as long as his or Tyler's but longer than the drummer's. The beard that was starting on his face was darker than the hair on his head, and his piercing eyes were an eerie cold blue that made Mason look away reflexively.

"Yep. Everything's fine. This is Sarah. I'm Mason." He stepped toward the men, noting the tall glasses they set down beside the half-empty bottle on the bar. Sarah didn't have time to be concerned for him as Mason pulled her along.

"Roche," the big guy said gruffly, his beefy paw enclosing Mason's long slender fingers. "I met your girl, good to see you again." He nodded once at Sarah before he focused beady black eyes on Mason, all the while grasping his hand firmly.

Roche looked down at his hand and gave it a final painful squeeze.

"Guitar player?" he asked.

Mason nodded.

"Are you the guy?"

He shrugged.

"He's the guy," Sarah laughed. She rubbed his shoulder. "Get used to it, baby."

"Hey, Sarah, Mason. I'm Paul." He shook her hand first, and when he turned to shake Mason's it was hard to look at him straight. He smelled of whiskey, but his eyes were like blue lasers boring into his skull. Mason squinted against another wave of pain as they shook hands and locked eyes. A twisting worm of memory stabbed a swirl of electricity through his head, but he couldn't place it.

"Nice to meet you," he managed, giving the man a passable handshake.

"Have we met?" Those blue eyes narrowed as the bearded man frowned at him.

Mason shook his head. "I don't think so." He'd seen him before; he knew he had. The vague memory couldn't pierce the throb in his head, however.

"Are you alright?" Paul asked, turning to transfer the contents of the bottle into the tall clear glasses. When he set it down, it was three-quarters empty. His eyes softened into a look of concern.

"Yeah," Mason nodded. "I get headaches sometimes. I'll be alright."

"Wanna beer?" The older man grinned under his fedora. "Devil's Brew. First batch. On the house."

"I'll take one. There are more of us outside, waiting to bring in the equipment," Sarah spoke up, rubbing soft unseen circles on Mason's back with the tips of her fingers.

The bearded man seemed to move without moving, and in a startling blink he stood beside Mason.

"Call them in," he said. "You guys need help?"

Before they could respond, Paul called out. "Jessica! Kris! Could you come down here?"

Mason turned, finally having a chance to survey the club.

"Wow," he whistled. "This place is awesome. Didn't this used to be a coffee shop?" Mason had stopped in before; it was right on his way to work. They hadn't had very good breakfast selections, and the place had been wide open and empty and a little creepy. He had never stopped again; there was a Starbucks on the way too.

"Still is," Roche gulped at the sipping whiskey. "Get drunk at night and come back in the morning for coffee. Stupid brilliant, right?" The bearded man clenched his jaw visibly and gave the older guy a strange look while two figures descended the stairs to the right of the stage. Mason watched them, marveling at the wide balcony.

"This is an incredible remodel," he said, his eyes going from balcony to stage.

"Thanks," the two men said together.

Mason's eyes went wide. "You guys did this? It must have taken forever."

"Almost two days," the round older man chuckled, and he clinked his glass against Paul's. Paul didn't smile, but he did drink.

"These two lose track of time when they're working," a soft sweet voice said behind him. Mason turned and extended his hand to the newcomers, shaking her hand first.

"I'm Mason," he nodded at the pretty blonde. "This is Sarah. Nice to meet you."

"Jessica." She had a firm handshake for a girl. "You ever hear of the lost weekend?"

Mason laughed and nodded. Half the room looked confused as Jessica and Sarah shook hands, and he explained as he hid his surprise at the wispy handshake he got from the guy with the gray eyes and the dark blue polo.

"John Lennon, his mistress and a handful of musician friends spent over a year doing God knows what in a Los Angeles hotel room. When they talked about that year, they called it the lost weekend. Mason," he said, looking into the intelligent grey sparkle.

The man smiled. "Kris. Good to meet you."

Jessica slid behind the bar like a pilot with a stack of yellowed log books sliding into the cockpit. "What can I get you two?"

Mason nodded at his pretty girl.

"One Devil's Brew, please," she smiled.

"Make that two," he nodded again.

Jessica slid the bottles to them, and they drank together. Sarah lowered the bottle and blinked, her eyes widening.

"That's good," she said, taking another sip.

"Mmm-hmm," Mason took a longer drink. "Coffee. And chocolate." He set the bottle on the bar, half empty. "That's delicious. Do you guys sell cases?"

Kris was shaking his head, but Paul nodded.

"Yeah," he said. "We've got over a hundred half racks bottled and boxed. We'll throw in a couple cases if you guys put on a good show."

The older man showed his teeth. "Otherwise you'll have to pay for it," he growled.

"We're going to bring some stuff in." Mason grabbed Sarah's hand and pulled her halfway to the door before he finished the sentence; but he stopped to ease the door open, remembering the bell. It still clanged, twice, and he heard it muffled on the other side of the door after it swung shut behind them. Fierce lances of fire stabbed his brain, and he squinted against the pain.

When Mason opened his eyes, Sarah was holding out her car keys, her brow furrowed in concern.

"We'll get the equipment," she assured him. "Your medicine jar is under the seat. Go for a drive, baby. Get your head straight."

He hesitated, and then took the keys gratefully. "Have I told you how wonderful you are?"

Up on her tip-toes, she kissed him lightly. "Yes. But I don't mind hearing it over and over."

Mason passed his friends on the sidewalk. "I'll be back in a few, they're ready."

Jason's white cargo van stood with every door open, and musical equipment littered the sidewalk by each opening. They began to heft the items they had unloaded, guitar cases and mixing board and the first pieces of an endless drum kit.

Cal had indeed arrived, and he called out. "Hey Mason."

"What's up, Cal." Mason slammed the car door shut and keyed the ignition, reaching under the seat with his left hand. He unscrewed the lid of the wide-mouthed canning jar and selected a purple plastic container instead of the orange or green as he pulled away from the curb. Little round smiling pieces of animated chocolate waved at him happily from the label of the airtight container. The lid made a quiet pop, and the dank, heavy scent of purple cannabis filled the car.

Purple meant indica, green meant sativa, and orange was for roaches. Sarah's car never smelled like weed, and now neither did Mason's. She had organized everything he had from all the medical marijuana dispensaries he had shopped, and now he had a jar for home and a jar for his car. Or her car. He smoked as he drove, thinking how hard he was falling for her and happy for it. He made a right turn and another and drove a few aimless blocks.

Half the joint was gone as he turned again, and his headache was lifting finally. Two more blocks and he turned right at a light going yellow and drove through a few more green lights. Passing through a wide open intersection, Mason dropped the joint as it burned his finger.

Suddenly his pulse was racing as an eerie déjà vu swept over Mason. His eyes went wide, and he saw a memory unfold as he passed through the green light. He thought that image had been drowned forever in gallons of beer.

Mason pulled over and stopped, finding the smoking roach as his heart threatened to pound from his chest.

He knew where he was suddenly. He was pretty sure he knew where he had seen the bearded man, too.

CHAPTER 12

Kris watched his friend open the door, the brass bell jangling once and then again as he swung it swiftly closed. Paul turned to the crew.

"There are people waiting," he frowned. "Lots of people."

"Well," the devil showed his teeth. "Let 'em in. Let's get this party started."

"Jess, Kris, Roche, to the bars please." Paul held up an orange numbered ticket. "Each one of these is worth a bottle of Devil's Brew. Take the ticket, tear it up and throw it away. Matt, I'll help you at the door until the line is reasonable enough for you to handle on your own."

"Remember," Paul gave Matt a sharp look, "Five bucks a head and one ticket per person, no matter how hot she is."

Matt nodded and Paul opened the door to one last jangle of the bell as he propped it open for the long night ahead. He was lost for a while in a stream of ID's and orange tickets and five and ten and twenty dollar bills. They blocked the entrance while they worked their respective registers, one on either side of the wide open doorway. Transaction completed, step aside to let the customers pass, then block and check identification.

"What if I want to leave?" A young man in a shirt too small to quite reach his painted-on jeans asked him.

Paul frowned. "You won't want to."

He handed Paul a five dollar bill. "What if I want to leave and come back? Do I get a stamp?"

His frown deepened. "Tell your bartender to give you half of this when you redeem it." He thrust the orange ticket at the man. "It's worth a free beer. Keep the part of the ticket they give you if you want to leave and come back."

The man made a face. "I don't like beer."

Paul stepped aside to let him pass. "Don't drink it then."

Noting the thinning crowd, Paul looked behind him. Flashing lights and loud music and the sea of faces disoriented him for a heartbeat, and he turned and spoke to Matt loudly while blocking and ignoring the next customer.

"Take over, big guy," he shouted. "I need to check on the bars."

Matt nodded wordlessly and moved to block the whole entrance as

Paul weaved his way to the new bar.

"Roche!" The devil was moving from one task to the next with a speed and economy of motion that was just a touch unnatural. He was in his element, surfing a sea of cash and liquor, grinning as he looked up at Paul. He glided across the rubber weaves of the matted floor to plunk a beer and a shot in front of the Walker. In ten seconds they were both empty.

"Did you find your demon?" Roche hollered.

Paul frowned, glanced left and right and leaned forward over the bar. "There is a suspicious lack of demon activity here tonight."

Roche nodded and poured him another shot. "That's good, isn't it?"

Paul drank and savored the burn at the back of his throat.

"No," he frowned. "It's suspicious."

The devil leaned in closer. "Relax, Walker. It's the bell. It's magick." He winked conspiratorially.

"It helps keep the demons out?" Paul asked.

"It quiets them down. A lot. It does keep the devils out. Among other things." Roche poured him another shot. "Have you seen that kid Mason since they started playing?"

The way the devil changed the subject right when Paul had a mind full of questions annoyed him, especially when it worked. Paul turned to view the stage.

Six musicians threw up a wall of sound, a guitar heavy version of Katy Perry's "I Kissed A Girl". Guitars and keyboards hit some of the chords hard together, trading off light and airy fills for screeching distorted snippets. Paul had heard the song, he liked it; he liked it even more the way they rocked it up. Watching the lead guitar player was a whole different story than listening to him.

Mason's face was ashen, covered in a sheen of sweat. Long strands of hair clung to his face in wet chunks, the rest plastered to his head and neck. He was wearing ripped jeans and a black concert tee, and the shirt hung limp and glossy with perspiration. His eyes were dark hollows, staring down intently at his hands while he played. The other band members seemed helplessly concerned for the flagging musician, all eyes glancing repeatedly his way.

The dance floor was full, a sea of swaying bouncing young flesh. The only time Mason ever looked at anything but his skilled hands was to steal a glance at the crowd losing itself in the music.

Paul thought, *the poor guy doesn't want to disappoint them.*

Mason continued playing, sweat dripping onto his guitar and the stage.

The crowd danced on, oblivious.

"He looks awful," Paul turned back to Roche. The devil was gone, blurring along from bar to cash register, pouring shots and cocktails and draught beers. There was another shot on the bar, and Paul drank it and called out to Roche. "Be back!"

The Walker needed some air. The place was packed: good for business, but not so conducive to clear thinking. Besides, there wasn't a demon in sight.

Wending his way through clusters of people, Paul felt more than one soft firm ass rub against him as he passed. He frowned and held his breath through one hovering cloud of fragrance after another. His hand fell on Matt's shoulder as he came behind him. There were only a few people in line; he was fine.

"I need to step out." Paul didn't wait for a reply, stepping past him and stopping on the sidewalk to let his face feel the cool moist evening air. Breathing in deep, he exhaled with a heavy sigh as his eyes searched the shadows. He frowned and checked the key, opening the watch face with the touch of a button.

It was time; the countdown was complete. The demon symbol pulsed with light. Paul scanned his surroundings. There were people walking on the sidewalk, but their demons were all normal toy-sized harmlessness. No tall nasty demons walked beside them, waiting to take over the show.

The Walker closed his eyes. He thought of a demon, thought of separating it from its host and taking off its horned red head. Opening his eyes, he stood still in the same spot and frowned. He saw a light then, or the lighted space between buildings grow brighter suddenly, and he thought he saw a flicker of movement as well. Remembering to walk like a normal person, the Walker King approached the narrow passageway.

As the length of the walkway hove into view, he definitely saw something, a figure cloaked in shadows. It seemed to be pushing against the solid concrete outer wall at regular intervals. Paul entered the foot alley, his shadow lengthening before him. The figure turned and darted off, entering the wide alley behind the club. With a glance over his shoulder, he knew no one was watching. Paul blinked out of existence in one place and into existence in another to turn the same corner a moment later.

Pressing frantically against the rear wall of the building again and again, the figure was close enough when he rounded the corner that he could see its face. He also saw the thick rope of energy attached to its chest, and it was enough to know that it was a demon. Strangely, it wore an overcoat of thin wool, dark and frayed at the hem. It didn't run when he came around the corner, but turned and peered at him with red and black eyes that were alive with intelligence.

They stood there looking at each other, and recognition seemed to dawn in their eyes in the same startling instant. It had grown tall, tall as a man, although not as tall as the Walker. It seemed to have grown into its height as well, no longer awkward or bent on its feet. It was the first demon Paul had ever faced. Its face was no longer twisted or hateful, having matured into the open and curious features of a young man happy to find his own way in the world. The small horns sprouting from its forehead made it look more vulnerable rather than threatening somehow, its red skin lightened to a pink that could almost pass for human. Almost.

It was the intelligence in its eyes that gave him pause. Paul had been around enough demons to know them by the crazed look of obsession in their eyes. He had lumped the whole lot into vile creatures of only one emotional dimension with single-minded purpose. This demon looked at him with bright eyes full of recognition, touched with fear. Then it dropped smoothly to one knee before him and bowed its head.

"All hail the Walker King." It spoke, head bowed and voice low and strong. It didn't sound like a demon either, although its voice was too smooth and honeyed to be human. Paul thought of what Roche sounded like in Hell, or how Lilia might sound on Earth. He stared at the top of its round bald head, thinking how easy it would be to just chop off its head and go back to work. It raised its eyes and looked up at him then, and the thought was chased from his mind by a frigid wave that climbed his spine.

"Rise, demon." Paul spoke through clenched jaws, half hoping that the monster would come at him so he could end this all with a sudden sword.

It didn't come at him, rising slowly instead to spread it's clawed hands ingratiatingly.

"Please don't kill me," it said simply. "He needs me."

The Walker frowned, his hand itching for the heft of sharp steel, the drag on the blade when its arc met spine.

"Who?" Paul grimaced. "Who needs you?"

The demon's eyes went round in disbelief for a moment, and Paul wondered if it was surprised that the Walker King didn't know everything or if it was just the first time anyone had directly addressed the being.

It's face softened then, and Paul thought it was actually going to smile.

Instead it spoke.

"Mason," it said. "Mason needs me. I am not his demon any more, I am his friend. I help him, I don't hurt him now. He needs me."

The demon nodded eagerly, went on. "Sometimes he looks right at me, talks to me. He can't hear me clearly, or at all perhaps. The only way I can tell him things is if he guesses at what I am trying to tell him. Then he sees me nod or hears me say 'yes' clearly. He doesn't see me and hear me like… like this."

Paul nodded. He was right, then; this was the first true interaction the demon had had with anyone since chasing Paul and Kris. It was both awkward and eager as it spoke to him, and Paul felt his heart soften for the creature with compassion.

"What kind of things do you tell him?" Paul asked, wondering how a demon might lift you up.

The demon spread his hands. "I tell him that it's not his fault, that he's a good person. I tell him he can do and be whatever he wants."

"What?" Paul asked. "What isn't his fault?"

He looked at Paul with sincere curiosity for a long moment, and then shrugged. "He doesn't understand like you do. I just tell him he didn't kill anybody. I can't explain to him that he just played a part in someone else's transformation. It's too complicated. He doesn't know that he helped to make a Walker, or that that Walker went on to become King of the Walkers. He knows you survived unscathed by some miracle, and that's all."

The Walker's eyes didn't leave the black and scarlet stare as he let the demon's words sink in.

"That's all he needs to know," he said abruptly. He frowned again. "What have you been feeding off of, if not Mason?"

For the first time, the demon stood up straight and proud before the Walker King. A smile played at the corners of his lips.

"I feed off his demons," he replied. "All the little bastards that try to tell him that he's stupid and worthless and untalented, I feed off them and then I feed myself and Mason with their energy."

"You feed your host?" Paul's eyes were wide with wonder.

The demon nodded enthusiastically. "I love him, he is brilliant. He would never let himself play well before; all the voices in his head were holding him back. The talent was there the whole time, the ability and the desire within him constantly at war with the negative self-image he had because of his demons." He sighed and looked at the street, shame darkening his youthful features. "I was the worst of them all. He thought he killed you, and I was created from that guilt. Anything horrible I said made me stronger and more hateful and self-righteous, and I was going to take over my host easily long before most demons would make the attempt. He was consumed by guilt; it was only possible for me to become what I became because of his conscience."

"A good man lives with many demons," Paul agreed solemnly.

"And a great man lives with even more," the demon responded. "May I ask you something, Walker King?"

Paul arched an eyebrow, curious. "What?"

"Why do you tolerate a demon on your shoulder?" The demon was looking not at Paul but at his right shoulder, a frown on his face.

"I can help with that," he nodded at the voice Paul needed to hear. "I have fed from other demons besides Mason's."

The Walker frowned fiercely in sudden anger.

"Leave it alone," he snapped. "You fancy yourself a Walker, demon?"

Paul stood tall over the demon, glowering down at him.

"I didn't ask to be a demon," he responded simply. "I am proud of the demons I have killed. They were doing no good at all, and I have seen much good come of their absence. I was the worst of all, and my change made me see how terrible and how wrong I had been. I wanted to make it right."

"When did you change?" Paul asked.

The demon shrugged. "The moment I saw you alive and well, my whole existence was thrown into question. If you were unhurt, I was unjustified at a conceptual level. Just as I was about to take everything I ever wanted from my guilty host, I realized that you looked just like the image I was using to haunt Mason day and night. And you were looking right at me. You could see me."

"So you tried to kill me."

He shrugged again. "I was a demon; all I knew was hate and anger. I longed for violence, but I couldn't touch anything. Then when you looked at me, I felt strong and powerful. I guess I thought that if I killed you my existence would be justified, by some twisted hateful logic."

Paul nodded. "A self-fulfilling prophecy." That's what most demons turned out to be, in his experience.

"Then I got confused," The demon looked away, remembering. "I wandered around, thinking, seeing the world for the first time. I ran into some…friends, demons who had survived their hosts or been displaced like me. They were lost, wandering idiots who had no purpose. They told me about Walkers, and to stay away from them. Then they tried to feed off me, and I got away. I followed my connection back to Mason and decided I wanted to make right what I had done to him. I used the same method the demons had tried on me and began to consume Mason's demons. When I got my strength back, I started to feed him. I changed my hateful single-minded chant into a voice that encourages him constantly in every aspect of his life."

The demon smiled and looked up at the Walker King. "I feed off other demons when they get in the way, too. Sarah's, the other band members'. They all seem so much happier. Even if you kill me now, even if I have no soul and this is it, I am glad I lived. I am glad I got to see the change in Mason."

"I'm not going to kill you," the Walker said, somewhat to his own surprise. "Don't ever tell a human about Walkers or demons."

The demon's eyes grew round, hopeful and happy. "Of course, never. Thank you, I…thank you."

"Wait here," Paul turned on his heel and strode up the alley. "Mason needs you."

Back inside, he was struck by a wall of bright lights and a cacophony of sound that made him long for the civilized calm of conversing in an alleyway with a demon. Writhing bodies pressed against him again and again as he made his way to the stage. Paul waited, still in a turbulent sea of drunken dance, watching Sarah sing about a girl being eaten by a shark and a lion and a cement mixer in bright happy tones. She stole a worried look at Mason from time to time, but neither of them missed a note or skipped a beat as he listened.

The Walker remembered how impressed he had been with the band's smooth segues, and he stepped to the edge of the stage while they dove into the final chorus. He got Sarah's attention, then Tyler's, and pointed at Mason. She nodded and stepped to the edge of the stage to kneel and bring herself eye level with Paul.

She sang the final words of the song into the bulb of braided mesh, and then another voice broke in at almost the same instant as the song changed.

Robert sang the opening line of "I Gotta Feeling" in a bouncy rhythm as the drunken bodies swayed to the new beat, the lone thump of the bass drum.

Sarah was looking at Paul watching Mason.

"I think I can help," Paul hollered over the music. "Do you need him?" He nodded at the guitarist.

She shook her head, clicked a switch on the base of the mic. "That's why Rob went into this song, he saw you. We're taking a break after this anyway."

Sarah flipped the switch on again and sang her scant part suddenly, perfectly, still looking in his eyes.

Paul switched his attention to Mason as Tyler helped him past Sarah and Mikie and Robert and Jason's drums, and soon Paul was helping Mason down the steps he had built at the edge of the stage. Pressing through the mindless throng was more difficult with the musician in tow, and Paul almost let his impatience get the best of him as they were jostled repeatedly.

Then he closed his eyes, took a deep breath and imagined a path widening before them. Opening them, he was pleasantly unsurprised to see the crowd parting. He carried Mason almost bodily through the gap. Outside, he breathed in the welcome fresh air while he felt his charge start to shiver beside him.

"Come on, just a little further." At his voice, the musician looked up at Paul as if just realizing he was no longer on stage. His face was stark exhausted confusion; looking at Paul, his eyes suddenly widened with fear. He stiffened and tried desperately to pull away. What little strength he had remaining strained feebly against Paul's inescapable grasp.

"Don't hurt me," Mason sagged in his arm, his face a blanched sheen of sweat. "I'm sorry."

Paul knelt and let Mason fall on his shoulder. He rose, bearing the weight easily as he turned his head and spoke quiet but fierce.

"I'm not going to hurt you," Paul assured him. "Relax."

The Walker didn't think him lucid enough to clearly register nor remember should anything strange happen, but he walked like a normal person just the same. Carrying him like a sack of potatoes, he rounded the corner to see the demon emerge from the shadows. Concern darkened his youthful crimson visage as he rushed forward.

"Mason!" The form over his shoulder stirred, and Paul knelt to help him sit on the ground. The demon was there, kneeling beside him to put a hand on his shoulder and run the other through his hair. Paul watched the man's hair ruffle as he stirred again.

"You can touch him." Paul was still kneeling, but he was watching the monster more than the man.

The demon gazed almost adoringly at Mason, smiling as his face flushed and his eyelids fluttered. Nodding, he continued to stroke the man's hair.

"Sometimes," he said quietly, watching the man intently. "When I really need to, I can do things. If it helps Mason."

"What kind of things?" Paul asked.

The demon turned to look at him, an odd smile playing about his mouth. The Walker glanced at Mason and realized that his eyes were wide open and lit with awareness.

"Paul?" His voice was strong, and he sat up straight and frowned. "Can you see Daemon?"

CHAPTER 13

Business was good. Cal smiled as he visited the restroom for the third time in ten minutes, two fellows trailing behind him. The pocket that had been stuffed with little baggies was nearly empty, the pocket that had begun the evening flat bulged with cash. He made the exchange with practiced smoothness and felt the sigh of relief that only he could see under his cool exterior.

Cal's freedom to party came only when enough customers felt free to spend, and selling everything he had brought to sell meant he could do more than maintain tonight.

That meant a trip to his car. Cal wasn't about to lock himself in a stall and sniffle away like these other jokers. He stepped out of the bathroom, looking coolly left, then right. His eyes met two beady black eyes as he felt a huge hand grip his upper arm like a vice. Suddenly, he was hauled through the sea of flesh that flowed over every square foot of the place toward a doorway in the back. His face nearly flattened against the sign that read "OFFICE" at eye level, but the door swung open before him just in time.

Cal was shoved through the open doorway and into the room that lie beyond. Stumbling, he caught his balance and turned to face his assailant.

He watched the big man close the door quietly behind him and then stand blocking it. It was the owner. Cal didn't remember his name, but did recall seeing him when he was helping the band unload.

He had been across the room then, and he had been sitting at the bar and drinking. Up close, the guy was a monster. His broad shoulders and huge arms made him seem taller than he was, and his round belly didn't make him look fat or slow; it just made him look that much more imposing. He balled up one meaty paw into a fist and smacked it into his open palm while the slim young man eyed him warily.

"Business is good, huh?" The beefy man growled at him.

That's funny, Call thought, *that's what I was just thinking.*

As if in reply, the man's frowning face stretched into a wicked sneer.

Cal grinned his winningest smile. "I'm sure I have no idea what you're talking about."

A lot of cocaine and a lot of people had raced in and out of his life, but Cal had never seen anyone move so fast. One moment they were a stride apart, and the next the big man held him aloft by the throat. Cal's hands gripped the man's huge forearm, lifting his weight off his neck while his feet kicked feebly at the floor.

"Oh," he squeaked. "You mean the cocaine."

The man let go and Cal landed on his feet, dazed but balanced.

"This is my club," the man growled. "You want to sling here, I get my cut."

Cal shook his head. "I need all the cash I have to re-up. If I'm short, I'm out of business."

Black eyes narrowed, and Cal backed up a step.

"I could just beat the crap out of you and take whatever you've got," the man said lightly. "Or call the cops."

Cal shook his head again. "Nobody wants that. I come with the band. If you bring them back, I bring clients back. Let's work something out for next time."

Putting his hands on his hips, the man frowned thoughtfully. "How much product do you have left?"

"Just enough to party with my friends."

The man grinned. "Let's be friends. I'm Roche. You're..." beady black eyes seemed to bore into his brain. "...Cal, right? Nice to meet you, Cal. Let me show you my war room. I've got plans for you and your friends."

Cal smiled as he followed Roche to the table in the room adjacent. There was a thin square mirror pane and short plastic straw already keeping a razor blade company on the table.

CHAPTER 14

Mason felt his eyes go wide with wonder.

"Paul?" he asked. "Can you see Daemon?"

Paul was frowning through his beard. "Yes, Mason. I can see your demon."

Although he didn't need it, they helped Mason to his feet; Paul under one elbow and Daemon under the other. The demon was a fuzzy hologram to him, nearly fading from view entirely as he took his hand from Mason's elbow and stepped back. Mason could see that Daemon was smiling, and he smiled back briefly.

When he turned to face Paul's strange look, Mason shook his head at him.

"He's not my demon anymore," he said, glancing again at Daemon. He could barely make out the vague outlines of his companion now. "He's my helper, he's my friend. That's why I named him Daemon, that's what they call a demon that helps someone realize their talent."

"He's not my demon," Mason said again. "He's more like my angel now that…"

Mason trailed off and arched an eyebrow curiously at Paul.

The other man's frown softened as he nodded and finished his sentence for him.

"…now that you know you didn't kill me?"

Mason nodded, unsurprised. If Paul could talk to Daemon, he surely knew who had been driving the car that fateful day. Mason's hands were still shaking a little, and he thrust them in his jean pockets so no one would notice. His fingers felt a familiar shape in his left front pocket, and he pulled it out without thinking.

Paul watched, a curious frown on his face. The purple plastic cylinder with a gray twist cap was as unfamiliar to Paul as it was recognizable to Mason. Longer than his middle finger, it kept its contents a secret until he twisted the cap. Then the sweet dank smell of cannabis filled the air between them, a smile tugging at his mouth as he watched Paul's nose crinkle.

"What is that?" Paul sniffed. "Weed squared?"

Mason smiled and slid the joint from its container. He held it by the filter, a thick piece of paper folded over and then back again and then rolled around itself. The filter was an inch long and not quite as big around as a pencil where the paper held it in circular shape. From there, the cigarette widened in a cone shape and the end was as big around as his little finger.

"It looks like a little baseball bat," Paul mused. "Did you roll that monster?"

Mason shook his head and spun the joint gently between his fingers up and down the shaft. The fat, folded-over end opened up at his careful worrying fingers, dried green ground up sinsemilla showing as it did.

"I have a medical marijuana card," Mason explained. "I get migraine headaches something fierce if I don't smoke it. I buy these already rolled at the dispensary I go to."

Sparking his lighter and touching the flame to its fat tip, Mason inhaled briefly and puffed out a cloud of white smoke.

"The Love Shack," he said, puffing again. "Best pot shop in the city."

Mason held the smoking white miniature baseball bat out to Paul. "Want some?"

To his surprise, Paul took it from him and took a long hit that turned the fat cherry to a blazing ember. He held it in as he passed it back, and Mason watched the whites of his eyes go almost completely red. When he exhaled, his shoulders and face relaxed with a visible sigh despite the almost complete absence of smoke.

Paul closed his eyes as his face relaxed into a sweet momentary serenity; but when he opened them, his eyes were clear and his frown was back.

Mason passed him the joint again. "So what happened? Why aren't you…you know, dead?"

With a shrug, Paul took another long strong pull. The smoke puffed and curled around his beard as he pulled it away from his lips and held it out to Mason again. "I was somehow unhurt by the accident."

Mason took three short puffs and held it in, his voice straining when he spoke. "And now you see demons?"

Paul nodded and glanced at Daemon.

The demon seemed pleased with their exchange.

"What do you do?" Mason blew out white smoke and puffed again. "I asked Daemon about it, but he's hard to understand when it comes to details. What do you do when you see a demon?"

He shrugged again and took the joint from Mason. "Mostly I leave them alone. Sometimes people need help dealing with their demons, so I try to."

Paul took a long intense drag and closed his eyes again.

"Help," he held his breath, his voice pinched. "I try to help."

Mason was feeling a little high. Finally. He chuckled.

"Like a therapist?" he asked.

When Paul opened his eyes and looked at him, they were glazed and red again. He blew out a thin puff of smoke and blinked, and his eyes were clear blue on stark white once more.

"Something like that," Paul frowned. He glanced at the shimmering form watching them smoke and talk, nodded firmly.

"Your demon—" he began, then stopped short. "Daemon is having trouble getting inside. I can help. Go back inside. We'll catch up with you."

Mason stubbed out the joint and contained it again within the airtight tube. He held it out to Paul, and he surprised Mason again by taking it.

A few steps up the alley, Mason turned to ask what Paul was going to do.

They were gone.

CHAPTER 15

Cal watched his new friend cause the rapid disappearance of the little white line he had cut for him. Then he watched him switch the rolled up dollar bill to his other nostril and snort the line Cal had cut for himself. The big man stood straight and sniffed, showing Cal his pointed canines.

Pulling the baggie from his pocket again, Cal shook another quarter gram onto the mirror and leaned over to taste his white mistress. Not bothering to form a traditional line, he chased the scattered powder across the smooth surface until it was gone.

"What the hell is going on in here?" Cal stood and turned at the sudden voice.

The bearded guy, Roche's partner, stood well within the room, watching them with a frown. Cal swore he hadn't been there a moment ago, hadn't opened or closed any of the doors cut into the walls far from where he was now standing.

Cal turned to see if the big guy was as surprised by the man's appearance as he was.

Roche struck his fist on the table so hard Cal was glad there was no more cocaine on the jostled mirror.

"You bring that in here?!" he roared, glaring at Paul.

Cal looked closely, but couldn't see what he might be holding or bringing with him.

Paul glanced pointedly at the mirror and then at Cal.

"It's for Mason," he said curtly. "You need to get back to the bar."

The big man pressed his fists into the table as his face reddened with anger. Then he sighed and nodded, ushering Cal towards the door.

Paul preceded them brusquely, slamming the door shut behind him.

Cal paused, his hand on the door knob. He was just starting to like the old guy. "What's with him?" he asked.

"Paul?" Roche shrugged his beefy shoulders. "He's alright; he just… lost his girl."

"Well, I hope he finds her," Cal quipped, turning the knob and swinging open the door.

Cocking his head to one side, Roche looked at him curiously with penetrating black eyes.

"Me too," he said seriously, nodding.

CHAPTER 16

Kris finished wiping down the bar and upended his tip jar over the smooth clean surface. It was so stuffed with dollar bills that nothing moved despite gravity, and he had to stick his hand in the wide glass gallon container to start the money spill. Neat stacks started to form as he counted, twenty flattened dollars to a stack. He had almost two hundred dollars tallied when Paul appeared suddenly across the bar. Kris brightened deliberately and grinned, trying to coax a smile from his friend.

"You know, for a Walker you sure don't do much actual walking," he joked.

Paul frowned. "I walk between worlds," he responded seriously. "That's what a Walker does." He eyed the pile and stacks of money. "What does a dead guy do with four hundred dollars?"

"He buys nice things for the girl who makes him feel alive," Kris shrugged. "It's more like five."

Kris could see his friend working his jaw despite his whiskers. "She's not a girl," Paul reminded him sternly. "She's a dragon."

Shaking his head, Kris grabbed a bottle of the scotch he had seen Paul downing earlier. "It's not polite to call her that," he murmured, pouring a tall glass of the smelly stuff and sliding it in front of the Walker.

"Sorry." Paul grimaced. "She's not a girl, buddy, she's a devil." He drank half the glass in one gulp and set the remainder on the bar with a thud. "Thanks," he said, licking his lips. "You ready to go?"

Kris had enjoyed tending bar, to his surprise, but the evening had been one long exercise in looking forward to the night alone with Jessica. He had forgotten about Paul. Deliberately brightening again, he smiled and nodded enthusiastically.

"Yeah," he said. "Just let me finish counting this and turning it into manageable bills."

In the time it took for him to say it, Paul did it. He moved so fast that bills flew in his wake, but not one hit the floor as he gathered and counted. Blurring past the open register, he stopped before Kris with a small stack of exchanged bills in one hand and the rest of his drink in the other, miniature brown ocean sloshing about in its world of glass.

"Five hundred, thirty-two dollars," the Walker said, emptying the glass.

Kris took the money and stuffed it in his front pocket, trying not to let on how much it unnerved him when Paul used his abilities like that.

"Don't worry," Paul said, misreading him. "This won't take long at all. In fact, it will be like we never left." His hand fell on Kris' shoulder; and in the moment he felt the weight of it, the world went white. The Guide waited for a shift or a landscape of new colors, but the world stayed white.

The Guide looked around, curious. They were in a huge wide open space, the floor below them and the distant walls and ceiling all made of the same strange substance. It seemed like light and cloud woven together in a flowing pattern alive with energy. Breathing in the crisp clean air, Kris smelled dried lavender and the sweet sweaty scent of burnt white sage. Turning, he realized there were two structures behind him, matching sheet metal sheds that rose in odd ordinariness from the liquid light floor.

The sheds stood side by side, ten feet wide and ten feet tall at their twin peaked roofs. Sliding double doors lay open on both structures, twenty feet of interior length lighted by the flowing clouded floor. One was lined with shelves of tall sturdy plastic, most of the shelving bare or shadowed by contents stacked or piled haphazardly. The other looked to be quarters of some kind. He could see a desk and swivel chair, a sofa and love seat and easy chair. Beyond that was a long oak table with chairs lining its length. It all looked brand new, untouched, as though no one had ever sat in the inviting furniture.

"What is this place?" he asked, turning to Paul.

Paul frowned. "This is where I became King of the Walkers," he said quietly. "This is an angel's personal creation, her private space. No one can enter here but God."

"What about the angel?" Kris asked.

The Walker considered a moment before answering. "She is currently indisposed."

"Indisposed?" Kris raised an eyebrow.

"I believe she is imprisoned," Paul sighed. "We shouldn't have to worry about her for a couple hundred years or so."

Kris smiled and played along. "Who would imprison an angel?"

"Roche," Paul responded brusquely.

The Guide realized Paul wasn't joking. "Are we going to free her?"

"No." The Walker grimaced. "She would kill us all."

"An angel?" Kris was confused.

Paul turned and began to walk to the shed with the neat rows of shelving. "A lot happened while you were…falling in love with Jessica."

The Guide followed him into the open space.

"We're not falling in love." He smiled to himself. "We're rising."

"What?" Paul glanced over his shoulder.

Kris shook his head. "Nothing."

Through the wide entrance, the contents of the shelves became distinct objects instead of misshapen shadows. One shelf had a pile of swords of all kinds. Some were thick relics from times when blades won battles and war made kings. Others were sleek sharp katana and samurai swords, long curved blades from the Middle East and several unique rough-hewn but formidable tribal swords that looked to be iron. There were dozens of them, and some looked stained with red or purple blood.

Kris was a Guide. There were some things he just knew; he didn't know how he knew them, he just did.

"Those are Walker weapons," he said quietly.

Paul nodded. "Turns out we can die."

"What?" Kris was aghast. "Who…?"

"I killed quite a few of them," he responded flatly.

Kris thought he sounded more smug than penitent. He looked at Paul, thinking how his friend seemed a stranger. He even looked different, his beard and lengthening hair coupling with the fierce frenzied look that always seemed to narrow his blue eyes nowadays.

He gestured at the shelves around them as it began to make sense. The heaps of clothes were armor, brown and black suede and leather overcoats piled with actual plate and chain mail along with the occasional woven leather and bone breastplate.

Beyond the shelving on one side was an open corner with more strange objects piled on the liquid light floor. One heap was a blazing fire, the flames dancing over thick links of chain while also apparently emanating from it. The other pile also looked like chain, but the links were made of a flowing lighted energy that resembled the liquid light floor. Behind the two haphazard piles of luminous chains, both lighted and shadowed by the cool white and the hot red, was an equally disorganized pile of swords. These blades were like nothing he had seen before, long and curved pieces of shimmering metal.

"Devil swords." Paul followed his gaze.

Kris let his confusion twist his features. "What the hell, Paul? What is all this?"

"Let's go next door." The Walker led him out of one structure and into the other. "We've got some catching up to do."

They settled on overstuffed couches of dark soft leather. Paul told him all that he had missed spending the evening with Jessica, and he learned much of Roche and the Walkers and the dangerous angel by the time he finished.

"Why did you declare yourself Walker King?" Kris was confused about Paul's decision.

His entire range of expression had become degrees of frowning, and Paul's frown deepened. "Everyone else seemed to want to control the production, and the best outcome I could see just meant going back to the way things were before."

"What's wrong with the way things were before?" Kris shrugged.

"One guy was in charge of the Walkers, and he was appointed by the Council of Angels." Paul grimaced. "He kept Walkers isolated and uninformed and was able to further his own mad agenda with no one to keep him in check."

"So you declared yourself king?" He heard the sarcasm in his voice and let it be. He was the Walker's Guide, after all. "Now you're the one guy in charge? That's not mad at all."

Paul shook his head solemnly. "Things are going to change, and you're going to help me change them. We will talk to every Walker on Earth, we will find out what every individual in the community struggles with and we will bring Walkers together. We will solve the problems of the Walker community together and eliminate or nullify any threats facing individuals or the family. Then I will step down and we will elect a new king."

Kris chuckled. "Are you assuming they will elect you?"

"No." Paul grimaced. "I would refuse. I don't want this, Kris. It needs to be done. I'm the only one who can do it." He held his hand out, palm up, platinum watch gleaming quietly with polished power. "I can't do it without you, though. I need your help, buddy."

Kris nodded. "I am your Guide, Walker King."

"No." Paul shook his head again. "I am not your king. You are my Guide, which makes you King of the Guides."

"No." Kris echoed flatly. "I don't want to be King of anything." *Except maybe Jessica's heart.*

"Tough shit," Paul snapped. "These people need a leader, the Walkers need one of their own and so do the Guides."

"What about the Watchers?" Kris didn't think it appropriate for a king to pout, but he was not pleased. "Do they need a king too?"

"They do," Paul replied calmly. "Andre has embraced his role. It was easier for him; the Watchers communicate more and can see more of the past and present and probable futures. They have been preparing for this since before I became a Walker."

"So what do we do?" Kris was glad he was sitting down. His head was spinning.

Paul nodded, and Kris let his mind stray again to his heart. He felt guilty counting the seconds until he could gather his love up in his arms again. After a long moment of pleasant imaginings, he looked at his friend. The pain in Paul's eyes was tempered only by the frown on his face, and it was easy to see only the frown and think him an angry man. Before he could respond, Kris spoke again.

"You don't want to be king," Kris said quietly. It was not a question but a realization. "You want to find Brenna."

Paul nodded, but did not speak that part of his mind. "First we are going to talk to Echor."

Kris felt his eyes widen as Paul stood abruptly. "The mad murderous angel? Uh, no thanks."

"Think about it," Paul urged, looking down at him still seated. "Why did she do it? Why did Roche do it all those years ago? That damned devil plays it too close to the vest; he only tells me what he thinks I need to know. If there is something wrong with the Walker world, it needs to be dealt with by Walkers." He grimaced. "Not by a mad angelic devil or devilish angel."

"Aye," Kris tried to sound solemn. "It needs must be dealt with." He stood reluctantly.

"What?" The Walker narrowed his eyes. "What the hell did you just say?"

"Nothing." Kris smiled weakly. "I thought that's how kings talked to each other."

Paul frowned, unfazed at his attempt at levity.

The Guide tried to match his frown. Maybe that's what kings did. "What makes you think the angel will tell you anything?"

"When I was with her, it felt like I was a part of her." The Walker's frown turned thoughtful. "That's why I'm concerned, there really is something going on. I saw it. I need to ask her about what I saw."

"What makes you think she'll tell you anything?" Kris asked again.

"I have to ask."

Kris shrugged. "Well, it can't hurt to ask."

"It can, though," Paul replied. "She is dangerous, for both of us. Don't look her in the eye." He was suddenly swathed in leather as his armor appeared. "I hate to say anything, but…"

Paul gestured at the Guide's plain jeans and polo shirt.

He closed his eyes and imagined himself clothed in the familiar robe, and when he opened them he was.

Paul's hand fell on his shoulder.

The room was a dark rusted red stone, smoothed to bare walls and floors in a cube. Twenty-four feet long and wide and tall, the rock room was illumined by a lone figure. A woman stood in the center of one wall, weeping quietly and glowing like a florescent tube. Waves of warm liquid light flowed from her, bathing the room in its brilliance. Stacked along every other wall were oak and iron chests, some of them thrown open to reveal mounds of glinting gold and jewels, diamond tiaras and thick gold crowns, chalices of gold and silver inlaid with gemstones.

"What is this place?" Kris spoke before he thought.

The woman raised her head and looked at him; and in the same moment that her beauty overwhelmed his senses, he saw the manacles at her wrists.

She smiled, and he was glad to see Jessica spring to mind. Good fortune had given his heart to the devil before it could be claimed and ravaged by the wicked love of an angel. Paul had described her in both forms, and Kris had been hoping to see the angel in all her wondrous splendor. Seeing her, he was glad she was in human form. She was breathtaking, impossibly flawless beauty truly illumined from within by a love so great it had become a mad fiery rage as she fell.

"This is Roche's trophy room." Her voice was as breathtaking as her face and form, a voice that could only belong to an angel. It took a moment for Kris to separate the words from the sound as his whole being resounded with her musical tones.

Looking almost helplessly to Paul, the Guide was glad for once to see the Walker frowning fiercely.

Paul narrowed his eyes. "This is Roche's personal space," he spoke to Kris as though she hadn't answered and wasn't there.

"So," Kris raised an eyebrow, "no one can enter here but God?"

The Walker nodded as the angel's musical laughter filled the room. It was light and wondrous and touched by melancholy.

"No one but God," she intoned with a solemnness that did not match her bitter smile. "And Roche and the Walker King and who knows who else. Have you come to claim this space as your own as well, Walker? Are mine not enough?"

Paul's frown deepened. "You weren't using them," he answered flatly.

"And this place?" Her voice was too beautiful to sound accusatory. "Does Roche know you are here?"

Kris felt the sudden urge to apologize, to grab Paul and drag him from this place, to do anything that might please the angel. Instead he clenched his jaw tightly and stared at the floor.

The Walker responded with a question of his own. "Why were you trying to end Walkers?"

When she smiled it was like a magnet to the Guide's stare. Unbidden, his eyes rose to drink in her beauty again.

"Take off these chains," she murmured, "and maybe I'll show you." Her eyes shifted from Paul to Kris, and the Guide suddenly found himself stepping toward her. His feet moved with no direction from him, and it took Paul stepping between them to stop him. As Kris bumped into his friend, his mind came back to him suddenly and he averted his gaze once more.

Shaking his head to clear it, his eyes met Paul's.

"Don't look her in the eyes," the Walker reminded him firmly.

Kris could only nod, unable to find his voice.

Paul turned to the angel. "You still want to kill us all, don't you?"

"Take off these chains and I'll show you," she said again, an edge to her sonorous voice.

"I told you she wouldn't help," Kris muttered, eyes fixed on the floor.

"There's something wrong, I saw it in you," Paul pressed insistently. "If you tell me I might be able to make it right."

Her laughter filled the space again, light and musical and mocking. "And what would you do, Walker King? What could you do?"

Paul took a step towards her, and Kris looked at him in alarm. Again relieved to see the familiar frown, he saw the anger lighting Paul's eyes as well. He dropped his gaze to the stone floor.

"I might come up with a solution that doesn't include genocide," Paul snapped.

"The Walker hubris has found its culmination in you, hasn't it?" Her voice sounded more amused than upset. "Walkers are not a race, they are an aberration. The whole universe follows the rules. Either you are human or you are supernatural. Only Walkers cross that line, and only trouble comes of it. The human mind is not equipped to properly wield supernatural powers."

The Walker snorted in derision. "I could say the same about a certain mad murderous angel."

Her smile was one of gentle tolerance then. "The human mind's inability to see the big picture often leads to erroneous conclusions. You are making my point for me, Walker. Such a narrow perspective should never wield great power. A human with supernatural powers is like a baby with a pistol."

"The Walker's perspective is narrow because they are intentionally kept in the dark." Paul's voice was angry, rising in volume as he spoke. "You are in chains because of what you have done. My people are in chains because of what they might hypothetically do if set free. The reason Walkers are human is because we are capable of having compassion for the human condition. You have never had that kind of compassion, and you never will. You treat us like animals, caging us because you arrogantly assume you understand us. That is not compassion, angel. That is cruelty."

Kris watched his friend standing there glaring at the angel. For the first time he began to see how his friend had changed, and found himself impressed rather than annoyed. He still seemed a stranger to him, but now he was a stranger he wanted to get to know better.

The Guide risked a glance at the angel. Her eyes were on Paul, her flawless features twisted into an expression of consternation. Then her face relaxed, her eyes widened, and she smiled. Kris felt his heart go out to her, his body aching to follow, and he quickly averted his eyes once more.

"The Stone Walker." Her voice was as beautiful as her face, touched with awe. "Perhaps you are right, Walker King. Even angels can create what they don't want when they put all their energy into preventing it. Maybe you are indeed the one."

Kris raised his eyes from the stone floor to Paul's face. His frown was still fierce, his eyes still demanding and angry.

Echor sighed, a gentle sound of relief or resignation. "I will show you what you wish to see, Walker King."

"You aren't going anywhere," Paul growled, his voice low and slow.

"I don't have to," she answered simply.

A hole appeared in the wall to her left and to their right, or it seemed to. Jagged and uneven, it was tall and wide enough for a man to leap through easily. From where they stood, only darkness revealed itself through the sudden gaping opening.

Kris watched Paul look from the hole to the angel and back again, his eyes wary.

"Go ahead, Stone Walker," she spoke in a quiet and musical and impossibly beautiful voice. "See what you came to see."

Another glance at the angel and Paul turned to walk to the jagged portal. Kris heard the Walker's breath catch suddenly as he neared the wall. Coming up behind him, the Guide followed his friend's gaze.

At first he just saw movement far below, like a writhing mass of living dark on darker. Then his eyes adjusted, and Kris felt his dead heart skip a beat.

There were demons everywhere, male and female and big and small. They crawled over each other, clawing and biting ferociously as they did. Their numbers were endless, a shifting sea of violence and shades of red. While he watched, one particularly large monster grabbed another by the leg and dangled it before him in midair. His huge maw gaped open, full of sharp and jagged fangs. Bite by disgusting bite, he ate the smaller demon like a chocolate bar as purple blood streamed down his face to drip unchecked on his broad muscled chest.

The demon grew visibly with each bite, and when he was done he raised his eyes and looked right at Kris.

CHAPTER 17

Mason hefted the hard rectangular guitar case and slid it smoothly into the back seat of Sarah's Honda car. Swinging the door shut, he turned and smiled and took her in his arms.

"You are amazing," he murmured in her ear.

She relaxed into him, her petite frame melting in his embrace.

"Takes one to know one," she whispered, arms encircling his waist.

"Do you want to go home?" He breathed her in, thought of her naked skin on his with a soft smile.

Sarah raised her chin to look at him. "I thought there was an after-party coming together."

"You are my after-party," he sighed, gazing down at her light green eyes, round with love.

She smiled up at him, pressing her small firm breasts into his stomach with quiet insistence. "This is an awesome place," she said.

"It is," he nodded in agreement. "It's cool that we were the first band to play here."

Her smile softened his heart as always. "Maybe we should stay for the after-party. The more we stick in their minds, the more gigs we might play here."

"You're so smart." He clutched her to him again, burying her face in his chest and resting his chin on top of her head.

"Good thinking," Mason said. "Let's go back inside."

He made no move to let her go, however; and it was a long sweet forever moment before they disengaged.

Hand in hand, they walked back into the club.

"Oh," Sarah stopped abruptly, remembering. "I'm sorry, lover. You have a migraine, don't you?"

Mason shook his head, pulling her along gently. "No, I'm great. I was hurting pretty bad earlier but..." he trailed off. "...it passed," he finished quietly.

Falling back into step beside him, Sarah glanced up at Mason. "Was it...was it Daemon?"

He nodded, his eyes still straight ahead. At the mention of the name, Mason became more aware of the shadowy form pacing him watchfully. Smiling, he thought of his life not so long ago as he walked between his two guardian angels.

"He was having trouble getting inside," he shrugged. "When that bearded dude took me out for some fresh air, Daemon found me and helped me."

"Paul," she reminded him. "The other guy is Kris; the girl's name is Jessica."

"Yeah, thanks," he said, stopping just short of the entrance, under the sign that read *The Devil's Brew.* "Do you remember the older guy's name? The grumpy dude with the fangs?"

She giggled. "You noticed that?"

Mason shrugged. "How could you not? That guy doesn't smile, he shows you his teeth."

"Roche," she was still giggling. "His name is Roche."

"What kind of name is that?"

Sarah smiled her pretty smile at him. "Sounds French to me, probably his last name."

"Roche," he repeated. "Paul, Kris and Jessica."

She nodded, and he leaned over to kiss her forehead for a long moment.

"Is he here?" she asked quietly as he pulled away. "Is Daemon here now?"

"Yeah." Mason glanced at his demonic savior.

Sarah followed his glance, obviously not seeing him. "Thank you, Daemon. Thank you for taking care of my love."

The hazy figure came more clearly into focus then, and Mason could see him grin with pride at her gratitude. "You made him smile."

"Awww," she crooned. "I'm glad."

Pushing the metal and glass door open, Mason held it for Sarah to walk through first. Glancing at the demon, he nodded for him to follow. Striding through the doorway, Daemon's grin widened further at the consideration. Mason knew he could walk through walls as simply as he walked through the open doorway, but it seemed the demon was more visible to him the more he treated him like a person.

Daemon never asked anything of him, as far as Mason could tell; but every acknowledgement he enjoyed just compelled him to find more opportunities to acknowledge him. Indeed, he saw Daemon's features come into slightly sharper focus as he passed.

Mason followed them inside.

"You kids done loading up?" A voice called out across the strangely quiet club. Mason turned, nodded to the old guy.

Roche, he thought fiercely. *Roche, Paul, Kris, Jessica.* He smiled inwardly, pleased with himself. *Not bad for a pothead.*

The mountain of a man trundled out from behind the bar and crossed the room swiftly to lock the door after them.

"Let's get this party started," he roared.

Cal had been seated at a table with his brother and Jason, talking quietly but excitedly to them. He stood and crossed to the bar, reaching it and taking a stool as Roche slipped behind the bar again.

"Is everybody cool?" Cal's gaze swept the sparsely populated space. His hand slipped into the inside pocket of his leather jacket as Roche nodded across the bar at him.

Mason exchanged a glance with Sarah, and they moved together to the bar. Cal was already cutting lines when they arrived and settled on padded stools. They watched him, the razor tattooing a rhythmic *tink! tink! tink!* against the mirror's smooth surface.

Jessica joined the scene quietly, emerging from the office and closing the door behind her. She had changed into jeans and a modest top that hugged her slim frame, and was a cute study in shades of blue. Approaching the bar, she glanced at the mirror and crinkled her tiny nose in momentary distaste.

Cal made to slide the powdered energy toward his friends. A low growl from Roche reversed its course. Three lines lay parallel to each other on the reflective surface, but after the big man leaned over and sniffed and stood again they were gone.

Cal frowned momentarily, reaching into his pocket to grab the bag and upend it over the mirror. The smile returned to his face as Mason watched his friend cut three new lines.

The mirror came to them then, and Mason glanced at Sarah.

"I've got a bit of a headache," he lied. "I better not."

He saw Cal relax with visible relief.

Sarah shook her head.

"Thanks Cal," she said. "I'm good."

Cal shrugged and leaned over the surface, clearing it as Roche had.

"You kids want a drink?" Roche thumbed his nose happily, showing them his teeth.

Mason nodded. "Thanks. I'll have a beer."

"Me too, please." Sarah's smile was as beautiful as her voice.

The older man drummed his fingers on the bar impatiently.

"This ain't a movie, kids," he growled. "What kind?"

Mason grinned. "Two PBR's, please."

Popping the tops, he slid the bottles across the bar to them. "That was quite a show, you two. How long you been playing together?"

They smiled at each other before Sarah responded.

"About a week," she shrugged.

Cal lingered a moment before drifting to the table where his brother and Jason sat drinking. He took the mirror with him.

Roche was nodding his approval. "You were born to play together. You should be my house band."

"Don't you mean *our* house band?" A voice behind them made them turn to see the two men coming down the stairs.

Paul, Mason thought fiercely. *Kris.*

"Sorry." The big man did not sound sorry. "I forget I have a manager now." A bottle had appeared before him, scotch that was old enough to legally drink itself. Roche poured a generous helping into one glass, then another. He slid one down the bar in Paul's general direction.

It seemed there was no way for the bearded man to intercept the swift slide, yet in a blink he stood at the bar lifting it to his lips. A moment later it was sliding past them again, empty.

While the glass was refilled and slid across the bar once more, Kris moved to Jessica's side.

Mason felt Sarah's hand find his knee under the bar. Glancing her way with a soft smile, he saw Paul behind her lifting the intoxicating liquid to his lips. Behind him, Kris had his arm about Jessica's shoulders, nuzzling her blonde hair as she giggled and rubbed his stomach.

Setting his glass on the bar, Paul turned his head to meet Mason's eyes. He saw a mixture of anger and anxiety in the bearded man's face, but his bright blue eyes were somewhere else.

"What do you think?" Paul asked, his voice flat. "Want to rock this house three nights a week?"

He watched Sarah's eyes close and then grow impossibly wide as she blinked her excitement at him. Her sly smile and slight nod put him in charge.

Mason glanced at the table where Tyler and Cal spoke excitedly to each other over an empty reflective surface. Framed between them, Jason sat quietly. The corners of his mouth were upturned just enough to show that he was thoroughly enjoying the moment in his way.

"Would you guys come over here." The words seemed a question, but Mason didn't make it sound like one.

The two musicians rose immediately, but Cal lingered in his chair for a moment. He glanced at Roche warily, and when Mason turned the big man was showing Cal his teeth across the bar. Looking back again, he saw Cal rising to join the others.

"Bring that mirror," Roche barked.

Cal frowned, but turned and retraced his steps to retrieve the pane. By the time he laid it on the bar and reached hand into pocket, he was bright charismatic Cal again.

They fell into a loose semi-circle around Mason and Sarah, Cal at the bar beside Mason while Tyler and Jason stood to face the couple.

Turning his back to Cal cutting lines on the bar, Mason could see Sarah looking at him the same way Tyler and Jason were. He could see Roche out of the corner of his eye, but the big man seemed to be paying more attention to Cal clinking the razor blade on glass.

"These guys want us to be their house band," Mason addressed his attentive bandmates. He saw Paul frown deeply and take a long drink, his thoughts apparently elsewhere. Behind him, Kris murmured something in his girl's ear and she looked up at him and smiled a smile that looked like it was meant only for her lover.

Mason looked at each of the musicians in turn as he spoke.

"We would play here at least three nights a week; we'd play all their special functions." His eyes found Tyler's, then Jason's. "I think it sounds like a no-brainer, this place is great." Mason met Sarah's eyes then.

"This place is awesome," Tyler bobbed up and down, his knees like springs. He grinned at Mason and then at Roche across the bar.

The big man took a drink of scotch, thumbed his nose and nodded a curt minuscule nod. He swung his big head suddenly and barked at the couple behind Paul. "You two want a beer, or do you need to get a room?"

They held their pose for a moment, not realizing they were being addressed. Kris had his right hand tangled in her blonde hair while his left cupped her chin lovingly. Jessica had her arms wrapped loosely about his waist, her blue eyes looking up at him like he was the first sunrise she had ever seen. When a long moment had passed and no one spoke, they felt the eyes of the room on them finally and turned together.

"They're so cute," Sarah crooned.

Tyler and Jason chuckled, their doped state making them sound like Beavis and Butthead.

Kris flushed a bit, which made even Paul laugh for some reason. It came out like a bark, a sharp humorless report.

"We've already got a room." Jessica was unperturbed and unashamed, her arms still wrapped about her love. Her warm smile and sleepy blue eyes found each of them briefly. "It was nice to meet you all. Great show. Sounds like it's going to happen again. I look forward to it. Good night, everyone."

Watching her while she spoke, Kris shrugged when she finished and gave the room one sweeping glance.

"Good night," he said.

They turned, smiling, to clasp each other's hands and head for the door in the back while the room echoed their goodnight sentiments. As the door closed behind them, Mason felt Sarah's hand squeeze his knee gently.

He tilted his beer and met her eyes.

"Mikie and Rob aren't here," Mason said, turning to Tyler and Jason. "I don't know if we should talk about this or make a decision without them."

Both men nodded solemnly, but Mason could see it in their eyes.

I know, he thought to himself. *Fuck them.*

"Not to interrupt or anything…" Cal's voice sounded behind him, and Mason turned. His hands were flat on the bar before him on either side of the mirrored pane. There was a fresh set of perfect lines on the smooth surface.

"Here, Roche." Cal slid straw and surface in front of the big man. "Have a couple more."

Abandoning his drink on the bar, the big man hovered his big head over the glass to disappear one line up each nostril.

Cal watched him, smiling; and when he stood up straight he started talking.

"These four could play a show themselves no problem." He spoke smoothly and evenly, the practiced tone of a good salesman with a good product. "It would be more rock than tonight's show, AC/DC and Metallica, Black Sabbath and Led Zeppelin. People would love it, though; people always love it when Mason and Sarah play together. If you can keep this core group busy enough, and pay them enough, I'm willing to bet they would all commit right now with or without tweedledum and whatshisface."

Frowning to keep from smiling, Mason leaned toward Roche to speak.

Sarah squeezed his knee again, harder this time, and he was still. When he glanced at her she shrugged prettily and nodded to Roche. Mason saw that he was focused on Cal, staring him down with beady black eyes while thumbing his nose distractedly.

Finally, Roche showed Cal his teeth. "We should talk numbers, then."

Cal looked to Mason.

Sarah's hand sliding gently up and down his inner thigh felt pretty encouraging.

He shrugged and nodded at Cal.

"Okay." Cal brought a piece of paper from his back pocket, unfolded it three times and laid it flat on the bar. It was halfway filled with writing already, names of band members and numbers with dollar signs along with a calendar neatly drawn by hand.

"Let's talk numbers," he grinned.

CHAPTER 18

"It's important to keep a routine." William glanced at his face in the mirror before sticking the toothbrush in his mouth. He looked alert and rested, dark brown eyes almond-shaped windows of intelligence. Working his strong jaw as he brushed perfect white teeth, lines creased his broad forehead over a long straight nose. His thick dark hair was cut short, the same way it had been three hundred years ago.

William spit out a mouthful of toothpaste and met eyes with the woman standing behind him in the mirror.

"It makes me appear human," he said.

Then, more quietly: "It makes me feel human."

He tried to hold her open gaze.

She was beautiful, which made it harder.

William felt her eyes on his back as he bent to splash water on his face. He tried not to think of her olive skin, her dark round eyes, her perfect heart-shaped lips.

"You're not human, though," she reminded him gently.

It did him no good to focus on her words; her voice was beautiful too. It only made him think of her long dark hair, flowing smooth and silky like her voice; and her eyes, always gentle and kind like her words.

Pulling the towel away from his skin and hanging it neatly on its rack, William turned to face her. Swathed in leather from the waist down, thick black pants and boots, he was naked from the waist up. Over the years he had seen many women react to his muscled arms and torso in one way or another. With each passing decade it seemed the women he met were more demonstrative and somehow equally less appreciative. The subtle sensuality that had made him so love loving women when he was a young man had given way to an overt sexuality that found him loathing his own desire for them over the centuries.

The world had changed, and he did not know how to change with it.

She was still looking at him. There was no hunger in her eyes, they were round and dark and beautiful and they stayed trained on his while she spoke. "You have two today, same as yesterday. In the morning, in about two hours, one in Reno. This afternoon, it looks like about Four P.M., you have another out in Fernley."

William grabbed a dark blue long-sleeved shirt from the hook he had hung it from and shrugged into it. Never taking his eyes off hers, he buttoned the front and tried to focus on her words.

She was beautiful, which made it harder.

"It looks like the one this morning will be in one of the big casinos downtown, you might want me to come along to distract and re-mind folks," she continued.

He nodded, finally tearing his eyes away from her perfect lovely face.

She fell silent as he turned to face the mirror image of himself running a comb through his thick dark short hair. He needed a shave. He needed his space and some quiet more, however; so he closed his eyes and thought the stubble gone, saw his own chin and jaw smooth and shaved.

Opening his eyes, he saw his thought become reality.

Her smile matched his frown as he turned to exit the bathroom, slight and strained. She swiveled in place without turning, floated a step toward him without walking, smiled up at him while he donned his leather jacket.

"The one in Fernley is alone in a hotel room," she continued, watching his frown deepen. "I can go if you like, but I thought you might like the afternoon to yourself afterwards."

William knew what she meant. He stood looking down at her, wondering how she could be so gentle and kind and understanding. He wished he could just see the perfect business partner that she was. That was the way God had designed it; that should be the way William saw it.

She was beautiful, which made it harder.

"That's fine, I can handle it myself, take the afternoon off." He turned it back around on her, though she was no more likely to express a need or a desire than he was.

William made for the front door.

"Where are you going?" Her smile fell.

"To Reno." He didn't mean to sound so gruff. "I'm going to ride in, stop for breakfast on the way."

She was still watching him.

"You're welcome to join me." He tried to make his voice gentle for her.

"That's alright." She smiled her kind smile. "I'll meet you at the casino."

William dipped to retrieve his motorcycle helmet where he had dropped it after his last ride. Hand on the door, he hesitated a moment.

"Vanessa, I..." he turned his head.

She was gone.

Soon he was alone on the highway, the steady thrumming report of his Harley Davidson filling his ears and pushing away his thoughts. There was a stereo system built into the bike that would flood the lonely road with songs of his choice. He rarely turned it on, thrilling quietly instead to the engine's deafening rhythmic thunder.

More than once, he felt he was being watched. William resisted the urge to turn his head or twist in his leather seat. Feeling eyes on you is just something you get used to. Watchers and angels were just the prying eyes he knew about.

Who knew how often God was watching, but God?

Who knew what else was out there?

William kept his eyes on the road and his mind on the pulsing between his legs and in his ears.

The engine roared on, sipping fuel and eating up the miles.

CHAPTER 19

The spirits were with him this morning. Chase grasped the black round ball at the end of the polished stainless steel arm and pulled. Lights flashed, bells rang, and the rolling display locked into place section by section until four identical symbols stood in place along one mismatched one. More bells rang, more lights flashed, and a shower of dollar coins clanked into the tray to join the small mountain already piled there.

Easing back on his stool, Chase regarded the slot machine warily. He let his eyes go out of focus a little, flashing lights blurring to colored clouds. Watching the spirits was like watching a fish swimming in a stream. He saw movement more than he saw features, and the three indistinct swirling forms he saw seemed to think this machine was a good place to be. Ripples of energy pulsed around and into and through the machine, and Chase watched as intently as he could without focusing his eyes and losing the vision.

"One more," he murmured quietly. "One more decent payout, and we'll play some poker." The spirits swirled and danced joyously about the glass and plastic and steel machine for a moment, then plunged as one into it. To Chase's eyes, the slot machine glowed with a pulsing yellow light that brightened as he watched.

He knew it would look strange to anyone watching, him staring dumbly at a slot machine and muttering to himself under his breath. He also knew that if anyone was watching it wouldn't work; the spirits would dash away like quicksilver fish flashing through the air, and Chase would know immediately. So he waited, watching; and when it glowed its brightest ethereal glow, he dropped three coins in the slot and pulled the lever with a practiced smooth tug.

Going for a big payout was never the objective with the slots. They were just a way to work his way up to the tables. When he woke with little memory of the night before and less than five dollars in his pocket, as he had this morning, he went straight to the quarter slot machines. On a good day, like today, he could have breakfast in his belly and be playing the dollar slots within an hour. Another hour sipping vodka and following the spirits from one slot to the next, and a couple hundred dollars weighed in his pockets while more collected in the tray.

This time three symbols matched, the other two different from the three but identical to each other; Chase watched the spirits, he watched the stream of coins; he paid little attention to the symbols. When the silver stream ended, he began shoveling dollar coins into his bulging front pockets. The weight tugged at his belted slacks, and Chase cast about with his eyes. He glimpsed the spirits as they swam off, heading for the exit.

They would wait for him, there or on the street, apparently staking out the next casino while he filled huge paper cups with dollar coins and changed them to manageable bills.

Soon Chase stood on the sidewalk, the spirits swirling about his head and shoulders while the morning sun coaxed spent vodka from his pores. Neither anxious nor bored, he waited for the spirits to move and then moved with them. Walking casually but purposefully, his feet carried him forward as his thoughts swirled noisily in his head.

Maybe today was the day. Maybe today the spirits would push harder than ever, and Chase would see all his imaginings come true. Passing shops and casinos coming alive, he saw himself in his mind's eye holding up a huge over-sized check with a huge over-sized dollar amount. Every day ended for him with an evening decided by the day's gambling. A hundred in his pocket meant a cheap hotel room and a bottle of decent vodka while he watched cartoons and pictured a better tomorrow. A thousand was a nice room and a pretty girl or boy to share it with. Sometimes he bought their drinks, sometimes he bought their bodies. Chase knew he was not the kind of man who could pay with his name, so he paid cash. It was easy to imagine what he would be doing in a few hours if he had a hundred, five hundred, a thousand, five thousand…

A faint half-smile crinkled one watery blue eye as his thoughts reached further than his winnings had ever taken him. He often wondered what he would do with a quarter or half million dollars. Would he drink himself to death with top shelf vodka in a posh casino penthouse, surrounded by tall windows and nude bodies? Or would he buy a nice place out in Silver Springs and go to school, try to make something of himself and his good fortune?

It wasn't so bad to consider either option. That's what he did, losing himself in his imaginings and following the subtle light forms in a pleasant haze.

The spirits hesitated before a set of revolving glass doors, streams of energy swirling in place in the warm morning air. Chase stood and watched them, oblivious to the scant early foot traffic. He caught a look at himself in the reflection from the spinning glass every few seconds.

The black iron-free slacks he had bought a couple days ago looked like they could use an ironing, the forest green polo shirt he had bought at the same time was wilting a bit at the collar. They didn't look bad on his slim frame, and his thick sandy hair was mussed just enough to give the overall impression of a careless drunk. It seemed to disarm other players when he came to the table looking a little disoriented.

In a flash of flowing light, the spirits shot suddenly through the glass without awaiting another revolution. Chase followed, finding them inside expressing impatience with an urgent beckoning only he could see. They led him to a table with three players and a dealer, swirling around the seat they wanted him to take without settling themselves in it.

He pulled the chair out, nodding to the fat bearded man in plaid to his left and then the two men in suits seated to his right. He sat, nodded to the dealer. She was a cute girl, shoulder length black hair that sprung forth in tight curls. A light dusting of freckles across her nose and cheeks punctuated her sun-kissed complexion, and her hazel eyes showed more smile than her lips did.

"Two hundred in five dollar chips, please." Chase laid ten twenties in front of her on the table. Then she did smile, pushing the chips in stacks across the table to him.

Chase lost fifty dollars of it in the first two hands, staring off into space and tossing chips. The third hand he barely glanced at his cards, then stared at a flashing slot machine in the distance and let his eyes go out of focus. Watching from the corners of his eyes, he saw a swirling stream of energy encircling each of the other players about the shoulders. Clear as day, he saw their cards, like there was a projector screen above each of their heads. The deck had turned for all of them at once, but Chase had the straight flush to beat their full houses and high straight.

Tossing chips in almost absently, Chase let the fat man lead the rounds of betting.

He pulled the winnings toward him a minute later, up two hundred dollars in one hand. Another ante, and the cards skimmed gracefully across the felt to him.

It went that way the next few hands, the energy swirling about the other players' shoulders while Chase had a clear view of all the cards in play. When one of the men had a better hand than Chase, the player felt compelled to fold. When he held a lower hand, he felt compelled to bet hard. People seemed easier for the spirits to influence, and soon he had a small mountain of multi-colored chips on the table before him.

Sipping a drink that was more melted ice than vodka, Chase watched the spirits dash away in all directions. Their flowing streams of energy went quicksilver to liquid white to gone in an instant.

The next round of cards was coming at him, and Chase frowned as he glanced at them without seeing. Someone was watching, the spirits only did that when someone was watching. It usually only happened when he was playing slots, staring with dulled focus at a machine for several minutes sometimes between pulls.

He stayed in for a couple rounds, tossing in chips while trying to scan the room about him in the most casual way possible. It was still early; there were less than twenty gamblers in the wide open space. Without turning around, Chase could see four other tables and the ends of perhaps a dozen rows of slot machines.

When the fat man with the beard drove up the betting, Chase folded and leaned back in his seat. He pretended to brood over his broken streak while trying to figure out if the guy in the biker gear was playing the slot machine he was sitting in front of at all.

Why would a leather-clad civilian have any interest in Chase? Even security had no reason to raise an eyebrow at his activities, not yet. He usually made it a point to be long gone before that became possible, anyway.

Chase anted up for another hand just to watch the guy a little longer. He lifted the corner of the cards in front of him and threw a ten dollar chip in the pot. One of the suits folded, but the other sat considering for a long moment. It gave Chase opportunity to size up the mystery man who kept glancing his way. It was a mite unnerving; he was obviously not well versed in subterfuge. He had yet to pull the arm on the idle machine flashing lights quietly before him.

The suit threw in a ten and then a five, and Chase let his displeasure show while the fat bearded fellow guffawed to his left.

"Streak's over, kid." The fat man's voice was thick with drink and extra pounds. He carefully and slowly tossed chips into the small pile: enough to call Chase, and then enough to call the suit, and then enough to raise them both another five dollars.

Chase was still frowning in consternation, letting the table think he was in the game with more than just his money, when he saw a woman approaching the guy who had been watching him. Petite and sexy and dark-haired, she wore a robe of simple white linen that made her look like a spiritual or religious devotee.

The leather-clad fellow had his attention on her completely as she neared, and Chase was happy to dismiss his previous behavior as wandering eyes while waiting on a girl.

"Fold," he said abruptly, gathering his chips.

He had to find the spirits. The remaining players at the table seemed both pleased and upset at his standing suddenly and nodding to each of them in turn. "Have a fun day, gentlemen."

He tossed a ten dollar chip and a quick smile at the bright dealer with the cute face.

Just as he was about to turn and walk away, Chase threw one last sideways glance at the man he had thought was watching him.

They were both watching now, standing side-by-side in a ridiculous leather and linen yin-yang. He was tall and stern and dark, she slight and open and bright.

Chase caught the woman's gaze, and her warm dark eyes widened in surprise. A cold chill climbed his spine.

He broke the eye contact, turned and walked on wooden legs any direction that would take him away from her.

CHAPTER 20

"He saw me." Vanessa sounded alarmed.

Vanessa never sounded alarmed.

The words 'that's impossible' tried to leap to his lips, but William quelled them. Instead he leaned toward her while they both watched the young man stalking away from them.

"Are you sure?" he asked.

She nodded, resolute, not taking her eyes off the retreating form.

"Where are his demons?" she asked.

William turned to her as he lost sight of the fellow.

"It's the damnedest thing." He shook his head. "They were there with him when I sat down. They were hard to see clearly, it was like they were constantly in motion. It looked like they were influencing the other players somehow, three huge demons looking over their shoulders and whispering in their ears. Huge, as in bigger than their host. They were flying or floating around, like they were unaffected by gravity. As soon as I started watching, trying to puzzle out what they were doing, they all three dashed off in different directions. I haven't seen them since."

"It's the damnedest thing," he said again.

Vanessa's expressive dark eyes met his, and they were round with wonder. She was nodding slowly, thoughtfully; and when she began speaking he tried to hear only her words and not the captivating timbre of her voice or the lovely hypnotizing lilt of her indigenous accent.

She was beautiful, which made it harder.

"He must be a sensitive, a seer," she spoke with slow measured certainty. "Amongst my people he could have been a shaman. Most white people who can see use their sight to take advantage of others around them under the guise of helping them. It appears he is at least an honest crook."

William settled back on the stool he had occupied earlier.

"His demons really were helping him win?" He was looking up at her now, and he was only slightly less aware of the fact that he was talking to someone no one else could see than he was of the fact that he didn't give a damn.

"They were making him win, surely," she nodded seriously. "Everyone has a symbiotic relationship with their demons, up to a certain point. Demons and angels keep us going, they keep us balanced, and they often keep us alive. We do the same for them, and each of us has our own unique set of steps as we dance with our demons. Most people can't see their demons or their angels, but even this rule must have exceptions. He probably doesn't see them as you do, or as I do. Your relationship with something influences and even determines your perception of it, the more so the more subtle the energy you are interacting with. Despite the obvious presence of evil in the world, very few of the evildoers actually think of themselves as evil."

She smiled. "Everyone is the protagonist in their own story."

"Not everyone sees themselves as some infallible good guy," William protested, startling two small old white ladies with tightly curled white hair and colorfully loud print dresses that floated about their veined ankles.

Vanessa smiled once more. "A good man always sees more evil in himself than he does in others; it's what helps him choose to be a good man. We all live by our own selfish motivations; those of us that would leave the world better for our place in it choose what we want carefully. We consider our words and our actions and how they might affect others before we make them manifest, and we are made to feel happy when we affect others in a positive fashion and unhappy when we affect others in a negative fashion. We learn from our mistakes and as we go about our way in the world we benefit countless others through our own selfish pursuit of happiness."

She was so full of words; and he was so impressed by her ability to express her views, William just sat quietly and smiled and tried to follow the gist of her thought. If he started questioning specifics of what she was saying, they would be here for hours and miss their appointment. He felt impatient, pent-up, and didn't understand how that was him pursuing his happiness; but he smiled and nodded occasionally and tried to listen.

She was beautiful, which made it harder.

"The rest of us don't see that far ahead," she went on, her open eyes not seeing the spell her words wound around his heart as she spoke. "We think that what we want is right because it is us wanting it, and those that are hurt by our inconsiderate methods of pursuit and choices of desire are twisted by our selfish perceptions into antagonist roles. All souls play both roles from time to time, and it is our experience with our own impetuousness on our journey down that gives us the compassion to deal with what may look like calculated evil on our way up."

William looked around before he spoke this time, kept his voice low so only she might hear. Vanessa leaned forward, although he hadn't meant for her to, and her delicious earthy flowery scent filled his nostrils pleasantly. It was a rare thing, her scent was somehow usually nonexistent or too light for him to detect. William didn't know why it came to him on the rare occasion, or what he was supposed to do with how it made him feel.

How can I smell a ghost? He thought absurdly to himself for the thousandth time this decade. Her lips were inches from his, her long silky midnight hair a dark waterfall between them. He felt a sudden stirring in his loins and a flush creeping up the back of his neck.

"So he doesn't see himself as a crook, using those…energies to his advantage." He whispered quickly and a little too loudly, but no one paid him any mind. He tried to keep his thoughts in front of his words and away from her lips and her eyes and her scent.

She was beautiful, which made it harder.

"He does not see himself as the cause of others' loss?" William asked.

"He's not," she responded. She didn't need to keep her voice down, but she did anyhow. Her whispers were sweet sounds to his longing ears, sounds meant just for him but words addressing the business at hand.

"Only a fool steps up to a gambling table thinking they have no advantage to press. The purpose of gambling is staking your good luck or personal strategy against others' good luck or personal strategy and thinking for some reason that you will come out on top." She was still inches from his face; and as she spoke he could smell her breath, fresh and fruity. "He is no more the villain than the stock trader who knows how to buy low and sell high is to the one who buys high and sells low."

William couldn't help but smile a little at that. Most of his spending money came from stock sales or dividends these days, and there was always more than enough lying about the house and locked in his wall safe.

Being immortal did have its advantages when it came to savings and stocks and bonds. He had never really considered all the mortals who had lost to his gains over the long years.

"Besides," Vanessa smiled a smile that made him remember how young she had been when she died, "he's not in danger of being consumed by his demons. Look at your key."

William had a good look around before he pulled the gold pocket watch from his leather jeans and pushed the small gold button to open the cover.

She was right. It wasn't a demon's visage burning its likeness into the face of the watch. It was a Walker's hat, glowing in gold luminescence.

"That can't be right." William looked up at her, shook his head unbelieving. "That one?"

Vanessa frowned, but only just a little. Her expression was comically youthful for a moment, a seventeen-year-old face bearing the weight of three centuries of wisdom. "Walkers are not what they used to be, William. Men are not what they used to be. Just as the changing world calls forth different aspects of our souls, different souls call forth a different kind of Walker."

"Times are certainly changing." His eyes found the floor, traced the loudly colored patterning absently. "Men who have been swinging swords for centuries now have a king who just picked up a blade for the first time last week."

William looked up, met her eyes again.

"Do you remember the last Walker we made?" Vanessa asked quietly.

Her smile was young and beautiful and ancient and wise.

"Jeremy," William recalled immediately. "He was a good man."

He smiled, nodded at the remembering. "He was a great cop; he was so quick to catch on. I'll bet he's the perfect Walker."

She stood up straight, her smile holding back a laugh.

When he looked a question at her, she only shook her head, still smiling.

"It's time." Vanessa nodded at the key in his hand.

William sighed, closed the gold cover and let the key disappear.

He held his hand out to her, palm up, and watched her long slender fingers cover less than half of his calloused mitt. William couldn't feel her touch, nor she his, but the closeness somehow made communicating silently and walking between worlds together easier. He tried not to think of how her skin would feel against his.

She was beautiful, which made it harder.

Thinking of the man he had been watching, William quested outward with his inner vision. He could see the man walking, making his way down the sidewalk, looking over his shoulder, walking faster.

William didn't even have to close his eyes anymore. The intersection the stranger was approaching appeared as clearly in his mind's eye as her hand in his appeared to his actual eyes. William thought them there together, and it was so. Standing beside Vanessa on the sidewalk, he looked down at her as pedestrians passed without a glance.

"Thank you." He knew she was keeping people from noticing him, and that she had done the same in the casino. Most folks she could easily send spiraling into the interminable cycles of their internal dialogue. Others had to have bits of memory replaced or erased, and Vanessa did it as routinely as William walked between worlds.

She called it 're-minding'.

There was no time for her to respond; the young man he had been watching was fast approaching. Panting and sweating, he looked up just as William let his hand fall on his shoulder.

William thought of home, and the trio disappeared.

CHAPTER 21

Chase nearly stumbled on the sudden thick carpeting underfoot, but he quickly had his feet under him and his wits about him. He couldn't shake the vice-like grip the biker dude had on his shoulder, holding him firmly in place whether he tried to move or not.

He glanced back and forth between them, the tall hard-faced man in black and the beautiful slender woman in white standing at his side. They had been holding hands a moment ago, in the street, but they weren't anymore.

"You can see me." Her accent was strange, her voice beautiful but accusatory.

"Yeah, sure." Chase shrugged. "Can't he see you?" He nodded at the tall man with the hard face.

"I can see her." The tall man's voice was as hard as his face. "Others can't. She is dead."

Chase swept his hand at her arm playfully, only to watch his fingers disappear as they passed through the unyielding image. He felt the blood drain from his face.

"I've seen ghosts and spirits my whole life." He heard his own voice quietly and simply state his life-long secret to the two odd strangers. "I've never seen one that looked so...real."

The dark-haired lady smiled. "You have seen lost souls and demons and angels, perhaps. If you have ever seen a ghost, or spirit in astral form, it is likely that you have failed to distinguish them from other living beings. A ghost is a soul with purpose and soul memory not currently residing in a body. What you see drifting about aimlessly or engaged in meaningless routine are lost souls, looking for purpose or a thread of memory in a world where they no longer belong."

The grip on his shoulder tightened, and Chase winced. "What you use to swindle people out of their money are demons."

Chase shook his head, adamant. "They're not, though. Not anymore. They used to haunt me, torment me. Now we work together, I try to figure out what they want and they keep me alive and safe. The spirits are my companions."

His shoulder felt like it was being crushed. Chase was beginning to crumple under the pain. He watched the two strangers exchange a glance, and the impossibly strong hand left his shoulder. Suddenly the hand was before him, palm up, a meaty calloused slab of flesh with an old-fashioned gold pocket watch resting lightly on it.

He eyed the pocket watch. It looked like real gold, and it looked antique as well. It was probably worth some money. There was something else about it, too, an ethereal glow that seemed to beckon to him with a cool rush of excitement and danger.

"Take it," the dark-haired woman breathed. She seemed enraptured by the sight of the glowing golden disc.

Chase felt his eyes widen. "I can have it?" He looked the question at the tall man with the impossible strength.

The man nodded, solemn. "You must take it."

There was a forever moment where Chase might have considered where he had been a minute ago or where he was now or how he had gotten here. He might have thought about why this strange pair was offering him an obviously valuable and possibly magickal antique gold pocket watch. He did think about the spirits, briefly, but only to wonder where they were. Bedazzled by the enchanted item, he let his mind fill with quiet wonder as his hand reached slowly toward it.

Before the long moment could end, before his hand could grasp the golden disc, Chase felt a push and then a pop above his belly, and pain arched his spine. Looking down, he saw a dagger buried to the hilt in his abdomen. He coughed, unwillingly, watching droplets of blood spray from his lips as his fingers curled around the smooth gold disc that the stranger held out.

"Take it," the man said, shoving the dagger deeper into his heart.

Chase gasped with pain.

"You must take it," he repeated, his voice low and calm.

CHAPTER 22

The engine's interminable thunder surrounded him like a chrysalis of sound. Filling his ears to the exclusion of all else, it made his very cells dance beneath his skin. William let his glance stray to the speedometer, suspecting he may be going too fast. He was, too, speeding along the lonely freeway at nearly a hundred miles per hour.

Easing up on the throttle, William let his thoughts race as noisily through his mind as the motorcycle raced down the road. After watching the human draw his last breath, he had carried the body to the spare bedroom and arranged it comfortably on the bed. Now they would wait for the key to do its work, changing human cells and thoughts and powers to those of a Walker.

William was fervently hoping for a complete metamorphosis. The man he had watched in the casino was simply not Walker material.

He thought then of Jeremy, the last man whose mortality he had taken. It was suddenly clear to him why Vanessa had mentioned him earlier. Jeremy had been a good man, a police officer who had made detective because he loved his job and was good at it. He kept to himself and lived a quiet personal life, preferring the company of books and weights to family and friends.

Vanessa had questioned him at length about his career in law enforcement during their time training him to walk between worlds. She had been trying to prove a theory over many years lived and many Walkers made. It was simple, and it made sense, which was why William suspected it may be true. It seemed to him that the only things that were truly eternal were simple things that made sense.

The idea was that a man or woman had to meet certain requirements to become a Walker. They had to be a soul on the way up, of strong moral fiber, with few or no social attachments. Often the friends a Walker had when he was human became his Guide and Watcher, but most lived such solitary lives that they had trouble filling both positions.

Vanessa insisted there was more to it than that, however, that there was another element to the human lives of Walker candidates. She described it as an insurmountable stumbling block that shouldn't be there, some twist of fate that stymied the continued pursuit of an important aspect of the soul's development.

They had seen her proven correct time and again, turning warriors into Walkers when their military careers were ended or ceilinged by bureaucratic foolishness. Jeremy had seemed on his way up, in every way, and Vanessa had tried to discover more about his situation while getting to know the man.

Riding his steed of chrome and steel and rubber and leather, William let the scene play out like a movie in his mind. He could see Vanessa, beautiful as always, sitting at the dinner table with the two Walkers and sipping her flask occasionally while they ate steaks and drank beer. He could see Jeremy, too: youthful and dark-haired, his broad shoulders and bulging biceps animated by a polite and quiet personality. He had looked more stoic than a young man should, which had made William take an instant liking to him.

"So what was the next step?" Vanessa's sweet voice rang clear in his memory. "What did you plan on becoming after detective?"

Jeremy had smiled softly, almost wistfully, staring at the plate of food before him. He shook his head slowly as he met eyes with hers across the stained oak table.

"There was no next step," he had replied.

"No?" She had arched her eyebrows prettily, surprised. "Is there nowhere to go from there?"

"Not for me." Jeremy had fiddled half-heartedly with his food, pushing a bit of steak from one side of the plate to the other and back again.

William could sense the man's discomfort.

Jeremy had set his fork on the table next to his plate and caught her gaze again.

"My captain approached me not long after I made detective," he had sighed. "He took me aside and told me that if he had known the truth about me he never would have promoted me to detective, and that it would not be long before he found a way to put me back in a uniform."

Chewing a particularly thick and sumptuous bit of meat, William had let Vanessa ask the question.

"If he had known about what?" Her brow had furrowed prettily with the query, teenaged face straining to express centuries of compassion.

The muscular new Walker had shifted uncomfortably in his seat, and his eyes had drifted back to his plate.

"If he had known I was gay," Jeremy had said quietly.

William had felt the delectable taste of steak turn to sawdust in his mouth, felt his jaws stop working at the mouthful of food. He remembered hearing Vanessa's voice, from far off, then Jeremy's. It had taken a forever moment for their words to register.

"That's silly," Vanessa had said dismissively. "Who would see you differently because of that?"

"William does," Jeremy had replied quietly.

When he came slowly back to his senses, William had realized that Vanessa was looking at him. He had tried to chew, tried to engage his jaws in the mechanical motion of breaking up the meat, only to find the task unbearably complicated. In one huge awkward gulp, he swallowed.

It had been all he could do to not break eye contact with her, to not edge his chair away from Jeremy's. A war raged within him, his heart and mind at odds with social programming from yesterday's yesterday.

"I may see you in a different light," William's voice had sounded wooden and hollow in his own ears as he spoke. His eyes were affixed to the salt and pepper grinders that sat side by side in the center of the table. "That does not mean I see you as less than before. If anything, I see me as something less as I look within."

William had been able to hold the man's gaze for a few seconds as he spoke sincerely: "My discomfort is my shortcoming, not yours. I apologize for it."

Jeremy had been nodding his slow stoic nod.

"Thank you, William," he had said quietly.

Her lovely dark eyes were round as Vanessa had looked from one man's shame to the other's. "How do you see him differently?" she had asked pointedly.

Tearing his eyes from the twin grinders, William had looked at Vanessa helplessly. With no idea what he might say, he had opened his mouth to speak.

"Vanessa." Jeremy spoke. His strong quiet voice had given William the opportunity he was looking for to shut his mouth.

He had done so, grateful.

"William grew up in a different time, in a different world." The young Walker had given him a nod of acknowledgment without meeting his eyes. "The way people act and treat each other has changed an awful lot over the last few hundred years. It can't possibly be easy to adjust to watching every conceivable facet of life on Earth shift and spin as you try to make your way in it."

Vanessa had smiled, her youthful face showing a touch of chagrin.

"I should be explaining this to you," she'd said. "I was born in another time as well, the same time and the same world as Walker William."

He was shaking his head slowly then; William had been able to see both of them without looking directly at either of them.

"Not the same world," Jeremy had argued quietly. "The same time, but not the same world. What did your people do with people like me in your time? What did they call us?"

"It was a term that meant 'other sex' or 'third sex'," she'd shrugged. "The only third sex people I knew of were shamans, seers, medicine men and midwives and the like."

"People you held in high regard, yes?"

Her nod was enough for Jeremy to press on in his quiet tones.

"It was not the same in William's world, nor is it now," Jeremy had said calmly. "Being homosexual still kills a lot of careers in the United States, and the prejudice hardly stops there. This country is still largely in tolerance mode on many of the issues it pretends to be accepting of, and homosexuality is among the least of them. Racism, sexism and classism are the cornerstones on which our society was built and the fuel on which it continues to function. I don't know about William, but I learned a lot about tolerance in the world I grew up in. I learned very little about acceptance. I saw even less."

William listened, wondering how there was no anger or bitterness in his tone.

"Tolerance is an ugly thing," Jeremy had continued. "When you tolerate something or someone, you allow it to exist despite the fact that you privately or publicly wish it didn't. A tolerant person is not someone who is happy to allow you to exist as you are; a tolerant person is someone who allows you to exist despite who you are. The tolerant person often sees themselves as being good by virtue of being tolerant. Yet how can it be good to wish something or someone didn't exist, even privately? When we teach generations of young people tolerance, we don't solve the problem of intolerance; we mask and perpetuate it. Acceptance is the solution to both intolerance and the ugly outgrowth of it that we call tolerance. Acceptance of someone or something means you give it as much right to exist and room to express itself as you do yourself. Acceptance means equal rights for everyone."

Vanessa had listened intently, leaning forward in her chair until she disappeared a bit into the table. William finally turned and looked at the young Walker with a new appreciation, and a bit of wonder.

"You may understand William's immortality," Jeremy's firm quiet voice had gone on, "but you can't understand his humanity. He has had to be in a state of constant adjustment for over three hundred years, living as a normal man in a society that continually changes all around him. I doubt that his upbringing was of a more liberal bent than mine, and there are probably many issues with yesterday's way of thinking that have never been shoved in his face like this."

"The routines he keeps," Jeremy had gestured to the food and drink between them, sustenance only for the soul in this house, "help him stay grounded in the world of men."

Vanessa had smiled. "You sound more like a Guide than a Walker."

"Not really." He'd shaken his head slowly from side to side. "I have no idea what your life experience has been, or what it's like now. I can understand a bit of what William has experienced just thinking of putting my new life together. I have no frame of reference for being a Guide other than seeing the experience from the outside. It must require a rare temperament to be a Guide. You are truly in the world but not of it. Most people would go a bit batty after just a few days of being invisible to most eyes and inaudible to most ears and unable to touch anything solid. Yet somehow you have existed in that state for hundreds of years, and in my experience you seem the most calm and peaceful person I have ever met."

Vanessa's smooth olive skin was not prone to flush, but she had smiled a pretty and flustered smile at the new Walker.

"You're right," she'd said, her full red lips still curled slightly in a smile that never failed to take William's breath away. "You have the compassion of a Walker."

At that, Jeremy had sighed and glanced at William before turning back to her. "I have enough compassion to know that William could probably use some time alone right now." His gentle gaze had come back to William. "Maybe go for a walk, or a ride?"

William had looked from one to the other, meeting their eyes each in turn for a full second.

"I'm fine," he'd bristled, looking down at the steak still left on his plate. He didn't need it, and now he didn't want it either.

A ride did sound good.

"You should go," Vanessa had urged him. "If you want to."

"The most considerate and compassionate among us should take advantage of the consideration of others on the rare occasion that it is offered." Jeremy was looking at Vanessa as he spoke.

William had stood then, suddenly, thanked them brusquely, and gone for a ride.

And now he rode the same highway, but he was a different man riding a different mount. Training Jeremy as a Walker after that had seen a slow change in him, and he was glad for it. Now seeing two men together seemed as romantic as a man and a woman to William, and as natural. He knew now that his discomfort and uneasiness had been his own soul crying out for evolution, and that Jeremy's path crossing his had been God answering that call.

Perhaps God worked in mysterious ways for others; for him, the people and events that came his way seemed to make a lot of sense. Not at first, but eventually.

He was going too fast again, eating up the miles more quickly than he needed to. Just as he crested a long smooth uprise, William saw a lone figure standing in the middle of the highway.

When he was a man, his eyes had been the only thing to fail him. Up close, his vision was clear and sharp. From ten feet away, he hadn't been able to tell whether a girl was pretty or plain; and at twenty feet, he couldn't tell whether the approaching blur was male or female. William had been as bad with a bow as he was good with a sword, an embarrassment with a rifle but a crack shot with a pistol. It had not taken long for him to realize that other men could see better than him, but the difference crystallized for William when he became a Walker. It was as if he had been given new eyes, although the same dark brown irises stared back at him from every mirror. Trees had once been colored blurs to him; now the shape of every leaf and needle and cone revealed itself to him, and it was a wonder. Nature had once been a vast explosion of colors for him, only to change in the space of one day to a fascinating array of curves and angles to delight his perfect eyes.

The Walker's sharp eyes could see the man in detail from nearly a mile away. Leather hat and overcoat were enough to tell him it was no ordinary man, and the face looked vaguely familiar.

Already downshifting, William recognized the face finally behind the new beard. He rolled to a stop beside the Stone Walker, killed the engine and removed his helmet.

William bowed his head as best he could while still straddling his steed.

"My king," he intoned gravely.

"Walker William." Paul's youthful face creased into a deep frown under his new whiskers. He looked older than he had when William had seen him before, which was of course impossible.

It wasn't the beard, or the lengthening hair; it was his eyes. Somehow the Walker King had gotten that long, cold, distant look in his eye that is the mark of the old immortal. William found himself wondering what eternal questions the new Walker wrestled with as he listened to him.

"I am a new Walker," the Stone Walker spoke in a level and matter-of-fact tone. "Yet I am also the Walker King. I do not have the luxury of learning from my mistakes over years or decades until I become a good Walker. I must be the perfect Walker and the best king I can be, for every mistake I make affects far too many people for me to make mistakes."

William resisted the urge to smile. The king seemed to be a very serious man.

"I would like to enlist your help," he went on. "You are among the oldest Walkers in the United States, and you have turned more humans successfully into Walkers than any other Walker in the country."

"Successfully?" William did allow himself a bit of a smile now; he had had no idea.

The Walker King's frown deepened.

"Accidents happen," he said dismissively.

The thought did not seem so easily dismissed from his mind, however, and he gazed off into the desert with a thoughtful forever stare.

"Walker William," he said again, coming back to himself suddenly. "There is a threat looming over all of us, a darkness of such power that it threatens the very fabric of reality. An army gathers even now with power and strength and numbers enough to overwhelm man and devil and angel alike. We Walkers are the only hope. You, me, our brothers and sisters, must form an army, the only army that can stand against this threat. Walker William, are you with me?"

William tried to assimilate and respond at the same time.

Words came out, useless and nonsensical: "My…um…grace…uh…"

The old Walker shook his head, as if to clear it. It had been a long time since he had met a king, longer since he had met one that fit the part.

"I am with you, my king."

CHAPTER 23

Kris lay on his back, gazing at the flat gray ceiling with a satisfied half-smile on his face. Stepping through the doorway was getting easier. Jessica lay beside him, her head on his chest while her fingers described faint patterns on his stomach. Her slim legs entangled his beneath the disarray of sheets and blankets covering them from the waist down. He could smell her hair, could feel the smooth skin of her back under his hand, and could taste the flavor of her on his lips from a thousand earnest kisses.

Moving his hand to stroke her soft blonde mane, Kris murmured softly into her hair. "Good morning, my sweet love. Did you sleep well?"

The smooth feel of her cheek brushing against his skin as she nodded sent a tingle of electricity through his body.

"I spend half the night having glorious, mind-blowing, soul-shaking sex with the man of my dreams," her words were the wind on his skin, healing his heart in passing, "and the other half sleeping in the sweet embrace of the love of my life. I slept amazingly well. And you, my darling man?"

"I slept great," he lied.

She turned her head to face him, blonde tresses falling attractively across her sculpted features.

"Liar," she frowned, staring at him with feigned consternation through an errant lock of honeyed hair.

Her cheeks puffed up for an instant as she blew at the lock of hair. It floated weightless over her cheek for a moment and fell back into place over her eyes. Her playful frown deepened.

"My dreams are different now," he smiled down at her, brushing the lock of hair from her eyes with a gentle touch. "I'm still adjusting to not sleeping like a human anymore. It's like I'm lucid all the time, going to sleep is not a break in consciousness as much as it is like walking into another room. Is that how it is for you? Do dragons dream?"

"I dream of flying," her voice was soft and sweet, "with the wind in my wings and the ground far below."

Her fingers continued to trace lazy patterns on his belly. "I don't know about other dragons, but I dream of flying. And you."

He smiled at her sweetness, tilted his head to land a light kiss on her forehead. "That sounds beautiful. I'm glad I am there with you."

"But you're not." Her playful frown was back. "You're off having meetings and classes and doing important Guide stuff."

Her fingers were still then, and her flat palm pressed itself warm against his belly.

"What's it like there?" Jessica breathed. 'Where do you go?"

Kris shrugged gently, so as not to disturb her head's perch. "It's different. It's like a colorless world of endless possibility, a drab concrete foundation for the glorious constant launch of beautiful colored rocket ships."

Her pretty young brow furrowed. "Purgatory? You go to Purgatory every night?"

"Some souls call it that," he acknowledged. "But most call it the Otherworld, and they say Purgatory is a different place altogether."

"What do you think?"

Kris smiled. "I think I would rather fall asleep with you in my arms and dream of flying with you. Instead I close my eyes here and open them in a place of infinite possibility governed by such strict rules and regulations that it is transformed into a place of interminable boredom. And without you there, if does feel like Purgatory."

Jessica's face was a cloud of touched concern as she turned her head to kiss his chest. "Awww…that's so sweet, and so sad."

She spoke into his chest, her voice muffled by his dead skin. "Do you have friends there?"

"Not really." He looked up and to the right, at the ceiling. "A couple, I guess. I spend most of my time alone."

When his eyes met hers again, the look of concern seemed genuine this time. "What do your friends think of you dating a dragon?"

"A friend is someone who wants you to be happy," he responded slowly. "If anyone doesn't like my being with you, they are no friend to me. Besides, I'm not dating a dragon…I am in love with the girl of my dreams, my sweet devil and my perfect angel. The fact that you are a dragon has nothing to do with my love for you, except perhaps in giving me opportunity to appreciate and adore another facet of your exquisite wonderfulness."

She giggled helplessly for a long sweet moment, and Kris let himself delight in her breath on his bare skin.

"Paul is my friend, Matt is my friend; they are both happy for us." Kris let his fingers tangle in her honeyed hair.

Her bright blue eyes were round, looking up at him. "So your friends in Purgatory don't like me, do they?"

"My friends in Purgatory don't know you," he sighed.

Kris glanced to the digital clock on the nightstand. "Don't you have to go to work?"

"Uncle Roche gave me the day off." Her clear blue eyes sparkled mischievously as her hand slid lower down his belly. "I was hoping to spend the day in bed with you."

Kris smiled and relaxed onto his pillow with a sigh. Letting his eyelids drift closed, he gave his full attention to her fingers on his skin, her breath on his chest. He lost himself in the delightful subtle seduction as every cell of his dead being silently sang his love for her.

"What did Paul want to see you about?" Her voice was soft and lovely, and her hand was still caressing his navel with enticing slow circles.

Gears spun free in his mind while he deliberately engaged his speaking mechanism.

It took a long moment, and Jessica spoke once more.

"He seemed awful grim when you guys came back downstairs." She was looking up at him, her round blue eyes full of concern again.

"Paul is pretty grim all the time now, Jess." He chuckled, trying to make light.

A frown darkened his thoughtful mien almost immediately.

"I'm king of the Guides now, I guess." Kris was still frowning.

Jessica's nod was solemn and unsurprised. Her hand drifted light up his torso to trace lazy spirals over his chest as he continued to speak.

"Paul is going to form an army of Walkers and I have to organize the Guides. A war is coming, and I have to play the part of general." His voice carried the displeasure he felt.

Jessica lay quiet, looking up at him and tracing designs on his heart.

"It's awful, Jess," he said. "All the demons that Walkers have been killing don't just go away, they don't cease to exist once cut off from the host and killed. They go...somewhere else. It's like they're rats in the walls between dimensions. They're trapped between levels of Hell, with nothing to do but fight and nothing to consume but each other."

Her eyes widened as he spoke; when he broke off they narrowed thoughtfully.

"That means demons have souls," she said quietly. "Apparently everyone in the Universe has a soul but dragons."

"What?" Kris was curious.

"Dragons don't have souls," she spoke quietly, solemnly, turning so her lips brushed his skin with every word. "Dragons are souls incarnate. Many dragons believe that it is the final stop for the soul before moving on to another reality altogether. That makes dragons the most advanced souls in the Universe if it is true. The angels say that dragons are souls broken beyond repair, cursed with power like no other and doomed to bring about their own eternal demise. Royal dragons keep track of their bloodlines, but others lay their eggs as far from their own territory as possible. There are dragon eggs all over Hell, waiting to hatch. Some take a thousand years, some a million; no one knows where all of the dragon eggs are or when they will hatch. Dragons live forever, until they are killed anyway. We get older slowly, very slowly; and when we die, we die. Our bodies disappear, no matter where we are, and a dragon's body is a dragon's soul. The body and the soul of a dragon are as one, and they die as one."

Kris was suddenly very serious. "I don't ever want to lose you. You are my way."

"You won't," she smiled. "Dragons are very hard to kill."

CHAPTER 24

"Let me know if you need any help," the Walker King offered before they went in.

William nodded his acknowledgement, tried not to smile.

They stood in a carpeted hallway lined with numbered doors. It was a nice enough hotel, loud colors unfaded and bright lights made brighter by the many mirrored walls. The door was painted a light blue, brass numbers reading three twenty-seven.

They had appeared together, a little high to remain invisible to security cameras and human eyes. In this state they were able to walk through the door like ghosts to stand side by side unseen by the room's three occupants.

Lying in bed were a man and woman, naked and clearly having just enjoyed each other's carnal company. The man was older, in his late fifties, with a well-trimmed beard and a long cultivated belly. His grey hair was thin and short, and the flesh under his jaw bulged out past the careful edges of his whiskers.

The girl was young, slim, with simple attractive features. The roots of her long red hair were a dull brown at her part, and her green eyes were milky and pale. Her naked body was darkened by long hours in the sun or in a tanning bed. She was covered by sheets and blankets from the waist down, and round silicone breasts with dark brown nipples rode high on her ribcage.

Her hand was drifting through his thinning hair while she leaned back on her other elbow. Jutting her implants forward seemed a part of her natural pose.

The man had his eyes closed halfway, a satisfied smile touching his mouth as her fingers touched his hair.

William exchanged an awkward glance with the Walker King before he focused his attention on the demon lying in bed on the other side of the man. She was both fully developed and generously proportioned. There were no sheets covering her nude form, kneeling beside the man to rest one hand on his shoulder while the other pressed into the mattress to support her weight. Smooth pale red skin stretched over her lean legs and generous hips and buttocks, straining over melons of breasts that hung swinging as she spoke.

"Feel that touch," she whispered, her demon voice sounding surprisingly sweet. "Feel that touch you don't deserve, think about the sex you should not have just had."

Long and thick and black, the demon's hair hung past wide red lips as her voice became more venomous. "Think about your daughter, feel that touch in your hair while you think about her. Think about your wife, your marriage. Think about that poor girl's father."

Turning his head, the man glanced disdainfully at the girl stroking his hair.

She met his eyes, smiled a fleeting smile and let her hand drift down over his belly to clutch him through the sheets. "You want to go again?"

His expression changed from disdain to a leering hunger. The man nodded wordlessly, leaning back further against the pillow and putting his hands behind his head. The movement caused his belly to jut forward while the sheet slid to puddle around her hand.

"Two hundred," she said flatly, lifting her hand from his crotch to run fingers through her hair.

The man's face reddened.

"I already paid you." There was anger in his voice.

"We already did it," she replied sweetly. "If you want to do it again, you have to pay me again."

A peal of cruel laughter split the air, the beautiful demon woman sitting back on her fleshy haunches and howling musical mockery that the man could surely hear on some level. His face reddened more, and the demon seductress leaned back to bring both hands to either side of her face. Her fingers brushed back her hair as her elbows squeezed together her breasts, and she grew just a little taller.

"Now." William spoke and moved at the same time, dashing around the bed to seize the startled demon at both wrists from behind. Hoping the other Walker knew how to follow, William thought *up* and closed his eyes.

When he opened his eyes, he released his hold on the demon and stepped back to manifest his longsword. He could see the cord, a smoky tendril of energy stretched taut from the figure before him to disappear across distance and dimensions.

William was pleased to see that the Walker King had followed, standing a step back from William's sudden sword.

They stood in a foot of snow, on a mountain that rose sharply above and below them, on a plateau twenty by thirty paces. The sun hung high in the sky above them, glinting off William's steel as it severed the cord.

Turning slowly, the demon stood with her hands on her hips and regarded the two Walkers. William's black leather pants and jacket stirred in the wind, and he heard the Walker King's black overcoat cracking like a whip with every gust.

William stepped back to stand beside his king, noticing that only he held a blade. They stood together and watched the demon girl watching them.

Still nude, the demon stood before them with an air of overtly sexual femininity. Her feet were shoulder width apart and buried in snow, but from calf to scalp her curves and crevasses were visible and inviting. Swaying slowly to some hellish tune only she could hear, she flattened her palm to run it in purposeful patterns under her breasts and over her hips.

"Is she going to attack?" The Walker King spoke, startling him.

"Probably not," William answered. "She is a sex demon, made more of guilt than anger. They usually only have the one weapon."

He watched her swaying form warily nonetheless, not one to be taken by surprise.

"Why are we here?" The king looked around them, gestured at the landscape.

William suppressed a smile.

"Demons hate the cold," he answered.

The nude form put her hands on her hips, twisted her pretty face into an ugly frown and spit on the snow. The spittle sizzled when it hit the cold powder, and a little cloud of steam rose from the spot. Looking back at her, William saw the smiling sexy demon swaying languidly again and cupping her voluptuous breasts between her hands.

William glanced at the new Walker, wondered what he was thinking behind those fierce blue eyes as they watched the demon dance.

"You want this one?" he asked.

The Walker King's cowboy hat moved, almost imperceptibly, as he shook his head no.

William rushed the demon with his longsword, letting his stride lend momentum to his swing, and the blade glinted in the sunlight again. Her pretty head floated in mid-air for a moment, expressing shock and gushing blood while dark hair drifted lazy in the wind. Then her body crumpled to the snow as her head fell to rest beside it, and the two pieces stained the white underfoot with purple blood.

Closing his eyes, William saw the plateau untouched by blood or body fragments; and when he opened them not a footprint dotted the snow. He disappeared the blade and turned to the new Walker.

"That was clean," the Walker King was nodding. "Why did you wait so long, in the hotel room?"

William let his frown match his king's. "A human deserves every chance, every moment to deal with their demons themselves. I never strike too early or too late."

He was nodding again. "Let me take you somewhere, Walker William."

William's frown deepened. "I have a busy schedule, my king. I just turned a new Walker."

The Walker King never stopped nodding.

"I know," he spoke brusquely. "Don't worry; this won't take any time at all."

His hand fell on William's shoulder.

CHAPTER 25

"I don't know, Sarah." Mason sat on the edge of the bed, guitar in his lap as he looked up at her. "Isn't this more of a Mikie kind of part?"

Sarah made a face, put her hands on her hips and shook her head. She looked so pretty standing there in her little blue dress, barefoot on the carpet.

"I don't want to do songs like this with Mikie; I want to do them with you." Her voice was firm and sweet at the same time, sweeter when she spoke again. "Will you please just try? For me?" Blinking pale green eyes rapidly at him, she coaxed a smile from him finally.

"Alright." Mason shook his head in resignation.

"It's not a big part." Her eyes were still blinking rapidly at him.

"I said alright." He let his tone show that he was becoming more annoyed that amused. "Flip my switch, baby."

She giggled and stepped to the amp, kneeling in front of it.

"What about the piano part?" Mason was thinking of the gentle keyed beginning of the Evanescence tune as the amplifier hummed to life.

Like any musician who played any instrument, Mason had a cheap keyboard propped unused and a bit dusty in the corner. Sarah stepped to it wordlessly and came to sit beside him on the bed. When she flipped a switch on the back of the electronic rectangle, a bank of red and green lights illuminated above the black and white keys.

"You play piano, too." He wasn't asking.

Mason was not sure whether to express shock over the keyboard's ancient batteries having juice or over Sarah's endless abilities.

She was looking at the instrument on her lap, pushing buttons and striking keys. "I started taking lessons when I was five. I can't remember a time when I couldn't play." She struck a key, kept the sound as she struck a half dozen more. Then came the slow haunting piano intro, joined the next bar by Sarah's own sultry strains. She was no Amy Lee, but her tone was dark and haunting in its own alluring way.

Mason was so transfixed by her easy playing and her soulful singing he almost forgot to start. Almost. He brought the crunchy riff from near silent to the point of overwhelming the scant piano notes as they gave way to the wall of sound. Sarah's voice rose above it, riding the wall in all its flinted, tortured glory.

The singing came easier than he had expected, as it seemed to always do these days. Their voices were perfectly suited to the call and response duet, and Mason was not surprised to catch a glimpse of Daemon watching them and smiling.

When the last notes died, she turned and grinned at him, her eyes wide. "That sounded great," she beamed.

Mason nodded. "You always sound great."

Leaning over his guitar to kiss his cheek lightly, Sarah kept her luminous eyes locked on him. "You sounded great."

He finally allowed himself a small smile.

"We did sound great," he chuckled.

"We should play it tonight." Sarah let her fingers dance over the keys, touching the first few notes of the song again.

Mason pulled the pack of Camel Lights from his pocket and flipped the box top open. Three joints rolled around with a half dozen cigarettes and a black Bic lighter. Placing one of the marijuana cigarettes between his lips, he chuckled again.

"Mikie would love that," he said, lighting the end and inhaling deeply. He held it out to Sarah.

"Fuck Mikie." A dark cloud passed over her pretty features as she accepted the joint and took a long pull. "He's been an asshole lately. Besides, I would never do a song like this with him."

She passed it back, still frowning "It would just feel...ecch."

Mason smoked thoughtfully, a suspicious worm burrowing into his brain.

"Did you two used to be together?" he asked.

Sarah rolled her pretty eyes and sighed.

"No, we were never together," she said. "We messed around for a while, and then we decided we should keep it purely professional between us."

Mason proffered the rolled sinsemilla. "You decided or he decided?"

"We decided." She pinched the joint between thumb and forefinger and took a small hit.

"We decided together." She took a bigger hit, held it in.

He frowned. "Sarah, was it your idea or his idea to stop sleeping together?"

A cloud of white-blue smoke streamed from between her lips to gather before her face. "It was my idea, I guess."

She held the joint out to him, narrowing her eyes as they met his.

"Why the twenty questions?"

Mason shrugged, watching smoke rise from the tip of the burning sativa. "Just adding things up…and some things Mikie said last night."

"See?" Sarah rose to lean the keyboard in the corner again, switching it off as she crossed the small room. "He's being a real asshole lately."

"Why didn't you tell me?" If his head had not been obscured by a thick cloud of smoke, she might have seen the hurt on his face. Instead her eyes were on the joint he was holding out to her.

"I thought you didn't care about the past." She frowned as she smoked, standing before him.

Mason looked up at her. "I do when I'm in a band with it." He reached up to take the joint again. "He's not really in the past if you see him every day." He smashed the burning cherry between calloused thumb and forefinger, wincing at the pain as he let it bite into him.

"Mason." Sarah spoke softly, quietly, as she dropped to her knees on the carpet at his feet. "The last few days have been a whirlwind for me. I have never fallen so hard so fast for anyone. I want to share everything with you, I want to tell you everything. We've had so little time together, I never really thought to tell you. You're right, though; I should have told you."

She took his hand in hers on his lap. "I should have told you something else too. I love you, Mason. You are my world now, and my world is yours."

The anger drained from him as she spoke, and by the time she finished he was blinking back sudden surprising tears.

"Sarah, I…" Looking down at her big green eyes, Mason reached for words, swallowed.

"I know it's soon," she shrugged. "But I also know it's true."

He disengaged his hand from hers long enough to set the Stratocaster flat on the bed beside him. Then he took her hand in his.

"Sarah." He frowned a little, so he wouldn't cry. "I love you too."

Leaning forward, he kissed her lightly on the forehead.

She was looking up at him mischievously now.

"Can we play 'Bring Me to Life' tonight?" She blinked prettily. "Please?"

"Yeah." Mason laughed. "Yeah, sure. Fuck Mikie."

Sarah sat next to him on the bed again, wrapping her arms around his waist and gazing at him in the most disarming way.

"I love you, Mason." She kissed him, and he let his ears thrill at her words as his lips thrilled at her kiss.

Daemon stood and watched for a minute, happy in their happiness. A faint smile touched his countenance, and with his raised brows and wide eyes he looked full of wonder and hope. Had a Walker been there to see, they might have described the demon's countenance as downright angelic.

A thought came into his mind then, and Daemon's eyes narrowed to angry slits as his lips curled into an ugly sneer. Fists clenched, he stalked through the closed doorway looking the perfect picture of loathing, like a demon ought to.

CHAPTER 26

"What is this place?" William turned in a slow circle, looking for seams or doors in the liquid luminescence all around him. It was beautiful and flowing, making him think of a sports arena with a cotton florescent dome and a field of living cloud. One structure stood alone near a wall. It appeared to be made of stone, but his squinting Walker eyes revealed it to be the same liquid light everything else here was made of. It was one room with no doors or windows within another room with no doors or windows.

The Walker King stood surrounded by the featureless beauty. "It was the Walker Angel's personal space, a place she created to bring all of the Walkers together…and kill them."

Paul's eyes fell on the distant structure, and his customary frown softened a bit. "Now it is a gathering place for Walkers. We will assemble here, and from here we will open a doorway between dimensions. That is where we will find our enemies."

William nodded toward the distant structure. "And what is that?"

"That," Paul glanced warily at the flowing light that shaped the building, "is for prisoners of war. It currently houses prisoners from the last war, devils that I have been getting information from."

William arched an eyebrow at the Walker King. "Information?"

Paul waved a hand dismissively. His frown deepened. "As I stated before, I am a new Walker. I have a great deal to learn. About everything."

The veteran Walker was finding it easy to be impressed by the new king's humility.

"How do you get information from them?" he asked.

"I briefly considered torture," Paul mused, crossing his arms across his chest. "Then I realized torture may not be much of a threat to someone who was literally born in hell."

Silence hung between them. William realized he was holding his breath.

"Also," Paul added, letting his hands drop to his sides, "I didn't have the stomach for even imagining it. I would have been incapable of performing it. I made them comfortable, gave them purpose, and waited."

William felt the tension and the held breath leave his body involuntarily.

He liked the Walker King even more. There was still a great deal to learn about him, however. William remained silent.

"Devils are just as likely to talk until your questions get answered without having to ask them as humans." The Walker King wasn't smiling, but he wasn't frowning either. He met William's unflinching immortal gaze with his own.

"Even devils have needs, desires," the Walker King was far away without breaking eye contact. "We all do."

It was William who looked away then.

"Even Walkers," he admitted grudgingly.

"Yes," Paul said. "Even Walkers."

He followed the older Walker's gaze at nothingness. "Perhaps especially Walkers."

William looked to his king again, cocked his head to one side. "What do you mean?"

"Well, Walkers are both human and supernatural." Paul's eyes found his again, icy blue chips of intelligence. "A new set of needs and desires gets stacked on top of the existing human needs and desires when the transformation occurs."

"Needs are removed in the transformation as well," William noted.

"Perhaps, but not nearly so many as are magnified or added," Paul countered, "including the need to appear to still have human needs even when you don't."

Four immortal eyes gazed into forever again, two minds lost in thought.

"The Walker is compassionate by nature, and by design," Paul spoke again. "The most needful among us must be the least needy."

William held his key aloft.

"I should be going," he said stiffly.

The king glanced at the timepiece. "There is no time here, Walker."

Looking closely at the key, William realized it was true. The earth time marker stood still.

When he glanced back, the king was gone.

CHAPTER 27

"A quarter ounce? That's it? You sure, man?" Youthful dark eyes gleamed under dark raised eyebrows. Two dark tattooed teardrops decorated his left cheek.

"Yeah, Raul, just a quarter ounce," Cal replied, smoothing his slacks as he took a seat on the sofa. "Thanks."

Dim and dark, the living room was spattered with bright colors cloaked in shadow. Framed religious prints shared wall space with tacked up pictures of fast cars, lethal weapons and naked women. The sofa he sat on was soft and covered in a patterned blanket of Christmas colors. The coffee table surface was a Mexican flag covered in glass. It had a small mound of cocaine, a rolled-up hundred dollar bill, an ashtray filled with roaches and a handgun neatly arrayed on the transparent surface.

"Go ahead, man," Raul waved his hand in the general direction of the cocaine and the gun. Raul's movements were frantic and friendly, and a smile lit his eyes and his face alike. He moved in one frantic fluid motion to kneel with his back to Cal. Opening the built-in cabinet under the giant wall-mounted flatscreen, Raul moved aside.

It gave Cal a clear view of the open safe.

There was a lot of cocaine in there. Some cash, too. And another gun. Cal had seen it a thousand times if he had seen it once. He had never seen it locked.

"That's it?" Raul threw a glance over his shoulder at the young pusher. "Just a quarter?"

"Yeah," Cal put on his winningest smile. "Just a quarter."

Raul closed the cabinet, not bothering to lock the safe. He tossed the bag on the table next to the gun. His hand made the same friendly frantic gesture at the mound on the table.

Setting a stack of twenties near the bag but away from the dark pistol, Cal nodded and smiled. He took a nice blow up the right side, then leaned back into the soft cushions and tilted his head back slightly. He counted the drips while Raul counted the money.

Cal wished he could buy more; he saw himself in his mind's eye, calmly removing money and blow from envelopes that had been cleverly stashed all about his apartment. Cal was never frantic; but when he had sized up what he had put aside, he had slammed his fist on the table and cursed. Taking on new business was supposed to be profitable. After paying the bills, there had been little left to restock.

His getaway nest egg was off limits.

"Cool, man," Raul grinned a friendly and frantic grin.

Cal snapped back to his awareness of the room. Raul was busy seizing a long roach from the ashtray and digging a lighter from his front jeans pocket. The money had disappeared.

Raul took a long pull from the cannabis cigarette, then proffered it to Cal with one hand while waving smoke frantically away from between them with the other.

Cal shook his head.

"I'm good." He slid the small bag of sunshine into his pocket. "Thanks."

CHAPTER 28

Kris lay on his back, one arm bent to cradle his head with its hand and the other wrapped about his love. Half of his torso was covered in Jessica, sprawled in sleep with her head on his chest. The rest of his chest was bare save for a few strands of honey blonde hair stretched out to tickle his dead skin.

They had talked and kissed and made love and fallen asleep in each other's arms. Kris had been thrust into that other world like a dreaming mortal, and had woke without remembering any doorway or most of his time spent asleep. He wasn't sure whether to be bothered or relieved by the transition, and Jessica had come awake while he was wondering. His wondering had evaporated under her touch and her kisses, and they had made languid love and lay spent in each other's arms once again; but when Jessica had drifted off, Kris got too caught up in his whirlwind thoughts to join her. Instead he lay there torn between his happy dream come true and his mounting concern for his best friend.

Jessica stirred, raising her head to give him a sleepy satisfied smile.

"Hey, lover," she purred, cuddling closer to him. "You okay?"

He smiled at her. "I'm with you. I'm far beyond okay."

Propping herself on one elbow, Jessica threw a glance at the bedside clock. "I should go make sure Uncle Roche hasn't accidentally poisoned any customers."

He lifted his eyebrows, sat up a little too much a little too quickly.

"Yeah?" Without meaning to, he eyed the doorway.

"Yeah." Jessica rolled off the mattress and stood up in one fluid motion. She stood stiff beside the bed, not looking at him, armored and naked at the same time. Her arms were crossed over her small breasts.

Kris scooted to the edge of the bed, standing up as she edged away. Standing there, naked and open, he looked down at her.

"Jessica, I love you," he said, matter-of-fact. "I'm sorry for not being completely present with you. I need you to know—"

Suddenly she was in his arms, so quick it startled him. Her naked skin pressed against his, devil blood pumping hot through her veins to warm her flesh.

"I know, my love." Her voice and her words soothed his heart; and with a deep penetrating look up at him, she put him back in the world that he belonged in. "You have a job to do, and I need to respect that. You love me so good, baby, you risk spoiling me."

Kris had his arms around her waist, and at her words he struck her ass with an open palm, just like she had taught him to. It made a resounding crack. He pulled her close to him again.

"Will that stop you from getting spoiled?" He nuzzled her ear with his nose.

A pleasant shudder ran up her spine, and she let him feel it.

"Whatever I did to deserve that," she breathed, "I am going to keep doing it."

Jessica licked her lips, and her eyes swirled red and black for a moment.

Smiling, Kris bent to cover her mouth with his own. He let himself feel her touch, her flesh, her sweet kisses. Then he stepped back and imagined his guide robe hanging loosely, as it did, about his frame.

When the robe appeared to cloak his body, Jessica made a face.

"Have fun at work today, honey," she sing-singed, blowing him a kiss.

He made as if to catch it, stowing it in the sleeves of his robe for later as his hands came together in them.

Closing his eyes, the Guide thought of Paul.

Nothing happened.

When he opened his eyes, Jessica stood there naked before him. He looked her up and down, slowly, hiding his perplexity behind his hunger.

"You are so sexy," he grinned.

Jessica flushed and feigned modesty while he closed his eyes and thought of Andre.

Kris felt the shift this time. He opened his eyes to another realm.

The walls and floor and ceiling were a drab gray stone-like material. This was not one of the many interminable walkways to be found in this place, lined with endless doorways behind which lie infinite possibilities. This was a high and wide room, a meeting hall for Guides or Watchers or Walkers or whatever else dwelt in this world.

He had materialized in the doorway, behind a small gathering of men seated with their backs to him. Every set of shoulders was swathed in a robe, and nearly every head sported thinning hair or none at all.

Standing before the men on a raised dais, Andre was the only one in the room who saw the Guide materialize in the entryway. And though Kris didn't make a sound, though Andre made no move to acknowledge him, the group moved as one to turn a dozen watchful gazes on him.

Nearly half of the men wore glasses, as did Andre. Kris found it an odd affectation for dead men with perfect eyes. He wondered if they all used quill pens like Andre too.

"You have your assignments." Andre's voice rose strong over the assemblage, and Kris was looking at the backs of their heads again as they turned en masse.

"Watch, record, and bring anything noteworthy immediately to me," the Watcher went on. He looked taller than before, or maybe just more sure of himself.

He took one last long look at the gathering. "Dismissed."

There was no rustling of robes, no friendly chatter. The Watchers simply disappeared, and a moment later Andre met eyes with Kris over a cluster of empty chairs.

"The King of the Guides," Andre spoke in the same tone of voice he had used to address his subordinates.

"Hello, Andre." Kris moved to meet him in the middle, sitting in one of the chairs. He indicated a chair nearby with a wave of his hand.

Andre hesitated for a moment, reluctant to relinquish the stage. He stepped down finally and crossed the room to sit with the Guide.

Kris waited until he was seated. "Sorry for interrupting."

The Watcher waved it off. "No worries. What's up?"

"I can't find Paul." Kris watched the Watcher, watched him frown while crossing and then uncrossing his arms in apparent agitation.

Andre sighed, shrugged and met eyes with Kris.

"He's probably in one of the angel's personal spaces," he explained. "Nobody can get to him there but God unless he brings them in."

"I've seen one of them." Kris nodded. "He took me there last night." His eyes found the floor as his hands burrowed further into the sleeves of his robe. "I don't understand what he's doing there."

"He's preparing, he's studying," Andre spoke with a touch of pride in his voice. "He is marshaling his forces and training himself to be the best warrior, Walker, and King he can be. Paul is spending a great deal of time in those spaces since he became king."

Kris couldn't help but laugh.

"It's only been three days," he reminded Andre.

The Watcher shook his head solemnly. "Paul has the platinum key, and he is learning to use it. Time already passed slowly in the angel's spaces; now there is nearly no time in them at all. The Walker King has been training for months, maybe years."

Kris let that sink in, stewing in his thoughts in silence. He raised his gaze to level it at the other dead man. "Where else could he be?"

Andre frowned. "What do you mean?"

"You said he's probably in one of the angel's personal spaces," Kris reminded him. "Where else could he be?"

The Watcher eyed him for a moment, as if considering something. Then he shrugged. "He could be in Hell, with the Dragon Queen."

CHAPTER 29

Matt sat slumped on the barstool, arms crossed over the smooth surface of the bar. His dark eyes explored the two fingers of tequila in his glass intently.

In one fluid motion, he drained the contents of the transparent container. His front pockets were stuffed with cash, and Matt twisted his body on the stool to fish a twenty from one of them.

"Hey, John." His words should have come out slurred, his movements more sloppy. Matt smiled vaguely at the man in sweatpants behind the bar, pushing the empty glass closer to his side of the counter.

"That's a lot of tequila, friend." He said it as he might say "it feels like rain" or "have a nice day". While he spoke, he also poured another generous helping of the yellowed liquid.

Matt nodded his agreement, drank it all in one draught, and set it close to the bartender again.

"My best friend just died," he said, his voice still not slurring.

Matt pushed the twenty closer to the bartender as well. "One more time."

With a shrug, the man palmed the bill and poured the drink.

"Sorry, buddy," he mumbled, turning his back to Matt and his attention to the register.

Matt didn't even like tequila all that much; he had just wanted that drunk. It wasn't coming, however, even as he quaffed the warm beverage once again.

It must be that damned key, he thought. His hand touched his shirt where it covered the dangling device.

It felt warm to the touch through the light cotton tee shirt.

Matt threw a glance at the bartender, who had busied himself with cleaning behind the counter. He pulled the chain from under his shirt until he held the key in his hand. It seemed to be glowing, pulsing with light, and definitely warmer than his skin.

Tucking it back under his shirt, Matt slid off the stool smoothly.

"Thanks, John," he said, the irritation in his voice directed at the slur that should have been there.

The bartender grunted a reply, then turned to watch the young man walk to the bathroom. He expected Matt to fall, or at least waver, and was surprised when he didn't. Soon minutes would pass and he would go investigate, expecting to find Matt sprawled passed out on the floor or against a toilet.

By then the small room would be empty; he would shrug, and return to the bar.

On the other side of the door in this moment, Matt stood in front of the wide mirror without seeing himself. Holding the key in one hand, he let its pulsing warmth permeate his closed fist. He closed his eyes, like he had seen Paul do.

He waited. He noticed he was holding his breath, and breathed. Then he thought of Paul, dark leather covering him from head to toe and a sword in each hand.

There was a wrenching and a shift, and for a moment his stomach felt like it had been turned inside out.

Matt opened his eyes to a swirling world of white, dark blurred forms in the dozens, and the persistent aching sting of sobriety.

He resisted the urge to vomit.

As his eyes swam into focus, they widened with wonder. The darkened forms were Walkers, lined up with recurve bows at the ready and arrows nocked. A row of targets hung thirty yards away, apparently suspended in mid-air by nothing.

"Remember," a solemn voice rose loud and stern to address the troops, "if it's not a bullseye, it's not a kill. If it's not a kill, it's a waste of time and arrows. There are too many of these monsters for our weapons not to find their mark every time."

The man strode purposefully behind his ranks as he spoke, swathed in black leather from head to toe. His back was to Matt at first, and he could see dark hair long and straight to his dusted shoulders from under his leather hat. When he turned, Matt saw that he had a full beard and a serious frown.

It took a moment for him to realize it was Paul.

When he reached the end of the line of men, Paul stood sideways as they all did. A long recurve bow appeared in his left hand, identical to the others.

As he drew the bowstring back to his cheek, his body forming a perfect cross, an arrow and target materialized.

With the ease of releasing a breath, Paul loosed the arrow. It found the red circle with a *thunk!*, burying itself deep in the imagined target.

Dozens of strings twanged, dozens of *thunks!* were muffled by the liquid light walls. A couple arrows missed targets altogether, a few struck the bullseye.

"Better." Paul was nodding and frowning at the same time. "Keep practicing."

Paul's bow and target dematerialized together. He motioned to one of the archers, another Walker in oiled black leather but with a different cut than the others'. Matt noted that his arrow had been one of the few to find its mark. After conferring a moment quietly, Paul raised his voice again to the troops.

"William will take over from here," he said. "My key is calling."

Brown and black cowboy hats tilted throughout the company in quiet assent, and most of the men went back to their shooting. One man broke away, approaching Paul as he turned and came towards Matt.

He looked like he had stepped through a time machine, the Walker that moved unhurried in Paul's wake. His duster and hat and boots were beaten and worn, unlike the new oiled look most of the leathered Walkers personified. They seemed to be of a distinctly Western cut, as were his denim jeans and buttoned collared shirt.

Matt couldn't see if there was a holster on the man's hip, nor did he see a horse tethered nearby, but either of those things would have seemed a lot more appropriate than the bow in the man's hand. It swung as he walked, slow and measured, to catch up with Paul as he neared.

Paul surprised Matt, proffering his hand and giving him a firm handshake.

"You got the message," Paul said. He didn't smile, but he wasn't frowning at him either. "Thanks for coming."

Matt nodded, feeling himself stand up a little straighter. He nodded again, casting his eyes over Paul's shoulder, to indicate the Walker approaching Paul.

The frown was back as Paul turned to the cowboy Walker.

"Samuel," he said, "this is my chief agent, Agent Matt."

Samuel touched the brim of his hat with the gloved hand not holding the bow.

"Agent," the cowboy said. His blue eyes were clear and bright and squinted.

Matt nodded at the cowboy. "Walker."

Still frowning, Paul asked, "How can I help you, Samuel?"

"Well." Samuel's words were as measured as his steps. "I'm just a bit curious as to why we are learning to shoot this way. The intent of a Walker is powerful; stance and form don't much matter when you can send an improperly shot arrow anywhere you can imagine just by imagining it."

He sounded just as Matt had expected him to, a slow southern drawl smoothed by decades riding the west. It was a little surreal, watching Paul and Samuel interact. One man was tall and slim, modern black duster and hat and boots almost glinting in the soft abundant light of this place. The other was short and stout, all in muted colors. One face was young and bearded, the other leathered by sun and riding and countless close shaves.

"The Walker's powers are strongest on Earth; the power of our foe is strongest in the lower realms. We must not take for granted any advantage we have become accustomed to having. We must train as any army, until we weapons that are Walkers are razor sharp." Paul seemed a completely different person, amplifying the surreal feeling for Matt. From the long hair and beard to his rigid posture and grave mien, Paul had transformed physically. His demeanor and attitude seemed to have morphed as well, and the look in his eye suggested a man with infinite patience who would wait for nothing.

The old cowboy touched his hat again, in acknowledgement. "That makes sense."

He looked down at the weapon in his hand a little disdainfully. "But bows?"

Paul arched an eyebrow, and Matt thought he might actually smile for a second. Maybe crack a joke or poke fun at Matt like the old Paul would.

Instead, Paul's frown deepened under his dark beard. "We are working on other options, like firearms."

The cowboy brightened visibly at that.

"There are issues, however," Paul went on, frowning. "The temperatures in the realms we will be battling in are too hot for regular gunpowder and casings, for one. We would need explosive charges in our bullets to properly decapitate a full-sized demon, and we risk blowing up the whole company before the fight begins."

Samuel looked down at the bow in his hand again.

Paul noticed. "The arrow designed by one of our generals in the East has a tip that spreads as it flies, becoming wide enough to sever a demon's head from its neck when properly placed. He has been using it successfully for centuries, as have the Walkers he has made. We need to be experts at pressing every advantage, Samuel."

The cowboy tipped his hat again. "Yes, sir."

Samuel returned to his place facing his target and took up shooting with a renewed vigor.

The Walker that Paul had left in charge was even more modern-looking than Paul. Swathed in dark oiled leather, it was a biker outfit more than it was a cowboy's. His leather jeans, jacket and boots were zippered and buckled with shiny steel that shone like chrome in the soft luminescence. His leather hat looked like a part of a uniform he only wore in service times, low and slim around the brim. There was a leather strap laced about his neck, thick and black protection just where the Walker most needed it.

The buckled and zippered Walker watched Paul watching Samuel shoot, caught his eye and gave him a respectful nod.

Paul stepped toward Matt, his hand falling on his shoulder. "You ready?"

"For what?" Matt asked the question and closed his eyes at the same time. He knew at least part of the answer: they were walking between worlds.

Somewhere between one world and the next, Paul's grave answer reached him: "The key is calling. We have a demon to kill."

When Matt opened his eyes, it was to a strange and familiar scene. They were in a bar, one he had never been to. The entryway they had materialized in was darkened enough to make it seem as though they had used the doorway.

Paul stepped into the dimly lit room, navigating the sparse seating to perch at the empty bar. There were two pool tables to the rear of the space, with a half dozen drinkers orbiting aimlessly around them.

Following the Walker's footsteps, Matt claimed a stool beside him.

The woman behind the bar was somewhere in her fifties, the weathered skin on her cheeks and nose shot with blood. Her mousy hair barely reached her shoulders, and it stood wiry and thin away from her skull.

She approached them with a friendly scowl.

"What can I get you boys?" she asked them.

Paul glanced his way. "You buying?"

Matt gave his friend a grin and a nod.

"Highland Park Thirty," Paul addressed the woman. "Tall. Neat."

She looked at Paul like he had asked for a unicorn.

"Chivas Twenty-Five?" Paul lifted one eyebrow hopefully.

The woman nodded.

"Beer," Matt grinned at her, charming her for no reason. "Whatever you've got on tap."

The Walker waited until the barkeep had put her attention elsewhere. He didn't reach into a pocket, didn't pull anything from up his sleeve. He just opened his hand between them, palm up, so Matt could see the gleaming platinum watch.

Paul depressed the button, and the face flipped open soundlessly.

"Good," he frowned satisfactorily. "We have a few minutes."

Matt saw a watch with too many hands and a small glowing symbol in the shape of a skeleton key.

"How can you even tell?" Matt thought he saw one hand moving; but it could just be his eyes playing tricks on him, staring at it too long.

He blinked, shook his head.

"See the dark brown long hand?" Paul asked.

Matt nodded, squinting.

"That's Earth time." Paul continued to hold the watch in one hand while reaching for his drink with the other. "How is that Earth time, you ask?"

Matt hadn't asked. He wasn't really wondering either.

"Doesn't Earth have twenty-four time zones, expressing every hour of the day all the time?" Paul asked.

"Hey, yeah," Matt nodded. He took a drink from his beer.

"I got curious," Paul continued, "and did a little research. It turns out that it's tuned to the Walker holding the key. If I go to China, then go above or below, my key tells me the time in China, where I last was. You see the other longer hand next to it, the dark blue one?"

Matt looked closer, nodded again. He hadn't seen his friend this animated sine he had cut off his sister's head.

"That's time above," Paul explained. "It works on a similar principle, except that time zones above are different. The higher you go, the less time that passes relative to Earth time. The last time I went above I..."

Paul trailed off, and Matt turned to see why.

A young woman had entered, and was approaching the bar uncertainly. She was an attractive girl, with blonde hair all one length to her chin and parted to the side. Dark black leggings showed all the smooth curves of her slim legs, stirruped into black heels that made her on the tall side of her average height. A dark red top covered her torso to her neck and her arms to her wrists. The top clung as close to her contours as the leggings, displaying large rounded breasts over a slim waist and flat belly.

Clicking the watch closed and curling his fingers into a fist as it disappeared, Paul spoke before she got close enough to hear.

"There it is," he said. "Do you see it?"

Matt looked at her feet. They were small, and she navigated the floor between them with a smooth and feminine gait. He looked at her legs and where they came together, forming a "V" that flexed as she walked. He brought his eyes to the black clutch in her hand in passing, noticing in great detail the way her breasts bounced with her steps. Finally, his eyes found her face, watching him watching her.

Matt smiled, reflexively, and she smiled back.

The girl was too close to the bar now to ask Paul what he meant: "did I see what?" Instead he tried to think about it while he pulled a stool out from under the bar for her.

"Hi," Matt smiled again at the pretty girl.

She sat in the proffered seat, looked up at him with vulnerable blue eyes.

"Can I see your I.D.?" The graveled voice of the bartender prompted the girl to begin fishing about in her compact purse.

"I'll have a Cosmo, please," the girl set the laminated card on the stained wood surface.

"I'll buy that," Matt smiled at the pretty girl again, "along with another round for me and my buddy."

The young woman thanked him while she posited the card back into the clutch. She looked up at him again, a little doubtful and a little hopeful in her soft eyes.

"Are you Josh?" she asked.

Matt laughed.

"No, sorry. I'm Matt." He turned to Paul. "This is my buddy Paul."

Matt got a good look at Paul before the girl turned to acknowledge him. He was glaring murderously at Matt, his frown deepened to a grimace. Matt had a momentary picture in his head of Paul holding him a foot off the floor with one hand crushing his windpipe. His hand went involuntarily to his neck.

He remembered then what they were doing here. Kris had taught him to tune out the demons everyone seemed to carry. Matt only saw them now when he willed it, which is what he did as he swiveled on his barstool to face the girl again.

"Hi, I'm Tina." Matt's eyes fell on her demon as her words fell on his ears, and the next forever moment was all about not reacting to the beautiful monster for him.

He stood beside her with arms crossed over his bare hairless chest. Nearly as tall as her, the demon was stout and muscled. Leather pants and boots painted him in black from the waist down, but from the waist up his bare torso flexed and twitched in agitated time with the muscles of his jaw. Clenching his teeth through a judgmental snarl, he glared at the girl through scarlet eyes filled with loathing and anticipation.

"Hi, Tina. Nice to meet you." Paul moved between Matt and monster, reaching out to shake the girl's hand with one hand while holding his drink with the other.

The demon was used to being ignored. His scowl etched lines further into his face as he started his hellish rant. *"You are such a completely classic failure,"* he hissed at the girl. *"A real piece of work. You—"*

Matt watched the Walker work then, saw the reality of what was happening that no one else could see.

Paul reached behind the girl to set his emptied glass on the bar. Then his hands were a blur, grasping a thick ropish spiral of smoky energy that Matt hadn't noticed until the Walker seized it in one hand. It stretched between girl and demon, until a dagger materialized in Paul's other hand to sever it cleanly. The dagger disappeared as quickly as Paul continued to move, his arm wrapping about the monster's neck to catch it in the crook of his elbow and pull it close to him. With his arm bent rigid at his side, he grasped his overcoat for leverage as the demon struggled mightily against him.

"Excuse me," Paul said calmly. "I need to use the restroom."

Matt watched the Walker half-drag the scratching and flailing demon past him toward the men's room, barely wavering in his gait. Nails scratched at his armor, fists beat his back, and Paul showed no sign of acknowledging any of it.

Matt forced his attention back to the girl and the apparent normalcy of the situation. Something about her seemed different; her face was less clouded somehow. He grinned at her, wondering what she looked like naked.

"Paul and I were just wrapping up our business." He drank the rest of his beer and looked purposefully at his wrist. Matt had never worn a watch, and he didn't need one any more than anyone else with a wireless device that told him anything he needed to know with a swipe and a tap. Then the price of a lottery ticket began to be the cost of anything, and he had made a few purchases. He didn't carry the little blue box around with him or anything, but Matt knew that plenty of people knew the pricey signature style at a glance. The Atlas didn't help his chances with every girl, but it never hurt them.

"I've got a buddy having a party on his yacht this afternoon," he put away the watch, pulled out the grin again. "I'll miss the boat if I don't get going." Matt let it all hang in the air, in her newly opened mind.

She looked up at him, her eyes open wide and her lips parted slightly. She was holding her breath.

Matt stood up, digging into the front left pocket of his jeans and coming out with a wad of twenties. He uncrumpled five of them and set them on the bar, stuffed the remaining wad back into his pocket. Standing, towering over her a bit, he leaned in casually.

"You want to come?" he asked.

The Walker stepped from the back of the bar, slowing as he passed.

"Are we done here?" Paul glowered at Matt, still walking.

"Yep." Matt spoke to his leathered back. "See you tonight."

Paul held the door for a moment, letting a thin wiry guy with squared glasses and a tuft of brownish hair pass into the bar.

The girl watched Paul leave, then turned her gaze fully on Matt again. A devilish grin pulled at the corners of her mouth.

"Let's go," she stood beside him and grasped his hand. As they passed the new patron, she entwined her fingers with Matt's.

The man turned to watch them go, confused certainty twisting his features.

CHAPTER 30

"How we doing tonight, people?" The big devil was showing his teeth in happy anticipation of another night at Devil's Brew.

Kris smiled and nodded, watched Paul and Matt and Jessica nod or smile or comment. They were all gathered at the bar, preparing for the evening while band members moved equipment in the background.

"I ran out of change at the door last night," Matt pointed out. "I had to go to the bar twice. And people kept asking for a stamp."

Jessica handed him a vinyl zippered bag with a bank logo emblazoned across the front. "Uncle Roche sent me to the bank. You shouldn't run out again tonight. The stamp and the pad are in there too."

Matt opened the bulging pouch, pulled out the stamp and ink. Flipping the pad open, he stubbed the stamp against it a few times and then inked his wrist. Dark purple letters spelled *Devil's Brew* on his skin. He grinned at Jessica.

Sarah and Mason approached the group, and Sarah smiled at Roche as they neared.

"What's up, you two?" The devil's buoyant tone broadened Sarah's smile.

"You ready for tonight? Everyone feeling okay?" Roche looked at Mason pointedly.

Mason smiled then too. "Actually..."

Sarah shot him an irritated glance, a split second departure from the smile she turned back on Roche.

"Actually," she repeated. "Mikie called. He's not feeling so good. He won't be here tonight."

"Which one is Mikie?" Paul spoke up, frowning and watching the band members moving in equipment to see who was missing.

"He's the other guitar player," Sarah responded.

"How will that affect the show?" Paul asked. "You guys are still okay to play, right?"

Sarah nodded in solemnity. "We'll be fine."

"We'll be better." Mason corrected her. "Mikie transitions like an old lady. He makes everybody tense, too."

Sarah let her look of irritation show for a little longer this time.

"Well, then," Roche was beaming again. "What are we worried about?"

"No worries," Sarah reassured him. "We just wanted to let you know."

Kris watched the guitar player take the singer's hand.

"We're going to finish setting up," Mason said, pulling her away from the group.

"I need to make a booze run," Matt announced, rising from his stool.

"I'll come with," Paul stood as well.

Kris jumped to his feet, perhaps a little too quickly.

"Hang on, Paul," he said. "We need to talk."

Paul crossed his arms, frowned at the Guide. "What's up, Kris?"

He motioned to the office behind him. "Can I have a minute?"

Paul sighed, not hiding his impatience.

"Sure." He turned to Matt. "Go on ahead. I'll catch up."

Paul strode purposefully toward the closed door, not turning to see if Kris followed.

Once they were in the office, Paul closed the door and crossed his arms, waiting.

"You've been going on more demon hunts," Kris said.

He waited for Paul to speak, but he said nothing.

"Why haven't you been bringing your Guide?" It felt strange for Kris to refer to himself in the third person like that, but it made the question sound more like curiosity and less like hurt.

Paul let his hands drop to his sides.

"I thought Matt could use the training," he said. "And the company. He's pretty torn up about…things."

You're so torn up about it you can't even say her name, Kris thought to himself, but he didn't say it. Instead he said, "I've tried to find you, and couldn't come to wherever you were."

The Walker crossed his arms again, frowned irritation at Kris. "You were occupied with Jessica. I didn't have time to show you how to access my spaces. I'll show you later."

"And the next hunt?" Kris knew his friend; if he said he would do something, he would do it.

"I'll bring you on the next hunt," Paul sighed. "Is that all?"

"No! Wait!" Kris knew the Walker's way too well. "Andre said you've been spending time in Hell. A lot of time."

"The Dragon Queen has been…understanding of my situation." Paul bristled. He looked as though he was going to say something else; instead the Walker's eyes hardened to pained chips of ice.

"My personal affairs are my business," he snapped.

Then he disappeared.

*   *   *

Matt eased the little silver Hyundai into a parking spot, put it in park and set the brake. As his hand fell on the ignition, Paul appeared in the passenger seat. The Walker looked seriously pissed off, and Matt edged away unconsciously in his seat.

He killed the engine and palmed the keys, his eyes not leaving Paul's troubled countenance.

The Walker surprised him, closing his eyes and breathing in deep a couple of times. The muscles of his face relaxed; and when he opened his eyes, they were full of tears. It was a startling and complete transformation, and Matt's heart went out to his friend as understanding dawned.

He smells Brenna, Matt realized.

He was driving her car, without really thinking about it; Matt always drove Brenna's car whenever he wanted.

Paul arched an eyebrow at him. "Did you miss the boat again?"

Matt grinned. "I always do. We went back to my place instead. Thanks for bringing me along. Sorry I wasn't more help."

"You're an Agent," Paul frowned seriously. "Your job is to divert people's attention away from your Walker. You are not supposed to engage demons, buddy; you are there to draw attention away from me. I'd say you went above and beyond."

Matt grinned again. "That's what she said."

Paul's hand fell on his shoulder.

"There's something I want to show you," he said abruptly.

Eyes closed, Matt felt a shift and a tug and just a touch of nausea.

A sulfur scent filled his nostrils, and Matt opened his eyes.

They were in a post-apocalyptic landscape, charred rock jagged and dark all around them. Acrid smoke billowed from cracked fissures in the burnt stone near and far, filling the air with billowing clouds of stench.

"Look familiar?" Paul's voice in his ear shook him from the reverie of beholding Hell.

Matt rotated slowly in place, wishing he could respond in the negative.

"Yeah," he said. "This is where Brenna and I came when you and Kris… died."

"Changed," Matt corrected himself.

A form approached, emerging from the thick smoke gradually. Matt made out a female, then her crimson skin and forked tail. She had a sword scabbarded at her hip and a helm held in the crook of her elbow.

Paul's sudden sword made Matt and the devil both flinch as it materialized in his hand, gleaming in the sparse light of Hell.

"We don't want any trouble, devil," Paul waved the sword slowly in front of him, placing himself square between Matt and the devil.

"Nor do I, Walker King," the girl smiled. "You have already shown me that I am no threat to you. I approached you hoping to inquire after your companion."

Paul relaxed his readied stance, threw a glance over his shoulder at Matt. The gleaming sword still stood between them.

"Him?" he asked.

"No, Walker King," the girl smiled again, turned a deeper shade of crimson. "Your other companion. I believe he is called Andre."

The tip of the sword dipped nearly to the ground. "My Watcher? What about him?"

"I was wondering if…" she hesitated, and her orange on black eyes explored the charred rock between where she and the Walker stood.

She lifted her eyes to meet Paul's, flushed again as her slitted pupils widened. "I was wondering if he is in relationship, if he is beholden to anyone."

"You want a date with Andre?" Paul's sword disappeared in time with his words, as he eyed the devil more closely.

The tension in her body relaxed, and she smiled. "Essentially."

"I will speak with him," Paul nodded.

She bowed at the waist, smiled at each of them in turn. "Thank you, Walker King. I would be in your debt."

Matt was glad for the exchange. It gave him a few moments to examine the way he felt, an unfamiliar task for him. He remembered this place, this landscape, from the vision he had had when Paul was hit by that car. He had told Paul as much, and was glad for it. What little he knew he wanted to share, especially if it meant finding Brenna.

But what could Matt say to his friend about how he felt right now? How could he share how his soul sang as he stood there, watching the burnt landscape, listening to the distant crackling flames? How could he put into words the way his body felt buoyant and his heart felt happy? How could he say it?

He felt like he was home.

CHAPTER 31

The office door closed behind him, Cal was thrust from quiet spaciousness to loud rock and roll clamor. He let his eyes roam the club for a moment, the door at his back. A couple of folks caught his eye and nodded or winked or thumbed at a nose.

No one was in need, so far as he could see. No one but him, anyway. He had kept the lines small while sharing with Roche, and it had done no more than take the edge off.

Cal needed to go to his car and finish the job.

He kept his countenance clear and his gait measured as he made his way to the exit. A fist bump here and a handshake there, he stayed friendly without breaking stride.

Arriving early had afforded Cal his choice of parking, and his black Acura was swathed in shadows while being close to the club. He approached casually, hitting the remote to unlock the driver's door as he neared. The parking lights flashed while the door unlocked with a muffled thud.

There was a shadow behind the car that shouldn't have been there, and it moved when the lights flashed.

Cal stopped a few feet short of his car, peering into the darkness. There was noise behind him then, but he turned too late.

His knees buckled as a body drove full force at him, throwing Cal backward into a leg or a foot and then to the pavement.

Rather than grab at his assailant, Cal dug in his pocket. One flick of his wrist and he held a blade in his hand, a nice pocket knife he had bought for things like opening packages and doing the occasional bump on the gleaming three inch hunk of tempered steel.

Cal had learned to open it in one fluid motion, but he had never brandished it hoping to hurt anyone. That's just what he did now, though, reaching out in a smooth arc that hit something so hard it almost knocked the blade from his hand.

Someone cried out, a man; then they were both upon him.

"He's got a knife," one hissed at the other while strong hands grabbed and hit at him.

A strong blow connected to Cal's jaw, and he saw stars while the knife was wrestled from his weakened grip.

"Not anymore," another voice said.

There was a knee on his throat and another was crushing one of his wrists. Cal tried to breathe, heard his own voice wheezing. He flailed blindly and weakly with his free hand, until that was pinned too.

They were going through his pockets, talking to each other in hushed tones. Cal made out one phrase clearly as his assets were transferred and his precious air supply dwindled.

"I thought you said this guy was big-time, man."

The hard knee was still pressing on his throat, and Cal didn't hear anything after that.

CHAPTER 32

Kris tried to match everyone's sympathetic looks while Cal recounted the event.

"There were two of them," Cal's hand went to his throat. His voice sounded thin and strained. "They took my money and my…they took everything."

"Did you get a look at either of them?" Mason frowned as he spoke, anger battling concern to take over his features.

Kris watched Cal shake his head no, listened to the squeak that emanated from the young man's mouth.

Clearing his throat, Cal spoke more clearly. "No, they had masks on. They were both white dudes. I saw their hands. I heard them talking, too. They knew who I was."

Standing next to Mason, Sarah's countenance was clouded to a pretty scowl. "Did you recognize either of their voices?"

Kris felt a familiar hand on his shoulder, and he turned from the pusher's response to meet Paul's eyes. The Walker nodded toward the door in the back of the club, then dropped his hand from the Guide's shoulder to begin walking in that direction.

With one last sweeping glance, Kris let his eyes fall on each of the assemblage in turn. Jessica and Roche seemed awfully sympathetic for a couple of devils. Kris tried not to be annoyed at how caught up his girlfriend seemed to be in the drug dealer's story. Matt and the rest of the band joined the devils in not noticing as Kris disengaged to follow Paul to the office.

By the time Kris closed the door quietly behind them, Paul was in full Walker form. From his black leather cowboy hat pulled low on his brow to the supple dark boots under shifting black duster, his armor gleamed as if freshly oiled. One hand held a sword at the ready, the long slim bastard that Roche had given him. The other hand hovered at shoulder height between them, palm upturned to display the platinum pocket watch.

The Guide had to fight the urge to smile.

The demon symbol on the watch face was glowing bright red.

It was time for a demon hunt.

Kris closed his eyes, to help keep his face cool and to better see his robe in place of his clothes. When he opened them, he watched the key disappear as Paul's hand stretched out to fall on his shoulder.

The cool breath of no wind touched his face, a bright world of no color seared his eyes, and then they stood together on solid ground in a darkened room. Kris let his eyes adjust as Paul's hand left his shoulder.

"Where are we?" Kris kept his voice low as dozens of forms began to take shape around him.

"They can't hear or see us," Paul replied in a normal tone of voice, at conversation volume.

Kris started at the sound, relaxing as the meaning sunk in. He realized they were in a house, a spacious living room that opened up onto an open dining area. There were no lights on, but a dim glow found its way through an uncurtained window. It was enough to illuminate the people that lay in corners and against walls and even splayed out on the dingy carpet. They looked and smelled unwashed and unhealthy. Dirty clothes hung on sagging inert frames, the only signs of life the rise and fall of shallow breathing and the putrid stench of unwashed flesh.

"It's a drug den," Paul's voice still seemed too loud, even if only Kris could hear it. "A flop house, whatever. There are more and more of these, in virtually every city. The homes get foreclosed on and then abandoned, and the homeless people or druggies or meth labs move in when new owners don't. No one seems to notice, or care."

The Guide's eyes adjusted more as Paul spoke, until he could see into the shadows with his dead eyes. He started again, took an involuntary step back.

"There are more demons then humans," he gasped.

It was true, too; for every white or brown or black form, two or three crimson-skinned forms lounged around it. Many of them lay with an arm or leg strewn over their host, some lay bodily on a host's limb. Every one of them was nearly as large as the human they touched, which made it easy for him to mistake them until prehensile forked tails and scaled skin were revealed to his supernatural vision.

"We're only here for one," Paul responded.

The key appeared momentarily in his hand again, and Kris watched the rapidly moving hand counting down the final sixty seconds before it disappeared.

As if on cue, a shadowed form stirred and then sat up. His hair was dark and long and unwashed, his face darkened further by scattered patches of whiskers. Two demons continued to slumber near him, both of them shifting in sleep to keep contact with their host.

A third demon stood and stretched, coming awake as the man did. Man and monster rubbed their eyes in unison, and all four eyes seemed redder for the effort when they were done. The man slipped a little baggie from his pocket, one inch square of mostly empty with a little brownish-white powder fattening the bottom quarter inch of plastic zippered containment.

"Do it!" The awakened demon stood over the gaunt man, taloned hands on his knees. Angry eyes bored into his host, scarlet on hate on black. "Do it all! Before one of these scumbags wakes up and takes it from you. Do it all!"

The wretch cast a suspicious glance around the room, let his eyes focus on the baggie again. A slow smile spread his lips and then opened them, and missing teeth coupled with sunken cheeks made for a ghastly grin.

The smile only lasted a moment, as his eyes darted suspiciously at the other occupants of the dingy space once more. He reached his free hand into a jacket pocket and withdrew a short tube, a once white pen that had been dismantled and cut in half to leave him with a three inch snorter. It was darkened with use from unwashed fingers clutching it countless times.

Kris was still watching man and demon when Paul slipped silently behind the monster and wound his leathered arm about its neck.

The demon's eyes widened in alarm as the sparing light glinted off Paul's swinging sword. Kris caught a glimpse of the smoky tendril of energy between man and monster as it was cleaved in two. Like rubber bands, the two ropes of energy snapped back to disappear into each of them.

The Walker moved too quickly for the demon to react or for the Guide to assist. Paul released his captive, stepped back and swung his sword in a wide arc. The demon's head was removed with a quick, thick wet sound and hit the floor in time with its lifeless body.

As the demon's parts disappeared, Walker and Guide both watched the man with the baggie. He considered the powder with new eyes, holding it up in the sparing light and gazing sadly at it. He looked around the room one last time, with sympathy rather than suspicion.

With a sigh, the man stood and straightened, then made his way toward the front door. The baggie and snorting tube lay on the floor where he had let them fall.

As he neared the exit, the two sleeping demons that had lain beside him rose uncertainly and lumbered after him. Soon all three were gone, the door left standing open behind them.

When Kris felt Paul's gloved hand fall on his shoulder again, he closed his eyes. He did not like seeing what lurked between worlds.

The Guide opened his eyes to luminous light walls and floors, a stark and welcome contrast to the cloying sense of doom in the last place.

"You've been busy," Kris remarked as he followed the Walker into the familiar seating area. The couches were worn and scuffed, weapons had disappeared to be replaced with stacks of books. A large dry-erase board had been added, and both sides were covered in drawings and notations in a half-dozen different hands.

Paul nodded as he let his weight fall into a sofa, reached up to scratch his lengthening beard.

"Why all the books?" Kris motioned to the nearby stacks as he took a seat. "What's wrong with your Walker's Journal?"

Paul snorted derisively and pulled a bottle of scotch from thin air. He took a long draught and closed his eyes for a moment, letting the whiskey soak his soul.

"William said I should look elsewhere for the truth," Paul grimaced. "He was right, too. The versions of books I get to read in my journal are edited by the angels. It turns out even actual accounts of Walker duties are changed when they are permanently recorded."

"Read the description of my becoming Walker King sometime," Paul continued. "It's ridiculous and contradictory. Half of it sounds like the Walker Council planned and orchestrated the whole thing, the other half is all about how I acted without their permission and am not recognized as king by them."

He took another drink. "Those bastards just sat on their hands. They always do. It's why there is a problem in the first place. According to their own rules and proclamation, I should be in custody or rehumanized. And yet…"

Paul glanced up at the flowing light above them, as if in silent challenge.

Kris sat in stillness while his friend finished the bottle. It didn't take long.

"Why did you bring me here again?" Kris finally broke the silence.

Paul sighed and set the bottle aside. "William says I should keep you in the loop about everything. He said I should teach you to access my personal space and the training grounds. Do you know what all five hands on my key are tracking?"

The Guide furrowed his brow in consternation, to keep from grinning his happiness about being included.

"No," he responded slowly, thinking about it. "I guess I don't. The demon countdown, the time on earth and above and below. That's only four. What's the fifth one for?"

Paul was holding the timepiece up the for Guide's inspection as he began talking.

"The demon countdown hand actually has two other functions," Paul spoke excitedly, and his animation made Kris think of his friend before all this had happened. "It counts down to the creation of other Walkers or Agents."

"What's the fifth one for, Paul?" Kris asked again.

Paul's frown was back.

"It counts down my time as a Walker," he responded quietly.

CHAPTER 33

The little stone room had become a study in layers. Blood had stained the walls, droplets here and streaks and splatters there…then it had dried to a brown stain, only to be painted over with another set of bloody patterns that had dried and been painted again in red. The stone floor was much the same, dried brown drops from corner to corner. Countless pools of liquid life had puddled under the wooden stocks still holding a delicate neck and slim pair of wrists firmly in place.

The layers of scent were as real as the layers of gore. The putrid reek of death hung in the air, the sweet smell of freshly spilled blood mingled with the stench of the layered dried blood of a hundred deaths. Under that was the smell of the Dragon Queen, sulfur and sex twisted up with the tight knot of nervous devilish anxiety. Rising above it all was another odor: the smell of life, of youth, of beauty. Brenna's natural fragrance filled the room, her cocoa and cinnamon-flavored skin a blooming flower in a lifeless crypt.

There were layers of emotion hanging in the air even more palpably than any scent. The lovely little human seemed lost and confused, and physically was the picture of submission. Her body language suggested that the ancient torture device was unnecessary, that she would lie on the floor in a puddle of human helplessness if she were not held in place by the bindings. Every question she was asked was answered immediately. When her voice did sound, it was to reply to the devil's strange questions or to ask for her release. She never ignored the queen, never raised her voice, and never begged for anything. Although captive, although her posture suggested hopelessness, Brenna was somehow serene and confident in her captivity. Her steady eyes watched the devil's madness with a calm that only compounded it.

Lilia was another story. She threatened, she screamed and swore, she used every macabre tool on the wall to exact painful torture on the frail human form that disappeared with each fatal blow only to reappear completely unharmed and full of life moments later, held firm again in the wooden stocks. The queen was the one in control, from all outward appearances; yet the calm of her prisoner and the panicked tone of her own actions made her seem the captive more than the captor.

"What is your name, you little bitch?" Her voice was full and flinted, a jagged edge to it as she asked the same question over and over and expected different results.

Beautiful dark eyes looked up at her, Brenna raising her perfect little chin as high as her restraints would allow.

"My name is Brenna Blanco." She spoke as a teacher would speak to a slow student, or a level-headed adult to their senile parent. She drew the words out slowly, pronouncing them with endless patience.

Lilia crossed the room in three angry strides. She stood over her prisoner, her eyes of flame burning fury down at her. A pretty crinkle formed in Brenna's forehead as she raised her eyes further to regard the queen with her calm unbroken gaze.

"I still don't know your name, because you still haven't told me," Brenna continued in that low measured tone. "Nor do I know where I am, again because you have not told me. Perhaps if you tell me the answers you would like me to give you that would help. Then you could let me go and—"

She was silenced by a resounding smack, a scarlet blurred backhand that raised a red mark on the olive skin of her hollowed cheek.

Lilia's visage was twisted into a beautiful hateful hellish mask, sparks of rage burning in her eyes as her breasts heaved with each panicked breath.

"Let you go?!" she hissed, her full lips curled to sneer at the pretty girl. "I will never let you go, you stupid girl. I am Lilia, the Queen of Hell, and you will be my prisoner forever."

Her face came close enough to Brenna's that she could smell her hot brimstone breath. "Or until I destroy you for good."

The queen stood up straight and seemed to regain her composure a bit. A wicked smile curled one corner of her lips until a canine was showing.

"In the meantime," she said, stepping to the wall and selecting a small and sharp-looking dagger, "we will keep having our fun in your little cell. You will break, you will tell me who you are, and your pain will end forever one day. Until then, you and I will play our little game here while Mister Stone and I play our little games in my boudoir."

Brenna tried to stand, banging her head against the hard wood of the stocks. Her hands moved, but only a little; only as much as the wood would allow.

"Mister Stone?" Brenna's dark eyes were narrowed, a thin vertical crease drawn between them. "Paul? You know Paul?"

Her smile curled into a cruel sneer.

"Oh, yes. Intimately." She dragged the sharp blade across her palm lightly in anticipation. "No man can handle himself in the bedroom with a devil unless he's had experience with one. You trained your little human well, Ximena. But he's not human anymore."

She plunged forward suddenly, arcing the dagger under the wooden containment to bury the blade in Brenna's belly.

She gasped, but she did not cry out. Red human blood trickled from around the blade to stain her olive skin.

"He's not yours anymore, either," Lilia's face was a breath from Brenna's as she twisted the knife.

This time she did cry out, then collapsed a little as the blade was pulled free. Blood flowed from the gaping wound.

Brenna's eyelids fluttered; then her eyes opened to gaze at the queen, bright with lucidity.

"Please stop," she muttered, her voice a breathless whisper.

"Tell me my name, you devil bitch. Tell me where you are. Tell me who you are," Lilia chanted her broken record mantra.

Her big brown eyes widened as her voice spoke new answers. "Your name is Lilia."

Lilia nodded, her eyes widening as well. Her forked tongue flicked across her full lips in anticipation.

"I am in Hell," she said doubtfully.

The queen nodded again, her eyes flashing fire.

Brenna hesitated, sighed. "My name is Brenna Bl—"

Lilia stood, dragging the dagger across her throat, and another layer of life spilled onto the stone floor.

CHAPTER 34

The doorway was still there, but it was not nearly as foreboding. He didn't have to keep his dead eyes open as he walked through it or anything crazy like that, but it wasn't nearly as foreboding. Now that he knew he could dream, sometimes, the Guide could better appreciate a life of lucidity. Awake and alert, he closed his eyes and stepped through the portal and into his dead body.

Kris woke and stretched in the soft expanse of Jessica's bed. His hand expected to encounter warm devil flesh, then to pull it close to him, but he was alone on the mattress. A quick glance at the red glowing numbers on the alarm clock told him night was over, at least for the barista.

Jessica would be opening the door to the customers upstairs at six, like she did every morning, in ten minutes. Kris told himself he didn't want to disturb her morning routine as he closed his eyes and imagined his robe about him. He rose to his feet, swathed in the folds of otherworldly material.

He started to head to the expansive bathroom that he now shared with Jessica, then stopped and stood still. Kris closed his eyes again, thinking his hair clean and combed, his breath fresh and minty, his face shaved clean. There was a shift and a pull and he opened his eyes, ready for work.

Breathing a little to prepare for the walk between worlds, Kris thought again of stopping to say good morning to Jessica.

Nah, she's busy, he thought to himself.

He closed his eyes one more time and thought of Paul, wherever he might be. Kris noted that when he thought of his friend, he saw him in black hat and duster and boots with a sword in his hand. And frowning.

Not one to disappoint, Paul greeted him when he opened his eyes in his full Walker getup. He didn't have a weapon, but he was frowning.

"Kris, this is Walker William," Paul indicated the man standing next to him.

"Kris is my Guide," he said to the other man.

Kris disentangled his hands from the sleeves of his robe to proffer one to the Walker. "Nice to meet you."

The man stared at him, confused. He was an imposing figure, although not uncommonly tall or wide. His Walker armor was modern biker gear, oiled to shine like the chains and buckles adorning it. There were two other people in the room, a living room that looked like any other living room. The man standing on the other side of William was a young, unkempt-looking fellow. He looked as though he was at death's door, or had been recently, his eyes milky and sunken and his skin a pasty pale color.

Standing next to him was a woman. She was pretty, with a face that looked young and wise at the same time. She was looking at the hand Kris offered to William with the same perplexity as the Walker. Kris put it together when he saw her robe, so similar to his own.

"You're a Guide," Kris smiled.

He let his hand fall to his side. Maybe Walker William was too cool to shake hands.

Paul spoke again, nodding at the young picture of death. "That is Chase. He is a Walker in training."

The young man narrowed his blue eyes at Paul's words, intelligence spearing through the fog. His gaze shifted left and then right, landing on Kris.

Chase extended his hand and mumbled something.

William spoke, starting in a patient and explanatory tone: "He's a Guide. He can't—"

Kris shook the new Walker's hand, noting that it felt as weak and soggy as the man looked.

William exchanged a look with the woman that clearly had a great deal of subtext.

"You can feel his touch?" The woman's voice was strong and soft and confident, querying Chase.

The new Walker nodded.

"Is it because of Chase's abilities?" Now she queried Kris, taking a step towards him. "I am Vanessa. I am William's Guide."

"No, Vanessa," Kris tried not to beam too proudly. "I can touch anything, just like when I was alive." He saw a magazine on the coffee table, a picture of a group of motorcyclists riding off into the sunset on the cover. Kris took two steps and picked it up, holding it for her to see.

The girl's dark eyes went round, as did William's. They stole another glance at each other.

Paul cleared his throat, a little loudly.

"We were just leaving," he said. "Chase's key is counting down to his first demon."

Chase visibly sagged at the words, his shifty gaze looking at everyone and nothing.

Looking around, Kris was curious. "Where is his Guide?"

"No one showed up," William said uncertainly.

"Yet," Paul amended, frowning at some thought.

Kris squinted, trying to see the dead form of a Guide or Watcher hovering nearby. Three forms, shifting in shape and flitting quicksilver though the air, swirled in and out of the gathered group of immortals.

"What are those?" The Guide blinked, and they disappeared.

"What?" Paul and William spoke together, trying to track what Kris was seeing.

"I saw something for a second there." Kris squinted again, to no avail. "Like smoky shapes swimming though the air."

"Probably his demons," Paul spoke dismissively. "We need to go. Are you joining us?"

Vanessa spoke before Kris could answer. "Do you need me, William?"

"No." The Walker shook his head. "Easy job."

"Guide Kris," the woman turned to him, her youthful face and posture the picture of seriousness, "would you stay with me and teach me to…to touch things?"

Her eyes went to her Walker as she waited for his answer.

Kris smiled. "Sure, Vanessa. It shouldn't take too long. You just need to let go of your knowing that you can't do it, like anything else."

"You might teach him about re-minding mortals, if he doesn't know how already." William offered the suggestion before he broke the eye contact.

Vanessa brightened at the confusion that came over Kris' features.

"What's that?" he asked, curious.

No doors opened, no one said goodbye or walked away. Paul put one hand on William's shoulder and the other on the new Walker's.

Then they disappeared.

CHAPTER 35

Cal pushed the little line back and forth across the glass tabletop. He was the Cal that nobody saw, his hair disheveled and his eyes hollowed and shot with blood. Sitting on his sofa in gray sweatpants and a white wife-beater, the confidence and charisma that defined him to others was absent.

He was just another loser when the fat lines ran out. Pushing the powder with the razor, he could make it one long thin line or one fat short mound. Cal settled finally on one long thin line, and leaned over the table to snort it directly up his right nostril.

Leaning back onto the soft cushions, Cal tilted his head back to prevent a single speck of the powder from escaping. He thought for a moment of all the times a little bit of the drug had drifted out of his nose after he snorted it, all the times both nostrils were so packed with the pricey powder that they lacked the power to snort more.

If all of that was on the table in from of him, he would have no obligation but to sit here and snort coke all day. It certainly wouldn't be the first time.

The table was empty, however; and wishing and dreaming and hoping wasn't going to make anything appear on it.

Cal had to act. He had to shower and shave and put on some clothes and slick back his hair. He had to take the money he had set aside for bills and get into his car and go to Raul's house with it.

So that's what he did.

By the time he knocked on the door, he resembled himself again in almost every way. That one little line had barely qualified as maintenance, and the cokey gleam that usually made his tan eyes luminous was missing.

"Come in!" Raul's voice shouted over the television and through the front door.

Cal tried to flash a grin at him as he entered.

Sitting on the couch next to a thin Latina with long bleached hair, Raul cocked an eyebrow at Cal.

"Damn, Holmes, what happened to you?" When Raul spoke quickly, he was nearly guilty of speaking perfectly unaccented American English.

When he spoke slow and serious, like now, a heavy Mexican accent flecked his words. His customary way of addressing Cal constantly as "man" shifted slightly, and Cal became "Holmes" instead.

Cal grimaced. Apparently he was not as well put together as he had hoped.

"I got rolled," he answered simply.

For the first time since Cal had entered, Raul addressed the pretty girl sitting beside him.

"Beat it," he said to her.

Dutifully, the girl stood up and walked down the hallway to enter a room Cal had never been in.

"Have a seat, Holmes," Raul patted the cushion the girl had vacated.

Cal took the proffered seat. He followed Raul's hand with his eyes as he waved it at the pile of cocaine on the table, offering him a line as well.

Cal took that too.

Leaning back into the sofa, Cal closed his eyes and let the big line hit him. Flashbulbs went off behind his eyelids, and a not unpleasant tingle wound its way through his brain like an electric eel.

"You know who it was?" Raul's voice was still slow and serious, thick with border town Mexico or East L.A.

Cal shook his head, opened his eyes.

"No," he replied. "It was dark. It was two white guys, that's all I know."

"Fucking white people," Raul spat.

Cal burst out laughing while Raul grinned and chuckled along. It felt like he hadn't laughed for weeks. He clapped Raul on the back, grateful.

"I can't front you much." Raul was still smiling, but his voice was solemn and accented.

Still shaking with the laugh, Cal shook his head. "I don't need a front. I have money."

Raul nodded. "I should have known. How much you want, Holmes?"

"Half ounce." Cal dug in his front pocket for the carefully counted bills. He set them in a stack on the coffee table, away from the coke and the gun.

The money was in Raul's hand as he stood, moving from one hand to the other one bill at a time as he counted and walked. He reached the safe at the same time as he finished counting, and stuffed the money in his jeans pocket before kneeling in front of the containment unit. It was unlocked, and Cal could see the abundant contents over the dealer's hunched shoulder.

"You need a gun, Holmes?" Raul half-turned, two baggies in one hand while the other rested on his knee to balance him.

"I have a knife," Cal responded uncertainly.

"Did you cut the guys that rolled you?"

"One of them." Cal couldn't help but feel a touch of pride in his response.

"Did you kill him?"

Cal frowned. "No."

"Did they still rob you, Holmes?"

Cal's frown deepened. "Yeah."

"Do you need a gun, Holmes?" Raul removed a small squared dark pistol from the safe, then nudged it mostly shut.

Heaving a sigh, Cal admitted, "I've never shot a gun before. Not a real gun, anyway. Just pellet and BB guns, when I was a kid."

Raul handed the bags to Cal. With a few subtle movements of his hand, he dropped the magazine into his hand and pulled the slide to spit out the chambered round and lock it open.

"Same shit, Holmes, just louder and deadlier." Raul held the weapon out to him.

"This is a Glock nine millimeter, easy to shoot and not likely to jam no matter how many rounds you put through it." Raul's voice was back to being crisp and efficient and unaccented. "The clip holds seventeen rounds, which is seven more than California state law allows."

Cal took the empty pistol from him, holding it awkwardly. "So, don't get caught with this gun?"

Pushing the ejected round back into the clip, Raul held the little metal rectangle out to him. He shook his head. "Definitely do not get caught with this gun, Holmes."

Cal took the clip and set it gently on the glass tabletop. He looked up at Raul.

"Only point at what you are willing to shoot, even if you think the gun is empty." Raul came around the table to sit next to him on the sofa.

His fingers were curled around the handle unnaturally, except the finger that tentatively rested on the trigger. Cal pointed the barrel uncertainly at the floor.

"I'm not willing to shoot anything in your house," he pointed out.

Raul chuckled. "Take your finger off the trigger until you're ready to shoot. Point it straight, rest it under the slide. Good," His lively dark eyes watched Cal handle the weapon carefully, and Cal thought deeply about the meaning of the teardrop tattoos on Raul's face for the first time. Raul leaned forward to snort a line, like he was taking a sip of coffee.

"Now release the slide," Raul continued, rubbing absently at his nose for a moment and sniffling.

"Either pull it back all the way and let go or push down on that lever," he indicated a small piece of metal that was turned upward to catch a notch in the sliding mechanism.

Holding the gun firm in his left hand, Cal pulled back on the top half of the pistol until it wouldn't pull back any further. He let go, and the weapon responded with a satisfying clack as the metal slid home. The hammer was cocked and at the ready.

"Point at the TV," Raul instructed him. "Line up the front site between the two rear sites, until they are at equal height with equal light between them. Do you know which is your dominant eye?"

Cal nodded, closing his left eye as he raised the weapon.

Cal held the gun up with one hand, one finger along the body of the gun while the other three clutched the handle. He eyed the sites, lining them up as Raul had instructed, aiming at a cartoon character that looked like a blue cat on the television screen.

"Pull the trigger," Raul said.

Taking his eye off the sites for a moment, he cast an uncertain glance at Raul.

"Go ahead," the dealer urged him.

Now he was aiming at a character that looked a little like a goldfish, not in water but sitting on the cartoon couch next to the blue cat. Cal tugged on the trigger, watching the front site skew right as the hammer fell with a click.

"Keep ahold of it," Raul instructed him. "I'm going to pull the slide back to show you what kind of recoil to expect." He grasped the top of the pistol and pushed toward Cal, tipping him back a bit deeper into the sofa cushion.

"Do it again," Raul continued, "but move your finger so the first pad is centered on the trigger. You went a little right, which will be even more pronounced when you're shooting double action."

Cal looked at him again, this time questioning.

"When the hammer isn't cocked," Raul explained. "Just keep practicing. You'll get used to it."

CHAPTER 36

Andre hadn't really been a big fan of life. Life had been something to be borne with as much dignity as he could muster. There had been no pleasure or power or respect, no wild sex parties or coke parties or even just cocktail parties. When Andre was alive, he wasn't the guy you called when you were throwing a party. He was the guy you called when you needed a breaker box installed or a faulty outlet fixed. He was the guy you called when you needed a pear-shaped bespectacled bald man to arrive in his blue van and run some wires and light things up and present you with a reasonable bill. He was never the guy two hot girls thought of when they decided to have a threesome together.

Death had been way better right from the beginning. There still weren't any hot girls banging down his door, but there were a slew of benefits that he couldn't help but notice right away.

For one thing, he didn't have to shower or shave or brush his teeth anymore. He was dead; if he wanted fresh breath or a barber-close shave, he just had to think about it. He never got dirty; again, he was dead. There was nothing in this dimension for the dirt to stick to, and apparently whatever layer of reality Andre inhabited was as free of dust as it was of odor.

What's more, in death your work was your life, at least if you are a Watcher. The job is writing and reading most of the time, work that is best done alone. Andre was long accustomed to time alone, and to being expected to be precise in his thinking and diligent in his work even when he was the only one watching.

He could change his appearance too, although he had only dared to trim a few inches off his waist and add about a half-inch of hair back to the dwindling ring that crowned his shiny head. Little by little, he might transform himself into the striking young man that he had never been using just the power of his imagination.

Not all at once, though; he didn't want to seem vain.

The time Andre had spent being dead had been the most comfortable period in his life. It seemed strange that he would have to die to find some meaning to life. He was alone, in a simple home, with a challenging job that he was good at, just like when he was alive. Yet life here seemed more suited to him, and the gray walls and floors and endless hallways stretching every direction was the only place he had ever felt at home since he was born a pudgy bald baby.

Then Paul had become the King of the Walkers somehow, although every book Andre read clearly said there had not been a Walker King for centuries and that there certainly was not one now. Other Watchers started coming to Andre for answers and guidance and leadership in his first week on the job.

Now he hardly had time to keep up with his duties as Paul's Watcher. There were knocks on the door at all hours of this place's endless twilight, especially since word got around that Andre never slept. He couldn't attend or present a lecture without at least one Watcher or Guide trying to pull him aside.

It was wonderful. Andre had not loved his life, but he was thoroughly enjoying his death. He felt important. He felt appreciated.

There was a knock on the door, not the tentative hallmark tapping the Watcher's usually approached with but a loud *rap-rap-rap!*

Andre let his feathered quill be still and put his Watcher eyes on the other side of the gray door.

He loved being a Watcher. He couldn't help but think it as he closed his eyes to see who was calling. He could see anywhere in nearly any world by wanting to.

Andre sat up straight and hastened to the door. Opening it inward, he smiled up at his Walker.

"Walker Paul," Andre motioned for him to enter.

Paul hesitated, then seemed to decide to remain in the gray hallway. His full beard and long hair combined with his leathered garb to give him quite the otherworldly warrior king look. He acknowledged Andre's greeting with a frown and a nod.

"Are you available for a while? It really won't take long where we're going." Paul's tone and manner were so brusque that Andre felt honored for just being addressed.

"Of course." Andre stepped into the hallway and closed the door behind him, locking it with his intent that only he and God may enter. "I am your Watcher."

Paul seemed to bristle a bit at his words. Andre sort of understood why. He had tried to address Paul as "Walker King" or just "My King" a couple of times since Paul had taken the title in the manner that most kings do.

The way Paul had asked him to please just call him by his first name had been done in the tense and demanding tone of a king expecting to get his way. Andre had addressed him as "Walker Paul" in the few times they had interacted since then. He had wondered more than once if his desire for formality was the reason for the infrequency of those interactions.

If this wasn't going to take long, that meant they were going pretty far up or pretty far down. Andre's fascination with the afterlife did not end with his experience of it. He closed his eyes as the Walker King's heavy hand fell on his shoulder, not asking and not caring which direction they were headed.

After the subtle shift, the Watcher opened his eyes to a charred and burnt landscape of jagged red rock under layer upon layer of thick acrid smoke.

Andre allowed himself a little smile. He had been hoping for Hell. This was the only place that somehow engaged his sense of smell and brought it back to life. The Watcher realm, the beautiful levels above and even Earth were completely odorless to him now. It wasn't stale or unpleasant; it was simply an absence of smell. Hell, on the other hand, tickled his nostrils with sulfur and soot and brimstone; and he breathed deeply and regularly whenever they visited, despite his not actually needing to breathe.

The Walker King stood unmoving, cloaked in leather. Under the slowly turning brim of his hat, he seemed to be scanning the landscape in search of something. Andre considered taking the opportunity to appear his book and quill, but perished the thought. His Watcher eyes could come back to this moment, see it from all angles as many times and ways as he wanted. He found it easier to record in the comfort of his chambers these days, and preferred to stay in the moment even when he was simply observing.

There was a sound behind them, someone overturning a rock gently underfoot from far away. It seemed like a deliberate sound, like the words that followed it.

"Walker King," her voice was soft and deep and feminine, "I am at your service."

The devil approached a few more feet, then fell to one knee and bowed her head. Andre knew it was the devil girl he had watched Paul best before, though she was wearing a dark leather dress. It covered her shoulders to her knees with one piece of fabric that clung attractively to her modest curves. Her shoes were leather ankle boots that clasped together with two buckles and increased her height by four inches with pointed heels.

The way she was kneeling was clearly uncomfortable in that outfit. With one knee on the ground, the other had to hover just over the charred rock to prevent them from seeing up her dress.

The Walker King walked slowly toward the abject devil. Andre followed, staying back a bit as always. Just because he couldn't see it didn't mean he didn't know there was a knife in her boot. He was a Watcher; it was his job to know.

Paul approached to stand over her with a frown. He didn't manifest a weapon, to Andre's surprise.

"Rise, devil." His voice was sure and strong.

She stood to her full heeled height, a little taller than the Watcher but still shorter than the king. She kept her eyes averted while she swept burnt dust from her kneeling knee with one hand. Andre noticed that her talons were filed and painted to look like a human woman's. They were the color of a dark red wine or port, and her lips had been painted to match. Andre couldn't take his eyes off her; she had been sexy in battle regalia, but this was a whole other level.

"What is your name, devil?" Paul was still frowning.

Her dark slitted eyes rose from the ground to meet Andre's.

"Charine," she replied.

A thrill went up the Watcher's spine for some reason.

"Charine," Paul repeated, "may I introduce my Watcher, Watcher King Andre."

Andre stood there for a moment, dumbfounded. His reasons were two-fold: first, Paul's formal introduction was just the kind of thing Andre wanted so much from the Walker King; second, the captivating devil girl was looking at him with a mixture of hunger and awe. The Watcher was glad he was not prone to flush; now would have been the time.

He made sure to glide towards her calmly, rather than walking. Andre took the hand she proffered him and stooped a little to brush his lips over the surprisingly smooth crimson skin.

For an agonizing forever moment, the Watcher feared his action a little over the top. He paused with his lips against the lightly veined back of her delicate hand in that forever moment, second-guessing himself to his dead core. Then he lifted his eyes to meet hers.

Charine smiled a slow, soft and sexy smile, licking her lips slowly and then biting her lower lip with one pointed canine.

Andre smiled and stood up straight.

"How nice to meet you," he said, still holding her hand in his for a few pleasure-soaked seconds. She made no move to pull away.

"Watcher King Andre," she said, as he finally let her hand fall from his. He watched her bite her lower lip again, then nod as if making some inner resolution. "Would you like to go somewhere or to my chambers and have something to drink or smoke or whatever you might like?"

The Watcher was not particularly prone to questioning his perception of events. Still, he had to go back over what she had just said at least once with his Watcher's inner power of playback. Just to make sure.

He had rehearsed some scenario like this in his mind countless times, even if it had never happened to him. Andre knew what to do.

"That sounds like a great idea," he said coolly. He extended his crooked elbow to her.

Charine sighed, like she thought there had been some possibility that he would say no. She smiled and hooked her arm through his.

"I don't know how long I'll be," The Walker King's voice sounded behind him, and Andre started.

He had forgotten all about Paul.

"I can find my way home," Andre assured him, composing himself long enough to turn and smile at the Walker.

He needn't have bothered. Paul was gone at his words, leaving Andre alone in Hell with a devil and happier than ever.

The Watcher gladly turned his attention to Charine.

"Is your place far from here?" he asked.

She shook her head, still smiling and still biting her lip most attractively.

"Can I ask you a question?" He spoke as they walked in the direction she indicated.

Charine nodded solemnly.

"Why me?" he asked plaintively.

She pulled close as they walked. "You're so solemn and wise and sexy and bookish."

Andre let a few of the pounds he had mentally shaved off his body return to round his belly, and a small cluster of his new hairs loosed from their moorings to drift to the rock behind them while they moved forward together.

The Watcher smiled and thanked God for death.

CHAPTER 37

The riff should have been taking all of his attention, the fingering was so fast. Mason played effortlessly, hardly looking at his hands while Sarah hummed a few bars of melody. Her voice was a siren's sweet song.

"Can you sing those notes?" Sarah asked when she was done humming.

Mason shook his head, still playing the rapid fire note sequence over and over and over.

"I can't sing that," he mumbled.

"What?" Sarah leaned in close.

"I SAID I CAN'T SING THAT WAY," he said slowly and loudly into her ear.

"Not that way," she shook her head. "Just those notes."

Sarah sang the catchy melody again, in time and in key with Mason's interminable playing.

He took in a lungful of breath and tensed his stomach, straightened his spine and opened his mouth as if to sing.

Mason closed his mouth, shook his head again. His hands blurred over the frets in a loop that was a little dizzying to watch, even for him.

He looked away.

"Would you try please?" Sarah sang the notes once again, a pristine reproduction of the first two times.

She wasn't going to let up.

Mason gave it a try. It was haphazard and flat.

He tried again, in falsetto.

Sarah valiantly resisted the urge to laugh.

The guitar went silent.

"I told you I couldn't sing it," Mason snapped, reflexively spinning the volume knob on his new black Ibanez. The amp sat silent and still, like a good new amp should when the input volume is off.

Sarah put her hand on his knee. "I know, sweetie. I'm sorry."

"Don't talk down to me." Mason crossed his arms over his guitar, averted his eyes. "I'm not Rob or Mikie. I don't have some huge vocal range, I know. You don't have to laugh at me."

"I am not trying to talk down to you." Sarah tried to make her voice sound as sweet as she could. "I am sorry if it sounded that way. I was apologizing because it looked like I hurt your feelings. I don't ever want to do that. I love you, Mason. Not Rob or Mikie or anyone else. Just you. Especially you. Completely you. Totally you."

He was back, smiling and looking her in the eyes.

"It was kind of nice not having Mikie around last night," Mason ventured quietly.

No matter how Sarah felt, she was not going to disagree with him on anything. Not in this moment.

Besides, why not speak her truth?

"That guy is such a fucking pain in the ass," Sarah swore deliberately, to show she meant it. "He's totally controlling, and constantly accusing you and me and even Cal of being the controlling ones."

It wasn't the whole truth of the man, but it was the truth.

It was the part of the truth Mason needed to hear right now. He emphatically nodded his agreement. "I know, right? You and I just want what's best for the band. And Cal…well, dude has really stepped up."

"I guess you choose better friends than I do," Sarah sighed. She frowned playfully.

"He was a band member," Mason shrugged. "You needed a decent guitar player."

She laughed. "Not anymore. Now I have a phenomenal guitar player. Who also happens to be my very handsome boyfriend."

Mason picked at the strings of the muted guitar, making the tinny sounds without thinking about it. It was the simple C to A minor back and forth intro to Leonard Cohen's genius 'Hallelujah'.

"Are you saying you want to get rid of Mikie?" Mason asked while his arpeggio played the fourth and fifth, then the minor fall and the major lift.

Sarah shrugged, pretty even though she was frowning. "He seems to be getting rid of himself. He texted to say he wouldn't be there again tonight. I think we should kick him out, if he ever comes back. I think we should give his cut to Cal and ask him to manage us full-time."

The guitar was quiet again as Mason laid his palm gently across the strings, over the pickups.

"Really?" He couldn't help but smile a bit.

"Really," she nodded. "Then we should meet with Cal and talk to him about whether or not we should drop Rob as well."

"Really?" Mason was astounded. It was all he could say.

Sarah giggled, bit her lower lip for a moment. "I don't want you to join my band. I want to form our own band."

Mason stiffened. "I don't want to get rid of Jason or Tyler." His voice was stiff too.

"Neither do I."

"So…you want to join my band?" Mason relaxed, even laughed a little bit.

She gave another shrug. "You pick better band members. I thought we had covered that."

Mason laughed out loud then, the remaining guarded tension draining from him.

"Would you do something for me, love?" Sarah's voice was sweet and supplicating.

He raised an eyebrow in response and started to mindlessly strum the quiet guitar again. A slow F to A minor and back to F, then he fingered the single note melody to the final 'Hallelujah' that finished the chorus.

"Would you ask Daemon to help you sing that part? The one we were just playing?" Sarah put a hand on each of his knees.

She had grown accustomed to watching his head turn and his eyes go out of focus, especially when she mentioned the apparition. Daemon always seemed to be nearby, and Mason always seemed to know where he was.

Mason stared over her shoulder at his demon or his imagination, Sarah didn't know which. After a tense forever moment, he nodded and smiled.

"Then we'll ask him to take care of Rob like he did Don and Mikie," he said darkly.

Sarah slapped his knee lightly. "That's awful."

From the corner of his eye, Mason saw Daemon grin devilishly.

He played it again, and Sarah sang along this time.

"Hallelujah," she sang softly.

CHAPTER 38

Kris thought himself into his street clothes, jeans and tee shirt and hooded sweatshirt. He stepped from the office and into the coffee shop.

Busy behind the counter, Jessica did not notice his ghostly approach. Kris watched her for a moment, thinking how beautiful she was.

Jessica turned and started, surprised at him standing there.

"Sorry, baby," the Guide's dead face flushed. "I didn't mean to sneak up on you."

"How's your morning?" Jessica glided from behind the counter to encircle her arms about his waist and rest her head on his chest lightly.

Kris could smell her honeyed hair, delighted in the weight of her head on his chest.

"Better now." He pulled her closer, kissed her lightly on the forehead.

When her eyes looked up to meet his, it was like a circuit was completed in his head. "I'm worried about Paul, Jess. He's so withdrawn and distant, even when he's right there with me. Losing Brenna really punched a hole in his heart. He seems to be spending a lot of extra time in timeless places, and the time is not healing this wound. He's preparing for war, and I'm not certain his reasons or his preparations are adequate. Also, I think he might be—"

The little brass bell over the door jangled noisily, breaking his gushing stream of words.

Kris and Jessica both turned at the sound, surprised at the customer at this time of morning. It was a young man, about the Guide's age when he died. He wore black and red flannel over dark jeans that were painted onto his thin legs. The combat boots on his feet didn't seem to go with the thick plastic eyeglass frames perched on his nose. Before the door had contacted the jangly bell in its swing closed, the customer had a smartphone in one hand and was swiping busily away with the other.

The man put the phone in his pocket and looked over at the couple as he approached the register. Jessica disentangled from Kris to help the man. She reached the rear entrance to the waist-high bar and hit the swinging door just as the man called out.

"Kris?" The man was squinting dark eyes and leaning over the register in the Guide's direction. "Kris Reed?"

He didn't have time to think that the blood couldn't drain from his face, as Kris went white as the ghost he was.

"Hey Bill," he heard his own voice say woodenly, from very far away. "Long time no see."

In the time it took for the man to cross the room to pump Kris' lifelike hand, the Guide had chance enough to catch Jessica glaring at him. He focused on listening to the questions being posed to him and answering them in the best possible way.

"You live around here now?" Bill had finished shaking his hand and had stuffed both hands in his back pockets. It made him look awkward and gawky, even in the thick flannel.

"Nah," Kris shrugged. "Just passing through."

"Where you at nowadays?"

"Uh," Kris answered resolutely, "I travel a lot."

"Yeah?" His dark eyebrows shot up. "Sales?"

"Yep." The Guide smiled. "Sales."

"Hah!" He didn't laugh. He said "Hah!" "Me too."

He continued the uncomfortable interrogation. "What are you selling?"

Kris looked around, shrugged again. "Liquor and beer."

"Nice, nice," Bill's head bobbed up and down as he finally ran out of words.

The Guide sighed. "What about you, Bill?"

"Electronic components," he sighed. "I don't know what any of it is or how any of it works, but I can quote you a part number and a price on anything you need to make anything you need for laptops, cell phones, game consoles, alarm and surveillance systems—"

"Wow." Kris cut him off. "Sounds like you're busy too."

Bill fished in his front pocket for his phone again. The time display on the screen seemed to surprise him although he had just been looking at it two minutes ago.

"I gotta run," he flashed Kris a fake smile, then turned at last to approach the counter. "Can I get an iced coffee to go?"

Jessica was not her usual cheery self.

"We don't do iced coffee," she answered coldly. "Or coffee to go."

Once again, he dug in his pocket to retrieve his phone and consult the time despite the fact that once again not two minutes had passed.

Bill shrugged. "Uh, okay."

He waved to the Guide on his way out. "Take care, Kris."

The bell had not finished clanging when Jessica spoke.

"Are you serious?" she spat.

Her face was twisted into a mask of scorn, her voice a reptilian hiss. Now that he knew she was a devil and a dragon, Kris got lots of reminders. It was usually delightful.

Usually, but not always.

"You didn't change the way others see you?" she demanded.

Kris shook his head, following a stained trail of some distant yesterday's dried coffee dribbles on the floor with his eyes.

He shrugged. "I didn't even know I could do that."

"You have to do that," she retorted. "You're supposed to be dead."

Kris nodded, abashed.

He should have thought of that, she was totally right.

"You started to say something before," Jessica prompted, her face serene again and her voice only a touch edgy. "You think Paul might be…?"

He met her eyes for a moment, hoping they were blue. They were.

"I think Paul might be spending a lot of time with the Dragon Queen," he said quietly.

Jessica scowled again. "The Walker King is dating the Queen of Hell? Paul is fucking my mom? Do you know how many ways that's just wrong?"

Kris counted droplets in silence, the ghost of yesterday's coffee spill.

"Stay away from her," she hissed. "Tell Paul that he should do the same, if he knows what's good for him."

CHAPTER 39

The Guide didn't need time to think right now. He felt a little stirred up after talking with Jessica, and had excused himself to come to her apartments and work on his new face. For the first time, he had a moment where he missed normal life. Then his bright mind barraged his hurt heart with happy reminders, and he felt better.

Still, he could use a friend. Come to think of it, Paul probably could too.

He didn't want to change his clothes, but he also didn't know what Paul might be in the middle of. His friend could be very uptight and formal these days; better safe than sorry.

Kris closed his eyes and thought of his robe. It was only a moment before he felt the familiar otherworldly material against his dead skin.

Not bothering to open his eyes, he thought of Paul.

The Guide knew it before he opened his eyes again.

He hadn't gone anywhere.

"Shit!" He almost stamped his foot. *"Shit, shit, shit!"*

Kris closed his eyes, thought of Paul and the visualization the Walker had taught him to find him when he was in his personal spaces.

He still didn't go anywhere.

Kris didn't bother opening his eyes or cursing or stamping his foot.

Instead he thought of Andre.

The shift almost took him by surprise, and the heavy downward cant of the inward pull surprised him even more. Why was Andre in Hell?

When the Guide opened his eyes, he saw why.

The Watcher was standing nearby, shrouded in smoke and fatter and balder than ever. His arms encircled a petite devil with a long forked tail and short sharp canines that showed between the playful kisses she was exchanging with Andre. The Watcher's big belly pressed roundly into her small breasts, mashing them together and upward with the help of her leather bustier.

It was hard to tell which was smiling wider, the introverted dead man or the fanged devil lady.

Kris cleared his throat politely.

Andre disengaged from the embrace, but not completely. When they turned to face Kris, they hooked the little finger of his left hand through the little finger of her right hand and stood as near as possible to each other.

"Charine," Andre spoke, looking down at her and smiling. "Meet the King of the Guides, Guide Kris."

Kris nodded politely. "Nice to meet you."

He turned his attention to the Watcher. "Andre, do you know where Paul is?"

Andre looked a little miffed that Kris hadn't used his or Paul's proper titles, or some version of them. He answered anyway.

"He's with the Dragon Queen," the Watcher replied coolly. "He and I have been traveling down here together quite a bit to pursue our perspective courtships."

He grinned down at Charine at his mention of her. She grinned back.

"What do you mean, quite a bit?" Kris felt his brow furrow. "I just saw you yesterday."

The Watcher turned to look deeply into the demon's fiery reptilian eyes. "Earth time," he scoffed.

She giggled.

Andre returned his attention to the Guide.

"The Walker King will be here soon," he said. "The army is set to gather for the first strike. I thought that was why you were here, so we could all go in together."

"No." Kris folded his hands in his sleeves. "I didn't know. The first strike? Already? Now?"

"You really need to stop spending so much time on Earth," Andre chided him. "The afterlife is passing you by."

The Guide was not sure what he was about to say, though he opened his mouth to hotly retort.

"Ho, Guide King! Ho, Watcher King!" A strong voice cut through the thick miasmatic atmosphere. It was followed by its owner, swathed in black leather and transformed by a full beard and hair that swept past his shoulders.

They looked at each other a moment.

Paul looked closely at his Guide's face. "Kris?"

Kris laughed. "Sorry."

He closed his eyes and put his features back the way God and his DNA had intended. He wondered why Andre hadn't noticed. He also wondered if Paul realized that he himself was virtually unrecognizable next to the man he had been a week ago.

"I was about to call you." Paul held up the platinum key. "It's time."

"I know," Kris nodded. His glance at Andre was not completely without venom.

The Watcher disengaged from the devil finally, kissing her one last time. He stepped away from her and towards Paul and Kris. As soon as they were both within reach, the Walker stretched out a hand to each of their shoulders.

Kris felt the shift behind closed eyelids. Unbidden, the thought came to him of a deep sea diver jettisoning his dive weights and rising naturally and swiftly to an environment with a breathable atmosphere and comfortable pressure. The Guide wondered if they could possibly rise too far too fast. He saw the white light through his eyelids, noted that his mood seemed to have been lifted along with his soul.

"Walkers, ho!" Paul's voice rang out as Kris opened his eyes to the dark assemblage. There were less than a hundred Walkers gathered, and they began to beat the flats of their swords against the leather of their own armor in response to the king's call. Despite their scant numbers, the patterned rhythmic clamor was deafening.

The Guide looked them over, wondering how Paul had chosen the troops from the thousands of choices offered. It obviously wasn't race or sex or size: Kris could see tall and short, big and small, light and dark, men and women. He knew the abilities of the average Walker; a regular human army would fall before the most inept demon hunter, if there was such a thing as an inept Walker out there. What kind of lethal talents did this elite group have?

The Guide had never had much of a stomach for real violence, in life or in death. He was surprised to find himself looking forward to the gore he knew lie ahead.

"Watchers, to me!" Andre's voice boomed out like Kris had never heard beside him, startling the Guide. They stepped from the nonexistent shadows, dozens of robed men and women appearing suddenly while somehow giving the impression they had been there the whole time.

Kris found Andre was less annoying this high up, and forgave the Watcher his theatrics as he gathered them around him and began giving instruction.

Finding a quiet place in his mind, Kris ordered his thoughts and then broadcast them to the other Guides. They were all there, one for each Walker, most of them tuned into a slightly lower frequency to avoid cluttering up the personal space.

'Guides,' he thought clearly. *'The Watchers will be looking ahead, scouting every square inch of where we are going and monitoring the big picture. They will work as one mind, assuring that the battle progresses as anticipated and eliminating the element of enemy surprise.'*

He could feel the Guides listening, a hundred sharp minds at full attention. They didn't need to be coddled or encouraged or micro-managed. There was no need for shouting. Kris sent out his thoughts, and each Guide picked them up.

'We Guides must think both for ourselves and for our Walker. Watch his or her back and look for the best opponent set-ups and communicate with your Walker without getting in the way. Your jobs are the hardest of all, and each of you is expected to perform that job perfectly.' Kris smiled inwardly. *'In other words, ladies and gentlemen, business as usual.'*

There was a ripple of mental laughter that existed only for the Guide network.

Kris had one last thought for them. *'Any questions?'*

There weren't. Kris was not surprised. There were reasons that a certain type of person became Guides. It made them ridiculously easy to manage.

He returned his attention to the battle staging area, where Andre appeared to be leading a corporate quarterly meeting to one side while Paul seemed to be the center of attention at an antique weapons convention to the other. The Guide allowed his mental eye roll to be broadcast as he signed out.

"…just not sure about bringing an untested weapon to a new battle scenario," Paul was explaining to another Walker as Kris hovered nearby and out of the way. The Walker was shorter than the king, his skin leathered and his eyes set in a permanent squint from a long life of sun before sunglasses. His cowboy hat was a weathered brown, like the rest of his outfit, and Kris suspected that hat had ridden that head even in life. Cowboy was not a look for this man; it was a way of life.

As if to demonstrate the Guide's thoughts, the stocky Walker swept his duster aside with a quick fluid movement and snatched a gigantic revolver from the holster at his hip.

"It's all about caliper and round style," the cowboy drawled, reversing the weapon to hold it by the silver cannon of a barrel and proffer the handle to his king. "This here is a forty-four, loaded with hollow points made of a synthetic polymer. The rounds explode on impact without requiring an explosive charge. It's what I always use."

Paul took the pistol, hefting its considerable weight tentatively for a moment. The gathered Walkers watched, murmuring amongst themselves.

He planted his left foot forward and grasped the gun with both hands, pointing his right index finger along the barrel. Knees bent slightly, Paul leaned almost imperceptibly forward into the weight of the lethal hunk of metal. Left eye closed, he lined up the sights with his right eye to aim at the blank shifting light wall in the distance.

The cowboy broke away from the group, walking as slowly and deliberately as he had spoken. He waved his hand in the general direction that Paul was aiming the gun, and a full-sized leather-clad demon appeared.

Nearly six feet tall, the demon was male and muscled and scowling. His face and stance and snarl dripped with malevolence, although he seemed as startled at his own sudden appearance as Paul did.

"My last hunt was a hate demon, ready to erupt with violence," the cowboy tipped his hat in the general direction of the Walker King. "I thought it would help demonstrate my point, so I brought it with me."

The demon seemed to realize that it was standing alone in front of an army of supernatural demon killers. To its credit, it did not look for an exit. Instead, it launched itself at the crowd of weapons and cowboy hats, running full speed to cover twenty yards.

Paul raised the gun again, falling back into the same two-handed stance naturally. Kris wondered where he had found time to learn to shoot a weapon he didn't plan to use, then let the thought be perished with the loud *boom!* the weapon made.

Coming fast, the slavering demon had covered half the distance by the time Paul squeezed off the shot. The round took the monster by its sinewy shoulder, and the shoulder exploded in a shower of purple blood. The demon's advance became a glorious tornado of crimson flesh and purple gore as the round's momentum spun it bodily and sent it sprawling to the liquid light floor.

As the demon rose to its feet, Kris saw that the cowboy once again stood near the Walker King. Paul handed the weapon back to its rightful owner.

In one moment, the demon stood there holding one arm tight to his torso with the other. Attached by only a patchy scrap of flesh, the arm hung uselessly in the demon's grasp under the tangle of purple stained hamburger meat that used to be his shoulder. In the next moment the demon rushed forward again, arm dangling and dripping a trail of fat purple droplets.

It didn't even seem as though the cowboy moved. Holding the gun at his hip, he tilted the barrel slightly and fired off a round. It was so swift, the sound and concussive force took Kris by surprise. He watched the demon's head explode in a disgusting cloud of purple blood and blackened bone.

Its lifeless body dropped unceremoniously to the clouds underfoot, and disappeared to wherever demons go.

"Bring it," Paul wasn't smiling, but he wasn't frowning either. "You say you can keep the rounds cool in Hell?"

The cowboy nodded.

"Same way I load my ammunition." He tapped his temple with his free trigger finger. "That way I never run out."

Paul nodded, then turned to his right. William was there, either appearing all of the sudden or having been there all along. Kris was not surprised.

"You want him with the archers or with the ground troops?" Paul asked William.

"On the ground," William answered immediately, and the cowboy's hat nodded his agreement. The biker Walker turned to the cowboy with a wry smile, his harness boots clanking with the movement.

"Don't shoot any Walkers, Samuel," he said.

"Don't worry about me, sword swinger. Last time I missed what I was aiming at, your Guide was still a babe in a teepee." The cowboy's drawl was accompanied by a wry smile of his own.

William arched a dark eyebrow doubtfully, but he did not respond except to smile.

A loud clang rang out, and then another, as Paul moved before the assemblage. He had a sword in each hand, one ancient and one modern, and he struck them together one last time with another resounding clang as he turned to face his troops.

"Through the ages, courageous warriors have been chosen to watch over mankind in a most sacred capacity." Paul's voice carried strong and sure to every ear, as the Watchers gathered to join the Walkers in listening. "Walkers are a special breed of men and women, compassionate souls capable of great violence in their service to humanity. The violence does not stain our rising souls, and the absence of gratitude in those we serve does not bitter our hearts. We are Walkers; that is enough."

Paul's swords had disappeared when he began speaking. Now a hundred swords manifested in killing hands to beat the blades against leather.

"The tireless efforts of your brothers and sisters have created a problem that you are all well aware of by now." The clamor died the moment Paul began speaking again.

"Walkers," he intoned gravely. "We have rats in the walls, so to speak. Today we are not individual hunters; today we are an exterminating army. Keep your line of attack frontal and progressive and keep your movements as simple and precise as possible. You are fighting shoulder to shoulder with the best of the best and the fastest of the fastest. Our only enemy of any formidability on this battle field is our own lack of organization. Press forward, let your Guide watch your back, and stain your swords from tip to hilt with demon blood."

Another clamor arose, along with an excited whoop or two. The Walker King turned his back to the assemblage and held his left hand before him, palm up. The platinum pocket watch rested placid in his open hand, emanating a soft glow that was easily lost in the abundance of light in this place.

A portal opened in the far wall, a twenty foot square doorway cut suddenly in the woven luminescence.

There was no pausing for consideration with this small army. The king neither turned around nor gave any sign to the warriors. He dashed forward in a black flash, short sword and bastard sword blinking into existence to glint in the otherworldly light before he disappeared through the opening. Standing amidst the suddenly mobilized army was a bit like standing in the middle of a racetrack with Indie cars blurring past at over two hundred miles an hour. The folds of the Guide's robe drifted with the supernatural wind, stirring and then still as the last Walker blurred by.

Kris was left standing there alone.

The Guide thought of Paul, casting out his intention like a fishing line. He felt an internal tug, and allowed it to pull him to the Walker King's side. There was no way he could move as fast as Paul unless the Guide linked his consciousness to the Walker's. Kris could feel Paul's quicksilver thoughts as he came to hover at the Walker's flank. He felt no desire to pry those thoughts into revealing themselves to him; he was a Guide, not a Watcher. Kris believed that was why Guides got this ability while Watchers didn't, and Vanessa had voiced the same opinion when they spoke. The other powers she had shown him had frightened him a little. Not prying came as naturally to the Guide's personality as not breathing, and directing anyone's thoughts but his own seemed a highly inappropriate invasion to him. Vanessa had considered that very attitude a prerequisite for learning the skill.

He found himself immediately and completely in the midst of battle. Looking behind him, the Guide could see the swath of violence cut by Paul's swinging sister swords. A dozen demons lay in rapidly pooling puddles of their own blood, fading from existence as Kris watched. Beyond them was the wide doorway Paul had opened, a lighted square that dwindled in the distance with Paul's lightning advance. A score of archers were posted up at the portal, loosing arrows with the calm regularity of a clock ticking.

Being linked to Paul as he was, Kris could see the world as the Walker saw it. He could split a second into so many long moments it nearly seemed that time was standing still. The Guide watched one of the archers nock her bow slowly, watched the specially designed arrow materialize between her fingers as she brought the string to her cheek. She loosed the arrow in the same instant, but to the Guide's eyes it looked as though she held it for a long moment and then slowly straightened the fingers that clutched the string. He saw the shaft begin its forward trajectory as the string went from a less than sign to a straight taught line.

When the arrow cleared the body of the bow, the tip changed in flight. Two slim sharp pieces of metal expanded from their snug housing in the wooden shaft to form a lethal "V" that flanked the center point. Kris couldn't tell whether the arrow was activated by passing through the bow or by flying through the air, but he could track the arrow's path easily as it flew.

The flying "V" caught a large lumbering monster by the throat, neatly decapitating it. The body stood there, trembling and headless, seven feet of rippling muscles that would have been eight feet if not for the missing head. Once the arrow cleared its target, it disappeared before it could hit the charred rock behind it.

Kris returned his attention to the archer as the body fell, saw her nocking another arrow. Or perhaps it was the same one, returning to her over and over as she nocked and loosed, nocked and loosed. Kris knew he had only watched for a total of about three seconds, but it seemed so ridiculously longer than that. He realized that Paul did not necessarily move all that fast; everything else just moved really slow.

Then he turned to watch the Walker King slashing and hacking and cutting a path through what looked like an endless river of oversized demons. Bodies fell at his feet like rain. The Guide could not follow the path of either swinging sword.

Scratch that, he thought inwardly. *Paul is just fast.*

'Behind you,' the Guide directed the next thought at the Walker King, as Paul slowed his progress to dispatch a pair of slavering monstrosities blocking his path. Both demons were nearly ten feet tall, and Kris had time to wonder how the Walker was going to dispatch them properly from his modest six foot height.

Either Paul knew the third giant was coming up behind him, or he treated the Guide's thought as his own. Whichever it was, the added body was calculated into the next lethal formula. The Walker leapt backward suddenly without looking, at the same speed he had been advancing. Planting his feet on the broad ripped naked chest of the crimson monster sneaking up on him, Paul launched himself at the hulking opponents before him.

Both demons reached out, in the same instant two swords flashed. Their twin snarls were locked in place as a giant head fell to either side. Paul hit the falling bodies together, springing nearly straight up in a slow backward somersault that was a quiet turning wonder to behold. The Walker King landed on his feet behind the third demon, his short sword disappeared and his bastard held firmly in both hands perpendicular to his body.

The blade had sliced the automobile-sized demon down the middle, and the Guide watched the two neatly cleaved halves of his gargantuan body begin to fall away from each other. Purple blood dribbled and spurted from the twin open wounds that the demon had become. Then blood and tissue zigzagged back and forth between the falling mirror image chunks of crimson gore, the halves stopped falling away from each other, and the hateful life came back into the monster's eyes as its flesh began to knit itself back together.

Paul leapt easily straight up in the air, hovering eye-to-eye with the taloned monster. The enlivened demon made a lunging grab for him just as Paul's single blade flashed. It bit into the sinewed neck at an angle, taking off the demon's head and part of one shoulder in passing. The reaching hands fell, lifeless, with the body.

The Walker King landed neatly on his feet and turned to the Guide. His hat and overcoat were soaked in purple blood, and a couple of pieces of unidentifiable hunks of flesh clung to the leather. A wide splotch of demon blood was drying on Paul's face, painting his forehead and cheek on one side. His beard was matted with it, wet and purple and dripping.

"Thanks," he said, tipping his bloody hat with his bloody glove. In the same instant that Kris identified the piece of gore on Paul's shoulder, he realized that the Walker was smiling. It was the first time he had seen him smile in what seemed a lifetime.

The Guide felt his stomach turn.

The piece of gore was part of an eyeball. Lifeless, it watched him watch the Walker appear his sudden short sword, then it was gone with that quicksilver fast dash that Kris still needed to get used to.

Battle raged all around him, but it wasn't until that moment standing alone on the battlefield that Kris heard the sounds of the bloodshed. It was like he had been watching a silent movie in the slow-motion full-color

Walker's cut edition, and his eyes had been too overwhelmed with the visual cacophony to extend awareness to his other senses. Now it hit him all at once, the smells of blood and brimstone climbing into his nostrils as the sounds of death bombarded his ears.

He was too far from the archers to hear the twangs of their bowstrings, but he heard the *thunk! thunk! thunk!* of shafts finding their targets with sickening regularity. Louder were the swords and shouts of the advancing ground troops, hacking their way through a grotesque horde of monsters whose smallest member outweighed the largest Walker by at least fifty pounds. None were as fast as Paul, and only two others wielded twin blades. They were still fast, though; and a human eye would have seen little but headless crimson monsters dropping to the ground like blades of grass before a team of lawnmowers.

Another sound punctuated the hacking and hollering, a loud regular booming noise. For a brief moment, Kris feared that a hundred foot tall demon would emerge from the shadows to smash Walkers under his explosive footfalls. Then the Guide realized it was Samuel, the lone gunman, gliding swiftly forward along with the other Walkers and squeezing off shots from his hip. Every *boom!* was accompanied by a nearby explosion of purple gore, and a headless body dropping to the ground in time with the next *boom!*

The worst sounds came from the demon horde. They howled and screamed and shrieked, gnashing their teeth and swinging taloned hands like sets of swords. Every one of them was at least seven feet tall, even the females, grown proportionately gigantic to tower easily over the tallest Walker. The largest of them were hulking monsters twelve feet tall, a few rare walls of supernatural flesh. Most were somewhere in between. They healed like Walkers in this place, any less than lethal wound closing in seconds. It looked like a couple classrooms of children had donned cowboy hats and dusters to clash with an army of full-grown heavyweight MMA fighters in monster make-up with the power of regeneration.

At first glance, the scene would surely have appeared terribly unfair to the casual observer. Then the casual observer would have seen one of the little people behead five of the giants in the space it required to take a breath. Perhaps the casual observer might then have realized it was indeed unfair; the monsters did not stand a chance.

Despite their size and home field advantage, the demons could not get a win. Every time one grabbed a Walker, it lost an arm and then a head. Most times they just weren't fast enough; the remaining instances, they just weren't strong enough. Their abilities matched their size, but not the raw explosive power of the Walker's supernatural strength.

The Guide stood there for a long moment, watching the carefully orchestrated slaughter from behind as it pushed forward. At any given time, hundreds of headless bodies and disembodied heads were on the ground or falling to the ground or slowly dematerializing. The Walkers were lucky their opponents disappeared after the last bit of purple life pumped from them. Otherwise they would be climbing over mountains of bodies and swimming a river of blood.

The landscape seemed to be a long wide valley of rock and smoke, fifty to a hundred feet of charred and hellish but mostly even terrain bookended on either side with swiftly rising rock walls. Hellish fires burned intermittently throughout the long and wide space, casting light and shadow and thick clouds of smoke in every direction. Not even the supernatural eye could see through the thick dark haze churning and roiling thirty feet above their heads, but Kris suspected there was a rock ceiling up there somewhere that much resembled the rock floor he stood on.

The wide valley stretched far in either direction, curving out of sight no matter which way he turned. The Guide watched the archers behind him as they continued to fire those nasty-looking arrows with lethal precision and clockwork regularity. He couldn't hear the arrows thunking home any longer, and the sounds of hacking and slashing punctuated by the lone gunman's endless rounds were fading in the other distance.

What had minutes ago been a wide valley crawling with so many demons that they had been stacked two and even three deep was now just a stretch of bare charred rock that burned somehow in random places. Kris stood there for another moment, thinking of how Guides seemed to loathe bloodshed as thoroughly as Walkers relished it. It was as if they were two parts of the same function, two sides of the same coin.

Like demons and angels.

The question was, was Kris the angel or the demon? Or was it not so clear? He thought of Paul and the Dragon Queen, then remembered Jessica and reminded himself not to judge. He was a Guide, not a Watcher.

With a thought, he was flanking Paul's swift forward movement again. He couldn't help but admire the Walker King's strategy as well as his fighting ability. Paul drove his spearhead assault through the middle of the sometimes wide and sometimes narrow valley. Gore dovetailed behind him like water behind a speedboat, his swinging blades moving faster than his own eyes could see. It opened up the valley behind him, allowing the next three to five Walkers to have a little more swinging room to cut down any demons that came close enough to lose their heads in passing.

The first few lines of Walkers never slowed, advancing their way through the Walker King's bloody wake. It was the last few that took more care moving forward, as they picked their way through tangled heaps of bodies and endless puddles of blood. The rear lines made sure every last demon was dead and disappearing, that any sign of life was quickly and completely extinguished. Then they moved on.

"I missed you." Paul's eyes didn't move left or right to acknowledge the Guide's reappearance as he slashed and swung through the monster horde. Kris didn't mind; he could see that Paul was busy.

'I've got the easiest job here,' Kris answered Paul mentally, his voice silent to everyone but his Walker just as his body was only visible to Paul right now. No need to clutter the battlefield with superfluous sights and sounds. That was the Walker's domain. *'My Walker makes other Walkers look like ordinary men and women.'*

'Have you seen where they go?' Paul answered him with a strong and clear thought, so strong and clear it was like his voice ringing clearly in the Guide's ear.

Kris smiled inwardly, proud of his Walker.

'Have I seen where what go?' Kris knew it was a stupid question the moment he thought it at the Walker, but he couldn't recall the transmission.

Paul's flashing blades did not stop flashing, but he did throw a quick eye roll at the Guide.

The demons, of course.

'No,' Kris thought. *'They just disappear, like when you kill them on Earth.'* He couldn't see the Walker frown in response, but he could sense his frustration.

'Does this tunnel go on forever?' Paul's thoughts were as strong as his swords.

'Let me check,' Kris released his bond with Paul for the moment and filled his mind with the thought of Andre and company.

The Guide found himself back in the bright woven luminescence of the staging ground. The Watchers gathered in a wide semicircle around the portal, scribbling in leather bound tomes with dancing feather quills or just watching. The archers continued to fire, and Kris saw their purpose more clearly.

To the left side of the portal, a sea of grotesque monsters rippled and surged and writhed as one gigantic disgusting organism. To the right, the path was lifeless rock with the occasional guttering flame throwing a dancing play of light and shadow over the hard bare footing. The direction the Walker army had taken was being kept clear by the archers, who paid little mind to the demons to their collective left. They shot straight ahead and occasionally to the right, as the stray monster slipped through the steady frontal barrage. Not a single demon passed to come up behind the advancing army.

"It's a wide loop," Andre said, appearing suddenly behind him. "As long as they keep moving forward, they will reach the doorway again from that side." The Watcher pointed to the left, at the writhing mass of crimson flesh.

Kris sighed. "How long will it take?"

The Watcher shrugged. "About three or four hours."

"Have you seen how fast they are advancing?" Kris had estimated that Paul was leading the assault at nearly a hundred miles an hour.

Andre looked at the Guide with disgust. "I've seen," he retorted. "It will probably take about three or four hours."

The Watcher did not seem pleased to be repeating himself.

"Is that all?" he asked icily.

"Have you seen where they're going?" Kris doubted the Watcher had seen anything he hadn't, but he had to ask.

The Watcher shrugged again. "They just disappear, like demons are supposed to."

Kris let his contempt show in his face for an answer.

"Is that all?" Andre asked again.

The Guide let himself be annoyed, even in this high place. "Is there something you need to get back to? Standing around? Watching? Losing your hair? Why are you still getting fatter and balder, Andre? You're dead."

Andre stiffened. "Yes, Guide. I need to get back to Watching." He winked out of existence for a moment, only to reappear near a gaggle of Watchers. They looked downright honored to be in his presence, and the Watcher stole a glance over his shoulder to make sure Kris noticed.

Kris, in turn, made sure he was gone by the time the Watcher looked back.

At Paul's flank again, Kris relayed the news telepathically while the Walker sliced and diced at the rapidly renewing resource of fresh demons to slaughter.

'It's a big loop,' Kris shot him a mental image of the army nearing the portal from the other direction. *'It should take a few hours to clear.'* He

considered for a moment. *'It really is like rats in the walls.'*

Paul spun and danced through the killing field, blood flying with his every movement as chunks of flesh flew in every direction. Neither a scrap of leather nor a patch of flesh showed through the layers of gore the Walker had painted himself with.

At first Kris misjudged his reaction to the news when Paul frowned at the Guide's thought. He figured the Walker was unhappy that the battle stretched so far ahead. Then the Guide watched Paul slice a fourteen foot tall demon into six pieces without slowing down, and caught the smile on his stained face.

Good God, Paul was disappointed that this was only going to last a few hours. Kris felt his dead stomach turn for the hundredth time in an hour.

'Does Andre know where they're going?' There was no slowing or stilling of Paul's physical activity, despite the calm clarity of his thoughts.

Kris shook his head, chided himself for being an idiot.

'No,' he thought deliberately. *'They're just disappearing. We don't know if they are going somewhere or if they are just dissolving once and for all.'*

There was tension in his thoughts, but no clear answer. After a bit, Kris stopped monitoring Paul's mental state and just rode alone in his murderous wake. From time to time he called out to Paul mentally, flashing him an image of some monster coming up on him. Mostly he just watched as hundreds dead became thousands turned to hundreds of thousands turned to millions.

He hated violence.

CHAPTER 40

Cal rapped lightly on the wooden entry, chambering his charming smile to fire it at the opening door. Sarah smiled back, ushering him into the small but clean apartment. Mason sat on a small sofa at the foot of the twin bed, quietly strumming the chord pattern to Bob Seger's "Still The Same" on the unamplified instrument. He looked up and gave Cal a curt nod, not interrupting the rhythmic wave of his right hand.

He spied a little dining nook inside the tiny kitchen through the door to his right, and Cal took three quick steps to retrieve a straight-backed chair that looked like it might have been all the rage in 1979. The pusher planted the chair between Mason and the dark television set. He put the straight back to Mason, so he could sit backwards in the chair, with a leg on either side.

"I'm coming tonight, you know," Cal reminded them as Sarah took up the remaining space on the loveseat next to Mason. He looked around at what little there was to look at, his sweeping glance ending at the coffee table.

Cal hated wooden coffee tables.

"You guys miss me? You want some blow?" Cal might have snorted a little too much cocaine on the long drive. He was talking pretty fast. "Do you have a decent surface?"

Sarah gave him another friendly smile, and Mason's hands began to move more precisely over the fretboard.

"We're good, Cal." Sarah glanced at the guitarist, who nodded his agreement in time with the flowing arpeggio he was playing.

Cal took a deep breath and settled back into his cool customary groove. "So, what's up?"

The soulful singer stole another look at Mason, who smiled and nodded and kept picking away.

There was a brief cloud of annoyance that passed over Sarah's face, but the sun soon came out again. She smiled at Cal and spread her hands.

"We want you to manage the band," she said.

Mason nodded again slowly.

There was a purse on the wooden coffee table between them, a little white clutch that looked as though it might go nicely with jeans or a dress. It certainty went with Sarah's light blue sundress, spattered in white stars. The clutch sat next to an empty ashtray, a pack of Camel lights and a wooden box with some kind of carving on it.

Sarah reached into the purse and pulled out an envelope. She set it on the stained surface between them, pushed it across the wood towards Cal.

Cal eyed the envelope. He knew what it was.

"What's that?" he asked.

Mason finally stopped playing. "That's your cut from last night, if you officially accept."

"First things first." Cal rubbed his hands together and nodded at Mason, one eyebrow raised in expectation.

Mason laughed. "Grab a CD case from the shelf behind you if you want to cut a line, buddy. We're good, man. For real."

As if to demonstrate, Mason seized the wooden box from the table and flipped the lid open. The sharp piney smell of unsmoked marijuana tickled the pusher's nose. Another moment and Mason had a joint in his mouth and was holding the flickering flame of a lighter to its tip.

The smell was overwhelming as the smoke filled the air. Mason puffed hard on the cannabis cigarette, then handed it to Sarah. She took a long steady pull, burning the cherry bright and holding it until she sputtered. She proffered the weed to Cal across the table.

Cal shook his head and reached over his shoulder to grab an empty compact disc case. It was a Beastie Boys album. Was there anything Mason didn't listen to?

"I wasn't talking about drugs," Cal explained, tipping the first bag his fingers had brushed in his full pocket. White powder obscured a part of the airplane in the picture under the plastic. "I was talking about that song you were playing."

He didn't need to chop it up or line it out. Cal pulled his companion tube of metal from his pocket and snorted up the mound. Just because he wasn't talking about drugs didn't mean more drugs were a bad idea.

Cal loved cocaine as much as he hated wooden coffee tables and the clouded confusion of pot. As if to illustrate, he tapped out another little mound and tooted it up the other nostril.

"That song you were just playing," Cal sniffled. "What was that?"

Mason and Sarah exchanged a smile as the joint changed hands once more. The guitar player's hands moved to the wound steel strings, and that smooth quiet rhythmic arpeggio found its way to Cal's ear again. He smiled softly, listening and savoring the numb tastelessness in the back of his throat.

Then Sarah started softly humming over the quiet notes, and Cal felt chills run up his spine as tears sprang to his eyes.

"Holy shit, you guys," Cal's eyes were wide with wonder and cocaine. "What is that? I've never heard it before."

"That's because we haven't finished writing it yet." Sarah stopped crooning to answer the question and hold the joint to Mason's lips while he played. Then she took a long series of short puffs and began humming the sweet lullaby as smoke gathered around her pixie face.

Cal knew enough about musical equipment to get what he wanted. He went to the amp that was as nearby as every other item in the studio and uncoiled the cord plugged into the input.

"Plug in," Cal held the male jack out to Mason. "I need to hear that louder."

Sarah and Mason exchanged another knowing glance. They had both written songs before that they thought were great. They had both learned that it can be hard to tell the difference between a great song and one that seemed great because you wrote it.

There was no mistaking it: this was a great song.

The guitar player stopped picking and took the cord from Cal's hand to click it into place. Cal turned to throw the switch on the amp and twisted the volume knob back to three. He wanted to hear Sarah too.

"Give me a little gain, please." Mason struck a power chord, then another, adjusting the volume and tone knobs on the new guitar.

Then it filled the air, that haunting tune that had captivated him in even its tinny quiet unamplified version. Sarah came in as the loop came around, her voice full and soulful. She was distinctly singing the same melody, still with no words.

The music changed, moving smoothly into the next song section and carrying the siren's sweet voice to a wider and deeper place.

Now there were words, scant as they may have been.

"Oh, oh, oh, my demon," Sarah had tears in her eyes, but her voice rang out clear. She sang the same words, but with a different melody. "Oh-oh-oh, my demon…"

His gold iPhone was in Cal's hand before he knew it, and he understood now why his camera needed to be accessible with a swipe and a tap. He also understood why he needed a video camera on his phone, when all he had needed a few years ago was a pager.

The recording started when they began the wordless verse again and continued through until Sarah had sung the haunting chorus once more.

They both stopped at the same time, and the room was quiet.

"That's all we've got so far," Sarah shrugged.

She leaned over to kiss Mason on the cheek, but he turned and met her lips in a slow sweet kiss.

Cal blackened the screen and pocketed his phone.

"That's totally going on YouTube," he grinned.

Mason set the guitar aside, stood up and stepped past Cal to power off the amplifier. He grabbed the pack of cigarettes from the table as he sat down, put one in his mouth and lit it. The air was once again filled with smoke, this time accompanied by the offensive stench of tobacco. Cal had never understood cigarettes. At least pot got you high, even if it was a sticky gooey uncomfortable kind of high.

"Don't you have to ask our permission?" Mason blew out a plume of blue-white smoke, deliberately in the other direction. Cal watched it swirl around the corner and felt it sneaking up behind him.

"Nope." Cal grinned at him and snatched up the envelope. "I'm your manager."

CHAPTER 41

"Let me get this straight." Roche had his arms crossed before him and his teeth bared slightly. His words were not so much words as they were intelligible growls, escaping between clenched jaws. "Last night your rhythm guitar player called in sick and is apparently still not coming despite lack of an adequate explanation. Today your keyboard player smashed his hands in a window, which may or may not be viable as an excuse in the city. Who opens their windows in San Francisco? Who smashes their hands in a window?"

There were eight of them on the other side of the bar, Kris concentrating on looking like himself to his inner circle while appearing different to others at the same time. Paul sat to his left, drinking whiskey like it was water and allowing himself to be lost in his thoughts. He wasn't frowning, so he was probably thinking of slaughter. Jessica sat to the Guide's right, her hands carefully folded in her lap. She had the serene composure of someone who had endured countless similar angry rants.

To Paul's left, directly in line with the devil's verbal barrage, were the four remaining band members and their new manager. Sarah, Mason and Cal sat at the bar and attentively absorbed the violent communication. Tyler and Jason stood behind them, both of them looking unusually interested in their own shoes.

No one answered Roche's questions.

"This one looked like living death for half the show the other night," Roche waved a beefy hand in Mason's direction, nearly knocking over the bottle of scotch he was sharing with Paul. "Your band members are dropping like flies, and your star can barely keep it together."

Mason stiffened and let his dark eyes rise to meet Roche's over the bar.

"I kept it together." He looked over his shoulder at the demon Paul had told Kris to ignore. "You don't have to worry about me."

The guitar player straightened in his chair and met the devil's eyes again. "And Sarah's the star."

Roche drained the glass of tan intoxicant before him. "Point taken."

He set the glass not-so-gently back on the bar, bared his teeth again.

"Do I have anything to worry about?" He glanced at the guitar player's crimson companion. "Besides that?"

Cal threw a confused look over his shoulder.

"You don't have anything to worry about," he grinned. "We just wanted to let you know."

The devil pounded his fist on the wooden surface between them.

"Don't bother me with trivialities, just put on a good show." He refilled his tall glass and then leaned his girth in Paul's direction to fill the Walker's glass as well. The bottle was drained before the glass was full.

Roche glared at the pusher. "What are you so happy about, cokey?"

Cal laughed, his good mood not so easily ruined.

"These two recorded the better part of a hit song about four hours ago, grumpy," the band manager responded proudly. "It already has over a hundred thousand hits on YouTube and hundreds of comments."

"Can we hear the song?" Jessica asked.

Sarah flushed. "Oh, no. It's not done."

"You can watch the video." Cal pulled his phone from his pocket and swiped right. "I made sure to tag it at the end with the club name and address and what time the show starts tonight."

The little crowd huddled around the tiny screen, even Paul leaning forward to have a look. They were all quiet while the music played, a small sound in a big space. Then Sarah's recorded voice said, "That's all we've got so far." After that was a five second screen shot of a flyer from tonight's show.

"Busy night ahead." Roche hid his smile behind the drink. "You need help setting up?"

"We're good," Cal waved his hand.

Everyone had something to do, and they all moved to do it. Kris pulled Paul aside as the others disappeared.

"Where's Matt?" the Guide asked. It was good to see Paul in street clothes instead of layered in leather and gore.

"He's helping William prepare for the next strike," Paul retorted. "Matt has a surprisingly good mind for strategy."

"Matt?" Kris was careful not to raise his voice. "He's mortal. He can't go above with you."

Paul frowned. He had trimmed his beard back, though his hair was still way too long for him to have only been growing it for a week. His frown was easier to see now, for better or worse.

"He's with Andre," he answered brusquely. "And I don't think they are above."

"Does Matt have a thing for devil ass now too?" Kris was not so careful about not raising his voice this time, but no one heard.

Paul's stare was devoid of anger or defensiveness. He looked exhausted.

"It seems we all do," he sighed.

The Guide had had it. "Goddammit Paul, what the Hell is going on with you? I'm supposed to know more about you now, not less. I'm trying to respect your privacy, as you obviously don't want me around any more than necessary, but…well, goddamn!"

He had kept his voice low, but Kris felt his dead heart pounding angry in his chest.

Paul looked around, then held up the ancient watch that had changed everything.

He clicked it open, speaking slowly and quietly.

"You remember I was telling you about the five hands and their purposes?" Paul asked.

The Walker's eyes looked so sad, Kris had to look at the watch.

The Guide nodded.

"I told you what the fifth hand does."

He nodded again.

"What I didn't tell you is how much time I have left." Paul was looking at the face of the timepiece as well.

Kris could see the fifth hand, small and red and easy to miss. He would've noticed it before if it had been moving, he was sure of it. It was moving now, moving backwards like the demon countdown did when the hunt was on, counting down to something that the Guide was not sure he wanted to know.

"I am running out of time, buddy," Paul sighed. "Apparently the Universe is not pleased with the way I am doing things, or maybe the Walker Council actually made a decision. Either way, I've got about three or four hours Earth time left. And then…"

He shrugged, resigned to the fate he had brought upon himself.

"Change course," Kris sputtered. "Call off the next attack."

Paul was shaking his head. "Almost every decision I have made has been made with an eye on that countdown. I would have been dead or dehumanized long ago if I hadn't followed this path. This is what needs to be done, Kris."

The Guide felt Paul's hand on his shoulder, and for a moment he thought they were going somewhere.

"The rapid countdown started when I became king," Paul spoke quietly to his friend. "My hope is that it counts down to a Walker victory as well. Whatever happens, know that I lived a hundred lifetimes in the time I had."

The Walker sighed again. "I am ready for whatever is coming."

Kris looked at his friend, tears in his eyes.

Paul was saying goodbye.

The watch was still there between them, three hands moving slowly forward while one counted too quickly backwards.

The red demon hand was the only one that stood absolutely still, and only for a moment.

A glow began to come from the numbered face, a symbol the Guide had never seen illuminated. It looked like a cowboy hat, a Walker's hat. The hand began ticking and the countdown began; not for a hunt, but for a transformation.

"Hey guys," Mason's voice startled Kris, but not Paul. The key disappeared as the Walker's arm fell to his side.

"Sorry to interrupt," the guitar player cast a cautious glance around them to make sure no one was within earshot.

"He's a part of your…other life, isn't he?" Mason addressed Paul, indicating Kris.

The Walker looked as confused by the question as Kris felt.

Paul nodded slowly. "Yes. He is."

"Daemon said something big is happening in some other world, or some other part of the world." The guitarist wrung his talented hands. "He says I am supposed to help somehow."

Paul shook his head.

"What is going on has nothing to do with you or your demon," he answered crisply. "It sounds like you two are communicating pretty freely."

The Walker's frown was not at all friendly as he added, "Perhaps too freely."

Kris saw the demon approaching, eyes downcast as he wended a path across the room that ensured that anyone who could see him would see him.

"Walker King," the demon's voice was both otherworldly and somehow completely normal at the same time.

Kris backed a step away from it, instinctively.

"An angel came to me," the demon went on, solemn. "He told me that Mason would come to walk between worlds."

Kris narrowed his eyes, his customary response to anyone claiming to talk to God or an angel.

"What was this angel's name?" The Walker seemed skeptical, but not so much as the Guide.

The demon raised his eyes to meet the Walker's briefly.

"Andal," he said. His eyes found the floor again.

Paul nodded. He looked at Mason. "Come find me when you are done here."

A chill ran up the Guide's dead spine. When the man and his demon were out of earshot, he turned to Paul.

"What are you doing?" he demanded.

Their lengthy aside had not gone unnoticed. Jessica was stealing regular surreptitious glances at them while she set the island bar up for the night, and Roche was standing behind the bar and drying the same glass he had been for the last several minutes, looking at anything but them.

'I've become pretty tuned in to the key,' Paul's voice came softly in his head, startling Kris.

The Walker's eyes strayed meaningfully to the two devils, and Kris nodded imperceptibly.

'That decision bought me almost a full hour in Earth time. That's an eternity in Hell.' Paul's voice sounded again in his head.

'Is that what you want? An eternity in Hell? Is that where we're going?' Kris was hoping the last snoot full of acrid brimstone and sulfur he had endured would be the last he would have to endure. He was a Guide; he knew the state of his soul. No matter what happened in the next few hours, Kris was not slated for Hell.

Not anytime soon, anyway.

"Come on," Paul headed for the stairs. "I'll help you set up the bar."

In Kris' mind he said, *'The Watchers found the demon horde. They all seem to have shown up in another space like the one we found them in last time, only lower.'*

'What are you going to do?' The Guide climbed the stairs behind Paul.

'We have to fight them now.' The Walker's thoughts felt urgent and tense as he reached the top of the stairs. *'There seem to be more of them, and they are preparing for battle. Matt says they are forming barricades at regular intervals, smashing rocks into clubs and piling stones to hurl or sling at us.'*

They both went behind the bar. Kris reached into his pocket for the few keys he still needed, one of them fitted to the upstairs cash register.

'Why can't you just leave them there?' Kris thought it best to stick with the private transmissions. Devils had notoriously good hearing.

Paul stopped facing liquor bottles and frowned.

'They're spilling out into Hell,' the thought came. *'They are trying to attach themselves to devils. The Dragon Queen is not pleased. She is demanding that the Walker army finish what they started, and I am inclined to agree.'*

He busied his hands again. *'For my own reasons.'*

Paul was at his side then, his hand on his shoulder.

"I have somewhere I need to go before I..." he paused, startled at the sound of his own voice.

'I have something I need to do,' his voice sounded in the Guide's head. *'Will you come with me?'*

Kris looked around the bar. He did have a lot to do.

'It will only take a minute.' Paul's hand was still on his shoulder.

The Guide nodded, closing his eyes and bracing himself for the smell of sulfur.

The shift came, but there was no odor at all.

He knew where they were before he opened his eyes. Paul had a room in this place, as did the Guide. The one who spent the most time here was Andre.

The door opened almost the instant Paul knocked on it. Andre looked as he always looked, the loose folds of robe doing nothing to hide his belly. The Watcher greeted Paul with an ingratiating smile, then turned to Kris with disdain.

The Guide hadn't noticed Paul changing into his Walker outfit when they shifted, and only now did he realize he was the only one in street clothes.

He closed his eyes and changed his outfit.

Andre stepped into the hall wordlessly, like he sensed something important was afoot.

The Guide felt it too.

Paul let a hand fall on each of their shoulders.

"I'm not sure if this is going to work," he frowned. Then he closed his eyes.

The dead duo followed suit.

There was light then, a light that was so bright Kris thought he had opened his eyes. Then he actually opened them, and the brilliance blinded him for a moment. The first thing he saw when his eyes began to adjust to the intense illumination was Andre.

The Watcher seemed to be glowing, and he was definitely smiling. Kris wondered why he had found himself so annoyed with the Watcher. Andre was Andre; Kris saw nothing but calm acceptance of that as he looked at the Watcher in this place of light.

"Paul," It was Andre that spoke first. Even his voice sounded somehow pleasing to the Guide's ear. "Where are we?"

Paul wasn't looking at Andre, and apparently he wasn't listening to him either. He was staring at a big ball of particularly bright light that was hovering some distance away.

The Watcher followed Paul's gaze. His eyes widened in wonder.

"God?" Andre asked. His voice was whispered awe.

Kris felt his brow furrow.

That's silly, he thought. *There's no such thing.*

"No," Paul answered. "That is an Original Angel. He was created when the thought of God first came to God, when the idea of a Supreme Being had to be personified so the next level up would remain free of discord. Is that about right?"

Kris felt a sense of loving amusement coming from the glowing orb, and a soft sexless soothing voice issued forth from it.

"That's about right, Walker King," it said. "You have been doing your research."

Andre began to kneel, but the voice stopped him.

"That won't be necessary," it crooned.

The Watcher stood there instead, his hands dangling uselessly at his sides, smiling at the oversized light bulb. He was awestruck.

Kris frowned. He didn't get it.

"Where is Brenna?" Paul tossed the question at the light, and Kris felt his heart dropping to his stomach. In his final hours, his fate sealed and the fates of two armies uncertain in his mind, Paul didn't come here to meet God.

He came here to find Brenna.

The Watcher shot a disgusted look at the Walker King. "Of all the things you could ask him…"

Kris smiled. He thought it was sweet.

"You are asking the wrong question, Walker King." The light was not agreeing with Andre; it was simply stating a fact. "The right question will bring you the answer you seek by leading you to a new question."

The Walker King looked beaten. Kris didn't have to read the thoughts in Paul's shaking head to know what he was thinking.

We are all but pawns in someone else's game, the Guide thought sadly to himself. He raised his voice to address the light.

"What question should Paul be asking?" Kris ventured patiently.

Again came that sense of loving amusement, followed by an answer. "Who is Brenna, Guide. That is what your friend wants to know."

Working his jaw, Paul turned to Kris with a look of frustrated bewilderment.

The Guide shrugged.

"Who is Brenna?" Paul's voice was strained and thin.

"When I was created, another was created as well." Kris marveled at the voice, somehow in his head and in his ears at the same time. It was not booming or soft, nor male or female. It was just a voice.

"I was to reign in the highest realms, she in the lowest. I took the job I was given by those whose belief shaped and maintained me, and for some time I have had little to do but contemplate my elevated existence." The voice sounded neither pleased nor displeased with its situation.

"My counterpart's job was admittedly harder, and even more thankless than mine," the voice continued. "She bore up under it, however, and learned to manage Hell with efficiency. Not long ago, a few hundred years of your Earth time, she turned the reins over to her oldest friend. Thus did the Dragon Princess become the Dragon Queen."

Paul crossed his arms and let his frown deepen. "What does this have to do with Brenna?"

"One of the conditions my counterpart accepted was that she would never return to Hell or attempt to regain her throne. The one you know as Lilia could not have ruled effectively if she was not given full and complete dominion. My counterpart could not transfer her powers as she did her title, however; she would have ceased to exist, as would anyone trying to wield her power. She found a way to contain and conceal them somewhere outside of herself, not anticipating that the Dragon Queen might be so consumed with the looming threat that she would try to find it. When my counterpart was recently sent to Hell in human form through no design of her own, the looming threat seemed imminent to the Dragon Queen." The voice went on as if it hadn't heard the Walker. It was measured and calm, without sex but not without emotion. The Guide tried to identify the light's emotional tone as he pieced together the story of its simple words.

"My counterpart has many names," the voice said. "I know her as Ximena, as does the Dragon Queen. You know her as Brenna, and in the human form taken by the Queen of Hell when she renounced her throne."

"Brenna is a devil," Kris murmured under his breath.

"No," Andre corrected him, even in his exalted state. "Brenna is *The* Devil."

Paul ignored both of them. "Is that why she bled purple and disappeared?"

"Now begin the right questions." The voice spoke again, and Kris identified the tone that strung together its words.

It was love. It neither spoke down at or up to the Walker. The voice was explaining just the way Paul needed it to, because the voice was love. Kris felt a tension release inside of him with the realization.

"The one you know as Brenna is fully human. Being fully human, she was vulnerable like a human," the voice explained patiently. "She was given a talisman inhabited by a demon you had killed. You cut a demon's head off, Walker, one that had possessed the human body of Brenna Blanco."

The voice paused before its final proclamation.

"You did not kill your love," it said at last. "She is not lost."

Something in Paul seemed to relax at the light's words. Kris glanced at the Walker to see a tear slip from one eye to trace its way unnoticed into his beard.

His face was set as Paul asked the next right question.

"Where is Ximena?"

"Stay your path, Walker King." The voice and the light both seemed to be fading. "It will lead you to what you seek."

The light was gone.

It wasn't, though, not really. Kris could sense it all around him, could feel it within him. He saw it in the lighted luminescence of the sturdy clouded surface underfoot, and in the Walker's eyes when they met his own.

"Don't go," Andre moaned piteously.

"What did you see?" Paul's voice was clear and crisp and somehow brighter. Something in him had changed. His question was addressed to Andre.

"I saw God," The Watcher replied with disgust. "How do you not know God when you see him?"

"What did God look like?" the Walker persisted. "Specifically?"

"Well...he looked like God," he sputtered. "Old and wise, with a long flowing robe, full white hair and beard...the way God is supposed to look..."

The Watcher trailed off. "Why? Isn't that what you saw?"

Paul smiled at Kris. It wasn't a big smile; he wasn't brimming over with joy or anything. It was just a small upturn at the corners of his mouth, yet it conveyed all the love and gratitude Paul had for his best friend and the role he played in his life.

"What did you see?" Paul asked him quietly.

The smile was gone, but the love wasn't. It never had been, Kris saw that now.

The Guide felt his own heart swell.

"I saw a ball of light," he answered honestly.

The Watcher glared at him.

CHAPTER 42

Cal was keeping both eyes on the excited crowd tonight. One eye was already trained as a customer radar; the pusher could spot a user at twenty paces and broker a deal in thirty seconds. The other eye was watching for suspicious characters. He was not in the mood for any unpleasant surprises.

Long ago, he had trained himself not to let his hand stray protectively to his money pocket or his powder pocket. His new job was to pretend that the cold lethal hunk of metal jammed into the front of his slacks wasn't there. It surprised him how often his hand began to reach for it, just to touch it.

He resisted the urge.

The band sounded better than ever tonight, and Cal would not have thought they were one number down if he didn't know them. He liked the clean and tight sound the four of them created together. The pusher stood there and watched them from time to time, turning on his two peripheral radars and being proud of his new legit job.

He had thought of going out to his car more than once; but he hadn't been in the black yet, and people were still flooding the entrance. Now, finally, his money pocket bulged fatter than his powder pocket, and the crowd was at the bar and on the dance floor.

Making his way to the glass doorway, Cal scanned the bar surreptitiously. No one was following him.

There was a cluster of vapers and smokers outside, making no effort at discretion as they passed a pot pipe. Cal crinkled his nose and made for his car. He had parked in the same spot as last night, without thinking about it. A wave of deja vu swept over him, and Cal's knees turned rubber for a moment as his eyes imagined a shadow shifting behind his Acura.

Refusing to break stride, he slipped his left hand under his dark buttoned shirt. As his hand closed around the grip of the pistol, the shadow moved again.

He had sat in his car for an hour, pulling the handgun from his waistband and chambering a round. Cal didn't like the direction the barrel pointed when he carried it that way, so he didn't feel comfortable walking around with the thing ready to fire. He had to be quick and comfortable about chambering a round, releasing the magazine and ejecting the round, pushing the round back into the clip and sliding the clip home. So he did it over and over, sitting in his car in a park, until the gun and its mechanisms were familiar to his hands.

When the shadow came from behind the car, Cal's hands moved smoothly to produce the unmistakable click and clack that a semiautomatic weapon makes when it becomes lethal. The shadow hesitated, and Cal heard footfalls behind him. He turned as quickly as he could, meeting the second attacker face-to-face for a moment before they went down together. The barrel of the gun was poking something, and it wasn't Cal, so he pulled the trigger twice. The sound was loud and immediate, but muffled for being squashed between them. Both brief rapid concussive blows had been like a surprising punch to his belly, and he lay there dazed and worried under his twitching attacker as the other approached. Cal felt weight on top of him, but it was dead weight. He rolled, and it slid easily to one side.

The other man was upon him, swinging his fists. They were wide and sloppy swings, slow roundhouses from both sides. Cal tried to pull the trigger again, but the gun wasn't in his hand anymore. One clumsy fist caught his left cheek, and the pusher's head rocked to the right to catch the following punch square on his jaw. Cal had regained his knee, but it went out from under him as he reeled from the second blow. He saw nothing but white starbursts for a long confusing moment, and he forgot entirely where he was.

Another fist came at him just as the reality of the situation returned to Cal. It was strange and magickal, the clenched fingers moving toward him and away from him at the same time. Cal saw the men who grabbed his jacket to pull the attacker off him.

Standing, slowly, shaky, Cal glanced at the entrance to the club. The smokers had disappeared, not having any interest in a scuffle or a police encounter. No wonder nearly half the murders in the city went unsolved. Cal turned back to his saviors, the two men that had pulled the other man off Cal and the three men emerging from the shadows behind them.

The pusher's brow furrowed. "Raul?"

His boyish face grinned in response. "It sounded like you needed a little more help than I gave you."

Cal glared at the masked man struggling between Raul's comrades. Both men had jeans and wife-beaters on, with handguns tucked into their waistbands; the sleeves on their arms were made of ink, and some of the patterns on one matched the other. Cal looked to see if Raul and the other two tattooed angels were blatantly packing as well. They were.

One of the men reached up with a free hand to yank the ski mask from the attacker's head.

"You know this piece of shit, Holmes?" Raul's accent was stronger than ever, probably how he always sounded when he hung out with other gun-toting color-wearing tatted up Latinos. Cal didn't mind; it was nice to have friends.

"No." Cal shook his head. White guy, longish hair, clean shaven, didn't look like anyone he knew.

Raul moved to the inert form on the pavement, sidestepping a puddle of blood forming in the street.

He rolled the body over, pulled off the mask. "How about this one?"

Cal felt the blood drain from his face.

It was Mikie. His cheeks were drawn from cocaine and death, but that was him. No wonder he hadn't shown up to play; he'd been too busy rolling Cal and doing his coke.

Sonofabitch.

"I knew that piece of shit," Cal muttered.

Bending to retrieve the weapon that Cal had dropped, Raul offered it to him. "You want to finish it?"

The full reality of the situation came crashing in on him then. He had just murdered Mikie. The gun he had used, the cocaine he had, the whole ball of wax made calling the cops an inevitable prison sentence.

Cal gulped, swallowing the feeling.

Fuck it, he thought to himself. *In for a penny, in for a pound.*

He took the gun and fired three quick rounds into his assailant's chest.

CHAPTER 43

Mason needed a moment to himself, a moment long enough to get away from the clamor of drunken club goers and needy band members and his ever-present girlfriend. He found it in the alley behind the bar, the same alley he had smoked with Paul in.

He pulled a joint out of his cigarette pack and lit it, inhaling the deliciously distinct flavor of Holy Grail. Mason was glad at the thought that neither Daemon nor Sarah had seen him slip out during the break. He was glad for their presence in his life, but it got hard to remember that moment to moment when they were constantly by his side. His sweet inner garden of loneliness had grown overgrown and neglected.

The cool night air felt good on his face, his skin relieved to be out from under the stage lights. Mason puffed languidly on the cannabis cigarette, listening to the jukebox in his head as it began to play an old bluesy favorite. His growing talent had him far more interested in tone and structure and composition these days, and he was constantly going back over the contents of his musical memory looking for things he hadn't seen before. In addition to that, riding in Cal's car was always a choice between no music and the pusher's favorite band.

Smiling softly, he pulled the smoke deep into his lungs and listened to the memory of Great White's "House of Broken Love" in his mind. It had been tugging at the corner of his brain ever since the last time he had chosen music in Cal's car. When Jack Russell's silky smooth voice began singing, Mason's foot began to tap softly on the pavement in time with the nonexistent music.

There was a bit of a clamor around the corner, voices raised in good-natured disagreement and laughter. Mason tuned it out, hoping he would be left alone with his smoke and his song.

It was not to be. Footsteps were sounding in the alley, the unmistakable click of high heels falling at irregular drunken intervals. Mason thought of extinguishing the joint, then thought better of it. He smoked and waited, listening to the steps growing louder as they drew closer. The song faded to the customary volume of the jukebox in his mind, continuing its endless playlist.

She came around the corner with a giggle and a hiccup. One hand came to her face as she came into view, brushing long blonde hair behind her ear. The red and black stilettos on her feet made her almost as tall as Mason, and he could see the muscles of her bare legs flex and shift as she moved. A skin tight tube of thin material painted her wide hips and bulbous buttocks and clung to her flat belly and small breasts. Her eyes were blue and bright and mischievous.

"I thought I smelled Mary Jane," she cooed, clicking a few steps closer. Her voice was nasal and flat. Mason tried not to think of Sarah's sultry tones.

He held the remaining half of the joint out to her. "Want some?"

In his mind, the band played on. The guitar solo was starting, the main reason Mason had punched in the unseen combination of mental keys that had brought up the song and started it playing.

"Oh, that's good," the smiling blonde took another hit before handing it back to him.

"Yep." Mason puffed away, blew out smoke rings in the still night air. A very small amount of his attention was on the exchange. As far as he was concerned, she was talking about the solo he was listening intently to.

She was peering at him closely. Nonetheless, she ignored the hand he held out to her.

"Hey," her blue eyes went from a pretty almond shape to round seas of surprise, "you're that guitar player."

She pivoted in place, as if to address a nearby friend and say, 'he's that guitar player!'

They were alone in the alley, however, so she turned back to him and said it again. "You're that guitar player."

"Yep." He took another hit, held it out to her again.

She accepted it this time, the mischievous glint in her eye brightening. "I saw you on YouTube; that was awesome." She took a small puff.

"You and that girl are going to be famous." When she said "that girl", she took the tone of voice one might use in a first-hand recollection of some personal holocaust tragedy.

Her heels clicked as she shifted, moving almost imperceptibly closer to Mason.

"You're cute," she giggled.

He took the joint back from her, playing his strong silent card and waiting to see where she would go with it.

"In a few years you will have a million rock star stories to tell," she bit her lip, and her light eyes gleamed with drunken daring. "But you'll never forget this one."

The pretty blonde kicked off her heels and stood barefoot in front of him for a deliciously pregnant forever moment, biting her lower lip and looking up at him. Then she was on her knees, fumbling with his black leather belted jeans.

Mason put the joint between his lips and reached down, unbuckling and unbuttoning. He tangled the fingers of one hand in her blonde mane and pinched the dwindling joint carefully between the thumb and forefinger of the other. He smoked and smiled as she took him in her mouth with a moan.

It had taken awhile for Daemon to find Sarah when the band broke. He had assumed finding her would mean finding Mason, so he had tuned in to her lovely frequency. The draw had brought him to the door of the ladies' room, where he had waited politely.

When she came out, he followed her, feeling bad that she couldn't see him. When she went out the front door in her rubber-soled sandals, he flanked her as respectfully as he could. Mason must have told her to meet him outside.

Sarah's steps were nearly as silent as Daemon's, and they reached the end of the alley at the same time. She froze, her eyes on Mason with his back to her.

The singer and the demon stood there side-by-side in silent static horror.

Then Sarah turned and walked quietly back up the alley.

Daemon followed.

There was a lone tear on her face, a malevolent scowl on his.

CHAPTER 44

Just as the top of the head of the last customer descending from the stairs dipped from the Guide's view, Paul appeared across the bar from him.

He was still in his street clothes, but Paul had that unmistakable forever stare that old Walkers get. Kris wondered if he was dreading the coming storm or if he looked forward to it. Probably a bit of both.

"You ready?" Paul still had a distance in his blue eyes, even when he looked right at him.

Kris shrugged. "Sure."

The Walker was not so self-absorbed that he missed the uncertain tone in which Kris replied. "What's on your mind?"

He shrugged again. "It's nothing. It's foolish…it's nothing compared to what you've got on your plate."

Paul surprised him, sliding onto a barstool and propping his elbows on the bar. "Talk to me."

Maybe Paul had also realized that this may be the last words they would exchange in this manner in this lifetime. Face to face and alone, they had navigated the treacherous paths of dating and working and living as young normal men in an old and strange world. Since they had both become something much different than normal young men, they hadn't had opportunity for a lot of lengthy asides. Kris missed their talks; it was nice to think that maybe Paul missed them as well.

Kris smiled to soften the blow his words were about to deal.

"I've been thinking…you know, when the clock runs out on you…" He shrugged once more. "What happens to me? What's a Guide without a Walker?"

Paul grimaced. "I've thought about that too, buddy. Even in a best case scenario, our soul schedules are on a much different timeline now."

Kris looked at him, confused. He remembered a time not so long ago when he was the one having to explain things to Paul. "What do you mean?"

"I spent too much time trying to find Brenna by trying to figure out the whole goddamned Universe," Paul spoke through his frown. "I didn't realize my soul would only rise for so long until I had been at it for some time. One of the reasons I was able to finally visit the highest realm a soul can survive intact is because my own soul was peaking."

Paul laughed, a forced chuckle that sounded pained. "It's all been downhill from there."

"So that was really God?" the Guide asked doubtfully.

"No." Paul answered quickly.

He seemed to reconsider.

"Yes," Paul sighed. "I suppose so."

"What did you see?" The Guide wondered if it was a ball of light or some old geezer. Maybe it had been Brenna.

Paul was staring at nothingness, lost in some thought that he might not feel like sharing.

What if he had seen Brenna? Kris thought. *What a mind fuck that would be.*

He shouldn't have asked.

Loud heavy footfalls sounded, someone or something big rushing up the staircase.

Roche skipped the last two steps and bounded into the space. His eyes were narrowed and his nostrils were flared. One corner of his mouth was lifted to show a sharp canine.

"I know what you two are up to," he growled, his eyes swirling scarlet.

Paul's sword was suddenly there, as sharp as his voice.

"Are you going to try and stop me?" he asked.

"Of course not, jackass," Roche countered. "I'm here to help."

"How can you help?" Paul relaxed his stance but kept the sword. "You're in exile."

"The Dragon Queen offered to lift my exile if I brought her your head and hand," Roche mused in a quiet growl. "And this."

The devil slowly raised one meaty paw, straightening three thick fingers as it reached shoulder height between them. A small agate oval dropped to the end of the length of silver chain still pinched between the devil's thumb and forefinger.

"That's Brenna's," Paul breathed. "Where did you get that?"

"This amulet belongs to Ximena," Roche sighed. "The Dragon Queen was asking around about it more than ever recently, and I knew I could find it. In exchange for your platinum upgrade, and the ensuing continued existence of Walkers, I agreed to find and take the artifact that contained Ximena's powers. I did not, however, agree to give it to the Dragon Queen."

An evil smile showed them both the devil's sharp biting teeth, and his voice held a touch of awe as he spoke the name again. "Ximena always could draw up an airtight contract like no one else."

Roche's eyes were narrowed to black and red slits as he eyed Paul. "I did not know who she was until I took your Agent's key and went looking for the artifact. I expected to search the worlds, and I found it in my own backyard. Your pretty perfect Brenna-"

"I know," Paul cut him off. "She's the devil."

He sounded unusually calm for someone making such a pronouncement.

"I am fully aware of what you know, Walker King, and where you have been. You have walked between worlds as no other, and twisted time to suit your purpose." The devil looked and spoke like a proud father counting off his son's achievements.

Paul's eyes widened, and his relaxed sword disappeared to be replaced by the ticking timepiece.

"Shit," he swore fiercely. "Time."

Quick steps ascending the stairs had them all three turning to see. Mason stopped at the last step, sensing he was intruding.

"Take it," Roche thrust the necklace at Paul. "She needs it."

Paul took the stone and chain, glaring accusing daggers at the devil but not speaking.

"Hey, guys," Mason threw a quick smile in their general direction. "Sorry to interrupt. Have you seen Sarah?"

He lowered his voice for the next question. "Or Daemon?"

Kris shook his head. "Great show."

"Thanks." Mason's attention shifted to Paul.

"No." Paul crossed the space between them in three quick strides; his feet hardly seemed to touch the floor. "Don't worry about them."

Kris could see that Paul had one hand on the guitar player's shoulder, but he couldn't see what Paul's other hand was doing until Mason collapsed into the Walker's arms. Roche just stood there, his arms crossed across his chest.

Paul pulled the dagger free, and Kris saw the bloodstained blade flash in the sparing bar light before it disappeared.

Roche nodded and moved to the stairs.

"We're not done, devil," Paul growled at his wide retreating back.

"No, we're not." Roche stopped and turned. "But you are. Best of luck, Walker King. Give Ximena my regards."

The devil descended the stairs, leaving more slowly than he had come.

Gaping at Paul over the bar, Kris watched him gather the lifeless body in his arms and toss Mason over his shoulder like a sack of potatoes. Blood dripped onto the floor to quickly form an alarmingly large puddle.

Paul glanced at the blood, then at Kris.

"Sorry," he winced. "I'll clean that up in a minute. Be right back."

He was gone.

Before Kris could draw a breath Paul stood in the same place he had just vacated. He looked questioning at the clean carpet where the blood had puddled.

Kris shrugged. "I've learned some things too."

It looked like Paul was about to smile.

He frowned instead. "It's time, buddy."

"I know." The Guide felt the robe materialize against his skin.

Kris cast out his mental line, felt Paul snag it. He didn't need to cross the room or place his hand on the Guide's shoulder one last time.

They both closed their eyes to walk between worlds.

By the time Kris opened his eyes, the Walker King was striding away from him swathed in oiled leather. He was rapidly approaching a knot of Walkers practicing swordplay, the liquid glow underfoot. The luminous walls made their swinging swords flash with light. Matt stood with Walker William, watching two men clang away in a friendly spar.

The Guide remembered the bottomless flask he hadn't had much use for since partially reclaiming his humanity. Another thought and he held the cold metal in his hand. Kris untwisted the cap and let his Adam's apple bob up and down a few times before recapping it.

Wiping his mouth with the sleeve of his robe, Kris smiled crookedly as a wave of dizziness swayed him.

That was pretty good stuff.

'*Guides,*' he broadcasted mentally, serious and sober. '*This is not the same situation we encountered last time. The demons are prepared. We are lower, so the demons will be stronger and faster while our Walkers will be slower and weaker.*'

'*Not your Walker.*'

The thought came at him with a spiteful tone, an anonymous comment in a sea of attentive minds.

Kris waited, rather than respond.

'*Your Walker's soul is falling.*'

'*Your Walker carouses with the Queen of Hell.*'

'*Your Walker turned his back on God.*'

They were all different voices, overlapping in the network of Guide minds. Then came the first voice again, the spite turned to sneer.

'Your Walker has gone immortal mad.'

'Enough.' Kris felt as though his heart might break. *'Do your Walkers not wish to follow him?'*

There was a mental grumbling, then a clear and clearly unhappy answer.

'Our Walkers will follow him anywhere, to a man.' A general murmur of assent followed.

A wise older woman's voice sounded in his head for the first time. *'The women feel the same.'*

Kris smiled inwardly.

'Then do your jobs,' he commanded coldly. *'Report any unusual demon activity or Walkers in trouble to me immediately. Dismissed.'*

Matt was examining Samuel's pistol with care when the Guide came up behind him and clapped him on the back. There was something different about Matt, something other than the shaggy uncut dark mane of hair and the patchy whiskers on his face. He shot Kris a quick smile and returned his attention to the antique revolver, reversing it to hold the handle out to its owner.

"You and that beautiful gun should lead the assault with Paul," Matt nodded to the cowboy as he holstered the hefty piece. He turned to Kris. "I'm having the Walkers pair up, at least in the beginning. One will press forward while the other guards his or her back. One Guide should watch the pair while the other Guide looks for clues as to where the dispatched demons are going. There have already been reports of demons in the lowest realm, and if a chance to follow a fleeing or fading enemy presents itself, I have instructed the Walker teams to take it. Have your Guides report back to Paul or William or me if a Walker team shifts in battle."

Kris eyed him with a suspicious kind of awe. Matt had changed; he was a part of an elite army of supernaturals. Not just a part, but an officer of some kind. The gathered Walkers all seemed to move around him or William or Paul as focal points, and none seemed to question Matt's hatless head or the status that went with it. When he spoke, they listened. When he joked with them, they laughed. And when he reached out his hand, a nearby Walker slapped the hilt of his sword into Matt's waiting palm without hesitation. The lone human raised the blade over his head and began to address the army.

"Walkers!" Matt's voice was strong and confident. He already had most of their attention; the rest turned at his voice, Paul and William among them. "Many of you fought in the first wave behind the Walker King, many of you did not. Consider yourselves equally unprepared for the battle ahead. This situation will be different in every way, and the lot of you has been chosen for your skills as warriors. Thus are you all equally prepared as well."

Kris tuned out the speech and the man reluctantly. He communicated what he needed to over the invisible Guide network, using the miraculous ability like a perfunctory tool. The Guide noted with relief that Andre and his Watcher ilk were either elsewhere or invisible.

One short speech had given way to another, and Paul was wrapping that up to a collective uproar of clanging swords and shouting voices. There were twice as many Walkers present as there had been at the first strike. The army had taken on a more worldly feel, the cowboy hats in the crowd outnumbered by turbans and samurai or tribal headdresses. They were as fearsome in their war garb as the Western Walkers.

A doorway opened once again. This time black acrid smoke poured through the opening. Perhaps the demons had found more things to burn that made easily picking them off from a convenient vantage point with arrows impossible; or maybe this realm was just so densely choked with smoke as part of its more malefic nature. Either way, the shortsighted effect was the same.

Kris felt the wave of heat hit him as Walkers leapt or dropped carefully from the lip of the portal to disappear in pairs into the obscured realm beyond. There were no archers this time, he hadn't noticed until now. Hopefully they knew what they were up against; the Guide certainly didn't.

As the last of the supernatural army were enveloped in smoke, Kris thought of Paul. Instantly, he was behind the Walker King and to his right. He wasn't the only one, however; Samuel was there, too. He followed Paul step for step, only slightly off to the side. His Guide drifted along in his wake, just to the cowboy's right. Kris had appeared between Samuel and his Guide.

Samuel began to turn, then Kris was caught in a wave of emotion that spoke a clear message with no words: *NO DANGER.* The gunman went back to methodically exploding demon heads to Paul's right.

That was not at all like his communication with Paul. Kris pivoted to thank the other Guide, and was surprised that he was surprised to see a woman. She appeared to be in her late thirties or early forties, but that would just be her age when she died. Had she changed her appearance at all over the centuries she had guided Samuel, even that age might be misrepresented. Shorter still than Samuel, she had narrow shoulders and broad hips. The voluminous Guide robe was not voluminous enough to cover her shapely form.

He smiled. *'Thanks. I'm Kris.'*

'I know.' The thought was crystal clear. Even her mental voice sounded feminine. *'Nice to meet you, King of the Guides. I am Guide Mary.'*

'Exactly what level of formality would you like to communicate on, Guide Mary?' He made sure the thought had a tone of friendly mirth.

Her hair was pinned carefully atop her head, mousy brown tresses wound about itself so that not a strand dared escape. Her eyes were a shade darker than her hair, and they crinkled when she smiled. *'None would suffice, Kris.'*

The Guide nodded.

'Excellent, Mary.' He smiled back. *'What's the situation?'*

Disentangling her hands from the sleeves of her robe, she gestured at their Walkers. His eyes followed the motion.

'Progress is slower,' her voice came softly in his head

The Walker King was his usual brutal self, spinning two swords like fast-forwarded helicopter blades at an ocean of crimson flesh. He moved forward, but at a steady measured gait. It was faster than a human could move, but for the Walker it was hardly more than walking pace. Samuel's pistol was firing faster than before, and more than one exploding spray of purple gore spattered the swordsman or the gunman as the Guide looked on.

Fighting the urge to lose his bellyful of mysterious flask juice, Kris turned his attention again to Mary.

Another thought-feeling hit him, and although there were no words it was a clear danger message: *BEHIND YOU. THEN TO YOUR LEFT.*

Although he knew he was in no danger, the message was so strong and immediate. It felt like his own, an intense thought-feeling that he couldn't deny or think away. Kris whirled, a moment after Samuel.

BOOM! Click. BOOM! A demon exploded in the Guide's face, blinding him with gore but not staining him with it.

The message was for the Walker, of course. Kris smiled a little sheepishly at the older Guide. *'What is that communication? Why do you communicate differently with me?'*

Her eyes didn't just crinkle when she smiled, her whole wise face lit up.

'He's a cowboy,' her voice in his head replied. *'He lives by intuition. You want clear concise words.'*

Kris nodded. *'Do you have them covered?'*

She returned his nod. *'What are you up to?'*

'I'm going to try to link up mentally with a demon that is about to be killed,' he replied. Kris hoped he sounded more confident in the idea than he felt.

There was that smile again. *'To see where it goes. Clever.'*

Her hands were intertwined in the sleeves of her robe again, her eyes watching the slaughter.

'That one,' her voice came in his mind, along with the flash image of a hulking monster loping toward Paul.

The Guide cast out his thought, trying to mingle feeling with it like Mary seemed to do. He felt the demon's hate as he attached to him.

The hulking monster nearly halted as it neared Paul, its round angry eyes glazing over. Kris looked out from behind its hateful eyes, watching his friend approach with a sword in each hand and a slight smile pulling at the corners of his mouth. He hadn't realized until this moment how terrifying his best friend could look when he was bathed in blood and lost in the dance of battle.

The Walker King leapt and slashed, and the Guide's world went black.

CHAPTER 45

William fought as quickly as he could, striking one beheading blow after another with precision and without pause. It was not long before he caught up with Paul and Samuel. Even with his Walker vision, he couldn't see the killing pair until he was nearly upon them, zeroing in on their location in the thick smoke by listening to the gunfire.

He saw Samuel first, jogging along and cutting a lethal swath through the demon horde ahead of him and slightly off to the right. The cowboy's speed was impressive, his short denimed legs pushing him forward rapidly with powerful strides. William swung his blade expertly and almost absently, beheading two demons that stood too close together for too long with one powerful swing of his longsword.

Running to keep up with them, slashing and stabbing ahead and to the right, William dared a quick glance at his flanking Walker. Short and lithe, the man never stopped moving. His stern face was unmistakably Japanese, hair trimmed short to his head while a sprinkle of whiskers dotted his upper lip. He wielded two swords like the Walker King did. They were two long curved narrow blades, and they flashed a hypnotizing light work show in the sparkling illumination of raging fire that dotted the landscape. Although his weapons were much like the score of samurai that now swelled their ranks, he did not wear the light and colorful armor that they did. His simple cloth robe looked like it belonged on a simple human priest, or a Guide, except that it spun and swished in time with his rapid violent unceasing movement.

Mikeo was fine. William brought his whole attention to bear again on fortifying the king's flank. There was Samuel, loping along. His boot would touch the ground, and he would push forward and up. While in the air, between strides, he would squeeze off a half dozen rapid fire rounds. The next boot would touch the charred rock underfoot for a moment as six headless bodies dropped, and then he was aloft and firing once more.

William was thinking that the gunman was a magnificent killing machine when he glimpsed Paul just beyond the cowboy. The Walker King moved amazingly fast, turning and leaping and ducking, all while chopping demons to pieces with swords that never slowed enough to be seen. He was covered in gore; not just blood like the others and William himself, but actual chunks of flesh that stuck to his overcoat and oozed slowly down rivulets of more liquid gore.

Just as William and his partner caught up, a wall of stacked rock loomed beyond the smoke and sea of bodies.

"Walkers, to the wall!" Paul's voice sounded, and the four of them came together at the base of the piled stones. They fought there for a few bloody moments, five swords and one pistol cutting down demons by the dozen. Then they stood alone together, looking up at a wall that disappeared into the miasma overhead, their feet in rapidly evaporating puddles of sticky purple blood.

A low rumble started, and the four killing machines had just enough time to exchange glances before being buried in tumbling stone.

CHAPTER 46

Mason woke with a start, his hand going reflexively to his wounded abdomen. There was no pain, his searching fingers found no cut under his shirt. The smell of beer spilt or sweated out or both assaulted his nostrils.

"You're awake." The voice was what a snake would sound like if it could talk, a dry papery hiss. Mason started at the sound, twisting in the bunk he was laying in. The mattress was firm but comfortable, and someone had thrown covers over him. Squinting in the dim light, he could only tell that four walls were close and three dim forms were closer.

He sat up, shivering involuntarily. Those shadows had horns. All three of them.

"Mason." It was that reptilian voice again. He thought it sounded somehow familiar. Two of the shapes were huddled together, but the other sat in a corner alone. That was the one talking to him.

"Mason," it said again, rising to its feet. "Can you walk? Can you fight?"

Scooting back, away from the slowly approaching shadow with the two pointed horns and the leathery voice, Mason realized he didn't need to squint. A thought that was somehow his own and not his own sounded in his head. *I want to see this room clearly.*

As if a light switch had been thrown, every detail of the room was suddenly made clear to him. The gray brick of the walls that looked like dark woven smoke, the gray blankets covering him, the three red-skinned horn-headed monsters looking at him curiously. Stacks of empty unlabeled bottles lined one wall, mirrored on the far wall by cases of beer that had been bottled and labeled. Glass jugs were everywhere, filled with what would soon be beer under a mountain of dark froth. The spouts on the jugs were carefully fitted to fill the room with the stink of the concoction at every imaginable stage. The capped bottles were labled with tall proud lettering that said "Devil's Brew".

The bunk wouldn't allow him to back away any further, so Mason searched the face that belonged to the voice that knew his name.

"Daemon?" Now he scooted closer. "Daemon? Is that you?"

The other two monsters looked at the third with undisguised contempt.

Daemon nodded, not some mirage glimpsed through a haze of uncertainty but a solid three-dimensional monster.

"Can you fight?" the demon asked again.

"Well…" Mason shrugged helplessly. "…I don't know anything about fighting, so I would say no."

The other two had a different look to them, more hard and reptilian. Maybe Daemon just looked monstrous in a way that had become familiar to him. They turned their collective sneer on Mason.

"Can you stand?" Daemon ignored the other two.

Mason stood up. "Yeah, sure."

Daemon touched the wall. "Picture you and I standing on the other side of this wall."

"Okay." He looked at the demon doubtfully.

"Close your eyes. Imagine it as vividly as possible."

The other two burst out laughing then, one chuckling darkly and the other howling a high-pitched death rattle of mirth.

"The demon is teaching the baby Walker how to walk," the chuckling one said between guffaws.

"The demon has a *name*," the other shrieked.

Mason closed his eyes, trying to tune them out. He realized he didn't know what it looked like on the other side of this wall, and he opened his eyes again to regard Daemon and ignore the others.

"What does it look like on the other side of this wall?" The chortling monsters howled with a fresh wave of cruel laughter, and began to mock the conversation they were trying to have.

"Oh demon," one crooned effeminately, "What do I do?"

"Close your eyes," the other sing-songed, "dream of a better place. Believe it, baby Walker, believe it with all your heart…"

"Oh demon," the first widened his reptilian eyes and then blinked them rapidly, "what would I do without you?"

They were laughing hysterically again, and Daemon even seemed a bit annoyed with Mason. He frowned, closed his eyes, and thought intensely of he and the demon on the other side of the wall.

He opened his eyes to a world of light. It was too much at first, woven colors dancing and shifting all around him and even underfoot. Then his eyes adjusted, and he saw that the other half of the strange space was filled with thick black smoke. It seemed to disappear when it touched the luminous floor or ceiling or walls, so it wasn't threatening to engulf the entire room no matter how thick it poured into the space. That's what it was doing, Mason saw, it was pouring through a hole that had been torn in the far wall of light.

Daemon came around the other side of the small building of dark woven light that he assumed they had just been inside. He was holding a pile of black leather in one hand, a cowboy hat on top of folded oiled layers. The other hand held a sword, a clean beautiful double-edged longsword nearly as tall as the demon holding it.

Feeling his eyes go wide, Mason seized the sword as Daemon held both hands out toward him. It felt lighter than it looked, or maybe his skinny arms were somehow stronger. He swung and stabbed the empty air a few times, awkwardly, like a guitarist with a sword.

"Good," Daemon's papery voice was brusque. "You can fight. Put this on."

Mason regarded his companion warily, letting the tip of the longsword dip into the clouded light underfoot.

"I don't know how to fight," he reiterated.

Daemon opened his mouth to respond, but Mason raised the sword and pointed it at him.

"And," Mason gritted through his teeth, "what the hell is wrong with you? I can see you and talk to you like you're a real person, and you're talking to me like I'm your little bitch. What the hell, Daemon?"

Still holding out the pile of leather, the demon averted his eyes. "I saw what you did to Sarah. You shouldn't have done that."

"What?" Mason thought back, remembered. "That had nothing to do with Sarah."

"You shouldn't have done that," he said again. "Put this on. We have to go."

CHAPTER 47

Riding a demon's death from one world to another was quite a bit different than walking between worlds on the coattails of a leather duster. There was an inky blackness that seemed to go on forever, where the only thing Kris had to hold onto was the tenuous mental link he had with the monster tumbling with him through the void.

For a while it seemed they were floating in timeless spaciousness; then a pull somewhat like gravity asserted itself, and they were falling. As if gaining mass and momentum at the same time, the Guide and the demon were pulled inexorably in a directionless direction. A strange sensation followed, like he was being pressed bodily into a silken spider's web or a giant malleable soap bubble. That gravity-like force pulled him from the other side, while the strange soft unyielding wall he pressed against wrapped about him like a second skin.

There was a soft soundless sigh and a pressure change. It felt like it felt when his ears popped, only it was his whole being that popped. Kris didn't feel like he was walking through a doorway; he felt as though he was being pushed through a wall. Colors and smells and sounds assaulted his senses in a kaleidoscope of pleasant confusion as he regained body and awareness on the other side.

Smoke above and charred rock below, Kris didn't need to see the fires that burned on every horizon or breathe in the brimstone stench to know where they were. He saw blurred forms in the distant sky, shrouded in smoke. The hoarse shrieks and guttural cries of fear and triumph combined with clanging metal indicated a fray nearby.

The demon he had ridden here was either unaware of the Guide or unconcerned with his presence. It stood with its broad wide back to him, flexing its muscles and stretching its limbs as if they were coursing with raw power. The tall monster growled and smacked its lips grotesquely, the thick cords of sinew standing out above and below his leather kilt in stark definition. It roared, a primal bestial cry that sent a chill down the Guide's dead spine, and dashed off in the direction of the sounds of steel and slaughter.

Kris watched it go, marveling at the smooth powerful movements that propelled the demon so quickly away from him. Suddenly a shadow swept from the smoke, descending on the demon with such speed that the muscled monster seemed to be moving in slow motion. The Guide didn't get a clear image of the shape until it landed bodily in the space the demon had just occupied a moment before.

It was a big beautiful black dragon, crushing the demon with its massive bulk as it struck the ground. From the tip of its tail to the end of its snout, it had to be at least thirty feet long as it stretched its long serpentine body to crawl slowly from the small crater its landing had described in the stone. The demon was not visible under the slithering mound of scaled flesh at first, then the dragon reached back behind its straightening body with a mouth open to reveal jagged rows of pointed teeth.

Pushing its snout under its own scaled belly, the beast snapped its head around violently. It stood with its back legs in the rock concavity it had caused, its tail arching up behind it in a scorpion's question mark. Its front legs were straight on the ground, and its shoulders were a good foot taller than the Guide's head. The long neck snaking straight out from the shoulders was straight, the strong muscles taut from the strain of holding the other monster aloft clutched in its jaws.

The demon didn't seem to have much fight left in him. He hung limp from the dragon's crushing maw, his abdomen pierced and bleeding in dozens of places, one arm smashed into a useless tangle of black bone and purple gore that dangled uselessly from his shoulder. The other arm was prying at the dragon's jaw, but without any results besides jagged bleeding cuts all over his taloned hand and muscled forearm.

With a slow and almost playful motion, the dragon shook its head slowly from side to side. The demon's arms and legs danced listlessly with the movement, then blurred in a lifeless rag doll whirlwind of fangs and flesh and lifeless limbs as the dragon shook its head with increasing violence and speed. Blood flew in every direction, clouds and droplets of purple arcing through the air to stain the nearby rock. Then the smashed and useless arm went flying too, thunking unceremoniously on the hellish ground to twitch and bleed.

When the dragon stopped shaking its head, the demon looked truly done. Its eyes were open, dead scarlet orbs wide to stare at nothing. What little of its flesh that had not been shredded by the dragon's teeth was mottled in its own dark lifeblood, and more blood coursed from endless wounds to further stain the skin. One arm was entirely gone, and its shoulder was a hellish mass of purpled hamburger.

Unable to turn from the wondrous slaughter, Kris watched the light begin to come back into the demon's eyes as it hung there in the dragon's mouth. The shoulder became a tiny little arm that grew from the mangled mess like a flower sprouting from a pile of dung. Kris almost felt sorry for the hateful demon; its miraculous healing ability was doing nothing but prolonging its gruesome suffering.

With a deft snap of its neck, the dragon released the demon from its mouth to send it flying straight up. Spinning and bleeding and howling, the monster peaked just before disappearing into the thick acrid smoke ceiling, hanging suspended in midair for a brief forever moment. Then it fell; and as it did, the dragon arched its back and shot a burst of flame from its mouth. A steady stream of red and orange fire erupted continuously from the dragon's unhinged jaw at the falling demon. One second he was above the fire, looking down at his hot fate with scarlet eyes widened in horror. The next second he was engulfed in flames, screaming and burning. Then the fire was gone and so was he, vaporized into nothingness. Not even ashes remained.

The dragon swung its head around, narrow eyes regarding the Guide coldly.

CHAPTER 48

William let out a long whistle, the whistle he had used to call his mount before his mount became a black on chrome Harley Davidson Switchback. The dragon turned in his direction, coming up on its haunches and whipping its tail behind it with a sound that was akin to Samuel's gunfire. William approached cautiously, the gunslinger to his right and the samurai to his left. William and Mikeo held their swords before them at the ready, and Samuel's hand hovered over his holstered pistol prepared to draw. Looking past the scaled black monster, William could see Kris well enough to see the stark relief on his face.

Stepping from the thick bank of dark smoke, Paul clanged his swords together and called out to the dragon.

"You there!" he shouted calmly. "I am the Stone Walker, the Walker King in this realm and all others. Bend your knee or feel my wrath."

Without hesitation, the serpentine monster rocked back on its haunches and opened its mouth wide to spew forth a fresh stream of caustic flame. The fire leapt forward to scorch the already dark rock where Paul's feet had stood only a moment before, melting the jagged edges of stone to a smooth scorched level surface.

Faster than demons, quicker than devils, the Walker King was also speedier than dragon fire. His blurred path described a lazy arc, a flash of leather that seemed to be standing still, dashing left and arriving at the dragon's side all in the same split second.

Paul leaned his shoulder into his flash forward and struck the dragon from the side bodily. They rolled violently a few times, black leather and blacker scales caught in a hateful tumbling embrace. Paul's black hat flew from the tornado of violence to tumble to the ground and lie still. Razor sharp teeth and talons snapped and swiped at the Walker while two flashing blades swung and stabbed at the screeching dragon.

Before they could roll to a stop, the dragon got its back legs under it and launched itself bodily into the sky. It unfurled its wings and flapped them with a resounding report, disappearing into the roiling smoke overhead. Paul crouched on the rock the monster had launched itself from as the dragon's feet left the ground, peering after its departing form with the careful eye of a hunter tracking his prey. Then he exploded upward with a powerful leap that left a series of fresh fissures in the charred stone, leather duster fluttering like a cape at his back.

Paul disappeared, engulfed in smoke on the tail end of the same second that the clouded miasma enveloped the dragon.

William stood with Samuel and Mikeo, six eyes squinting at the sky overhead to catch a glimpse of anything. Kris covered the space between them with a thought, and stood with the Walkers to stare at the sky.

The first thing to hit the ground was Paul's short sword. It landed near where he had tussled with the dragon, a few feet from where his cowboy hat had come to rest. William exchanged a concerned glance with the Guide, but Mikeo and Samuel did not take their eyes from the sky. The next thing to strike the rock was the dragon's right taloned front leg. It had been cleaved just below the elbow, cleanly sliced through scales and sinew and bone. It landed with a splat and lay there, lifeless and bleeding.

William smiled.

Paul descended though the cloud cover then, landing on his feet and crouching to cushion the blow. Blood sprayed downward as he struck, forming a red and purple ring of wet on the rock around him. Three long gashes had been torn open across the wide back of his armor, and the flayed skin underneath was still knitting itself back together. The torn layers of muscle were laced with ripped strands of fat and a scratched pair of ribs, and the whole mess was full of blood and mangled scraps of leather.

The Walker King breathed in, and William watched the damaged ribs move with it. Then the dragon's body hit the ground to Paul's left with a lifeless *whump!* The head struck the ground to his right, dead eyes staring forever at nothing. The Walker King exhaled, his skin under the damaged duster whole again. He stood up, looked at the body to his left and the head to his right, then stepped to retrieve his hat from the ground. Placing the leather carefully on his head, he reached out toward the short sword lying on the rock nearby as soon as his hand was free.

The sword leapt through the air and into his waiting outstretched hand.

Paul approached the Walkers and the Guide with a sword in each hand, his features painted in purple blood.

As he got closer, William could see that Paul's armor had been attacked from the front as well. The entire right side of his duster hung in tattered shreds, and the skin along his muscled abdomen was exposed. Surely his belly had been a mess of shredded flesh a moment ago, but it was whole and healthy now.

"Is everyone alright?" Paul spoke as he neared the group, his eyes on his Guide. William almost laughed; the four of them stood here undamaged while the Walker King's once formidable armor hung in useless bloody tatters.

The Guide nodded in answer to the question, gulping audibly before speaking.

"Yeah," he said, obviously shaken. "We're alright."

None of the Walkers responded. They were fine.

"Do we need to scour this entire realm for demons?" Paul addressed the group. "Or do we just head in the direction of the delicious sounds of battle?"

William heard the clanging and shrieking and shouting in the distance. It did seem to be concentrated, at the group's two o'clock position.

"The demons have found the dragon tunnels; they are flooding the subterranean city." Vanessa materialized beside William, answering the Walker King's question as the other two Guides coalesced into living form next to their respective Walkers.

Samuel's Guide spoke next, her voice much like the cowboy's in cadence. "The dragons are trying to drive them out, run them over open ground and flame them, but more demons keep finding tunnels and entering them."

Mikeo's Guide was a petite Japanese woman, with the fierce beauty of a royal courtesan. Her contribution was not a string of words but a series of images that showed the dragons taking their humanoid devil forms to fight in the underground tunnels and narrow city streets hewn in stone. The dragons could move and live in the subterranean pockets of space in their fire-breathing forms, but even the smallest dragon was cramped for fighting space there. The Guide's projection showed one dragon after another putting down fire and flight to take up snarls and swords in their devil bodies. Armed and armored, devils moved into tunnels and fissures with battle cries raised in rage.

Her broadcast gave them a dragon's eyes view, looking down on the mostly armed demons appearing from the thick choking smoke to stream into tunnels not being guarded by dragons or scouted by devils. Some of them did try to dash past a dragon and into the mouth of a tunnel the beast was watching. The sentinel dragon would leap forward to flame the demon or snatch it up with sword-like talons and bite its head off with one powerful snap of its razored jaws. Demons would flow into the unguarded entry while the dragon dealt with the one brave dead demon; and when the dragon turned its attention to another, a passing demon would bend to pick up the fallen's sword.

Their strategy was as clear as the projected images. The Walker quartet turned as one towards the thickest sounds of battle. Before Paul could dash off, Kris thought a private question at him.

'Why did you battle that dragon?' The tone of the Guide's thought was neither accusatory nor reprimanding.

Paul turned to him with a raised eyebrow, letting the others wait a moment. *'It looked like it wanted to take a bite out of my best friend and my most valuable source of guidance.'*

'They can't hurt me, can they?' Suddenly the distant clamor didn't sound so distant.

'In this place, probably.' Paul's thought came at him, the calm and honest response sending icy prickles down his spine. *'I wasn't willing to take the chance.'*

Then the Walkers were gone, and a moment later their Guides were as well. Only Kris remained, and he took one last look around at the dragon pieces and the ring of blood already blackening and bubbling in the heat. They were all slowly fading, following the dragon soul into nothingness.

He thought it amusing that the three Walkers Paul had grown closest to all had women as Guides. Not that women were not often Guides; the percentages tended to lean towards men, that was all. Most Guides were the Walker's best friend from life, often a service buddy or fellow police officer or intelligence agent. Every generation had warriors, and most of the warriors that became Walkers in the modern West had some armed forces or elite security training. Paul was a rare exception, learning to fight and lead after becoming an immortal.

Kris chuckled quietly at an inner thought, and didn't see the harm in voicing it aloud to see if it sounded funnier that way.

"Paul's Guide would have probably been Brenna if she hadn't turned out to be a devil," he muttered.

He chuckled again, then corrected himself, as Andre wasn't here to do it for him. "Not a devil. *The Devil.*"

Still chuckling to himself, he corrected himself aloud on one more point.

"Not Brenna," he said, louder. "Ximena."

There was a crackle of electricity in the air around him, and Kris smelled ozone and brimstone and sulfur and sage pleasantly mixed together. The dead hairs stood up on the back of his dead neck.

He liked the way that sounded. He liked the way that felt. He liked the way that smelled.

"Ximena," he said again, for no particular reason.

A network of blue electricity pulsed through the air around him, smoke cleared, and that pleasant swirl of odor came to him again. This time it smelled less of sulfur and brimstone and more like clean white sage. There was a new smell too, a smell that made him smile for some reason. It was the smell of cocoa and cinnamon blended together and browned to perfection in bright sunlight.

Yeah, he had definitely caused that.

Kris was pretty sure what he was doing now, but still far from certain.

"Ximena," he said again, stepping back as a flash of light seared his eyes.

Kris blinked rapidly, trying to regain his vision.

Then his eyes adjusted, and a form stepped from the light.

"Brenna?" Kris exclaimed.

His eyes filled with tears, and he rushed forward to embrace her.

CHAPTER 49

William was proud to see that they were not the only Walkers that had made it this far. The Guides were all just as clever as Vanessa had proved herself to be over the centuries, each in their own way. It had been a wonder to witness the interactions between Walkers and Guides these past months of inter-dimensional training. Each Walker's experience of the life was unique, and much of that unique experience could be attributed to the sacred relationship each Walker had with his or her Guide.

Walkers from all corners of the globe fought their way deeper into Hell, finding entrance to the subterranean passages with the help of their Guides. They employed diversionary tactics similar to the invading demon horde, one Walker engaging a sentinel dragon while their partner rushed an entrance. Simple speed won out then, the fastest flying dragon unable to catch the Walker's sprinting escape. The Walkers weren't cooperating with the dragons, but they weren't attacking them either. The most aggressive move he saw a Walker make toward a dragon was to push a massive muscled demon forcefully in one's direction. It distracted the serpentine monster and allowed the Walker and his partner to enter a nearby fissure unmolested.

Pleased, William eyed the entrance Paul was striding toward. The Walker King seemed unafraid as he walked boldly forward, his tattered armor dancing a frayed swaying dance over his mostly exposed upper body.

A dragon guarded the wide entrance, crouching over the opening poised to spew its crematory breath all over the steps that led to the darkened chasm. William was watching Paul carefully, wondering what his battle-loving king was planning. A flicker of movement above and behind the dragon caught his attention at the same time that it caught the scaled creature's. Two short and beefy demons were coming up behind the dragon, and they leapt as it whipped its head about to confront them. Each grabbed a leathery wing and bit or tugged on it.

Paul walked casually through the wide fissure in the rock, stones dropping about him from the tussle that raged above him. He disappeared into the darkness. Mikeo and Samuel were right behind him, and

William slipped through the portal after them. His perfect eyes adjusted immediately, showing him a tunnel that narrowed to as little as eight feet in rough uneven diameter to as much as twelve feet. Its serpentine path wound slightly left and slightly right and back again, straight enough for his eyes to see it turn sharply left about half a mile off. Between the band of Walkers and the place where the tunnel curved out of sight, there were three or four hundred demons and devils locked in combat.

William watched a pair of blurred warriors zig-zagging through the length of tunnel. One was a Western Walker, a modern-looking face swathed in a cowboy's brown leather. The other looked ancient and Middle Eastern, with dark layered fabric wound about her lithe lean body and a curved sword in each hand.

The cowboy stepped light on the level walkway, dodging left and right in an unpredictable pattern that left a trail of precisely beheaded demons at each turn with a longsword. Flat level surface was the one place the dashing woman's feet hardly touched. Using her speed to defy gravity, she ran up and down the walls and across the low ceiling to produce a dizzy kaleidoscope of flashing steel and spraying blood.

William noted with pride the way they worked together, and that neither of them so much as brushed rudely past the dragon devils. Their only prey was demons, and the monsters were dropping dead with satisfying regularity as far as his eye could see.

Taking the lead, Paul dashed amazingly quickly to that distant turn. One moment William was shoulder to shoulder with him, the next he was standing calm a half a mile away. Seven headless demons dropped dead in his wake; another was obliterated by his dash into a momentary cloud of purple blood. Samuel and Mikeo followed, performing their own version of the lethal dance the two Walkers occupying the space already were doing. Samuel exchanged a curt nod with the cowboy as they momentarily shared a stretch of space, and Mikeo crisscrossed the walls and ceiling to playfully clang swords with the stern speedy woman. William followed, taking out as many demons as Paul had while not engaging any dragons. He was again pleased to see that the others had done the same.

Turning the corner, William saw another long stretch of tunnel burrowing further into the depths of Hell. It was similarly populated with dragon devils and demons, though many more of one than the other. The four Walkers that formed a neat phalanx which moved with lethal regularity from one end of the visible stretch of tunnel to the other probably had something to do with that. They looked like they had stepped from the same time period in the same army, a Mongol warrior facing each direction of the compass with his back to his fierce brothers. A square of calm empty space stayed between their backs, while a flurry of violence erupted continuously before each of them. Each armored warrior slashed violently and effectively with a long curved saber. When beheading the closest demon meant stepping from the square, a curved blade would disappear and be replaced by a bow that fired one expanding arrow after another at the enemy. When firing a bow, each of the fighters held several shafts in their hand while shooting, sometimes loosing two or three arrows with one pull.

The phalanx moved toward them suddenly, all four walkers moving as one up the narrow passage. As they approached, two of them stepped away from each other enough to admit the new group of Walkers into the square of peace between them.

They were offering them an escort.

William stepped aside to let the others go first, but Paul and Samuel leapt the phalanx as one to fight their way up the tunnel. William stepped into the space and watched Mikeo back into place to make it a five man formation.

Then one of the stout warriors, the tallest among them, turned with a fluid motion and stepped into the peaceful space. His sword disappeared, and he gave William a nod that looked more like a bow. The space closed behind him as he turned, and they walked casually between the small but solid wall of Walkers.

"Batu." William returned the nod as respectfully as possible, not hoping to match the warrior's regal air. His armor and body language resembled that of his men, but up close the differences were immediately apparent. Where the others had silky black hair, his long mane was a deep ruddy brown. His eyes were a dark penetrating green, and a spray of freckles across his nose gave him a youthful complexion.

"How are you faring?" William asked.

It was difficult to see the set of the man's mouth past his long flowing dark beard streaked with natural red tones and wet unnatural purple splotches.

"We are well," Batu spoke carefully and slowly, without accent. "The demons, not so much. We are pushing forward soon. The dragons seem to be annoyed with our presence and participation."

He stroked his beard with a gloved hand, smearing demon blood further down the dark tresses and all over the black leather. Pulling his wet and sticky hand away from his face, he seemed amused looking at the purple liquid life force. He made a tight fist and watched globules drip to the hot rock underfoot. The entire time he moved casually in step with the mobile safe space, paying no mind to the clamor all about.

"Perhaps it is because we are more effective warriors than they are." Batu's observation was not without humor or pride. "The dragons seem frustrated to be fighting in their devil guises."

"Thank you again for the arrows; that was a stroke of genius." William kept pace as Batu did. "It's too bad we couldn't line up the archers again. That was very effective."

Batu waved his hand dismissively. "By arrow, by saber, by bare hand, no matter. I will fight with pride and with pleasure, in any imaginable circumstances. I am no whining dragon. The same goes for my men."

It seemed like the truth; William could see the ring of violence around them. Even with more demons streaming in behind them, the demon population in this stretch of space was getting sparse.

Their escort was nearing the next bend. "Did your Watchers come up with this strategy? It is much like the pair of Walkers we passed before you."

Batu nodded, once. "They are cleaning up nicely back there. We took our cue from them."

Now he was shaking his head slowly to answer the first question more completely. "I have seen no Watchers since the battle began."

The formation paused as the tunnel turned sharply right, fighting in place in all directions. One curved blade beheaded a demon that was backing toward the warriors, trading clanging blows with a devil two feet shorter than him. The purple blood showered the devil, splattering his face and eyes as he drove forward. The devil dragged a forearm across its eyes and hissed at the killer Walker.

"You should probably move on," William advised the other leader as he stepped from the safe place.

"Soon." Batu switched places with Mikeo, and the formation moved murderously away back the way they had come.

The next section of tunnel was a mess of demons overwhelming the devils two to one. William moved immediately to the nearest unmatched clashing of swords, beheading a demon with his straight long blade as it reared back to swing an axe at the devil. Then Paul moved past and rapidly down the passageway, motioning for the others to follow.

They did enough damage in passing to give the well-armored devils a fighting chance, moved swiftly through the next section of tunnel and then the next. Paul led the way as if he knew where he was going, but William knew the king's stride looked purposeful even when he was utterly lost. Either way, William and the others followed without question and without a scratch on them.

Somewhere along with way Paul thought to think his armor whole again, and so it was.

William wondered if the kevlar vest he wore under his zippered armored jacket would give a dragon's claws any more pause than Paul's tee shirt had.

Probably not.

At last they came to a widening of the tunnel that led to the expanse of an underground city. They were several miles deep now, by William's reckoning.

The ceiling rose high above them to disappear in black smoke, making the large carved out cavern appear much like the surface they had left behind. The space was tighter, however, as William could see from one end of the city to another from their vantage point.

It appeared that every tunnel let out in the choked upper atmosphere of the city carved in stone. William could see other openings along the wall, all wide portals with a rock ledge on which one could look down upon the city. It would have been a magnificent sight on a peaceful day, every structure a small castle forged from rock and inlaid with gemstones of every size and variety imaginable. Each castle was missing something, something William couldn't put his finger on. They formed a spiral of burnt beautiful architecture, with one wide street between the plots of darkened land. The spiral led to a castle that rose high above them all, surrounded in a moat of black boiling oil and orchards of unidentifiable trees that burned eternal.

The central castle was a black burnt color, with glittering black gemstones melted into the rock in dazzling patterns. As William stood on the wide ledge with the other Walkers, looking at the black castle, he realized what was missing. There were no doors in the structures, no place for a humanoid to walk up a path and enter on foot. This city was made by and for dragons; that explained the lack of doors as well as the fifty foot drop between the ledge they stood on and the city below.

This was the place where you put on your dragon form, if you weren't already in it, and launched off the ledge to fly into the city. Instead the Walkers approached the drop, one by one, and calmly stepped over the side. Being out in the open right now was not a good idea, as this was not the beautiful dark kingdom it might have been on a peaceful day.

Demons clogged the wide single spiral street, streaming toward the giant black castle in the center of it all. A few devils fought them on the ground with swords, trying to stave off the horde as hundreds of demons approached the moat, dove in, or pulled themselves out dripping on the other side. Most of the dragon army had taken their natural monstrous forms, and darkened the sky on leathered wings or lit up the street with raging flame.

Three dragons guarded the central castle, one patrolling the moat and spitting fire at the oiled demons as they pulled themselves from the bubbling liquid. There were dozens of scorched huddled forms still smoldering on the shore, and fire danced lazily on the surface of the moat in several places. Another dragon flew a tight circle around the final spiral of the street, vaporizing demons in short bursts of white hot flame in groups of two or three and then rising too high in the sky for sword or spear. The third dragon was certainly the largest in the city. It sat poised on the tallest flat roof of the castle, watching the battle rage all around it. Sixty feet long from tip to tip, the dark red monster turned slowly in place, whipping its two-ton tail. A bolt of flame issued from its mouth from time to time, but they were angry errant bursts that were aimed at nothing and scorched only the sky.

Paul must have seen the scattered pairs of Walkers dotting the spiral street, or maybe he just figured this all had to end at the great dragon castle. William hoped it was the former; even if the entire Walker army was here, they would be outnumbered by winged flamethrowers. After seeing what the dragon had done to Paul, the fastest among them, William had no desire to see the dragons turn on the Walkers in this open space.

They killed demons and dodged flames, all four veteran Walkers claiming a section of the wide spiraling path as their killing swath. Only when a devil stood in their way did they step left or right, beheading the demons that stood blocking the path and leaving the rest alone. William had seen a dozen Walker duos fighting the demons in the street, and it was not long before they came upon two Western Walkers fighting back to back, one in a brown duster and cowboy hat wielding a broad straight short double-edged sword and the other swinging a long heavy battle axe swathed in black.

As they rounded the wide corner and the pair came into view, the Walker in brown leather jumped to a devil's aid. He put himself between a demon coming up behind a devil and swinging a curved blade at the vulnerable dragon devil's exposed neck. Two swords clanged loudly against each other as the Walker blocked the blow, but the cowboy's momentum drove him forward inexorably. He swung at the demon, knocking its blade aside and beheading it neatly, then struck the devil bodily and went down in a heap with it.

The Walker hastily rose to his feet.

The devil rolled, transforming mid-roll, and launched its dragon body to hover flapping its wings just beyond the Walker's reach. Disappearing his weapon momentarily, the cowboy held his empty gloved hands palms out in front of him to show respect and apology.

Its strong wings beating rhythmically, the small serpentine monster puffed its chest and unhinged its jaw. One moment the Walker was a dark blurred form outlined in orange flame, the next moment the flame and the Walker were both gone. The Walker's partner was running forward as the flames spewed forth, arriving a moment too late and leaping toward the hovering dragon as his buddy was turned to hot ash.

The dragon didn't have time to turn or breathe another burst of caustic breath; instead it opened its arms as if to embrace the Walker and cranked its maw open even further. It chomped down on the Walker's shoulder, and only because the cowboy dodged at the last moment. The Walker howled in pain, his armor useless against the dragon's fangs. He tried to swing his sword at the monster, but it had him in its grasp, arms pinned at his sides. Releasing its toothy hold on his shoulder, the dragon lifted its head and turned it slightly. The Walker's head disappeared into the powerful jaws with a sickening cracking sound.

Another dragon, a deep cobalt metallic blue scaled monster twice the size of the first, descended from the smoking sky. It squashed the smaller dragon to the rock, completely obscuring the Walker between them but for one leather-booted leg sticking out between the two sinewed torsos. The dragons leapt up and away from each other, one still holding the Walker's head in its mouth while the other dug long claws into his chest and pulled the other way. They snapped at each other angrily, and the Walker fell free for a moment. They had him again before he could fall, little chunks disappearing from his body in bloody sprays as their gnashing teeth clamped repeatedly and mercilessly down on his rag doll form.

By the time the Walker finally hit the ground, both arms and one leg were missing. His neck was spewing blood from where his head used to be, and his ribs were exposed under torn skin and muscle all down one side. The dragons pounced in unison, tearing flesh from the corpse and shrieking in the most disturbing way between bites. Then the smaller one tried to take a bite at the same time in the same place as the cobalt monster, and the larger dragon swiped at it with razor talons. They began to battle each other, oblivious to the four immortals watching.

Paul looked at his key for some reason, opening the antique watch face and then snapping it closed quickly. He glanced at William. "Get the Walkers out of here, all of them."

William sighed, relieved. He was afraid the king was about to declare war on the dragons, who were clearly frenzied by battle.

This was not a good place for Walkers or demons. Let the dragons have them; he needed to get his people out of here. William reached out his thoughts to Vanessa, delighting in the warm familiarity that was so old and so new to him all at the same time. Since she had learned to touch, he had become her favorite thing to lay her hands on; and her touch had become his favorite thing in all the worlds.

She was already there, of course; he just needed to tune in to her. The robe did nothing to hide her shapely form, and his recent memories of touching the bare beautiful skin under the thick cloth was a series of pleasant pictures that never quite left his mind. He tried not to smile as she materialized beside him.

She was beautiful, which made it harder.

"Let all the Guides know that their Walkers need to vacate the dragon city." William spoke urgently. "Tell them to head toward the surface using that tunnel." He pointed his gloved hand at a large ledge that would be easy to discern from the others.

"Two Walkers are in trouble near the central castle," Vanessa replied calmly.

William only had to glance at Samuel and Mikeo, and they were off. He looked around, noticing Paul no longer stood at his side either.

There he was, approaching the battling dragons at a slow confident pace with a sword in each hand. The other demons and devils fighting nearby stepped out of his way, clearing a path between him and the frenzied fray.

One pair stopped fighting altogether, the demon and devil exchanging a glance and a shrug and then relaxing their swords at their sides.

They wanted to watch this.

The Walker King was about fifteen feet away from the dragons when they noticed his deliberate approach. William was glad Paul had decided to repair his armor, but he wasn't sure what good it was going to do him. The big blue dragon was clearly dominating the smaller one, and William wished Paul had waited just a little longer to see if their battle would have been to the death.

Paul pointed his bastard sword at the dragons as they disentangled from each other. Their recent wounds were healing; and although they had inflicted them on each other, they stood side by side now as allies.

"You killed a Walker." Paul did not sound happy about the fact that he felt the need to point out.

The smaller dragon shrieked and chomped its jaws on open air, smoke issuing from its reptilian nostrils.

The blue one flicked a forked tongue between its lips and hissed too. Then the hiss became words, a leathery hateful voice.

"*Yesss…*" the dragon said slowly. *"He was deliciousss…"*

"What do you want, Walker King?" Devils were an odd bunch, William noted; they could be so formal and so rude all at the same time. *"An apology?"*

"No," Paul replied.

William saw the set of his shoulders and held his breath to hear the words he knew were coming.

"I want you to die." Paul clanged his swords together and took a step forward.

"Are you mad, Walker?" The cobalt monster was forty feet long and surely weighed several thousand pounds. The little one was small only by comparison; it was still several times the Walker's size. *"You are but one. We are two. We are dragonsss…"*

"Am I mad, dragon?" Paul took another step forward. He was in flame range now, judging by William's estimation.

When the Walker King stepped forward again, William was suddenly by his side. Both of the dragons started, and the small one reared back on its haunches. It sent a blast of flame at the Walkers, scorching the ground where they had just stood. William was upon it before it completed the fiery exhale, and he cut its foreleg off at the elbow as it turned to swipe at him with those razor-sharp talons. The limb began to grow back immediately, but not enough to hold off the carefully aimed longsword. Sharp and strong talons gripped his other arm, but the Walker set his jaw against the pain and used the dragon's grasp as leverage. William hacked at the most narrow and available section of scaled neck, then again in the same place, and the dragon's head fell to the ground. The grasping talons fell from his arm.

William turned to aid Paul, just as the cobalt monster launched itself into flight. The Walker King was on its back, his short sword buried to the hilt in its shoulder. He hung on to the handle of the short sword with one hand and hacked at the dragon's neck with the long double-edged battle axe he wielded with the other. It was only a moment before they were flying over the city, the dragon flapping its leathered wings while Paul rode the dragon like a trained steed.

William began to run. He was not as fast as Paul, but that did not make him slow by any means. There was thirty feet of bare rock between him and the nearest devil locked in combat with a demon. He dashed towards them, thrusting straight up before he reached the clashing hellions.

The leap was smooth and graceful, his arc peaking about sixty feet over the scorched rock street below. Soaring through the air, he saw Paul still riding the blue dragon over the city. The monster was pumping its wings furiously, rising nearly straight up despite the rivers of blood coursing from various open wounds about its head and neck. Paul's short sword was still sunk in the dragon's shoulder, but the Walker King was no longer gripping it. Instead he wielded the axe with both hands, hacking at the beast's neck in a contest between the blade's cutting power and the dragon's ability to mend.

His feet struck the flat roof of a small castle, and William ran across the even surface to jump even higher. He was headed straight for the king and the dragon, but he wasn't rising as fast as the winged monster. William cursed as his ascent slowed to nothing some hundred feet above the street. Then he was taken hard from his right side, and William felt teeth or talons tearing at the flesh of his sword arm. He pivoted at the wound, throwing his entire weight around in a way that twisted his already damaged arm nearly off his shoulder. Dropping his sword, he took the dragon's back and appeared his dagger to secure it between two of the monster's vertebrae with a downward stab of his good left hand.

Suddenly William was riding a dragon as well, hanging on to the hilt of the blade while his mangled sword arm twisted back into place and healed.

For a moment they were falling, dead weight dropping rapidly toward the street not so far below. William had time to think that maybe he had paralyzed the beast, driving his dagger so deep in its spine. Then it twisted awkwardly in the air, and he realized it meant to simply drop to the ground and turn him to paste. The second of impact, he yanked the dagger out and leapt free to roll on the level rock.

The dragon was on him immediately, gnashing its teeth at the spot where he had fallen. William's quick mind and quicker muscles sent him in a leap that landed him square on the monster's back again, facing the whipping pointed tail. As soon as his weight hit the scaled broad back of the enraged creature, it launched itself once again into flight. William sank his gloved fingers deep into the dragon's hard scales, squeezed his thighs around its muscled abdomen, and watched his dagger drop to the ground just as his sword had only a few long moments earlier.

Every time he loosened the grip of one of his hands or his clenched thighs, the dragon would pitch and spin and try to shake him off. That blasted tail kept whipping around as well, striking him in the face more than once. His motorcycle helmet may have come in handy right now, with his face a shredded mass of flesh and the dark rusty taste of his own blood filling his mouth.

He hung on, and the dragon climbed quick enough and high enough for him to realize that it meant to crush him against the ceiling if it could not crush him against the ground. Before long, they were enveloped in a smoke so thick William could not see his own gloved hand in front of his face. There was no way to tell how high the ceiling was, and he did not want to find out the hard way.

William steeled himself and pushed off with both hands and feet. The dragon twisted in mid-air and came for him. He still couldn't see, but neither could the dragon. In the split second that there was nothing but smoke between them, the Walker thought his blades back into his waiting hands. When the dragon hit him full force, his longsword pierced the center of its chest and was driven through its torso until the tip punched through the scales of its back. His dagger went hilt deep in the monster's throat just below its jaw. Talons raked across his back and legs, the dragon's jaws snapped at his face, and William held on to the handles of his weapons as desperately as he clung to his flagging consciousness.

The dragon flayed William from his shoulders to his knees over and over, long bloodied talons ripping out his guts and muscles and blood every time they grew back as they fell together from the sky.

CHAPTER 50

She felt stiff in his arms, and Kris had time to wonder if he should have been so quick to hug her before Brenna relaxed into his relieved friendly embrace.

"Does nobody know how to summon a goddamned devil anymore?" The annoyance in her voice was amused annoyance, and she was smiling when she pulled away from him.

Kris shrugged, happy and befuddled.

"Sorry," he said. "Is that really all it takes?"

She laughed and shook her head. "No, I'm just teasing you. Conditions had to be right, and I had to be ready to make a move. Anyone with a soul can open a doorway to the devil. The devil doesn't always come."

Their faces were both quite serious by the time she finished talking, and he found himself searching her familiar face for clues of her hidden nature.

Brenna is the devil, Kris thought to himself in the quiet hollows of his mind.

She smiled softly and nodded. "Yes, my friend, I am the devil. I apologize for having deceived you and your best friend; I thought that life was truly behind me."

He was looking at her with wide eyes.

Can she hear my thoughts? he wondered.

Brenna shook her head. "I can't read your mind, if that's what you're thinking. Not while I am confined to this form. I can't travel at the speed of thought like you either."

She smiled again. "So we should probably get going."

Kris continued to contemplate her perfect human features, memories of her doing ordinary human things flooding his mind.

"You were studying to be a nurse," he sputtered, stupidly.

She nodded solemnly.

"Brenna was." Her voice was tainted with a sadness that made the Guide's heart ache.

Kris smiled, remembering himself. "Brenna was a part of you, and I loved Brenna like a sister. It's nice to meet you, uh..." he held out his hand, wondering if he should go formal or traditional, Christian or Pagan. Surely not her counterpart's name reversed.

"Ximena." Her hand felt like Brenna's when she placed it in his, and her smile looked like Brenna's. "A pleasure, Guide Kris, King of the Guides and Guide to the Stone Walker."

He stuck out his elbow, noticing her tattered nightgown for the first time. It was stiff with dried blood; brown layers of human life had turned the scant scraps of material into stiff shredded cardboard.

"Shall we?" Kris asked.

Ximena must have noticed his look, and he was glad she couldn't read his mind. She looked down at her gory ensemble, which showed a lot more skin than it covered.

"Am I presentable?" It was Brenna's sweet voice, but there was a devilish gleam in her eye. "Will Paul be turned off by all this blood?"

"No." He tried not to answer too quickly. "He will probably find you more sexy than ever."

Kris could admit that his friend would feel that way; he didn't have to admit that he felt the same. "You can borrow my robe if you want."

"That's okay." She hooked her arm through his. "I'm no more keen on walking around Hell in a big clunky robe than you probably are traversing it in your boxers."

"Where are we going, then?" She was shorter than him in her bare feet, and a little horizontal line creased her smooth forehead as her round dark eyes looked up at him. Kris knew the answer before he asked the question, but he wanted to know more before they got moving.

"We need to find Paul," she replied. Her eyes were round and dark and swirling with thoughts only the devil knew.

"We need to save him from the Dragon Queen," she said, more urgently. She took his hand in hers, still looking up at him with an honest and open face. "We need to save him from himself."

Kris nodded, remembering the countdown ticking away in his best friend's head.

"Ximena," he said, slowly. "About Paul…"

"And the Dragon Queen?" She cut him off. "I know, Kris. Please understand that you can expect more of me than you might the average modern American female. I saw the first man promise his love to the first woman, and I saw that love live in his heart even as his lust for another grew in his loins. My love for Paul lives deep in my soul, and his love for me runs just as deep. I know he still loves me because he is a part of me that I am not willing to live without, and he is not willing to let anything stand between us. Do you know what he has gone through just to find me, just to make sure my soul was not lost? Do you know what he has given up?"

The Guide blinked back tears.

He had been prepared to extend sympathy to the devil. Now he felt a touch of shame that Jessica had not crossed his mind in some time now. "You really love him."

She smiled. "We really love each other. That's how it works."

"Let's go, then." The Guide could not boast that level of loyalty to Paul. Kris had doubted him more than once since Paul had lost his pretty moral compass.

The compass itself had apparently never lost faith.

They walked, the sounds of battle coming closer.

Kris had so many questions he was having trouble ordering them in his mind.

Ximena spoke first. "You don't happen to have my necklace, do you?" Her eyes were on the scorched rock ahead of them, her voice casual with the question. It was somehow comforting to see her hand go to her throat with the familiar gesture, even if it was bare.

"No." Kris shook his head. "Roche had it for some reason. He gave it to Paul to give to you."

Ximena laughed aloud. "For every evil that one does, he always balances it with good. Roche can be a true bastard, particularly when the fall is upon him, but he's saved the world as many times as he's endangered it."

The temperature seemed to rise with every step they took, the clamor of combat growing louder.

"How does Matt figure into all of this?" Kris wondered aloud. "Is he really your brother?"

"Matthew was my master of arms and my closest confidante. I would have chosen him to succeed me, but his soul was on the rise. It was time for him to pass from one realm into another, so he asked to accompany me to Earth." Ximena watched the ground ahead of them as she spoke, her voice still calm and matter-of-fact.

"Matt?" Kris couldn't help but be a little astonished. "You wanted Matt to run Hell?"

She glanced sideways at him. "In your realm, Matt was a new soul, full of life but not yet wise to the ways of the world. In Hell he was an ancient devil who struck fear into the hearts of those who spoke only fear, inspired love in the devils on the rise and evoked awe in all of us."

There was emotion in her voice now; love for some being that Kris had only seen a facet of. "When a soul is born into a new realm, it invariably loses all conscious memory of what it was before."

She frowned. "No matter how magnificent."

"What would happen if Matt returned to Hell?"

Ximena's smile was wide and open and without candor. "He has returned, though, hasn't he?"

Kris nodded.

"Does he seem to be somehow more than he was before?" she asked.

Kris nodded again, dumbly.

There was so much that he didn't know.

"Just as this place is so much less than it was before," Ximena said quietly.

He glanced over at her, her short legs keeping a strident pace with his long steps. The ghost of a smile still played about her lips, but there was a touch of sadness to it.

Scanning the smoky horizon in every direction, the Guide tried to imagine Hell as something other than a wretched and scorched wasteland. He waited for her to elaborate, but she seemed to be darkening as she thought of it.

Maybe one of his questions would take her mind off whatever clouded her countenance.

"So, do you know everything?" It was something he had wondered more than once since he found out who she was.

She kept her eyes on the path ahead, nodding once.

"Pretty much." She shrugged.

The Guide was almost swelling with pride as he posed the next question. "What would I most want to know about the world if I had the sense to ask the question?"

Ximena stopped walking suddenly and turned to look up at him.

"Good question." She grinned.

"Should I sit down?" Kris felt even more pride at her praise.

"No." She was still smiling. "You do not have much use for news that might break your heart or crush your soul; besides, there's less of that in all the worlds than you may think, when you get a little perspective on things."

She took his hand, kindly, like a friend.

"What you would most want to know is not who your father is, but who your father isn't." Ximena let the words sink in, still smiling and still holding his hand.

He understood the riddle immediately, if that's what it was.

She was right; it did not matter who it had been. Kris thought of his own light hair and gray eyes, then his father's thick dark mane and eyes.

"Doug isn't my dad." It wasn't a question, but he did have one. "Did he know?"

Ximena shook her head. "He was so consumed with his own cycle of lust and guilt that he never considered the possibility that he had married someone much like himself."

Kris burst out laughing. It felt like a series of weights that had been stacked one on top of the other on his heart had been lifted. "She was cheating too?"

"Only in the beginning." Ximena squeezed his hand. "After she had you, she deliberately let herself go so she wouldn't be so attractive and wouldn't have much opportunity. Of course, she lost respect for her husband when he tried to be intimate with her because she saw herself as unapproachable. So your father found others who found his advances flattering, and she got her romance and fulfillment in fantasy."

Kris remembered the books he had seen lying about when he was a kid, painted cover depicting some bare-chested beefcake with locks that flowed longer and prettier than the hair of the invariably buxom girl he invariably held in his arms. Kris had learned more about sex from peeking into those pages than he had from looking at the most explicit pictures in his dad's magazines.

Kris shook his head. *Doug's* magazines.

He squeezed her hand back, still smiling.

"Thanks," he said. He meant it. "Anything else?"

"Just that you're in good company. There are a lot more examples of misplaced paternity than you might think, although there are even more examples of fathers who share the secret with the mother." She smiled. "It's generally done with the best of intentions, and nearly everyone who does it feels justified in doing it. If that makes you feel any better."

He frowned. "It really doesn't."

Ximena smiled, a little sadly. "Me either."

They began walking again, but they hadn't gone ten steps when a dragon emerged from the mist.

Ximena stepped boldly between the Guide and the monster. It was a little embarrassing, her being so tiny.

"Dragon, look upon me." Ximena stood fearless before it. The beast narrowed its reptilian eyes and lowered its head to the ground.

"Do you know me?" she asked it.

In answer, the dragon reared back on its haunches and screamed. A chill ran up the Guide's spine, and he thought he heard Ximena's soft calm voice under the deafening shriek.

"Just so you know," is what he thought he heard her say.

They moved at the same time, the dragon falling forward onto its tiny front legs and belching fire while Ximena ran to her left. Kris felt the heat of the flame scorching the place she had been, so near to him.

Though she moved at a normal human speed, Ximena seemed a master of that limited movement. She ran alongside the dragon and then over the top of it, so when its head snaked to its right she was on its left flank. She kicked at the flank almost playfully, and the beast whipped its head around to bite at her. With a subtle sidestep, she locked her arm around its neck at the base of its skull and clenched her wrist with her free hand.

Ximena did a simple graceful backflip and landed on her feet. Somewhere between her feet leaving the ground and landing on it again, there was a distinct cracking sound that sent another wave of ice down the Guide's back. Still holding the agog head tight, its black slitted dead eyes staring off into forever, Ximena did another backflip and then another. The reptilian neck made a few more disgusting sounds, and then the monster's head came off in her hands. It was accompanied by a sickening shower of purple blood.

She tossed the head aside and turned to him.

Ximena was painted in purple, except the white of her teeth as she stood there smiling. Kris couldn't help but think of Paul.

"Kris," she said calmly. "You're robe is on fire."

The Guide whirled and frantically batted the flame out.

"Sorry," she said as they began walking again. "I know how you hate violence."

They were close now.

He still wanted to ask her one more thing.

"Ximena?" he sounded out the new name carefully.

She looked over, still smiling and walking and dripping blood.

"Does knowing everything about everyone make you hate them all?"

"No." She smiled up at him. "It makes you love them all."

CHAPTER 51

There was light, but no sound. The light became colors, and the colors took shape, but the deafening silence remained. A thin scrap of dim consciousness floated over the battlefield, passing through dragons and demons like the ghost it had become. It reached in every direction for some memory or feeling or thought it might anchor its identity to.

Something pulled at the spirit, a force irresistible like gravity that spoke to it without words.

'Rise,' the force whispered voicelessly, 'Come home...'

The thought was the sweetest thought possible, and the home it hinted at was real. The spirit knew that, somehow, but it also knew something else. Without a mind to think, it resisted the irresistible force with a feeling. Concentrating on that feeling with every ounce of its immateriality, the feeling became a certainty.

Not yet.

That was the feeling, the certainty, the knowledge that kept the soul from rising out of the depths of Hell to ascend into Heaven's waiting embrace.

Not yet.

The spirit drifted, clinging to that certainty, until another force began to tug at it. It was weak at first, a subtle pull that brought with it the first sounds the spirit had heard in a seeming eternity. Then the power of the pull increased, and the sounds became loud enough to tell that it was the rushing river sound of a thousand voices all speaking in different tones and cadences at the same time.

As the new pull became stronger, the other weakened. The thousand voices became one; and as soon as the spirit heard that voice, it all came rushing back.

"William." Soft and sweet and worried, it was Vanessa's voice.

Like a rubber band being released, the spirit snapped back into the damaged body it had left behind.

William opened his eyes and said her name. That's what he tried to do, anyway. One eye opened, but the other remained a gash of shredded gore that used to be the left side of his face. Her name was not distinguishable when he spoke it, either; it came out as a three-syllable low moan.

He felt his body healing, that rapid-fire pain coursing through his cells that a mortal would never know. The pain of injury could not compare to the agony that healing the injury in a matter of seconds brought with it. It wasn't the first time his essence had been violently forced from his body due to excessive damage, but it never got easier. He counted the times he had resisted that magnetic force that called from above, stronger every time. He thought of how the moments he had spent listening to that voiceless message had changed him, and he lay there with the fire of resurrection burning through his every cell.

It was only a few seconds, and all he had to do was resist crying out while his powers made William himself once more. It took everything he had, biting against the pain.

"Not yet." His own voice startled him, whole again.

William sat up and blinked away the last of the blood obscuring his vision. He looked down at himself, his leather torn to bloody shreds but his flesh underneath it mended.

"William." He felt her arms around him and buried his face in her hair. He breathed in her woods and wildflowers smell, the scent that had exuded naturally from her more and more as she learned to touch and feel the world of humans again. It had always been his favorite smell, and having it tickle his nostrils pleasantly every time he was close to her now was worth waiting the centuries for. It filled him and cleansed him and made his healed body and his shocked spirit one whole again.

This is home, he thought happily, breathing her in. *This is my love.*

The thought surprised him, though it shouldn't have. Of course he loved Vanessa; he had loved her before the United States were states, or united. He had loved her in every moment since, as his Guide and his companion and as his friend. Any other feelings he had experienced had been useless conjecture, a series of "what ifs" that led in a frustratingly circuitous path where answers only brought them both to a deeper level of suffering.

Now that he knew her touch, he was coming to know her desires, but it was still so new to both of them. The centuries of working together so closely had surprisingly made their new intimacy something they both approached with great caution and respect, though he saw the same raging hunger mirrored in her eyes that lit his own. Through unspoken agreement, they were working slowly toward that greater closeness. Love was not a word he was ready to burden her with, even if the feeling felt as though it gave his heart wings.

William pulled away from her, brushed a dark strand of hair that had fallen across her face behind her ear.

"Vanessa." He smiled. He kissed her, felt her press her lips against his with an urgency he didn't mind savoring.

"It's alright," he said, standing and extending a hand to help her up. A few scraps of leather that had been stained stiff with his own blood or the dragon's fell as he stood, landing on the scorched rock with a series of soft splattering sounds. He looked down at the remnants of his armor and saw that the kevlar had not fared any better than the spelled leather. He removed the tattered scraps that had once been his leather armored jacket and let it fall to the ground, then the last remaining bits of the bulletproof vest. He closed his eyes and thought his armor whole, zippered jacket and pants and harness boots without a scratch or speck of blood.

William opened his eyes, swathed in flawless black oiled leather. "Where's Paul?" he asked Vanessa.

She extended a sleeved arm to point at one of the ledged tunnels. "He went in there, right after he killed the dragon you were fighting."

William had wondered what had happened to the beast; he was more pleased with the fact that Paul had not left him behind than he was with the knowledge of the dragon's death. He followed her finger to glimpse a narrow opening in the rock. It was not the passage William had instructed the advancing (or were they retreating?) army to take.

Vanessa pivoted to point at another passage. "The others went that way."

That was the one William had pointed them towards.

William sighed, then began to run. As his eye fell on his destination again, he saw that a gigantic red dragon was gliding toward the same ledge he was running at. He slowed his pace, then stopped and stood in the street to watch.

The dragon was enormous, almost too big to land on the wide ledge. Just before it struck the rock wall too hard and too fast, it transformed into a small hourglass-shaped she-devil with flowing hair the color of flame and a long curved sword in her hand. Her curved form was swathed in red chain mail that glinted beautifully as she moved. Dropping the last few feet to the ledge below, she hit the ground running. Coming to a stop, she threw one last look over her shoulder and then disappeared into the tunnel.

In the same moment that she slipped into the tunnel, another dragon followed the flight path she had described to land on the ledge. Half her size meant it was able to land in dragon form on the ledge. It was still gigantic, however, since half her size was equivalent to a city bus. Its deep metallic blue scales flexed and shifted, then it became a devil that was over six feet tall and wore a layer of plate armor over stacked layers of muscle to weigh in well over four hundred pounds altogether. The twin sharply curved blades he held in his hands did not look any less lethal for being shorter than most.

A third dragon approached as the second watched, and the second slipped into the passage as the black dragon came in for a landing. Somewhere between the size of the first and the second, this one looked nearly too large to touch down on the ledge as well. It changed form as the first had, in mid-air, dropping a dozen feet to roll into a smooth somersault and then to its feet.

William caught only a glimpse of the devil, tall and thin and wiry and covered in chain mail. His face was ghastly and twisted with rage, and two long thin horns jutted menacingly from his forehead like pointed spikes. His weapon was a long thin solid metal rod that was both pointed and barbed at each end. The sharp points spun about him slowly, the wicked six-inch barbs flashing in the wan light, as the devil disappeared into the mouth of the cave.

"Do not follow them." Vanessa's voice was full of concern and caution.

"I have to help Paul." William glanced at her, then back at the fateful opening.

"Not by dying again," she responded. "You must go to him."

Of course. All he had to do was close his eyes and think himself to wherever he wanted to go. Before he did, William took one last look at the ledge where he had seen the dragons follow Paul's path.

The ledge was cluttered with Watchers, men and women in nondescript robes all scribbling away in their books with quill pens. The feathers seemed to be moving in unison, and William saw Andre standing in their midst with the two male armed and armored devils. Andre would consult with the devils, then shout something William couldn't hear, and the feathers would move as one over the pages.

The Watcher sensed he was being watched, and looked behind him.

William met his eyes across the vast smoke-filled space between them, and he spat the foul taste in his mouth out as he held the Watcher's treacherous gaze. The spittle hit the hot rock and smoked and sizzled.

Andre shook off his accusing stare and turned to address the devils.

They leapt as one into the air and became dragons pumping their wings furiously and headed in his direction.

Closing his eyes, William thought of Paul.

He heard the sounds of battle all around him, and William opened his eyes in the same moment that he appeared his longsword. There was a demon before him, and two devils. They each seemed more interested in his sudden appearance than they did in each other. All three came at him, and William ducked and whirled an impromptu dance that separated each from their heads in turn.

Paul was beside him in a flash, pressing his wide back to William's and slashing impossibly fast with both blades.

"Nice of you to join us," Paul shouted over his shoulder. "The way you were dancing with that dragon, I thought you might not want to leave the party."

"Good dancer," William shouted back with brevity. "Terrible breath."

He cut off a demon's head unceremoniously.

"We've been betrayed," William shouted as he readied for the next kill.

Paul didn't even glance back. "Andre?"

"And a score of Watchers." William did not sense any surprise. "There are at least three pretty seriously old dragons on the way, too. A black one, a red one, and a blue one."

"Old?" Paul shouted only one word in response.

"Dragons never stop growing, but they grow slowly. They start out about the size of their devil form, which hatches as what we would call a young adult. They can transform almost immediately into either form, but one form ages slowly while the other grows slowly." William stepped forward and disarmed a demon with a zig of his sword and beheaded it on the zag.

"Dragons." It sounded like Paul was laughing. William couldn't say for sure; he had never heard him laugh before. "I should have learned more about dragons."

They fought on in relative silence, though both men tended to cry out from time to time in fury or triumph.

"Tell me about the old dragons you saw," Paul shouted after a while.

William finished a kill before he spoke. There were so many, they seemed to be inching forward at best. "The red one was the largest. She was the size of a house."

"She?" Again, Paul only shouted one word.

"She turned into a devil before she landed. She was way too big to fit."

Parry, thrust, swing, they just kept coming. William's brand new armor was a sticky wet mess.

"Red hair?" Paul shouted. "Black and orange eyes, like fire?"

Before he could answer, a low throaty flinted feminine voice split the air with an angry shout.

"Walker King! Stone Walker! Face me, you coward!" Her words echoed against the walls, and William saw Paul stiffen at the sound.

Paul caught William's eyes over his shoulder.

"Never mind," he muttered darkly. "Come on."

He was hard to follow; Paul was always so damned fast. They lost ground, maybe a hundred yards, ground that had been hard won. It didn't matter; William's place was at Paul's side, and he arrived there as quickly as he could. There was a clear stretch of tunnel between them and the three devils that stood abreast of each other. There were the three he had seen enter the cave, the fiery-haired she-devil between the thin one and the wall of a devil to her right. The tall and wiry one spun his long barbed spear casually before him, breathing heavy and gnashing his teeth. Both blades were smeared in red and purple blood.

A score of Watchers stood behind the devils, books held in one hand and quills at the ready.

"What the Hell is wrong with you, Lilia?" Paul addressed the female with a level of familiarity that seemed to surprise her companions as much as it did William.

"What's wrong with me? Are you blind, Walker, or just stupid?" She was still shouting though they were half a dozen strides through the quiet tunnel from her. "You flood my sacred city with demons? You murder dragons? In my realm?"

"We were helping you fight the demons until you turned on us!" Paul was shouting now too. There was clearly some bad blood between them.

"You brought the demons here! You killed the first dragon! *Dragons are souls!* You destroyed souls, Walker!" Her flinted voice went higher.

"You said you would help with the demons if we needed it!" Paul yelled. "We needed it, and you turned on us!"

"You killed a dragon!" she shrieked.

"I defended my Guide and myself against monsters drunk with blood lust," he spat. "I understand that a dragon's soul is sacred. Why do dragons not understand that others' are as well?"

"Dragons *are* souls!" she shrieked again, almost incoherently.

"Then step aside and you can keep yours," Paul replied calmly.

"You killed dragons!"

"You murdered Walkers!"

They shouted and moved at the same time, clashing in the open space with the deafening clang of sword on sword. Paul and Lilia stood transfixed, weapons locked against each other, looking deep into each other's eyes.

"I thought you loved me," she breathed, almost too quietly for William to hear. Her eyes looked wide and vulnerable.

"I never said that," Paul replied calmly. Then he pressed hard with his weapons, throwing both his weight and his strength behind it. Lilia was driven back several steps, tottering, until she stood fast between the devils again.

"The Walker army began to retreat upwards toward open ground," she said. She pronounced every word carefully, like she was making an important proclamation. While she seemed to be addressing Paul, as she was looking at him, the Walker King only chuckled as his army began to build behind him. It was clear they were not retreating.

Lilia turned her back on Paul and her attention to Andre.

"The Walker army began to retreat upwards toward open ground," she said again, a hint of annoyance in her flinted voice. "The Walker King and his sidekick were also driven back by the weapons of the royal devils."

Andre nodded, and a score of quill pens danced as one.

A strange ripple went through the air, the vertical hold on reality went haywire; and before William could contemplate how he felt about being called a sidekick, he was being driven back by two short curved blades wielded by a monster of a devil. He should have backed into the army that had been amassing behind them, but they were being driven back even more effectively by the many devils aligned now with the few demons that still crowded the passageway.

Paul was fighting the wiry devil with one whirling weapon, and somehow he was being driven back as well. It didn't make any sense, beyond the fact that they were being driven in the direction they had already been going; they had no reason to be falling back.

Nearby, Andre was arguing with Lilia, and William was able to maneuver his busily defensive position to overhear.

"…don't see why we can't just erase their souls and be done with it," Andre was asserting as William came into earshot. "We can deal with the demons and restore your city and let you get back to business as usual, all with a few orchestrated strokes of our pens."

"I said no, Watcher." Lilia's eyes danced fire, and when she poked a sharp finger at his chest he winced in pain. "We will drive the Walkers out in the open and the dragons will take care of them. This power you wield is only possible through me. You are not the vital component in this equation."

She turned away, dismissively, then whirled around again. "What makes you think it would work?"

William felt icy fingers down his spine, and a curved blade got dangerously close to his face. He had to duck and spin and dance away from his aggressive opponent, and he didn't hear the rest of what the she-devil said. He saw Andre shake his head and wag his finger at her in admonishment, and was able to catch the tail end of what he said in response.

"...cannot control emotion, just events and their specifics," he explained. "You know the rules."

After she had made a suitable show of her displeasure, Lilia turned and launched herself at Paul. The Walker army fought valiantly, losing ground but not losing lives, and the mouth of the tunnel came into view far too soon. The two devils fighting Paul fell back in time with the one battling William, and the Walker King stepped to his side rather than press the momentary advantage.

"What the Hell is going on?" Paul whispered violently.

"She means to drive us out in the open and kill us all."

"I know that." Paul frowned. "Why is it working?"

William opened his mouth to answer, and then snapped it shut when two figures materialized beside them. He recognized them: it was the new Walker that Paul had made and his demon. Paul had told William that it appeared that the demon had been granted Guide status, but they hadn't had time to discuss the possible repercussions of such an anomaly. The Walker King had stowed the transforming sleeper and his demon with the devils he held prisoner, explained the situation, and led William and the others off to war.

William hadn't thought of him again until now.

The new Walker stood on the scorched rock and turned a slow circle in the open space between the Walkers and the devils. His eyes were open wide, and his jaw was slack. He held a sword in his hand loosely, and the tip described a slow circle in the ground as he turned. His hazel eyes passed over William, glassy and unseeing.

"What is he doing here?" Paul snapped at the demon.

The demon straightened proudly. "We are here to fight, Walker King."

"He can't fight, he's in shock," William snapped. He couldn't believe he was debating with a demon.

"Heaven and Hell and devils and dragons on his first day, demon?" Paul was scolding the muscled monster. "What were you thinking? Get him out of here."

Neither of them paid attention to the Watchers or the devils consulting on the other side of the stupefied new Walker.

Lilia's voice rang out, angry and loud. "Prove it!"

She whirled about and pointed a finger at Mason. "That one!"

With a satisfied smile and not a moment's hesitation, Andre turned to the assembled Watchers and spoke. "The Dragon Queen took her fire-breathing form and burned New Walker Mason until even his soul was obliterated. The Stone Walker and Walker William stood helplessly immobile and watched."

Their quills danced together over paper, and William stood by Paul in frozen astonishment as the red dragon filled the tunnel.

The queen belched flame, a long searing stream of fire that engulfed Mason from head to toe. It burnt flesh and blood and bone, heart and talent and soul; first to ash and then to nothing. The new Walker disappeared forever in the long burst of soul-scorching flame, while William and Paul stood in frozen helplessness. For several moments after his shadowed form had burnt to nothing, the fire continued to spew forth from the dark red dragon's unhinged jaw.

Daemon bowed his head, tears in his eyes, and walked into the fire.

CHAPTER 52

They stood on a wide ledge overlooking the dragon city. It was overrun with demons, filling the streets and climbing stone walls to sack the castles. There was no clear order to their movements, and more demons continued to spill into the city from the tunnels above it. Not a step of street could be seen under their numerous taloned feet, and the castles looked like anthills covered in red busy shapes from here.

A few dragons remained, mostly flying out of reach of sword or spear but descending occasionally to flame a dozen demons crossing the road or clinging to a castle or emerging from the moat.

Kris stood watching the terribly beautiful scene. He looked down at the sheer drop that led to a long swim through a sea of demons. He pointed to a far wall.

"They went up that tunnel," he told Ximena.

"I know," she responded quietly.

She too was looking at the long drop and the overwhelming odds. Even if they fought their way through, how could they get up the other side?

"Do we need to go back the way we came?" Kris didn't much care for the trip down; Ximena had avoided violence whenever possible, but the times it had not been possible resulted in rapid lethal movements that considered nothing but efficiency and effectiveness. More than once she wrenched a sword from a demon's hand to behead the monster with its own weapon. She would drop the weapon immediately and resume moving down the passage unencumbered by its weight. Usually, she would dance past the weapon and take the demon's back, twisting its head until it popped off in her hands like a cork leaving a bottle.

She was searching the sky over the city with her eyes.

Kris followed her gaze, but all he could see was smoke.

Ximena smiled then, a broad smile that lit up her blood-soaked face.

"No," she replied, still smiling and gazing at the acrid cloud hanging over the city. "We don't need to go back."

The Guide had a mental image of her snuffing the flames of a thousand demon's lives to stack their bodies and climb over them to reach the opening.

He shuddered.

Then a figure began to take shape in the mist, the form of a dragon flapping its wings with an urgency that speeded it toward the ledge they stood on.

Kris shuddered again, although he had seen her deal with a dragon already. This dragon was huge, however; too big for her arms to even halfway encircle its sinewed neck. He looked at Ximena, wondering what she was about to do.

Ximena stood there, still smiling broadly, and watched the monster come in for a landing. Just before it reached the ledge, the huge dragon shifted the angle of its body and pumped its leathery wings. Kris could feel the warm downdraft on his face, could see the tatters of Ximena's outfit dance in the powerful wind. The giant black beast touched down quietly, gripping the edge of the stone platform with its rear talons. Even with the bulk of its body hanging over the ledge, Kris and Ximena had to back up a few steps as it settled its weight on its rear legs and folded its leathery wings behind its upright body.

One blast of flame and they would be ashes floating up the tunnel they had just traversed. Or it could just fall forward and smash them under tons of black scales and thick muscle. Kris tried to dismiss his imagination, at least for the moment.

"My Queen." The dragon's voice was low and leathery, thick with solemnity. *"You have returned."*

Kris got the sense that the only reason the dragon didn't bow was because it would crush them. He breathed; not because he had to, but because he still could.

"Laurentis," Ximena was still smiling broadly. "You know I am no longer your queen."

The black dragon stretched out his wings, his wingspan fifty feet of scaled leather. Rocking back on his haunches, he straightened his neck and blasted glorious fire into the already smoky air above them.

"You always were and always will be my queen," the dragon boomed.

The creature relaxed into his former slightly less menacing posture, and Kris felt his bunched shoulders relax. There was a burn spot on the Guide's robe that he couldn't get out of his mind.

"I am but an ordinary human, stripped of my powers," Ximena spoke up to the dragon. "Is there any way we might bother you for a ride?"

"Anything, my queen." The dragon's booming response drove the Guide's heart to joy and his mind to fear.

Two voices spoke in his head at the same time, silently intoning the same three words in two very different ways.

Ride a dragon? said one voice excitedly.

Ride a dragon? asked the other, in abject terror.

Ximena was motioning for him to step into the tunnel with her; and when they did, the dragon lowered itself as close to the ground as it could get. With a few quick strides and two leaps along his foreleg, Ximena ascended the dragon and settled sidesaddle on his wide back.

"Come on." She motioned to him.

Kris eyed the mountain of flesh.

"I think I'm good." He entwined his hands in the sleeves of his robe so they would stop shaking. "I'll meet you on the other side."

Kris started to disentangle his hands to point at the distant portal, thought better of it and just nodded in that direction.

"Kris!" It was Brenna, his friend, waving at him like she was coaxing him to ride a ferris wheel or something. Covered in blood, she grinned and motioned to him again. "Come *on!*"

He knew she was in a hurry, so was he. Kris could also tell that her urgency was as much for him as it was for Paul.

Ximena sat on the monstrous back, patting the scales in front of her and giggling like a little girl lost in the magick of the moment.

"Oh, hell," Kris muttered.

He steeled himself and carefully climbed the mountain of flesh.

The Guide sat down, his legs hanging to one side like hers. She was still grinning unabashedly at him.

"You might want to hang on," she murmured.

Kris began to unwind his hands from his sleeves in the same instant that the mighty dragon took wing. He started to slide sideways, and his scrabbling hands grabbed ineffectively at slippery scales.

Small strong hands gripped his robe, and suddenly he was sitting next to the devil on a dragon's back.

It was breathtaking. Even with the horrors of war below and the toxic cloud above, the majesty of the moment made his heart feel as though it might burst.

He turned to Ximena.

"Thank you," he breathed.

She didn't answer, just placed her hand over his and smiled at him.

The flight ended quickly, as he knew it would. It didn't matter; he could go back to the memory any time, now that he had it. They dismounted as soon as the dragon settled its massive bulk on the seemingly narrow ledge.

"Thank you, Laurentis," Ximena spoke to the dragon in farewell. "Wish us luck."

Suddenly the dragon was gone, a tall weathered devil standing in its place.

"I will do no such thing," he responded tersely. He was covered in black leather armor and was holding a long scimitar with the casual familiarity with which Kris held his own arm. "I will continue to serve my queen until I am dead or dismissed."

Kris looked from one devil to another, wondering just what kind of history these two had. The Guide knew her to be intelligent and thoughtful, considerate like no one he had known. He wondered how this dragon knew her; he marveled at how he must love her, to place his very soul in her service.

Ximena hesitated for a moment, perhaps considering the gravity of the situation even more deeply than Kris.

"Very well," she said finally. "My gratitude."

Turning her back, she ran as quickly as her legs would carry her up the passageway.

The tall devil ran past her in three quick strides and began cutting a path through the sea of demons. It was horrific: the devil was nearly as fast as a Walker and twice as brutal. He stabbed and stomped, punched and kicked as he ran, horned heads severed or exploding with every violent motion. Ximena ran behind him up the center of the tunnel, her bare feet throwing spatters of purple blood behind her with every sprinting step. Kris floated alongside her effortlessly.

"You can go on ahead if you want." Though she was running as fast as humanly possible, she was not panting or even breathing hard.

Kris shook his head. "I'll stay with you, if that's okay."

She flashed him a grin. "That's what I hoped you'd say."

"Ximena," he said after they had moved along rapidly in silence for a few minutes. "Can I ask you something?"

"Of course," she replied, calm and conversational.

"How long were you on Earth?"

"Not long," she responded thoughtfully. "Two hundred years, maybe three."

"Why did you go?"

She glanced over at him. "You sure know how to ask a loaded question, don't you?"

He shrugged and floated along. "I am a Guide."

"There were two prophecies," she said.

He marveled at how she navigated the slick stone and spoke so clearly at the same time. It must have bothered her, at least a little, because the next time she spoke it was in his head.

'Do you mind?' Her voice sounded the same in his head as it did in his ear.

'Not at all,' he responded in kind. Apparently she wasn't completely without extraordinary abilities. Or perhaps she had just spent a few decades learning telepathy. According to the books, it was possible for anyone to learn.

'There were two prophecies,' she repeated. *'One said that the Queen of Hell would marry the Stone Walker, one of the most violent figures in all the histories of all the realms. The other said that the Original Devil would only find love if she went to Earth.'* The devil continued to cut a wide path with his brutal onslaught, and Ximena continued to run as fast as Kris had ever seen a human run. Neither of them showed any signs of tiring.

'I did not want to have anything to do with the future Walker King; the prophecies all made him sound mad with power and thirsty for blood,' a slight smile upturned the corners of her mouth. *'So I chose love, like every soul should. I handed over the throne to a royal dragon that I had known for millennia, I gave up my position and my powers, and I came to Earth to fall in love with the man who would become the Walker King.'*

'Is that why Lilia seduced Paul? To make the prophecy come true?' Kris knew his friend hated feeling like a pawn more than anything.

She shot him a sly smile. *'You don't think my boyfriend is hot enough to bed the Queen of Hell?'*

He chuckled, but he saw that her eyes were not without pain. *'Lilia is clever and manipulative. She had many reasons to do what she did. You are correct, of course, in assuming that most or all of those reasons were underhanded.'*

'And Paul's reasons?' Kris didn't mean to formulate the thought loud enough for her to hear, but there it was.

Ximena stared straight ahead as she ran, kicking out purple droplets behind her and letting the pain show clear in her face now. He didn't think she was going to respond at first; then her voice sounded in his head.

'The Walker's healing power works in ways that can make the path a challenging one,' her thought came clear. *'Once a Walker is…spent, sexually, the healing abilities rush in to resurrect them to peak condition. The women*

seem to have little trouble with it, but other aspects of the Walker's life are often not...comfortable for them. They are all rising souls, so they handle themselves honorably, but they struggle.'

'Also, Paul thought I was dead and lost,' she continued. *'He kept searching for me, even after they got involved, but life without me was something I had promised he would never have to experience again. That promise meant a lot to both of us, and he was surely adrift without me.'*

She ran in silence for a while again, and Kris thought about how a vital part of his best friend had seemed to be lopped off along with Brenna's head.

'Don't think that means I forgive him,' she thought hotly, suddenly. *'I understand him, because that's what love is. I cannot forgive him until he does whatever it takes to heal the hurt I feel in my heart. Because that's what love is too.'*

Kris smiled as he floated along. *'He will, you know.'*

She looked happy again when she glanced his way. *'I know.'*

He could see the mouth of the tunnel, widening up ahead to the open ground. A score of Watchers stood with their backs to them, with three devils in their midst. Beyond them, out in the dangerous exposed terrain, some sixty tattered and burnt Walkers stood in loose battle formation and waited.

Paul and William were out front, swords at the ready.

They continued forward, until Kris heard the Dragon Queen raise her voice as they neared.

"The Walker King realized that he truly loved the Queen of Hell, and he threw down his swords to bow at her feet." Her voice was tense and strident.

"It won't work," Andre responded, standing at the head of the gathering of Watchers.

"Do it!" she screamed.

Andre sighed and nodded at the Watchers, repeating her words. "The Walker King realized that he truly loved the Queen of Hell, and he threw down his swords to bow at her feet."

The Watchers scribbled.

A ripple of energy went through the air, and Kris heard Ximena's breath catch beside him.

Her hand reached out, involuntarily, and clasped his.

Paul stared at Lilia for a dreadful forever moment while every member of both armies seemed to hold their breath along with Ximena.

Then he clanged his swords and chuckled darkly, and they breathed out as one.

His gaze shifting slightly, Paul's eyes widened suddenly.

He dropped his swords and brushed by Lilia at the speed of thought to fall to his knees before Ximena. Wrapping his arms tightly about her waist, he buried his blood-stained face in her blood-stained belly and let out a wretched sob.

"Brenna," he gasped, his voice muffled against her skin. His shoulders shook as her fingers tangled in his wet hair, and a tear streaked from each of her eyes to mingle with the blood on her face.

"No!" Lilia shrieked. She whirled on Andre. "The Dragon Queen burned the Walker King and Ximena to nothingness! *And their fucking souls!*"

Andre motioned to the Watchers. Their quills lifted as one.

Laurentis pushed the Guide away from him with one long arm, Paul and Ximena with the other. The long arms became wings as he transformed, and a burst of flame issued from his mouth to engulf the Watchers as they touched quills to paper.

The Watchers burned, to their pained surprise, but not for long. When the dragon's flame finally died down, every last Watcher was gone as if they had never been. There had not even been time enough for them to cry out, and all that remained on the scorched ground where they had stood was a thin skiff of drifting ash.

Lilia transformed and launched herself into the sky.

Kris turned from the sight of Ximena still holding Paul to see Lilia's companions rush William. The stout devil with two blades busily engaged the Walker while the other circled behind him, thrusting his spear at William's leathered body. The Walker fought with both speed and skill for several tense rounds of melee, dodging and deflecting with all his might.

Thrusting the barbed spear forward, the devil finally caught William square in the back. The Walker cried out as the devil leaned all his weight into the next thrust, and the wide barb ripped through William's body to poke gruesomely out his chest. Slower but still steady, he continued to fend off the dual attacks of the larger devil while the other yanked on the spear to drive the barb deeper into his chest.

William cried out again and dropped to his knees.

His eyes closed for a moment, and Kris held his breath as he watched William's body dangling lifelessly from the long spear.

Then Kris saw his jaw working, as William steeled himself to strike.

The next moment he was a flurry of motion, standing and spinning with such speed that the thin devil was thrown hard and far. The whirling spear caught the wide devil across the cheek, and William's sword was close behind it to claim his head.

CHAPTER 53

William pulled the spear hand over hand through his chest and felt the barb on the other end dig into his back painfully. He clenched his jaw, tugged, tugged again, and then pulled it free in a shower of his own blood. He flung the weapon aside, wincing as the wound mended. Turning to confront the devil that had speared him, he was pleased to see that the Walker army had engaged the enemies that had not burnt up or flown away.

Demons were fighting the Walkers on the ground; devils were transforming and taking flight to rain fire from above. The Walkers still worked in teams, one watching the sky while the other battled on the ground. William watched one pair of Walkers working together, the cowboy on the ground battling demons with a battle-axe while the samurai with the bow fired arrows at any flying forms that came near and many that didn't. Every dragon he could see had arrows sticking from them.

There he was, the devil that had put the painful hole in William's chest. The Walker advanced on him, noting with disappointment that the devil remained unarmed. Oh well, perhaps quick was better anyway. He didn't think that maybe the devil would transform into a menacing dragon before his eyes, until it did just that.

Fortunately it was not the only gigantic fire-breathing monster nearby, and the other was apparently with the small beautiful woman that had driven Paul to his knees. The woman motioned at one beast while smiling sweetly at the other, and the dragon by her side suddenly had the other in its jaws. It moved faster than something that big should be able to move, embracing the other dragon with hind legs that dug in with sharp talons while forelegs and teeth rent the top half of its victim to shreds. Shrieks of delight punctuated the sickening sounds of flesh turning into a disgusting dragon smoothie that drenched everyone nearby.

The demons had seemed to realize as one that the dragons were scorching them with their haphazard flames more often than the speedy Walkers. They began to make for the tunnel again, or disappear retreating into the haze. William saw that the woman with Paul had helped him to his feet, and now her head rested on his chest while his fingers moved through her hair. They looked so peaceful in the midst of such horror, William hesitated to approach them.

Paul turned his head and smiled. His eyes crinkled and his cheeks rounded and his teeth showed. William was happy to see the king looking so happy. A cloud that had hovered over him all the time they had known each other was suddenly gone, and it was as if a different man stood before him.

"Walker William," Paul said, disengaging enough for her to turn and see him, "I would like you to meet…"

He looked down at her in amused uncertainty; she shrugged, equally amused.

"Ximena," he finished.

She extended a small hand to him.

With blinding speed, a red blur cometed from the sky to send Paul and Ximena exploding in opposite directions. She rolled to her feet and never stopped moving, grabbing the short broadsword that Paul tossed at her from the air and dashing up the dragon's back and neck to bury it in her skull.

Meanwhile, Paul rose from the tumbled heap he had become with a sword in each hand. It had almost been instinct to toss Ximena one, as was his powerful leap that brought him eye to eye with the monster.

Her eye was as big as his head, and it twitched and rolled as he rose beside it. Then it narrowed, and the giant red head swung to swat him from the sky. Paul's fast twitch movement cleverly positioned his long straight blade between them, and her violent motion drove his bastard sword deep into her eye. Clear and purple slime exploded all over his face and hands, and the dragon shook her massive head rapidly from side to side.

Both Ximena and Paul were tossed about like rag dolls, each clinging desperately to the sword they had sunk into the dragon's head. After several mind-numbing, teeth-jarring shakes, Paul's sword came loose and he fell toward the charred rock below. Again the gigantic head came at him, again his sword pointed straight at the oncoming maw. Just before the dragon took Paul in her unhinged jaw with rows of sharp fangs larger than the sword that would enter her mouth first, Ximena grabbed the leathered pommel of the short sword with both hands and twisted.

The dragon reared back and screamed, and Paul's long blade slit her throat eighteen inches deep. Purple blood showered him blind, but he kept swinging. Blood was everywhere, and William could only see the tip of the blade flashing occasionally in the wet purple cloud. Bits of scaled skin and bloodied flesh flew this way and that, splattering the rock around them with dripping, quivering hunks of gore.

The dragon's head dropped to the ground, finally. Ximena rode it through the bloody bounce, yanking Paul's sword free as it settled.

Her body collapsed with such force that it shook the very rock William stood on.

CHAPTER 54

Jessica finished cleaning the downstairs bar and began setting it up to serve coffee instead of alcohol. It was so much easier to roll out of bed in the morning and have all of her prep work done, especially with the busy new second business. Her life on Earth had never been better, or busier, and she lost herself in happy thoughts of Kris as she stood there inspecting her own spotless work.

She gasped suddenly, her eyes rolling back into her head as she dropped to her knees.

When they rolled back into place, her eyes were crimson and black and filled with fiery rage.

Sliding the ring off her toe, she didn't bother to get undressed. Her dragon form ripped her clothes to shreds and destroyed the narrow bar around her as it took shape. Her dark red scaled tail swung in a wide circle, and little pieces of the bar flew in every direction until she stood on bare open floor surrounded by coffee-making shrapnel and grounds. Water spewed from the twisted and broken pipes that rose naked from the floor, dousing her in hot and cold water.

Taking a deep breath, she breathed fire as she turned again in a slow flaming circle. The tables caught fire, one by one, then the stage and the stairs leading to the upper landing. She was cut by the twisted pipes as she turned, but she paid no heed to the blood that flowed or the healing that followed. Steel and plastic and wood alike caught alight in the impossibly hot flames of dragon fire.

When the slow circle was done, she reared up on her haunches and screamed.

Then she disappeared.

CHAPTER 55

Kris watched Paul and Ximena fight off the demons that surrounded them, wondering if they were communicating telepathically or if their synergy was natural. She was not nearly as fast as Paul, but her economy of motion made her seem as though she was. Neither of them ever stopped moving or left the other's back unguarded, and they exchanged more than one smile as they slaughtered.

The dragons seemed to be gone from the sky, and the demons had fallen back enough to pose no danger unless they continued to advance.

Ximena reached a staying hand out to lay it on Paul's sword arm.

William was nearby, following their lead and adding to the tremendous body count; when they stopped killing, he did as well.

Kris saw her hand the sword back to Paul.

The Guide arrived at Paul's side at the same time as William.

"What is it?" the Guide asked.

"The Dragon Queen is dead, Hell has been ravaged enough," Ximena said, then raised her voice.

"Let there be no more killing," she proclaimed loudly. "Let the children of creator and the children of creation be at peace with each other. More killing is not the solution to this problem."

The sounds of battle were dying down, as several Walkers turned to the voice to see their king standing beside the speaker. Many disengaged, stepping closer to hear.

"I am Ximena, returned to Hell to restore order and deliver justice. Justice has been delivered; join me now in laying down your arms that we may begin restoring order, together." Her voice seemed to emanate from the rock as much as from her mouth. "Let every ear in every corner of Hell hear my voice, and know that I speak true: the Dragon Queen is dead, the war is ended. Let no more demons die on this day. Let no more Walkers die on this day. Let no more dragons die on this day. Hear my familiar voice, denizens of Hell. I am Ximena, returned to liberate you from the heavy chains of the dark dragon's rule."

Paul looked at her, his eyes going wide.

Ximena turned to him and smiled at him sweetly.

"Later," she spoke quietly to him. She let her smile fall. "I get the feeling we have a lot to talk about."

The Walker King looked down, frowning, then returned his eyes to hers and smiled tensely. He nodded.

"Do you happen to have my necklace?" Ximena was smiling sweetly at him again. "The one I always used to wear? It would make this a lot easier."

The Walker King nodded once more, the confusion fleeing his face. Wordlessly, he reached into his pocket and withdrew the simple agate oval dangling from a slim silver snake chain.

Ximena held out her palm, Paul dangled the necklace over it, and Kris watched.

And watched.

They had stopped mid-motion, the chain in Paul's gloved grasp and the gemstone an inch from Ximena's skin.

Kris tried to move, found that he couldn't. Even his eyeballs would not shift in his head, and focusing his attention on William just showed him a nearby peripheral blur.

The acrid ceiling of smoke began to glow with a bright ethereal illumination, and white glowing shapes began to descend slowly from the lighted clouds. Kris thought he counted nine illumined figures, and he was pretty sure they had wings. Details were hard for him to make out, but they were definitely glowing a brilliant white. Slowly and gracefully, they came closer as they came lower, and Kris strained his eyes to get a good look.

A strange stillness filled the air.

Then the flapping of leathery wings broke the eerie silence, and Kris recognized the dragon as it came to a landing at Paul and Ximena's feet. The dragon's head swung balefully from one side to the other, narrowed with rage and taking it all in.

Her head stilled mid-swing as her eyes fell on Kris, and her eyes narrowed further for a moment.

The dragon whipped her head about to regard Paul and Ximena's frozen bodies, then reared back and took in a deep fateful breath.

'No!' Kris screamed at her in his mind. He thought of the symbol that had burned itself into his palm, the pronouncement Roche had made. He thought of how reluctant he had been to learn to change another's thoughts. Then he brought everything within him to bear on bending the will of the woman he loved, reaching out with his powerful trained mind.

'Jessica! No!' Kris thought it fiercely at her. *'I command you to stop!'*

Her head swung his way again, her eyes afire with hate and hurt. For a moment Kris thought he had her; then her jaw began to crank open and he was thinking once again of the burnt spot on his robe.

Sadness swirled in her eyes with the blue and black and red as Jessica swiveled to face Paul and Ximena once again.

'*No!*' Kris let his tortured thought fill the dragon's mind. '*Please, Jessica! Don't!*'

She made no indication that she even heard him this time, dropping her weight to the ground and spewing fire at the helpless couple.

That's where his eyes were locked, unmoving, and it burned the image into his brain as surely as the flames burned his friends.

Kris watched their clothes melt away, then their skin, then their muscles and bones. Both of their healing abilities seemed to fight back at first, reforming bits of sinew in the scorching heat, and Kris felt hope flicker in him for a moment.

Then they became two dark hunks of charred bones, still burning as they fell.

Then they were ash.

Then the ash burned.

Dear Reader,

You got an apology from me at the end of the first book in this series; or at least, you got something resembling an apology. Leaving you wondering about what is going to happen next by cutting off the story where I did may not have made you super happy, but this book also had to end at some point. It's only the second of three installments, after all; in a manner of speaking, you could say you really just reached the end of the middle.

This story needed to be told; and if I set things up so you weren't interested in what was coming next, that would just be me not doing well describing this series of events. All you have to do in order to wrap things up and walk away with a feeling of satisfaction is read the last book.

It is a pretty satisfying ending, if I do say so myself. You might even call it epic, and you wouldn't be the first.

'Fall of the Walker King' is the final installment in this trilogy, and it's available now wherever you got this book from. All your questions will be answered, some happy and sad surprises await your discovery, and you will find out where all the folks you've been getting to know over the last couple books end up. I'll encourage you to grab your copy and get started on it one last time, while also asking that you read this to the end first.

If you haven't already subscribed to my newsletter, I would like to invite you to do that as well. You can find all my blog posts and short stories at JayNorry. com, along with samples from all my books; and you can easily subscribe to the newsletter there, to get news and sneak peeks and special offers available only to members.

As a reader, I always felt a certain kinship with an author when I enjoyed one or several of their books. I believed writers were special people, able to cast spells that affected readers like me deeply. Now I know readers are just as special as the writers, and equally important. Without a receiver, there is no point in giving; and without a reader, there is no point in writing. Readers grant writers a completion that we cannot give ourselves, simply by letting us into your lives for a little while; and I would be remiss to pass up this opportunity to express my gratitude.

May we get to know each other better with all the time and all the books to come.

Oh, and also…sorry for the ending.

Thanks for reading!

All the best,
Jay